MICHELLE MADOW

DIAMONDS ARE FOREVER

HARLEQUIN®TEEN

Recycling programs
for this product may
not exist in your area.

ISBN-13: 978-0-373-21152-4

Diamonds Are Forever

Printed in U.S.A.

"There's no easy way to say this."

Adrian looked closely at each of them, as though searching for the right words. He took a deep breath and said, "When Courtney found out about Britney, I promised there would be no more secrets. I wanted to have relationships with you, something that I think has been going well, with the Sundays we've spent together and our vacation over winter break."

"Okay…" Courtney's stomach twisted, feeling as if she wasn't going to like where he was headed with this.

"The Sundays have been going really well," Savannah added.

Adrian managed a tight-lipped smile. "There's something else you need to know. I didn't tell you originally because it involves other people. Now they're ready for you to know—they were actually ready weeks ago—but it was around the same time you found out about Britney." He directed that last part to Courtney. "I knew how hard that was on you—on all three of you—and I didn't want to drop anything else on you while you were grieving for your sister. But I'm not perfect. I've made mistakes, and keeping this from you is one of them."

"You mean there's something else you've been hiding?" Peyton rolled her eyes. "Why am I not surprised?"

"This is the last secret," he said. "I promise."

Praise for Michelle Madow and *The Secret Diamond Sisters*

"The exciting—and often terrifying—exploration of the Vegas strip is tempered by the more relatable plotline of the sisters trying to figure out their past…. *Gossip Girl* meets *The Princess Diaries* in a city that never sleeps."

—*Booklist*

"This quick and entertaining read is filled with glitz and glamour. The Vegas setting fascinates. The Diamond sisters are so different that at least one sibling will be completely relatable to readers, making the novel even more fun. Get ready for one crazy and fabulous ride."

—*RT Book Reviews*

"Highly addictive! Hold on tight, because *The Secret Diamond Sisters* throws you headfirst into the Vegas fast lane. A fun ride not to be missed!"

—Rachel Harris, author of *My Super Sweet Sixteenth Century*

Books by Michelle Madow
available from Harlequin TEEN

The Secret Diamond Sisters series

(in reading order)

The Secret Diamond Sisters
Diamonds in the Rough
Diamonds Are Forever

To Natashya Wilson, for helping me make this series better than I'd ever imagined it could be. I've learned so much from you—thank you for your belief in me and the Diamond sisters from the very beginning!

www.campusbuzz.com

Happy New Year!
Posted on Thursday 1/1 at 1:19 PM
Why does the year always feel like it goes by so fast? It seems like just yesterday that we were all starting the fall semester! And I don't know about you all, but winter break has been amazing, and I'm so not ready for school to start up again. But who would be, after spending Christmas and New Years partying in an exotic location? (Not telling you where, because this IS anonymous! ;) I'm so not ready to get back into school mode. Waking up early, studying...who needs that? At least we have a few days of break left...

1: Posted on Thursday 1/1 at 1:56 PM
Been seeing everyone's pictures from winter break and it's so not fair you all are doing such fun things while I've been stuck here!! Super jealous.

2: Posted on Thursday 1/1 at 2:09 PM
don't spend too much time being jealous—it could be worse! like oliver, who's been in the hospital for the entire break. I heard he's all messed up from the car crash and won't be back at school when it starts up.

3: Posted on Thursday 1/1 at 2:49 PM
Apparently Madison's been at the hospital every minute she can...

4: Posted on Thursday 1/1 at 2:55 PM

She must feel guilty, since she got in that huge fight with him at Savannah's party before he left!!!

5: Posted on Thursday 1/1 at 3:24 PM

The accident wasn't Madison's fault, and even though I was never friends with Oliver, I do feel bad for him. But the winner for the best new years has gotta be the Diamonds. Have you all seen their pics from rome? Fireworks at the coliseum, popping champagne on the streets . . I've gotta get there someday!

chapter 1: *Savannah*

If someone had told Savannah Diamond eight months ago that she would be in a private jet, flying from Las Vegas to LA to meet with a talent agent who wanted to manage her career as a YouTube singer, she wouldn't have believed them. Because eight months ago, she was living in a tiny apartment in a run-down neighborhood in Fairfield, California, with her two older sisters, Courtney and Peyton, and her mom, whose drinking had spiraled out of control. Then her father (whom she'd never met) had sent Mom to rehab, and Savannah and her sisters had discovered that their father was Adrian Diamond. Yes, *that* Adrian Diamond—the billionaire who owned multiple hotels in Las Vegas.

She and her sisters had been whisked away to live in the penthouse of their father's newest building on the Las Vegas Strip: The Diamond Hotel and Residences.

Their father had been quick to tell them about how Courtney had been kidnapped as an infant, and how their connection to him put them in danger. What he *hadn't* told them (and what Courtney had discovered a few weeks ago), was that Courtney had once had a twin sister, Britney, who'd been kidnapped along with Courtney. When their father took too long to pay the ransom, the kidnappers had taken Britney's life. Adrian had never forgiven himself.

Savannah hated that she'd been lied to for so long, but with so many opportunities in front of her, she believed that everything could only get better from here. Mom was out of rehab and was doing better than ever. Her father was finally part of her life, and she was enjoying getting to know him. She loved her new private school—the Goodman School—and for the first time, she fit in with a big group of friends. On top of all that, her YouTube channel was doing better than ever, thanks to the guys in One Connection Tweeting about it during her Sweet Sixteen party. And the hottest of the five of them, Perry Myles, frequently replied to her Tweets and had sent her a few text messages.

But while it might *sound* like something from a fairy tale, everything was still far from perfect. Her best friend from home, Evie, had become jealous of her new life, and they hadn't spoken since their fight during her Sweet Sixteen. And she still had feelings for Damien Sanders, who was making up for breaking her heart over the summer by helping her develop her YouTube channel. Also, Courtney and Peyton had made Savannah promise that the three of them wouldn't speak to Mom and Grandma until Courtney was ready, but giving them the silent treatment made Savannah feel so guilty, and she'd only lasted a week before she'd started talking to Mom and Grandma behind her sisters' backs.

Savannah had never broken a promise to her sisters. She hoped they wouldn't find out, but she feared it would happen eventually, and she'd barely been able to eat since that first phone call to Mom. Mom and Grandma had told Savannah that everything would be all right, and that if Courtney and Peyton found out, they would forgive her. Savannah wasn't so sure.

But right now, she had to relax and mentally prepare for her meeting with the talent agent. She also had to pay attention to Rebecca's chattering about her upcoming wedding to Adrian. Because while Savannah had been given a lot of freedom since moving to Las Vegas, she was still only sixteen, and Adrian didn't want her traveling alone (even though she had a personal bodyguard). So he'd sent her future stepmother, Rebecca, along. Which, of course, meant wedding talk. The wedding was already being dubbed "The Upcoming Wedding of the Year: A Romance to Rival William and Kate's," and Adrian and Rebecca were being called "The Duke and Duchess of Vegas" in tabloids everywhere.

"What do you think—matching bridesmaid dresses, or each of you picking a color and style that suits you?" Rebecca played with her huge heart-shaped engagement ring, which was apparently worth over a million dollars.

"Courtney, Peyton and I have such different styles. But don't bridesmaids wear matching dresses?"

"Most of the time," Rebecca said. "But I'm grateful that you and your sisters agreed to be bridesmaids, so I want to consider your opinions."

"I would pick blue," Savannah said, smoothing out her blue silk top. "It's my favorite because it matches my eyes. But watch out if you give Peyton a choice. The only color she wears is black—if that even *counts* as a color."

"Since it's going to be a bright spring wedding, I certainly don't plan on having my bridesmaids wear black." Rebecca smiled and checked her watch. "Anyway, we're almost there. Are you excited?"

"I'm nervous." Savannah bounced her knees and looked

out the window. They were no longer flying over desert, but dense clusters of houses—they must be getting closer to the city. "What if I mess up while talking to her, or she doesn't like me?"

"Just relax and be yourself," Rebecca said. "She's going to love you."

"It sounds easy when you say it like that." Savannah sighed. "But this is Lynda Caine—agent to some of the top YouTube stars all over the country. My mind will go blank the second I walk into her office."

"She wouldn't have invited you to meet with her if she wasn't serious about taking you on as a client," Rebecca reminded her. "This meeting is a formality. You've got this, Savannah."

Savannah took a deep breath. When Rebecca put it that way, it didn't sound as intimidating. But that didn't stop her nerves from feeling like they might burst.

This was Savannah's one chance, and she refused to mess it up.

"So that's the basics," Lynda Caine said from behind her desk. She looked so pristine in her beige suit, her hair pulled into a delicate top bun, and she looked Savannah straight in the eyes. "I'll want your cover songs up on iTunes, and for you to make joint videos with my other clients. Emily Nicole's told me how much she loves your videos, and that you chat on Twitter, so the two of you could make a great team. I'll also find brands to pitch you to for possible sponsorships—we'll get an idea of the demographics following you online to figure out where to book live shows, and I'm going to push for you to perform at VidCon this summer. How does all that sound?"

"It sounds amazing," Savannah said, breathless. "I love Emily Nicole's channel, so doing a video with her would be awesome. And I've always wanted to perform at VidCon." She tapped her fingers against her legs, glancing at Rebecca for confirmation. Rebecca *had* to say yes. This was the opportunity of a lifetime. How could she turn it down?

"And eventually Savannah will work with a cowriter and record original songs?" Rebecca asked.

Savannah clenched her fists, wishing Rebecca hadn't brought that up. Yes, it had always been her dream to record an album of her own. But that would *never* happen if Lynda decided her family was too pushy and didn't sign her because of it.

"That will come in time." Lynda smiled brightly. "But as I said earlier, first we need to get Savannah a secure enough following through her YouTube cover songs. She already has a healthy number of fans on YouTube, Twitter and Instagram, but those fans need to develop trust in her brand, and feel like they know her as a person. Once we see a bigger boost in Savannah's social media following, we'll record original songs."

"Perfect," Savannah jumped in, not wanting Rebecca to have another chance to mess this up. "I've been trying my best on Twitter and Instagram and everything—thanks to a good friend who helped me. But let me know anything else you want me to do on social media, and I will."

"Are you referring to Perry Myles from One Connection?" Lynda leaned forward, her eyes hungry.

"Perry helped me a lot when he Tweeted about my channel," she said, since it was the truth. "But it was a guy from my school—Damien—who helped me at first. Way before anyone heard about my channel, Damien had all these great ideas for me to spread word online. My YouTube channel would be nowhere without him."

Lynda raised an eyebrow. "Is Damien your boyfriend?"

"No." Savannah swallowed and looked down at her hands. "He's just a friend."

"And Perry...?" she asked. "In your segment on *My Fabulous Sweet Sixteen*, it looked like there might be something between you two."

"Seriously?" Savannah laughed. "No way. I mean, we Tweet and text sometimes, but he's one of the most famous people in the *world*. He could have any girl he wanted."

"And if that girl were you?" Lynda asked. "Being seen with Perry would be excellent publicity. You know how much his appearance at your party helped your channel—now imagine that tenfold." She paused, which gave Savannah just enough time to imagine Perry getting out of a limo at the Grammys—with her by his side. "*That's* what would happen if you pursued this opportunity."

Savannah's eyes widened. It was beyond cool whenever she saw a Tweet or text from Perry, since he was so famous that she'd never imagined he would know she existed. But he wasn't truly *interested* in her. Was he?

"Perry's cool and all," Savannah said. "But it would never work between us."

Lynda smiled, as if she knew something Savannah didn't. "Why do you say that?"

"Because..." She pressed her lips together, not wanting to say the first thought she had—that pursuing something with Perry would wreck the chance of *anything* happening between her and Damien. "He lives in a different country. And he's on a world tour, so we can't even see each other. Not that it matters, since we barely know each other."

"I thought the two of you Tweeted and texted?"

"It's just chitchat," Savannah said. "He's not interested in me. And even if he was, I follow gossip sites, so I know his reputation. He never dates anyone for longer than a few weeks, if that."

"You can't give those sites too much credit," Lynda said. "Yes, Perry's an international superstar, but he's only seventeen. You can't fault him for not having had a long-term relationship yet. And the two of you looked like you really clicked on your segment of *My Fabulous Sweet Sixteen*."

"It was my party, and he was paid to be there," she said. "Of course he was nice to me."

"You said yourself that he's stayed in contact with you since the party," Lynda said. "Was he paid to do that, too?"

"No," Savannah admitted. "But he's just being friendly. He has his choice of every girl in the *world*. Why would he pick me?"

"You're not giving yourself enough credit," Lynda said. "You keep coming up with reasons why it wouldn't work, but how do you know if you don't give it a try?"

"I guess I don't." Savannah shrugged.

"Exactly," Lynda said. "The One Connection world tour breaks in March. You could try seeing Perry again during that break, and in the meantime, get to know him better over the phone. The exposure could really help your career."

Savannah froze, not sure what to say. Because Perry wasn't the guy she was interested in—he wasn't the one she thought about all the time, wondering what it would be like if they ever dated. That guy was Damien.

Unfortunately, ever since her disastrous crush on him last summer, Damien had put her in the permanent "friend-zone."

"If Savannah's not interested in pursuing a relationship with Perry Myles, then she's not interested," Rebecca interrupted. "I thought we were here to discuss a media contract—not Savannah's social life."

"Networking is an important part of being successful,"

Lynda said. "Savannah asked if there was anything she could do that would help her career. My biggest suggestion right now is to pursue this connection with Perry Myles. But if you don't want to take my advice…"

"I'll do it." The words burst from Savannah's mouth, and she sat straighter, hoping she looked more confident than she felt. She was *not* losing this chance. "If you want me to get to know Perry better and see him in March, then I'll do everything I can to make it happen. I promise."

"All I ask is that you try." Lynda pulled a few papers out from a drawer in her desk and handed them over to Rebecca. "This contract outlines everything we've discussed. I'll need both of you to sign—assuming you're Savannah's official guardian?"

"I won't be until the wedding." Rebecca flipped through the pages. "Right now her official guardian is her father, Adrian Diamond. He'll want to have his lawyer look this over before he or Savannah signs anything."

Savannah deflated and sat back in her chair. What if in the time between now and the lawyer reading it, Lynda decided she didn't want to represent her anymore?

"Can I sign it now?" She held up the pen, ready to go. "Then we can bring it home and Adrian can sign it when he's ready?"

"Adrian wants you to wait," Rebecca said. "Nothing's going to change in the next few days."

Savannah crossed her arms and frowned, but she didn't want to argue with Rebecca in front of Lynda. Adrian's signature was the one that mattered, anyway.

Rebecca plucked one of Lynda's cards from the holder on her desk and added, "Adrian's lawyer will contact you if he has any questions."

"Of course," Lynda said. "I look forward to working with you."

They exchanged a few more pleasantries, and Lynda's assistant led them out of the building, where the limo was waiting. Savannah slid inside after Rebecca, feeling like she was able to breathe for the first time since waking up that morning.

"You have an offer of representation." Rebecca did a little shimmy dance with her shoulders as she buckled her seat belt. "Aren't you excited?"

"I would be if the contract was signed." Savannah leaned against the door and huffed. "But that went totally awful."

"Why do you think that?" Rebecca's hands went straight to her pearls—she seemed honestly surprised. "I thought it went well."

"Except that you kept giving Lynda a hard time," Savannah said. "Now she probably thinks we're too much trouble and will change her mind about representing me."

"I wasn't giving her a hard time," Rebecca said, soft and steady. "I was looking out for your best interests. It's routine to ask questions in a meeting like that, and then have a lawyer look over a contract. But Lynda *wants* to represent you. She wouldn't have offered you the contract otherwise. Although…" She paused, and Savannah had a feeling she wasn't going to like whatever Rebecca was going to say next. "I'm worried about what she said about Perry Myles. You shouldn't do anything that makes you uncomfortable."

"It doesn't make me uncomfortable," Savannah said. "Perry was nice to me at my party, and he's been nice to me ever since."

"You did seem to get along well," Rebecca agreed. "But are you really interested in him, or were you saying what you thought Lynda wanted to hear?"

"Who wouldn't be interested in Perry Myles?" Savannah

smiled, trying to shrug it off. "I just never thought I had a chance. But Lynda's right—I should try harder to reach out to him."

Plus, if Savannah told Rebecca that she was worried because she didn't want to mess up her non-relationship with Damien, then Rebecca might tell Lynda, and Lynda might second-guess how devoted Savannah was to her career. Besides, Damien and Perry didn't know each other. If Savannah tried harder with Perry, and nothing came of it, Damien would never know. And if she tried harder and something *did* come from it…well, she doubted that would happen.

If it did, she would deal with it then.

Worry crossed over Rebecca's eyes, and Savannah's heart raced. Was she not convincing enough? Maybe she should change the subject.

"I can't wait to shoot a video with Emily Nicole," she said. "I've been a fan of hers for years, and her channel is huge. She seems like a really fun person, too."

"I'm glad you're excited," Rebecca said. "And I'm sorry you thought I wasn't on your side in there. But I hope you know that I'm just trying to do what's best for you."

"Which is signing that contract with Lynda." Savannah squared her shoulders, looking Rebecca straight in the eye.

"And unless there's something seriously wrong in that contract, that's exactly what's going to happen," she said. "How about we have a big family dinner tonight to celebrate?"

"So this is really happening?" Savannah asked. "I'm a real singer with an agent?"

"You've always been a 'real singer.'" Rebecca smiled. "But yes, it's really happening."

"Then I *have* to text Courtney and Peyton." She grabbed her phone and told them in a group message. They didn't respond right away, so she opened her text chain with Damien and shared the news with him.

CONGRATS!!! he replied back immediately. Let's grab hot chocolate at the Lobby Bar when you get back, so you can tell me everything? ☺

Savannah smiled at the thought of seeing Damien, and she told him she would let him know when she landed. She was about to put her phone away when she remembered Lynda's advice—get to know Perry better.

A text right now would be a good start.

She opened her texts with Perry. The last message she'd sent was a picture of her at the Coliseum with her sisters, wishing him a Happy New Year from Rome. He'd texted her back from NYC, with a picture of him and his One Connection bandmate Noel in their hotel room, looking over at the crowd they were getting ready to perform to in a few hours for New Year's Rockin' Eve at Times Square.

He was so famous, and she was an amateur. But she drafted what she would say to him, anyway.

Hey! Just got out of a meeting at Caine Talent—Lynda Caine offered me a contract!! I know you're probably busy with your tour, but your tweeting about my channel is a huge reason why this happened, so I wanted to share the news and thank you again ☺

She stared at the text without sending it. She hadn't even gotten something big, like a record deal. It was just representation. Something Perry probably got *years* ago.

But everyone had to start somewhere, right? And Lynda had told her to try connecting more with Perry.

So she held her breath, and pressed Send.

chapter 2: *Courtney*

Courtney couldn't believe that Brett had talked her into watching the first three episodes of *The Walking Dead*. They were halfway through episode two, and the blood and gore was *so* not up her alley.

He pulled her closer, his arm fitting perfectly around her shoulders, and she snuggled into his side. "Is the show growing on you?" he asked, his green eyes sparkling. The way he looked at her warmed her heart every time—as if he cared about her more than anyone else in the world.

"Not really," she said, smiling in apology. "But I was just thinking about how I could get payback by making you watch the first three episodes of *Downton Abbey*."

He reached for the remote and pressed Pause. "We can turn it off," he said. "There are tons of other shows we can marathon. Have you ever seen *Lost*?"

"Nope." Courtney was really more of a reader than a TV-watcher—especially since they hadn't had cable in their apartment in Fairfield, California. She'd been at work when most shows were on, anyway. "But I'll give it a shot if it means more time spent with you."

"You have no idea how hard it was to pretend like you're only my friend when we were in Italy," he said, squeezing her hand.

"I *do* have an idea." She leaned closer to him and tilted her head up, her stomach fluttering at how there were only inches between them. "I loved Italy, and it's great that Adrian's so happy with your mom, but keeping away from you because our parents were watching drove me absolutely crazy."

"Not as crazy as it drove me," he teased, brushing his nose against hers.

"I wouldn't be so sure about that." Her gaze locked on his, her breath catching in anticipation of kissing him. After only a few seconds of restraint, he lowered his lips to hers. She wrapped her arms around his neck, her heart beating wildly as she kissed him back, feeling as if her body would melt into his. She wished she could feel this happy forever.

Then her cell buzzed, and she pulled back to rest her forehead against his. She glared at her phone. Reaching for it meant moving away from Brett, and she didn't want to do that.

"Whoever it is can wait," he murmured, burying his fingers in her hair and bringing his lips to hers again.

She closed her eyes, losing herself in his touch, wanting to take advantage of their time alone. But eventually, she found the strength to break away. "It could be Savannah telling me how it went with that agent," she said. "She was so excited before leaving this morning… I have to see if it's her."

"I know." He brushed his lips against hers, softer this time, and she leaned back into him. He was so intoxicating that she wanted to forget the rest of the world existed. But he untangled himself from her arms, reached for her phone and handed it to her. "The sooner you check, the sooner we can get back to where we left off."

"Right." Courtney's hand shook as she unlocked her phone and tapped the message icon. Just as she'd thought, the text was from Savannah.

The agent offered me a contract!! Just need dad's lawyer to look it over so he can sign it, and then it's official! Family dinner tonight to celebrate ☺

"Well?" Brett asked. "Good news, I hope?"

"She was offered a contract," Courtney said as she texted Savannah back, congratulating her. "We're doing a family dinner tonight to celebrate."

"And you don't sound thrilled because…you'll have to hold off on talking to Peyton about that college application you filled out for her?"

"You got it." She put her phone on vibrate and tossed it in her bag. "I was ready to talk with her about it tonight, but now that we'll be celebrating, I don't want to ruin Savannah's good mood. I guess it'll have to wait until tomorrow. And you know how much Peyton *hates* the idea of going to college, so I want to get it over with."

"What's the worst she can do?" Brett asked.

"I don't know." Courtney shrugged. "Tell our parents that we're together?"

"She wouldn't do that," he said. "She was egging me on to make a move on you the whole time we were in Italy. So was Savannah. Your sisters are our biggest fans."

"If only Adrian and your mom would see what they see," she mused, tracing her fingers along his palms. "It would be so much easier."

"We could always try to tell them again." He spoke faster,

as if the idea excited him. "Our parents are getting *married* in a few months. So we can't hide this from them forever. And once they realize that we've been together for a few weeks, and how well things are going, they'll have to support us. That was our plan when we decided to go for this, right?"

"I guess." Courtney's stomach dropped from thinking about it. "But honestly, I think the chances are higher that Peyton will decide she wants to go to college."

"I doubt that," he said. "You *filled out Peyton's application* for her. Most people would love to have someone do that. I don't think she'll be as mad as you think."

"You don't know her as well as I do," she said. "She'll probably yell at me, tell me I have no right to try controlling her future and delete the application."

He raised an eyebrow. "And would that be the first time Peyton's ever yelled at you?"

"No." She laughed. "Good point. And I did back the application up on the cloud."

"Then you'll be fine." He pulled her close again, his eyes blazing with an intensity that made her heart feel like it was going to beat out of her chest. "Now, where were we before we got interrupted?"

"Right about here…" Courtney leaned into him and pressed her lips to his once more. It wasn't long before he'd lowered her onto the couch, every inch of his body on hers. Her heart thumped harder. She'd never been this close to him before—but it felt so right that she didn't want to stop.

Someone knocked on the door. Brett bolted off her, his eyes panicked as he straightened his shirt. Courtney glanced at the door, sure she must look as confused as he did.

"It's probably Peyton." She sat up and ran her hands through her hair in an attempt to smooth it. She *hoped* it was Peyton. Because her lips felt swollen, and her cheeks felt flushed—she would bet that anyone would know from looking at her and Brett what had just been going on between them.

Whoever it was knocked again.

"Brett? Courtney?" Adrian's voice called from the other side of the door. "Are you two in there?"

Brett grabbed a textbook from the coffee table and opened it on his lap. "We're studying, right?" he said softly to Courtney, his voice surprisingly calm—as if they hadn't just been having a heavy make-out session on the couch.

"Of course." She gathered up a pile of flash cards and shuffled through them. It was good that she was so paranoid about having a cover story about hanging out with Brett. Plus, she really *had* wanted to get some studying done for their upcoming quiz in AP History. She'd just gotten…distracted.

Brett took a sip of water from the glass on the end table and lounged back on the couch. "Yeah, we're in here," he called back to Adrian.

They heard a key card slide into the slot, then Adrian opened the door and strolled into Brett's penthouse. As always, he wore a perfectly fitted navy suit, his blond hair slicked back as if he'd just come out of an important business meeting. But there was something different about him today. Usually he was a mask of calm—Courtney often had a rough time deciphering what was going on in his mind—but today, he seemed to be…glowing. He even grabbed a few M&M's from the bowl Brett kept in the foyer, which was surprising, since he rarely ate sweets.

"Peyton told me you would be here," he said, popping an M&M into his mouth. He glanced at the open textbook, then scrutinized the foot of space left on the couch between them.

"She did?" Courtney leaned even farther away from Brett, holding her flash cards so tightly that they bent. How could

Peyton have told Adrian where to find her without warning her first? Did she *want* Courtney and Brett to get caught?

"Yes, she did." Adrian looked back and forth between them. "She said you were studying."

"That's right," Brett jumped in. "Sorry we didn't answer when you knocked the first time. Courtney's pretty intense when she studies, and she didn't want to ruin her concentration until she finished reciting the answer to one of the short essay questions."

"I got it right," she squeaked, holding up a flash card as "proof."

"I'm not surprised, judging by your excellent grades last semester," Adrian said. "I didn't expect your transition to Goodman to go as well as it did. Your report card was impressive."

"Thank you." Courtney smiled, but when she looked down at her flash cards, guilt flooded her chest. She was proud of her grades last semester, but she had to keep them up if she wanted to get into Stanford. And if she kept making out with Brett instead of studying, that wasn't going to happen.

"Anyway, as proud as I am about your grades, that isn't why I came in here," Adrian said, situating himself in one of the chairs in the living room. "I have some good news."

"Cool." Brett closed the textbook and placed it on the coffee table. "What's up?"

"I just got back from seeing the Prescotts at the hospital," he said. "With everything that's happened to Oliver, Logan's been doing a lot of thinking recently, and he and I had the longest conversation we've had since the fallout at the grand opening last summer."

Courtney's eyes lowered at the mention of the grand opening. Because the "fallout"—when Logan had decided he didn't want to be business partners with Adrian for a major hotel they'd been planning in Macau—had been partly her fault.

"How's Oliver doing?" Courtney asked. She wanted to get the talk away from the grand opening, but she also truly wanted an update. She might not *like* Oliver, but she wouldn't wish what had happened to him on anyone.

"He's recovering," Adrian said. "His worst injury was his knee, but the surgery went well, and he should be able to walk on it soon. It seems that his biggest challenge is psychological. Logan wouldn't give me all the details, but it's clear that alcohol and drugs were why Oliver got into that accident. He's getting treatment, and is refusing to see anyone but his immediate family members."

"Not even Madison?" Courtney wasn't Madison's biggest fan, either, but apparently Oliver had left Savannah's party while drunk because of a huge fight with Madison. If Madison hadn't seen Oliver since that night, she must be a wreck.

"Are you friends with Madison?" Adrian looked taken aback, but it took him only a second to compose himself. "I've never seen you spend time with her."

"We have a lot of the same classes, and we're both student tutors," she said. "I'm not exactly *friends* with her, but I know she cares about Oliver."

"Logan didn't mention her, but since Oliver's only seen his immediate family, I'm guessing that doesn't include Madison." Adrian clasped his hands in his lap. "Anyway, Oliver's expected to make a full recovery, so everyone's grateful for that. But as I mentioned, Logan and I had a heart-to-heart this morning. After the scare he had with Oliver—especially in that first week, when the doctors weren't sure if he was going to make it—he apparently had a 'revelation.' He said he was hypocritical in judging my family, especially when Oliver has more troubles than any of you, and apologized for breaking off our partnership." He paused, glancing at Brett. "Logan said his snapping point was that black eye you gave Oliver before the midnight ribbon cutting—"

"Oliver was being a dick," Brett said, clenching his fists. "If you knew what happened, you would have wanted to punch him, too."

"I don't doubt it." Adrian chuckled. "But that's no way to work through a problem, and Rebecca was right to have grounded you for the rest of summer. I'm just glad there haven't been any reoccurrences of that behavior."

"It's the only time I've ever punched someone," Brett said. "I think my hand was as bruised as Oliver's face."

"I don't suppose you want to share *why* you punched him?"

"It doesn't matter now," Courtney jumped in. "It happened months ago. It's over."

No *way* was she telling Adrian about Oliver's bet to sleep with her and her sisters before the end of summer—and that he'd succeeded with Peyton and had been trying to make moves on Courtney, too.

"Well, I hope you'll work past your differences with Oliver," Adrian said. "Or at least be civil with him. Because Logan's revisiting the idea of us collaborating for the super hotel in Macau. If this goes through—which, judging from the way he was talking about it, it seems like it will—it should be our most successful hotel to date."

"That's amazing." Courtney smiled. She'd felt guilty about what had happened last summer, but she'd figured there was no fixing it, so she'd stopped dwelling on it. Now, relief flooded her veins that she hadn't messed everything up after all.

"Yes, it is," Adrian said. "We'll have two things to celebrate tonight—Savannah's offer from that agent, and the new hotel in Macau. Anyway, I have some phone calls to make, but I'll see you at dinner at eight at the Five Diamond."

"Sounds good," Courtney said.

"Congrats again," Brett added. "When you talked about the plans for the hotel last year, it sounded like it'll be awesome."

"It certainly will be." Adrian stood and headed for the door, flashing them one last smile. "Now I'll let you get back to that studying."

Once he was gone, Courtney let out a long breath and leaned back on the couch. "That was close," she said. "What was Peyton *thinking*, sending Adrian in here without warning us? I'm seriously going to strangle her." She stomped over to her bag and grabbed her cell, her chest heated.

She immediately saw two missed calls and three texts, all from Peyton.

1: Adrian just came over here and wants to talk to u! I told him ur at Brett's studying...so be sure ur STUDYING! ;)

2: PICK UP YOUR CELL!! I tried to delay him, but he's going to Brett's and I know ur prob NOT studying!

3: If you get caught, this SO isn't my fault.

"What happened?" Brett asked. "You're staring at your phone with the same horrified look you get whenever a zombie pops out on *The Walking Dead*."

"I am *such* an idiot!" Courtney threw her phone onto the couch and paced around the room. "I let my guard down, and we almost got caught. What if Adrian had come in here without knocking? Do you know how much trouble we would be in?"

"Relax." He stood and held her hands in his, steadying her. "Adrian and my mom always knock. It was close, but we were fine. He believed the studying cover-up."

Courtney glanced guiltily at the flash cards. "It shouldn't

have had to *be* a cover-up," she said. "Because we have that quiz in AP history about our winter-break reading, and I've barely reviewed for it. I needed to spend the afternoon studying. Instead, you talked me into watching that TV show."

"I thought we were having fun hanging out," he said softly. "I wasn't trying to mess up your studying."

"Well, we didn't get any studying done, and now we have that dinner tonight that'll probably take forever." She gathered her flash cards and textbook and shoved them into her bag. "*You* can ace a test by cramming the night before, but I've never been able to do that. And we're about to start second semester junior year. I can't let my grades drop. Especially since my PSAT scores weren't as high as I wanted them to be."

"Courtney." Brett wrapped his arms around her from behind. "You're right. If you want to study now, we'll study, okay? I don't want to distract you from doing well in school— I know how much your grades matter to you."

She closed her eyes and relaxed into his arms, wishing they could go back to ten minutes ago—before Adrian had almost busted them, when she wasn't thinking about anything except wanting to be with Brett. But she couldn't do that. So she spun to face him, gathering the courage to say what she needed. "It's more than my grades," she said, forcing each word out. "You heard Adrian—that big hotel deal with Logan is back on again. I can't mess it up for him a second time."

"We won't mess it up," Brett said, his gaze steady. "Because this whole thing with Adrian and my mom not wanting us to be together is stupid. We care about each other, and no matter how much they don't want us to feel that way, we can't ignore it. We shouldn't have to pretend anymore."

"So what do you want to do?" she asked.

"Tell them the truth."

"Just like that?" She shook her head, amazed by how easy

he made it sound. "I know we were planning on telling them eventually, but now that the hotel deal is back on again, it changes everything. And I can't get distracted this semester and let my grades drop."

"What are you saying?" He dropped his arms to his sides. "You don't want us to be together anymore?"

"After trying to keep my distance from you last semester, I know that won't work," she said. "But I do need time to think. And to study. Alone."

"Are you sure?" He reached for her, and before she could process what was happening, he was kissing her again, so softly, as if begging her to stay.

Her heart jumped, and she kissed him back, but only for a few seconds before pulling away. When she looked into his eyes, so full of how much he cared for her, she wished everything wasn't so complicated. But her family was counting on her—to be responsible, to get good grades, to follow the rules, to be the good example. And more important, she expected those things of herself.

"I'm sure," she choked out. "But I don't trust myself to get any studying done if I stay here, and I need to be ready for that quiz. I'm sorry."

"Don't be sorry." He traced her cheek with his fingers, and it took all her willpower not to lean into him and kiss him again. "I'll see you tonight, okay?"

"Okay." She zipped her bag closed, picked it up, and headed for the door. When she turned to have one more look at him, he still stood there, watching her, as if waiting for her to change her mind.

Part of her wanted to throw her stuff on the ground and resume where things had left off before Adrian interrupted them. But the bag of textbooks weighed on her back, reminding her about how much studying she had to do before dinner.

"See you tonight," she said softly, letting herself out. The door closed behind her, and she leaned against it, taking in a deep breath.

Even though they would see each other tonight, nothing could *happen*, because it would be a family dinner. Meaning they would have to pretend that everything between them— the depth of how much they cared for each other—didn't exist at all.

chapter 3: *Peyton*

After getting back from Savannah's celebration dinner, Peyton lay down on her bed and glared at the calendar pinned on her wall. There were less than twenty-four hours until the end of winter break. Sure, the Goodman School wasn't as torturous as Fairfield High, but she still didn't like sitting in classes all day or want to be there. Especially after all the fun she'd had in Italy.

She clicked on Dante Lazzaro's Facebook page for the hundredth time since returning home and scrolled through the pictures they'd taken together. Dante was the son of the owners of the resort they'd stayed in while in Tuscany. He was gorgeous and only a year older than her, and they'd hit it off immediately. But he was only a vacation fling. She'd been with him mainly to help her get over Jackson—her bodyguard, whom she'd fallen for over the past few months, and had stupidly managed to get fired because she kept pushing him to give in to his feelings for her.

It had all gone to hell on Thanksgiving Day, when she'd

found out about her mom keeping the secret about Courtney's twin sister, Britney. Peyton had gone to Jackson to talk. Once he saw how red her eyes were from crying, he'd taken her to a dive hotel on the Strip, where no one should have known who she was, so they could talk privately. They'd ended up admitting their feelings for each other, and some tourists had taken pictures of them having a clearly romantic conversation while drinking beers.

Adrian had seen the pictures, fired Jackson, and told them they couldn't see each other anymore. Jackson had gone back to his home in Nebraska. The last Peyton had heard from him was that he "needed space so he could get his life back on track." She hadn't wanted to be clingy and force him to talk to her, but it had been almost a month, and she missed him so much that it left a hole aching in her chest.

Not knowing what else to do, she'd tried getting over him by spending time with Dante in Italy. But Dante didn't look at her the way Jackson did—like he could see through her protective shield and straight to her core. Dante was supposed to help her get over Jackson, but he'd made her miss Jackson even more.

She shouldn't do it—she would only be torturing herself—but she typed Jackson's name into Facebook and clicked on his profile. She'd added him about two weeks ago, and his page still taunted her with the box that said Friend Request Sent. She slouched over her computer, staring hopelessly at the screen. His page had such intense privacy settings that all she could see was his profile picture of him and his family hanging out at a lake.

Maybe she should send him a message. She bit her lip, hovering her mouse over the message button. She just wanted to make sure she hadn't completely wrecked his future. If she had, and if he never wanted to speak to her again, she would rather he tell her. It would be better than this awful silence.

Then someone knocked on her door, and she clicked off his Facebook page.

"Peyton?" Courtney opened the door a crack. "Can I come in?"

"Sure." Peyton shut her laptop and pushed it to the side of her bed. "What's up?"

Courtney walked inside, clutching a red pocket folder to her chest, and sat down on the bed. She chewed her bottom lip, a telltale sign that she was nervous.

"What's in the folder?" Peyton prompted.

"A college application for UNLV." Courtney gingerly placed the folder down, unable to meet Peyton's eyes.

Peyton heaved a giant sigh and pushed her hair behind her ears. "I'm not going to college," she said. "Shoving forms in my face and asking me to fill them out won't change my mind."

"I'm not asking you to do anything," Courtney said. "I filled it out for you. It's all saved online—I made you an account—but I printed it so you can see what I did."

"You did *what*?"

"I filled out a college application for you," she repeated. "For UNLV. I knew you wouldn't do it yourself, and your SAT scores from when Adrian and Rebecca forced you to take the test were good."

"My SAT scores were *average*," Peyton said.

"Slightly above average," Courtney corrected her. "And UNLV is a good school, but it isn't Harvard or anything, so above average is fine, especially since you don't need a scholarship. And your grades have improved at Goodman. With a good essay, they might accept you."

"I knew there had to be a catch." Peyton laughed, stretched

her legs out, and leaned back into her pillows. "I'm not writing a college essay today. Or ever."

"I'm not asking you to," Courtney said. "Like I said, I completed the application for you."

"You wrote my essay?" Peyton smirked. "Isn't that breaking some kind of rule?"

"Don't tell anyone." Courtney took a deep breath and glanced at the door, as if afraid someone would overhear. "But yes. I wrote your essay. And it's pretty good." She pushed the folder closer to Peyton. "At least take a look. It'll only take a few minutes."

Unable to resist, Peyton picked up the folder and opened it. One side held the boring form with all her information filled out, and the other held an essay. She took it out and skimmed through it.

It was about how switching to Goodman, where she received individualized attention from teachers who cared, opened her eyes to the "joys of learning." This was proven by evidence of how her grades had improved in the past semester. The majority of the essay consisted of trying to convince the applications committee to look past her below-average grades from Fairfield High and see potential in what she could do in the future. Courtney had even written that Peyton wanted to be an education major so she could positively influence students the same way her teachers at Goodman had influenced her, going as far as listing three courses offered at UNLV and saying that Peyton couldn't wait to take them.

If Peyton had been an admissions person, she would have believed it.

"It's good, right?" Courtney asked.

"I guess." Peyton placed the essay back inside the folder. "Except that I don't want to go to college, and I definitely don't want to be an education major. I can't wait to get *out* of school. Why would I major in something that would keep me *in* a school for the rest of my life?" She shuddered. "That sounds awful."

"You're not declaring your major in your admissions essay," Courtney said. "This is just to convince them to let you in. Once you're in, you can choose not to declare your major, and take your general requirements until you figure out what you like best."

"But I don't want to go to college…" Why couldn't Courtney get this through her head?

"Applying doesn't mean you have to go," she said quickly. "I've done all the work for you. Just give me permission to click Send, and we'll see what happens." Peyton opened her mouth to protest, but Courtney continued. "If anything, do it for me," she said. "This is practice for my own college applications. If I can get *you* in, I should be able to get myself in somewhere, right?"

"So let me get this straight," Peyton said. "This is a game for you to see if you can get me into college? And if I get in, you won't care when I don't go?"

"Exactly." Courtney nodded. "So you'll do it?"

"You'll send it even if I say no, so fine, I'll do it," Peyton said. "As long as you promise not to bug me about going if I get in."

"Deal." Courtney bounced on the bed. "There's only one small thing you have to do, and then it'll be ready to send."

Peyton braced herself. Of course there had to be a catch. "What's that?"

"You need to get a teacher to write you a recommendation."

Peyton paused, waiting for Courtney to say she was kidding. But her sister's serious expression didn't change. "What teacher is going to recommend *me* for college?" she asked.

"The other students at school care about college applications. I don't. My teachers know that."

"What about Ms. Mandina?" Courtney said. "Your astronomy teacher—the one who helped you study for that test you did well on. She sees your potential. All you have to do is approach her after class and ask her if she would mind writing you a recommendation."

"And get her excited because she thinks I suddenly want to go to college?" Peyton crossed her arms. "I don't think so. What if she wants to have some long talk with me about how happy she is that I'm changing my mind? She'll know I don't mean it."

"Just tell her the truth," Courtney said.

"That my sister filled out my application for me, wrote my essay, and is using this as a practice run for her own applications next year?"

"Definitely *don't* tell her that." Courtney shook her head. "But let her know that you're giving yourself an option, and you'll see what happens when you hear back from the school. It's not a lie. You can even talk to her after class when you *know* she has another class coming in next, so you won't be stuck talking to her for too long. Please?"

Courtney widened her eyes, as if begging Peyton to give in. Peyton wanted to say no, but Courtney had gone through such a hard time after learning about Britney. If filling out a college application was keeping her mind off the twin sister she'd never gotten to know, then so be it.

"Fine, I'll do it," Peyton said. "But remember—this is *just* so you can see how you did on my application. Even if I get in, I'm not going."

"Great!" Courtney beamed and clapped her hands. "Once you get the recommendation, forward it to me and I'll upload it to your account."

"Will do," Peyton said, unable to muster up much enthusiasm.

"Great," Courtney said. "But anyway, Rebecca's coming over in five minutes to talk about bridesmaid dresses. You ready?"

"Tell me again why I agreed to do this?"

"Because Rebecca begged us to be bridesmaids on New Year's Eve during that ridiculously long six-course meal before the fireworks, and she wouldn't give up until we said yes? And because maybe you're realizing that she's not as awful as you originally thought?"

"I never thought she was *awful*," Peyton said. "Just annoying. She tells us how to dress, how to act, and wants to pick out our outfits for events…" She scrunched her nose. "I know she'll technically be our stepmother, but that doesn't mean she needs to act all motherly towards us. She knows our mom never did that, so why would we want her to?"

"How would you prefer her to act?" Courtney asked.

"I don't know." Peyton shrugged. "Normal?"

"Well, that was descriptive." Sarcasm leaked through Courtney's tone. "She's trying to reach out to us. And she's excited for the wedding."

"Excited?" Peyton raised an eyebrow. "More like obsessed. If I had to hear, 'That's so cute, we need to have something like it at the wedding!' one more time when we were in Italy, I might have lost it."

"She's about to have a princess fairy-tale wedding come true," Courtney said. "It's every woman's dream. You can't blame her for talking about it."

"It's *her* dream," Peyton corrected. "After being forced to hear about all this wedding stuff, I decided that if I get married, I'm going to elope."

The doorbell rang, and Peyton groaned, not wanting to

get up. Then Rebecca's voice echoed through the hall—she must have used her key to let herself in. "Girls? Are you in here?" she asked. "You remembered the appointment about the dresses, right?"

"Come on," Courtney said, pulling Peyton off the bed. "Weddings are romantic. It won't kill you to *pretend* to be interested."

Peyton wasn't sure about that, especially since her romantic life had dwindled to staring at a computer screen, wishing Jackson would accept her Facebook friend request.

It was probably a good thing that Courtney had walked in before she'd sent him that message.

In the living room, Rebecca was already showing Savannah a binder of color swatches, and her wedding planner was holding gold fabric up to Savannah's face.

"You're not making us wear gold, are you?" Peyton asked. "I hate gold."

"It's one of the colors I'm considering," Rebecca said. "If there's another you'd prefer, just let me know."

"How about black?" Peyton doubted Rebecca would go for it, but it was worth trying. "It goes with everything."

Savannah laughed and shared a smile with Rebecca, as if there was some inside joke Peyton didn't know about.

This was going to be a long, torturous afternoon. Scratch that. It would probably get worse every day until the wedding was finally over.

It was going to be a long, torturous next few *months*.

chapter 4: *Madison*

Madison Lockhart had been a walking disaster ever since Oliver's accident.

She'd let Oliver leave Savannah's party early, knowing he was drunk and about to drive, because she'd been too upset over learning about a bet he'd made to stop him. A better person *would* have stopped him. But she'd been crying in the bathroom while Oliver was speeding through a red light, getting his Maserati convertible totaled by an SUV.

She'd spent most of her time over break in the hospital waiting to see him. But once he'd woken up from his coma, Oliver had refused to have visitors who weren't family. Meaning he wouldn't see Madison. Now, after going through the first day of school without him, she'd had enough. She *had* to see him. And she refused to take no for an answer.

At least that's what she told herself as she marched through the hospital doors, her long dark hair snapping behind her, her huge Versace sunglasses covering her eyes. She moved her sunglasses onto her head, knowing that with her makeup done up for the first day back at school, she looked like a girl on a mission.

She spotted Oliver's fifteen-year-old sister, Brianna, sitting in the corner of the waiting room. Well, Brianna was actually Oliver's half sister—she was the result of an indiscretion on Oliver's dad's part. Normally Brianna would be at boarding school, summer camp, or at her mom's place in Santa Fe. But she'd been in Vegas a lot more since Oliver had landed in the hospital.

Brianna spotted Madison and lowered her iPad to her lap. "He's still not seeing anyone who's not family," she said.

"Maybe he'll change his mind once he realizes that I'm not leaving until he sees me," Madison said, lowering herself into the chair next to Brianna.

"I've been trying to convince him to see you," Brianna said. "But he's struggling through physical therapy—he still can't walk after the knee surgery—and he doesn't want anyone to see him this way. Especially you."

"Well, that's just stupid." Madison flicked her hair over her shoulder. "I've known him since kindergarten. I witnessed his chubby phase in seventh grade, and his shaved-head phase in ninth grade. I can handle seeing him with a knee brace."

"His face is also bruised and cut up from the glass," Brianna said. "I think he's more embarrassed about that than the knee."

"It'll heal," Madison said. "And I don't care about any of that. I just want to see him."

Her eyes filled with tears as she stared at the doors that led to the private patient rooms, hoping that by some miracle, a doctor would walk through and tell her that Oliver was ready to see her. She hated that their last words to each other had been said in anger. The days after his accident, when he was in the coma and she wasn't sure if he was going to make it, had been the most terrifying of her life. And while she was still upset about his bet with Peyton, she kept thinking about what he'd told her before leaving the party—that while the bet had put everything into motion, his feelings for her were real.

Had he been telling the truth? She wasn't sure. But she did know that she couldn't lose him. She wanted to be there for him, but how could she be when he kept refusing to see her?

Plus, Oliver was the only one besides her parents who knew that Adrian Diamond was her father, and that Peyton, Courtney and Savannah were her half sisters. Madison hadn't seen the Diamonds much since Savannah's Sweet Sixteen, due to winter break, but the secret had continued eating away at her. Oliver was the only one she could talk to about this. And his not wanting to see her hurt more than when she'd found out about the bet.

Brianna fiddled around on her iPad, not meeting Madison's eyes. "There's actually something I wanted to talk with you about," she said. "I haven't been able to yet because my dad or Ellen has always been around."

"What's up?" Madison asked.

"After Oliver was brought out of his coma, his mind was hazy from the medicine, and when it was only me and him in the room, he said something strange…" She looked around cautiously at the other two people in the waiting room—one asleep and one reading a magazine—and lowered her voice. "He said something about you being a Diamond, and having to keep it secret, and how he was the only one who knew and that he wanted me to make sure you were doing okay. I asked what he meant, but then he snapped back into focus and told me not to say anything because you'd be mad that he'd blown your secret. I promised him I wouldn't. But he sounded so worried, and now that I know you better, I have to ask—what did he mean?"

Madison felt like all the air had been sucked out of her

lungs. She could make something up, like Oliver calling her a "diamond" as a nickname. Or she could say that the pain medicine was messing with his mind, and that she had no idea what he meant.

But Madison had been drowning in the secret, and she needed to talk about it with someone who wasn't her parents. Months ago she might have told Damien, but now he was close with Savannah, so that wasn't an option. Larissa was a huge gossip, and she didn't feel right telling her other friends from school, because all it would take was one person to say something and then the secret would be out. Maybe she *should* tell Brianna.

"I wasn't sure if I should say anything, which is why I didn't for so long." Brianna pulled a leg up on her chair and faced Madison. "But when he told me, he sounded like he really wanted to make sure you were okay."

Madison swallowed, hating how her heart raced at the possibility of Oliver still caring about her—even if he was sending his sister to make sure she was okay instead of talking to her himself. "Don't be sorry," she said. "Oliver wouldn't have said anything to you if he didn't think I could trust you."

"You *can* trust me," Brianna said. "I won't tell anyone. I promise."

"All right." It was now or never. Madison took a deep breath, figuring she might as well get it over with. "In the beginning of the school year, I discovered that Adrian Diamond is my biological father."

"Omigod." Brianna's mouth dropped open. "No way. How did you find out? Do your parents know? Does Adrian know? Do the *Diamond sisters* know?"

"Keep your voice down," Madison hissed, scooting closer to Brianna. "I found out during a lab in my advanced genetics class, when I realized that my blood type didn't match my dad's. I asked my parents about it that night, and they told me the truth. My parents and Adrian have always known, but they weren't planning on telling me until I was old enough to access my trust fund…if they were ever really planning on telling me at all. No one else knows." She shook her head, unable to believe that this was her life. "My parents asked me not to tell anyone, but I broke down and told Oliver. We agreed that the Diamond girls needed to know. So I told my parents that if Adrian didn't tell them, I would.

"My mom talked to Adrian, but he said there were some major issues going on in their family, and he wanted to wait to tell them. I thought he was waiting until after Savannah's party, and was going to insist on telling them afterward. But then Oliver had his accident, and now we're here." She shrugged. "I still want to tell them the truth. But Oliver was there for me through this whole mess, and I'm not sure I can get through it without him."

Brianna's eyes were wide as saucers. "Wow." Her mouth opened and closed a few times, as if she wanted to say something, but wasn't sure where to start. "That's just…wow. I can't believe you've been keeping this to yourself for so long."

"I know," Madison said. "I wish Oliver would talk to me."

"He asks about you a lot," Brianna admitted.

"So why won't he see me?" Madison asked. "He won't even respond to my calls or texts. I don't get it."

"Give him time. He will when he's ready." Brianna focused on the floor, clearly not wanting to say more. "Anyway, have you talked to Adrian since finding all this stuff out?"

"No." Madison sighed and sat back in her chair. "I have no idea what to say to him. Besides, if he wants to talk to me, shouldn't *he* be the one to initiate it? He's supposed to be the parent here, not me."

"You're right," Brianna said. "And I guess marching up

to Adrian Diamond and confronting him is scary, even to someone as brave as you. But you should tell Peyton, Courtney and Savannah the truth. They deserve to know. They *are* your sisters."

"Half sisters," Madison corrected her.

"Oliver's my half brother," she said. "But it doesn't make him half as important."

"I know." Madison looked down at her hands. "I'm sorry. It's just all so strange. I've been an only child all my life, and now I have *sisters*. And I wasn't very nice to them when they moved here. I would probably be a terrible sister."

"I doubt that's true," Brianna said. "Just act the same way around them that you do around me. They'll love you."

"Maybe." Madison pulled her legs onto the chair and wrapped her arms around them. "But you didn't see what a bitch I was to them at first. They should hate me."

"You'll never know *what* they think if you don't tell them the truth."

"I know." Madison didn't like it, but Brianna was right.

"Let me know how it goes, okay?" Brianna said. "I have to go back to school soon, and I hate being so far away from everything that happens here."

"Is boarding school really that bad?" Madison asked, glad to change the subject.

"It's in the middle of nowhere, and the only guys I see are my teachers," she complained. "I want to live here and go to Goodman. Whenever I come to visit, it seems so fun and glamorous. But Ellen would hate it if I lived here, my dad doesn't want to make her upset and my mom thinks Vegas is a 'world of sin.'" She leaned back and frowned. "I'm stuck at boarding school, and it sucks."

"There's always college," Madison said. "Have you thought about applying to UNLV?"

Brianna perked up at the possibility, but the doctor came into the waiting room before she could answer.

"Oliver's out of physical therapy and is ready for visitors now," he said, glancing at Madison. "I'm afraid he's still seeing family members only."

"I've been here every day since his accident." Madison crossed her arms, keeping her gaze level with his. "Can I *please* see him?"

"He was specific with his request, and I can't go against it," the doctor said. "I'm sorry."

"I'll try getting him to change his mind again, but I doubt it'll work." Brianna stood up, stretched and grabbed her iPad. "You know Oliver—he's stubborn. Thanks for the talk, though. And good luck with what you were telling me."

"Thanks," Madison said, watching as the doctor escorted Brianna into the recovery wing. She stared blankly at the doors as they shut closed.

Why didn't Oliver want her to visit? Madison swallowed back tears, frustrated that she couldn't just *talk* to him. He was her best friend. Shouldn't he want to see her? Shouldn't he *miss* her? She definitely missed him—especially since school had started again today, and she'd been forced to see Peyton, Courtney and Savannah. How was she supposed to tell them the truth without knowing that Oliver would be there for her if it went terribly wrong?

A tear ran down her face, and she quickly wiped it away. She didn't want to cry—especially not in the waiting room. So she put her sunglasses back on, left the hospital and blasted the radio her entire drive home.

www.campusbuzz.com

High Schools > Nevada > Las Vegas > The Goodman School

Savannah Diamond is getting WAY more credit than she deserves!!!
Posted on Friday 1/16 at 4:20 PM
Like everyone else, I've watched Savannah Diamond's videos on her YouTube channel. And I know I'm not the first to say that I just DON'T GET IT. Someone please tell me WHY this girl is getting so much attention?! I can name so many YouTube artists who are WAY more talented and who aren't nearly as well known as Savannah.

1: Posted on Friday 1/16 at 4:42 PM
its because her daddys rich and everyones fascinated by the girl who came from nothing and is now a hotel heiress. clearly its not because of her "talent!!!!" shes a good singer and all, but the girl has no stage presence! shes BORING!!

2: Posted on Friday 1/16 at 4:58 PM
What are you all talking about?! Savannah's videos are amazing! Her voice is PERFECT. And yeah, she was shy around the camera at first. But she's getting better! Give her a chance.

3: Posted on Friday 1/16 at 5:13 PM
shes a good singer, sure. But she SUCKS on guitar!!! Go back to her fist few vids and watch. Pure entertainment (in a comedic way).

4: Posted on Friday 1/16 at 5:29 PM

whenever I watch one of her early videos I want to yell at her to PUT DOWN THE GUITAR!!! She might be decent if she wasn't attacking the poor instrument through every song!! At least in her recent ones she has someone else playing for her.

5: Posted on Friday 1/16 at 5:34 PM

You all are such bitches. Have you listened to her sing? She has perfect pitch. I'm telling you, that girl has natural talent and is going somewhere. You're all just jealous.

6: Posted on Friday 1/16 at 5:41 PM

Perfect pitch doesn't give her a personality. And whats up with her eyeshadow? She puts so much on it looks like she got punched in the face.

7: Posted on Friday 1/16 at 5:55 PM

hahahahahahaha you would think that considering how much money her dad has, she could afford to get her makeup professionally done for her videos!

8: Posted on Friday 1/16 at 6:09 PM

You all know the only reason she's so well known is because her daddy paid One Connection to perform at her sweet sixteen and tweet about her YouTube channel. ANYONE would be famous after that!!

9: Posted on Friday 1/16 at 6:58 PM

she thinks shes a hell of a lot hotter than she is, too. she looks like every other blonde teenage girl around here! nothing special. people only put up with her cause she's a Diamond.

chapter 5: *Savannah*

Courtney and Peyton still had no idea that Savannah had broken their pact and talked to Mom and Grandma, and Savannah planned on keeping it that way.

So when Grandma had asked them to visit over the long weekend in January for Courtney's birthday—using Aunt Sophie's illness to guilt-trip them into saying yes—Savannah had been relieved. Soon her sisters would be *forced* to talk to Mom and Grandma. Savannah wouldn't have to feel like she was going behind their backs anymore.

The limo got on the freeway—it wouldn't be long until they reached Grandma's new home in Napa. Courtney was staring contemplatively out the window, while Peyton had her headphones in, listening to a '90s rock band so loudly that they could all hear it. Savannah scrolled through Instagram to pass the time. She was commenting on a photo by a popular YouTuber when the phone buzzed with a text from Perry Myles. She smiled and opened it, having a good idea about what it would say. She was right:

We go on in 10! The crowd rocks tonight ☺ xx

Ever since Savannah had texted Perry after the meeting with her agent, he'd been texting her every night of the One Connection world tour. On days when they played a show, it was always when he was waiting in the greenroom. When he first did it, Savannah had thought it would be a one-time thing. But he'd continued with every stop, and the texts had become something special between them. She'd even looked his tour up and memorized where he'd be every night that week…although she made sure never to let *him* know that.

Where are you now?? ☺

Belgium… I've been craving waffles since we got here :P

I love waffles!! ☺

I thought pancakes were your fave?

Yeah, they are ☺ Especially the ones at the Grand Café at the Diamond. They're the best pancakes EVER!

Is that an invite for me to visit so I can try them? ;)

Savannah's fingers froze, and she stared at the text. What was the right reply? She wished she could ask Peyton, but the vibe in the limo was so awkward—Savannah could *feel* her sisters' anger toward Grandma and Mom. She didn't want to make things worse. So she would have to try her best at channeling Peyton herself.

If you ever get a break in your crazy schedule ;)

She pressed Send, and reread their conversation. Hopefully her response was okay. She didn't want Perry to think she was throwing herself at him, but she also didn't want to sound uninterested.

I always have time for you. Anyway, my manager's yelling at me to put my phone away…time to hit the stage! xx

Her heart flipped at the first line. *He would always have time for her.* It was hard to believe that Perry Myles was interested in her, but he *did* text her every night before performing. That had to mean something. But he also had to put his phone away, so she had to reply quickly.

Good luck tonight! I wish I was there <3

I wish you were here, too ;)

Savannah smiled at his reply, then returned to scrolling through Instagram. One of Perry's bandmates, Noel, had posted a picture of the five of them backstage, and while they would never see it because they had so many fans, Savannah liked the picture. She couldn't wait to see them live when they played Vegas this summer. In the meantime, Perry would text her when the show was over to tell her how it went. Although she'd come to learn that One Connection shows *always* went well. With seats that scalped for thousands of dollars, it was to be expected.

Eventually, the limo exited the freeway. Courtney was biting her nails—something she did only when she was *really* nervous—and Savannah tossed her phone into her bag. She wanted to say something to make Courtney feel better, but what? The guilt over her secret rose up in her throat once again, so Savannah stayed quiet, looking out the window and playing with the ends of her hair.

Peyton paused her music and took out her earbuds. "Are you guys ready?" she asked, looking mainly at Courtney.

"No." Courtney stopped chewing her nails and lowered her hands to her lap. "I have no idea what to say to them. I wouldn't even be visiting this weekend if Grandma hadn't sent us that email about how Aunt Sophie wanted us to come, and that this might be one of our last chances to see her before…"

She let the sentence hang, not needing to clarify what she meant. Aunt Sophie had stopped chemo at the start of the New Year, since it wasn't working. The three of them didn't know Aunt Sophie that well—she'd moved in with Grandma right before they'd come to Vegas, and prior to then they'd only seen her a handful of times when she'd visited during the holidays—but how could they refuse to come to Napa with Grandma holding Aunt Sophie's illness over their heads?

"Maybe it won't hurt to listen to them?" Savannah twisted her bracelets. "We can't stay mad at them forever."

"But I can't forgive them, either," Courtney said. "They lied to us. For our *entire lives*. I can't just get past that."

"You don't have to 'get past it.'" Peyton blew a bubble with her gum and sucked the air back in. "I sure as hell won't."

"I don't know." Savannah bit her lip. "Will you really never forgive Grandma? You're her favorite."

"No, I'm not." Courtney rested her head in her hand and sighed.

"I just keep worrying that Mom will relapse," Savannah said. "If she does, and it's because we haven't forgiven her… it'll be our fault."

"It's not our fault," Peyton said sharply. "Besides, Grandma would have said something if Mom were drinking again. But it seems like quitting her job, moving to the country, and doing yoga every day was cure enough. Oh, and us moving out so she didn't have to take care of us anymore. I'm sure that had something to do with it."

Savannah flinched. "I don't think that's it. I mean, the other stuff must have helped. But she misses us—I know it."

"How?" Courtney asked. "None of us have talked to her since Thanksgiving."

Savannah's heart stopped. "Right," she said, her sisters' gazes searing into her as she grasped for an excuse. "But before then, when we talked to her on Skype, I could tell she missed us. And when we saw her the day before Thanksgiving, she was really happy to see us. She tried cooking for us and everything."

"She did *try*," Courtney said, her forehead creased. "But being back in that house after what happened there, and seeing Mom and Grandma again…it'll be so strange. I don't think I'll ever look at them the same way. I'm just so grateful that the two of you have stood by me through all of this. Thank you."

"Of course," Peyton asked as the limo passed through the gates of Grandma's neighborhood. "We're all three in this together."

Savannah's stomach dropped. What would her sisters do if they knew about her secret phone calls with Mom and Grandma?

Hopefully they would never find out.

"You're going to have to say *something* to them, 'cause here they are." Peyton motioned to the house, where Grandma and Mom had stepped out to wait for them—Grandma smoothing out her dress, Mom wringing her hands.

The initial greeting went well. Courtney managed to be pleasant, as if she hadn't been giving Mom and Grandma the silent treatment since Thanksgiving. Peyton was a little sullen, but then again, when *wasn't* Peyton pouting over something?

"Thank you for not shutting me out these past few weeks,

like your sisters did," Mom whispered to Savannah while hugging her. "I appreciate it more than you know."

Savannah's heart jumped, and she checked to see if Courtney and Peyton had heard. But they were already on their way inside the house, and they didn't seem to have caught Mom's slip-up.

"Of course," she said, pulling away. "But you know Courtney and Peyton don't know I've been talking to you, right? So please don't say anything about it again? I don't want them to get mad at me."

"They shouldn't make that decision for you," she said. "But if you don't want me to mention it again, I won't."

"Thanks." Savannah smiled, glad that Mom still looked healthy. Her skin was clear, she no longer had circles under her eyes, and she'd kept off the weight she'd lost since rehab. Maybe Peyton was right, and Mom was better off living away from them?

As much as it hurt to think about, it might be true.

They went inside, and Grandma was the only one to be found in the living room,

"Your bags are in the guest room, and your sisters are down there getting settled in," she said. "Aunt Sophie's taking a nap, and her room's right above yours, so be quiet when you unpack, okay?"

"All right." Savannah wanted to stay with Mom and Grandma, but she also wanted to see how her sisters were doing. And she didn't want her sisters to think she was taking Mom and Grandma's side. "I'll be back up soon."

She headed down the steps and into the big bedroom that she and her sisters shared when they visited Grandma. She loved having her own room in the penthouse at the Diamond, but sometimes it got so quiet. She liked coming here and sharing the room with her sisters. This bedroom was about three

times bigger than the one they'd crammed into in their dilapi-
dated apartment in Fairfield, but it reminded her of old times.

Peyton was unpacking her stuff, but Courtney was nowhere to be found.

"Where's Courtney?" Savannah asked. "Is she okay?"

"I don't think so." Peyton shook her head. "She didn't say
anything when we got down here—she just went straight to
the bathroom. She looked like she did after finding her and
Britney's baby book. Really pissed off."

"Crap," Savannah said, glancing at the bathroom. "I guess
seeing Grandma and Mom didn't go as well as she made it
seem."

"You guessed right." Courtney stomped inside, slammed
the door and glared at Savannah. "What was that about with
Mom?"

Savannah opened her mouth, but nothing came out. Had
Courtney overheard what Mom had said? If she had…then
Savannah was screwed.

She decided to act clueless. "What was *what* about?" she
asked, sinking onto her bed and glancing at Peyton for help.

"I don't know what's going on." Peyton threw her hands up
and took a step away from Courtney. "Did I miss something?"

Savannah's chest tightened, her eyes darting back and forth
between her sisters. Courtney needed to stop glaring at her
like she was the worst person ever—like she *hated* her.

She swallowed and looked down at the carpet. "Is this about
the hug Mom gave me when we got here?" she asked. "Because I had to hug her back. I'm sorry."

"Stop lying." Courtney's voice echoed through the room.
"I'm sick of all the lies. I heard what she said to you. So just—
stop. Stop pretending like you don't know what I'm talking
about."

"What did she say?" Peyton crossed her arms. "What am I missing?"

Tears filled Savannah's eyes, and she tried swallowing them away. She couldn't say it—not without crying.

Leave it to Mom to talk without thinking and screw up everything.

"She thanked Savannah for not shutting her out these past few weeks," Courtney told Peyton. "Which means that Savannah must have broken our pact. She's been talking to Mom."

"Is that true?" Peyton asked Savannah.

"I couldn't *not* talk to her." Savannah sniffed and wiped away a tear. "She hates what she did, and wishes she could take it back. Us not talking to her was making her feel worse."

"She can't just 'take it back.'" Courtney paced around the room, her hands curled into fists. "Britney wasn't some small thing that slipped Mom's mind. She was our sister—she was my *twin*—and Mom didn't tell us about her because it was too hard for *her*. Don't you see how selfish that was?"

"I know," Savannah choked out. "I tried not talking to her—I really did. But she kept reaching out to us, and she's our *mom*. I couldn't ignore her."

"And I'm your sister," Courtney said. "Me, you and Peyton—we agreed to take space from Mom so she would know that she can't lie to us without any consequences. But you not being able to do it...it's like you don't care about what she did. Like you don't care about Britney."

"That's not true," Savannah said. "I do care about Britney, and I hate that Mom never told us about her."

"So why are you acting like she doesn't matter?"

"Because Britney's *dead!*" The moment she realized what she'd said, Savannah clasped her hands over her mouth, her eyes wide.

Courtney stopped pacing, her face pale. She stared at Savannah as if she didn't recognize her.

"What the hell, Savannah?" Peyton said. "When did you become such a bitch?"

"I didn't mean it like that," she mumbled, unable to meet her eyes. Her sisters were looking at her with so much betrayal that she wanted to bury herself under the covers. "Mom just kept reaching out to me, and I felt so bad ignoring her…"

"Mom kept reaching out to you because she knows you're the weakest of the three of us," Peyton said. "She knew you would give in."

"At least I *let* myself care about people," Savannah shot back. "You just push everyone away. Of course you had no problem shutting Mom out—shutting people out comes naturally to you."

There were three knocks on the door, and they all went silent, watching as whoever it was opened it and peeked her head through. Aunt Sophie. Her skin was wrinkled and hollow, with age spots all over it, and the circles around her eyes were so dark that they could have been bruises. In her ivory, flowing nightgown, she looked like a ghost who hadn't slept in weeks.

"Is everything okay in here?" she asked, her voice soft and frail.

"Aunt Sophie!" Courtney exclaimed. "Did our talking wake you up?"

"I wouldn't call what you were doing 'talking.'" Aunt Sophie laughed, although it turned into a hacking cough. She caught her breath, then said, "Yelling is more like it."

"We're so sorry," Courtney said, clasping her hands together. "We didn't mean to bother you."

"I know," Aunt Sophie said. "I opened my window this morning for some fresh air, and your window down here was open, too. Sound really travels out here in the country."

"How much did you hear?" Savannah asked.

"Everything." Aunt Sophie hobbled over to the closest bed—Savannah's—and sat down. She held her hand against her head, as if just that short walk had made her dizzy, and took a few long, steadying breaths. "As I understand from what I heard, the three of you made a group decision not to speak to your mom and grandma, and Savannah spoke to them anyway without telling you."

"We don't need to 'talk this out,' or whatever," Peyton said. "We've got it covered."

Aunt Sophie cracked a smile. "I disagree. It sounded like you were about to rip each other's hair out. And since I have to live here while everyone else is angry at each other, I think we do need to talk it out. Let's not make this weekend more stressful than it needs to be, okay?"

Savannah's cheeks turned red, and she fiddled with her bracelets, unable to look at Aunt Sophie. If she'd heard that entire conversation, then she must have heard what Savannah had yelled at Courtney—about Britney being dead. She'd never said anything so mean, ever. Especially not to her sister.

Aunt Sophie must think she was a terrible person.

"I want each of you to sit on your beds, and we'll discuss this—without yelling," Aunt Sophie said.

"Are you a psychologist now or something?" Peyton asked, although she did stomp over to her bed and sit.

"No—but I was a teen once, and your grandma and I had quite our share of fights as well," Aunt Sophie replied. "I know what it's like to fight with your sister. And when it came to your grandma and I, I was always the peacekeeper of the two."

"Like Courtney," Savannah said. "Well…like Courtney is normally. Peyton and I fight all the time about stupid things, but Courtney always fixes it."

"You're right," Courtney said. "I'm *always* there for both

of you. When you and Peyton fight over what music to listen to, or taking each other's stuff, or any of your stupid fights, I help you work it out. But now—the one time when I needed you to stand by me—you couldn't do it. And you lied to me about it."

"Which are you more upset about?" Aunt Sophie asked. "That Savannah talked to your mom and grandma, or that she kept it from you and Peyton?"

"Both." Courtney sniffed. "But not telling us makes it worse." She turned her focus to Savannah, her eyes full of so much anger that Savannah backed up against the wall. "How did you sit with us in the car today when I was talking about how grateful I was that you and Peyton kept your word, *knowing* that you hadn't? How could you lie to me like that?"

"I didn't mean to," Savannah said. "You made me promise not to talk to them. Then they wanted to talk to me, and I hated ignoring them, so I didn't. No one ever asked me if not talking to them was something *I* wanted to do."

"It's always about you, isn't it?" Courtney said.

Savannah blinked, and looked down at her lap. How could Courtney say that to her?

"We're supposed to be talking about this *without* fighting," Aunt Sophie reminded them. "I don't have the energy to deal with a fight like the one I overheard earlier—and I certainly don't want to be surrounded by this attitude all weekend."

"Sorry," Courtney said. "I knew we shouldn't have come here." She leaned against the wall, pulled her legs up to her chest and added, "But maybe it's best that we did. Otherwise we wouldn't have found out that Savannah's been lying to us."

"So I was correct," Aunt Sophie said. "It's the lying that upset you the most."

"I guess." Courtney shrugged. "It definitely made it worse."

"What was I supposed to do?" Savannah asked. "If I'd told

you about talking with Mom and Grandma, it wouldn't have changed anything. You still would have been mad."

"Yeah," Courtney said. "But not *as* mad. At least that way you wouldn't have been going behind my back for weeks, lying to me and making me think you had my back this entire time."

"I *do* have your back," Savannah insisted. "I just couldn't ignore Mom and Grandma, either."

"So you never should have promised that you would."

"Your sister makes a good point," Aunt Sophie said to Savannah. "When you made that promise, did you know you wouldn't be able to keep it?"

"No," Savannah said. "I wanted to stick to it. I swear it."

Peyton rolled her eyes. "So why didn't you?" she asked. "It wasn't hard—we live in a different state than Mom and Grandma. All you had to do was not pick up the phone when they called."

Savannah shook her head, amazed that Peyton didn't get it. "Maybe it wasn't hard for you," she said. "But it was for me. I kept thinking…what if Mom gets so upset by our ignoring her that she relapses? She kept calling and reaching out to us, so eventually I had to pick up, and once I started talking to her, I couldn't just stop again. But I've felt terrible about talking to her every time."

"You shouldn't feel bad about wanting to be there for your mom," Aunt Sophie said. "That was kind of you to do—especially considering the magnitude of her lies. It takes strength to forgive and love unconditionally, and you have that strength, Savannah. It's what makes you shine."

"Thank you." Savannah swallowed and glanced at her nails. She'd never had someone say something that nice to her before.

"I mean it," Aunt Sophie said. "It seems like the real problem here is that you didn't feel like you could be honest with your sisters."

"I know," Savannah said. "I was afraid. And I felt bad that I couldn't follow through with the promise that I'd made them." She took a deep breath and looked at both Peyton and Courtney. Peyton's eyes were hard, and Courtney's face was still red from the yelling she'd done earlier. "I hate when you guys are mad at me. I don't want to take sides between both of you and Mom and Grandma, but I should have told you the moment I realized I couldn't go through with the promise. And I shouldn't have said any of that stuff to you just now. I didn't mean it. I wasn't thinking, and it just came out. I'm sorry."

"It doesn't change what you did," Peyton said. "Or what you said."

"Is that fair, Peyton?" Aunt Sophie asked. "Of course Savannah can't take back what she said or did—that's how life works. There are no do-overs. Everyone makes mistakes, and if you can't forgive them, you'll end up pushing everyone away. That's no way to live. What's most important is intent. Do you think Savannah means what she's saying in her apology?"

"Sure." Peyton shrugged. "I guess."

"All right." Aunt Sophie nodded. "I suppose that's progress. Now, what about you, Courtney? Do you accept Savannah's apology?"

"I want to." Courtney focused on Savannah, and while her eyes were glassy, they weren't angry like they were earlier. "And I will. I know you didn't *want* to go behind my back, but it doesn't change that you did. I just hope in the future you'll be honest with me. Okay?"

"Okay." Savannah smiled. "I promise."

"Does this mean we'll be able to enjoy this weekend in peace?" Aunt Sophie asked. She coughed, took a few wheezing breaths, and cleared her throat. "After all, we do have Courtney's birthday to celebrate tomorrow."

"I'm going to be civil to Grandma and Mom," Courtney

said. "But that doesn't mean I forgive them. What they did by not telling me that Britney even *existed*…that's unforgivable."

"But you have to forgive them eventually," Savannah said. "Right?"

"I don't know." She grabbed her backpack and pulled it onto the bed. "But I do know we're celebrating my birthday tomorrow, and I have homework I need to do today."

"I supposed that's enough for now," Aunt Sophie said. "And I need to get some rest. Would one of you mind helping me up the stairs?"

"Of course." Courtney jumped up off her bed and helped Aunt Sophie up. "I'm so sorry that we bothered you."

"No need to apologize," she said. "I just hope I helped."

"You did," Savannah said, watching Courtney lead Aunt Sophie out of their room. Every step of Aunt Sophie's was slow, and she breathed heavily as she walked. She couldn't imagine how she'd come down here on her own.

"She seems really nice," she said to Peyton once Aunt Sophie and Courtney were up the steps.

"Yeah," Peyton agreed. "It sucks that she's so sick."

"I've never known what to say to her," Savannah said. "She's the first person I've ever known who *knows* she's dying. But after that conversation…I'm glad we're here this weekend."

"I'm glad we're here, too," Peyton said, pulling at the ends of her sleeves. "It's weird, though. Talking to her is almost like…talking to a ghost."

Savannah shivered, and they were both silent for a few seconds.

Then her phone buzzed with a text. Evie.

Hey, Savannah! I saw on Twitter that you're in California, and was hoping we could hang out? ☺

Savannah glared at her phone, clicked out of the text, tossed it onto her bed.

"Wow," Peyton said. "Whoever that was must have really pissed you off."

"It was Evie," Savannah said. "She wants to hang out."

"But you're still mad at her?"

Savannah thought back to the last time she'd spoken to Evie—the night of her Sweet Sixteen. Evie had known that Savannah had feelings for Damien, but she'd tried to flirt with him, anyway. After Savannah caught her, Evie had blown up. She'd called Savannah a selfish brat, and said that Savannah's YouTube channel was stupid because she only sang covers and no original songs. Then she'd tried to claim that her making moves on Damien was good for Savannah, because it would prove to Savannah whether or not Damien was worth it. It was so convoluted.

At least Damien hadn't fallen for it—he'd only been talking to Evie because he felt bad for her, because Evie had felt out of place at the party.

"I'm still mad at her," Savannah said. "I don't want to see her."

"What about everything Aunt Sophie said?" Peyton asked. "About forgiveness?"

"That was different," she said. "You and Courtney are my sisters—we *have* to forgive each other. I don't need to be friends with Evie."

"It's your call," Peyton said. "I'm just surprised."

Savannah frowned and glanced at her phone. If *Peyton* was telling her to forgive Evie, maybe she should? But then she reminded herself about the mean things Evie had said at the party, and the way she'd tried snuggling into Damien, and anger surged through her body.

"You lost touch with your friends from Fairfield," Savannah said. "Why shouldn't I do the same?"

"Because those 'friends' I had in Fairfield were never really my friends," Peyton said. "They were just people to hang out with and party with. But you and Evie were *best* friends. I always thought that you would have preferred to have her as a sister over me or Courtney."

"Don't be ridiculous," Savannah said. "I would never choose to have *anyone* as a sister besides you and Courtney."

"But you did always have more fun with her than you did with either of us," Peyton said. "And don't say it's not true, because I'll know you're lying."

Savannah shrugged, since she *did* have a lot of fun hanging out with Evie. They could talk and laugh about everything. It wasn't that she didn't have fun with her sisters, but it was different. Courtney was so responsible, and Peyton was so confident. Savannah always felt like everything she said was up for judgment or a lecture. But with Evie, she didn't have to worry about that.

Her phone buzzed with another text.

Or be a bitch and ignore me. Whatever.

It hadn't been ten minutes since the first message. Evie couldn't know that Savannah had seen it.

Except that Savannah had her phone on her constantly, and Evie knew that.

But did she have to be so mean about it?

"I don't want to talk about Evie." Savannah deleted their entire string of text messages and threw her phone back down onto the bed. "We're not friends anymore."

"Okay," Peyton said, although she didn't sound like she believed it.

chapter 6: *Courtney*

That night, Courtney had stayed true to her word to be civil to everyone, and they'd all marathon watched a television show—minus Aunt Sophie, who'd fallen asleep in the reclining chair. Courtney was the first to wake up the next morning, and when she checked her phone, there was a text message from Brett. She smiled when she saw that he'd sent it exactly at midnight.

HAPPY BIRTHDAY!! Can't wait for you to get back home so we can celebrate. Wish I was there with you, but I hope you're having a good time in California, and remember to call me if you need anything… I miss you!

She texted him back immediately, even though he was probably still asleep.

I miss you and wish you were here, too. So much. I'll see you first thing when I get home <3

She slid out of bed, making sure not to disturb Peyton and Savannah, grabbed her Kindle and tiptoed upstairs to the kitchen. The birds chirped outside, and she brewed some chai tea in the Keurig, glad to have time to herself. Despite her insistence that no one should make a big deal about her birthday, no one ever listened. There was always so much pressure to have the perfect happy day.

Well, Mom was usually a wreck on her birthday—which made sense now, since she was grieving for Britney—but Peyton and Savannah tried to make the day all about her. Courtney hated it. Her perfect day would consist of doing nothing but reading an incredible book.

She'd situated herself on the couch, Kindle in hand, and was blowing on her tea when Aunt Sophie emerged from her room. Courtney would never get used to seeing how sick Aunt Sophie looked, especially since she was Grandma's twin. Her wrinkled skin, sagging circles under her eyes and the wool hat she wore to hide her lack of hair made her look at least fifteen years older.

"I heard someone walking around, and given the time, I thought it might be you," Aunt Sophie said, settling into her favorite recliner. "Happy birthday. Is that chai tea I smell?"

"Yes," Courtney said. "This one's nearly cooled off enough to drink, and I haven't had any yet. If you want it, I can brew myself another."

"That would be lovely," she said. "Thank you."

Courtney handed the tea over, afraid Aunt Sophie's hands were shaking so much that she might drop it. Once she saw that she wouldn't, she went into the kitchen to get another cup. The Keurig had it ready in less than a minute, and she brought it back into the living room.

"I'm glad I was able to help you and your sisters work through your argument yesterday," Aunt Sophie said, sipping on her tea. "You've had quite a few changes to adjust to in the past few months, haven't you?"

"My entire *life* has changed," Courtney said. "I've been try-ing to make the best of it, but recently I feel like I don't know who I am anymore." Realizing how intense that sounded, she tried to smile and shrug it off. But it was too late. The words hung in the air, waiting for an explanation.

"And you truly don't see yourself forgiving your mom and grandma?"

Courtney took a deep breath and stared into her tea. "I don't *want* to still be mad at them," she said. "But right now, I don't know how not to be. Especially today, when I should be celebrating my seventeenth birthday with Britney. I should have been remembering her every year at this time. But be-cause Grandma and Mom lied to me, I didn't even know she *existed* until a few weeks ago."

"Your grandma and mom were wrong not to tell you about her," Aunt Sophie said. "I told them for years that they needed to, but they never listened."

"Thank you," she said. "That means a lot."

"But they did what they did because of love," Aunt So-phie said, her voice stronger than Courtney had heard so far. "They thought that by not telling you about Britney, it would spare you from wondering what life would have been like if she'd lived. It's a pain your grandma and mom have experi-enced every day."

"But Britney was my *twin*," Courtney said. "Keeping her from me was selfish. If I'd never found that baby book, they might have never told me about her, and then I never would have known the truth."

"Very true. But you *did* find that baby book, and now you do know the truth." Aunt Sophie lifted her mug to her lips and took a sip, her hand shaking. Courtney prepared herself to jump out of her seat in case she dropped it, but her aunt managed to place it back on the armrest and hold it steady. "At this point, what's in the past is done. Being angry at your mom and grandma won't change that. Ever since Thanksgiving, when you and your sisters left early and refused to speak with them, they've been beating themselves up over it. Savannah was right to worry that your mom would return to drinking—your grandma and I worried about it, as well. We were so grateful when Savannah offered her forgiveness."

"I know you wouldn't believe it after hearing our fight yesterday, but I'm grateful to Savannah for that, too," Courtney said, curling up on the couch. "The last thing I want is for Mom to relapse. But I can't force myself to forgive her and Grandma. Every time I think of them, I'm reminded of how they never told me about Britney, and I get angry all over again. I hate it."

"Neither of them can take back their actions," Aunt Sophie said softly. "But you need to ask yourself—do you want to look back and wish you'd handled this differently? Most of us go through life feeling invincible, but none of us know what day will be our last. Is holding on to your anger truly worth it?"

"When you put it that way, I know it's not," Courtney said. "But I can't just *forget* about what they did."

"I didn't ask you to forget," Aunt Sophie said. "You should never forget. But you should try to forgive."

Courtney couldn't meet her eyes, because she *wanted* to forgive Grandma and Mom. She missed talking with them—Grandma especially. But it was too fresh right now. Especially today, with her birthday as a reminder of how Britney was missing from their lives.

They sat in silence for a few seconds, sipping on their tea. Then Grandma's door opened, and Courtney watched as she walked into the living room, dressed and ready for the day.

While she and Aunt Sophie were identical, the two of them were more likely to pass as mother and daughter than twins.

"I thought I heard people out here," she said, smiling. "Happy birthday, Courtney. And Sophie—you're looking refreshed this morning."

Courtney would hardly describe Aunt Sophie as looking "refreshed," but she supposed it was all about perspective.

Soon Savannah came up to join them, followed by Mom. Courtney still wasn't used to Mom waking up before noon, but it was one of the many changes that had come with her journey to recovery.

"I'm going to get breakfast started," Grandma said. "French toast—Courtney's favorite, since she's the birthday girl. Will you girls get Peyton out of bed and up here to join us?"

Thirty minutes later, they were all sitting around the dining room table, the serving plates piled with French toast, eggs, fruit and bacon (the vegetarian kind for Courtney and regular for everyone else).

"So, girls," Grandma said after everyone had food on their plates. "Your mom and I recently received our invitations to your father's wedding."

Peyton's mouth dropped open, despite being in the middle of chewing her food. She swallowed quickly, and said, "They invited you? *Both* of you?"

"You're not actually going, are you?" Savannah chimed in.

"I don't see why we wouldn't," Grandma said.

Courtney could think of a lot of reasons. But she started with the most practical one. "There's going to be an open bar," she said, looking at Mom. "Is that something you're ready for? Especially since you haven't seen Adrian in so long...it might be a trigger."

"I talked with my doctor about it after receiving the invitation," she said. "She told me that with the support of Grandma, the three of you, and with my sponsor there, I'll be able to get through the event. She actually believes it will be good for me to attend."

"But it's more than the wedding." Courtney picked up a piece of fake bacon and tore it apart. "It's Las Vegas in general. Everywhere you turn in the Diamond there's a bar, or people drinking in the casino, or people walking around with drinks, or a mention of some sort of party. I can't imagine that'll be good for you."

"Which is why we'll stay at the Trump," Grandma said. "A non-gaming, family-friendly hotel."

"What about Aunt Sophie?" Courtney turned to Aunt Sophie, who had barely touched her French toast. "You won't be able to travel, will you? Or stay here alone?"

"Oh, don't worry about me," she said. "A nurse will stay with me here. I'll be perfectly fine."

"It sounds like a good plan." Savannah twisted a piece of hair around her finger and looked at Mom. "But are you going to be okay watching Adrian marry Rebecca?"

"You think I would be upset watching him marry her?" Mom smiled, as if she found the notion amusing.

"You were married to him once, and you do have kids with him," Courtney said. She'd pictured the wedding numerous times—Rebecca talked about it constantly, so she had to—and she couldn't imagine Mom and Grandma there. In fact, she couldn't imagine Mom having a *conversation* with Adrian, let alone being married to him. "Of course you might be upset watching him marry someone else."

She waved it away. "I've been over Adrian for years," she said. "And when I was married to him, I was friends with Rebecca. Some of the women Adrian introduced me to snubbed me because I hadn't grown up in their exclusive circle, but Rebecca was always welcoming and kind."

"Did you ever meet Ellen Prescott?" Peyton asked.

"Yep." Mom made a face and laughed. "She was one of the ones who snubbed me. The ringleader, actually."

"And you were friends with Rebecca?" asked Savannah, her fork dangling in the air. Courtney couldn't blame her for being stunned. Rebecca was so calm, organized and level-headed—the complete opposite of their mom.

"Sort of," Mom said. "I knew Adrian and Rebecca dated in high school, and I used to worry that their feelings for each other hadn't disappeared. When I first heard they were engaged, it stung, but that's in the past now. I really am happy for them."

"Oh." Savannah frowned and played with a loose thread on her place mat. "So…you don't want to get back together with Dad?"

Courtney was surprised at the sadness in her sister's voice. Mom and Adrian getting back together wasn't something she'd ever considered. From the photos she'd seen of her parents in her baby book, she knew they must have loved each other once, but they were so different and wrong for each other now.

"You girls can do simple math, so I'm sure you've realized that Adrian and I got married *after* finding out I was pregnant with Peyton," Mom said. "We used protection but… sometimes these things happen."

Peyton nearly choked on her eggs. "We don't need the details," she said. "But yeah, we figured as much."

"Adrian and I tried to make it work," she continued. "But it wasn't meant to be between us. Even before the…event that drove us apart…" She glanced at Courtney, and Courtney looked away, the reminder of Britney making her chest pang. "Adrian wasn't always faithful to me. I tried to ignore it, because at the end of the day, *I* was the one he was married to and came home to and claimed to love. But it couldn't have gone on much longer. He's always had a soft spot for Rebecca—she was his first love, after all—and I don't think those feelings ever went away. Hopefully he'll be different with her than he was with me. I think it's possible."

"He does really love her," Savannah said. "And she's been nice to us since we got to Vegas. Even Peyton doesn't mind her anymore."

"She gets annoying—especially now that *all* she talks about is the wedding—but whatever." Peyton shrugged. "I tune her out and she's not that bad."

"That might be the nicest thing you've ever said about her," Savannah said. "She does talk about the wedding a *lot*. More than I ever talked about my Sweet Sixteen party."

"Now that we're back to the wedding, what do you girls say?" Mom asked. "Is it all right if Grandma and I come?"

"I don't think it's a good idea," Courtney said before her sisters had a chance to speak up. Her mom deflated, and she searched for a reason—something other than the fact that she simply hadn't forgiven her. "We won't be able to spend time with you, because we'll be so busy doing bridesmaid stuff." She pushed her food around on her plate, knowing that the excuse sounded lame. She needed to add *something* to it. "Since you'll barely be able to see us, you shouldn't miss out on a weekend here with Aunt Sophie."

"If you prefer us not to come, we understand," Grandma said. "That's why we asked the three of you before sending in our RSVP."

"The wedding's in April, so no one has to decide right now," Aunt Sophie cut in. She sounded tired, as if the conversation with Courtney that morning and having breakfast with them had exhausted her, but she continued, anyway. "Why don't the three of you take a few days to figure out how you feel about it? You should all have a say. But for now, it's

Courtney's birthday. Let's talk about something more fun—like that trip to Italy you took in December. I've never been to Italy, and I've always wanted to see it, so spare no details."

With that, Savannah launched into describing their trip.

Courtney stayed silent for the rest of the meal. Because despite Aunt Sophie's advice—to forgive while she had the chance—Courtney wasn't sure she could. At least not now, or anytime soon.

chapter 7: *Peyton*

After the tension of the weekend—mainly between Courtney, Grandma and Mom—Peyton was glad to be back in Las
Vegas. She'd just settled onto her bed with her laptop to crank
out some last-minute homework when her cell buzzed. One
glance at the screen, and her heart jumped into her throat.

It was Jackson.

After all these weeks of silence, he was finally calling her.
She'd expected his first move to be a Facebook message or a
text. But for him to call...whatever he wanted to tell her *had*
to be good. He had to still care about her.

Did he think about her as much as she thought about him?

She took a deep breath before answering. "Hello?"

"Peyton?" the deep, familiar voice asked. Just hearing him
made her heart race. "It's Jackson."

"I know." She stood and paced around the room—she hated
standing still while talking on the phone. "What's up?"

"I'm in Vegas right now," he started, and she paused midstride. "I got here Saturday night, and spoke with your father yesterday."

"You spoke with my father?" she repeated, stunned at how so much had changed so quickly. "You're working for him again? You're moving back here?"

"No." He sounded so resolved, and she fell back onto her bed, her heart crushed all over again. "Things went well, but I'm leaving tonight. I just didn't want to go without seeing you."

"You're leaving?" Her voice caught, and she swallowed to get ahold of herself. "Again?"

"Yes," he said, so calmly that she had no idea what he was feeling. "Adrian told me you and your sisters got back in town about an hour ago. I understand if you don't want to see me, but I wanted to at least give you the choice."

"Of course I want to see you," she stammered. "Where are you?"

"In the Diamond," he said. "In your hall, actually. Right outside your door, with your guards."

She yanked off her baggy sweatshirt and hurried to her mirror. Why did he have to give her such little notice? When she'd imagined seeing him again, she assumed she would look fresh—not like she'd been woken up early to go to breakfast, forced to go with her family on a bike ride through Napa, and then flown back home. Her smudged makeup was ten hours old, and her hair was a mess, since she'd pulled it into a bun so she wouldn't play with it while doing her homework.

"Peyton?" Jackson said again. "It's all right if you need a few minutes. I'll be waiting here."

"A few minutes sounds good," she said. "I'll see you soon." She jammed her finger onto the end-call button, ran a brush through her hair and tried to salvage her makeup.

This was her chance to make things right with Jackson.

She could do this. She *had* to do this, otherwise she would be mad at herself forever.

But first, she had to text her sisters, since they were in their rooms and would definitely hear when he came in.

Jackson's here and wants to talk to me...we'll be in my room, so don't come in!! Will give you the 411 later ;)

She shoved her phone into the back pocket of her jeans, walked to the front entrance and opened the door.

Just like he'd said, Jackson was waiting with Savannah and Courtney's guards—Carl and Teddy—and Peyton's new, older guard, Dustin. In the months that Jackson had been her guard, Peyton had grown used to seeing him in his bodyguard uniform, but today he wore dark blue jeans, a black T-shirt and a leather jacket. Even though he was a few years older, he looked like he could pass for her age.

"Hey." She tried to sound nonchalant, despite the fact that every inch of her body was shaking.

"Hey." He moved closer to the door. Everything about his expression was neutral, so it was impossible to tell if he was excited to see her or not. Her blood ran cold—this couldn't be a good sign.

"Want to come in?" She swallowed, her throat ridiculously dry, and opened the door wider.

He did, and they walked to her room in silence. She felt like he was watching her, but every time she tried to catch his gaze, he looked away. He'd been in her room only once—the night of Halloween when she'd had a "costume emergency" because she couldn't decide what to wear, and had tried on her top three choices for him. They'd kissed that night, and while it wasn't their first kiss, it was the first time he hadn't pushed her away. Or at least he hadn't pushed her away *imme-*

diately. It hadn't taken him long to remind her that he worked for her father, and any other relationship between them was inappropriate.

"So," she said, closing the door to her room and facing him. "It's been a while." She forced herself to stay still and not wring her hands. She didn't want him to see how nervous she was.

He took a deep, pained breath and glanced at the ceiling. "I know," he said, his hazel eyes finding hers again. "I wanted to apologize for that."

"Okay." She smiled, since she'd never had someone declare that they wanted to apologize to her. Did he expect her to give him permission? "Go ahead."

He pulled at his sleeves. "Mind if we sit?"

"Sure." Peyton sat on her bed, but instead of joining her, Jackson chose the desk chair nearby. Dread twisted in her stomach. If he'd decided he wanted to be with her—to see if it could work between them—wouldn't he have joined her on the bed? She grabbed a small decorative pillow and placed it on her lap, then started picking at the corners.

"I spoke with your father yesterday," Jackson repeated what he'd told her on the phone. "He called and asked to see me— he bought me a round-trip ticket from Omaha and gave me a room for the weekend."

"No way," Peyton said. "I thought he hated you."

"It surprised me, too," he said. "Especially since the last time I saw him, he fired me and gave me no recommendations. I've been home since, trying to figure out how to get a job with that on my record."

"*Someone* would have to hire you," she said. The alternative— that she'd ruined Jackson's career—was too awful to think about. She'd never forgive herself if that were the case.

"With no reference and no acceptable explanation of why I got fired?" He leaned back in the chair and raised an eyebrow. "A bodyguard is not a position that people want to take a chance on, so it wasn't looking good. My best option seemed to be changing careers. Luckily, my old karate instructor heard me out about what happened and offered to let me assist with teaching a few classes at the studio."

"You were going to go from being a bodyguard for the daughter of one of the biggest hotel owners in the world to teaching karate at a studio in Nebraska?" Peyton scrunched her forehead. "I have a hard time picturing that."

"I was actually enjoying it, but it was only a temporary position while I was considering my options," he said. "Then Adrian called. I came straight here, and he told me that he'd had a change of heart. He said he still doesn't approve of my actions, but that for the most part, I did a good job, and he was impressed by my work ethic."

"So he wants to rehire you?" Peyton sat up straighter, excitement thrumming through her veins.

"No," he said, and she leaned back into the pillows, her hopes crushed again. "But he apologized for firing me without giving me a recommendation. He said that while he still stands by his decision, he was too harsh on me, and that he doesn't want to ruin my career."

"Wow," Peyton said, trying to sound cheerful. "That was nice of him."

"It was." Jackson rocked the swiveling desk chair back and forth. "I assumed you had something to do with it."

"I wish, but I don't think I did." She ran her hands through her hair, trying to figure out what could have caused Adrian's change of heart. "After everything that happened, Adrian made it clear that he didn't want to hear about you. I've only mentioned you to my sisters, and to Rebecca."

"Rebecca's the only person I can think of who could change his mind."

"But I don't see why she would bother," Peyton said. "I mean, she *did* ask me a few times while we were in Italy how I was handling everything, but I'm not exactly close to her." She thought about it, then shrugged it off. *How* this had happened didn't matter. All that mattered was that it *was* happening. "When will you start applying for a new job?" she asked. "There must be tons of people who need a bodyguard in Vegas."

"Adrian reached out to a connection and got me a job himself." He pressed his palms together, watching her closely. "I start tomorrow."

"That's amazing!" Peyton smiled and bounced her legs. "Who will you be working for?" A few possibilities crossed her mind—Logan Prescott, Steve Wynn, Sheldon Adelson— there were so many high-powered people connected to Adrian in Las Vegas. And the fact that Adrian would do this, despite how angry he'd been after seeing the photos of her and Jackson…it meant a lot.

"That's what I wanted to tell you." The seriousness in his voice made Peyton go still. "The job isn't in Las Vegas. It's in a town in upstate New York—Port Charles. They have some mob issues there and one of the guys in charge needs a new bodyguard for his kid. I'm taking the red-eye tonight."

The words felt like a stake through Peyton's heart. "Adrian did this on purpose, didn't he?" she said. "He got you a job far away to make sure we never see each other."

"Listen, Peyton." He rubbed his hands over his head and blew out a long breath. "I have feelings for you. You know it's true, because I told you that night at the Imperial Palace, and I would never lie to you about something so important."

"Really?" she asked. "Because when you dropped off the face of the planet, I thought you didn't care anymore. I thought you never wanted to talk to me again."

"As I told you, I needed time to think," he said. "And while I was home, I did a lot of thinking. I wanted to justify what had happened between us, but I kept coming back to the same conclusion—the way I let my guard down around you was unacceptable. My job was to protect you. Not to bring you to a bar so you could confide in me over a pitcher of beer."

"You listened when I needed someone to talk to," she said, scooting closer to him. "You were the only person I trusted who was there for me. There's nothing wrong with that."

"Besides the fact that until you turn eighteen, anything between us is illegal, what's 'wrong with that' is that I was your *bodyguard*." He set his jaw, sitting straighter. "Not your boyfriend."

"Well, you're not my bodyguard anymore." She hated how bitter she sounded, but there was no taking it back, so she might as well let it all out. "And even though I only have *two months* until my birthday, clearly you have no interest in being my boyfriend, either."

He raised an eyebrow. "I thought you didn't 'do' long-distance relationships. At least, that's what you told Mike when you broke up with him."

"You're comparing yourself to *Mike*?" Peyton laughed. "Mike and I had nothing in common except that we were attracted to each other, and he was a challenge because he hung out with a different group of friends than I did in Fairfield. But you get me on a deeper level. You saw the darkest parts of my life—the worst parts of *me*—and you didn't hate me. I didn't have to put on an act with you."

"But you were forced to let me in," he said. "I read your file, and I watched you for months before you even knew I existed. I knew you before we exchanged a single word. And I know that if you try to let people in on your own, you'll connect with them more than you thought you could." She opened her mouth to argue, but he cut her off. "Plus, you said yourself that you like a challenge. That's why you went for Mike, and for Oliver, and for that Australian teacher of yours."

"Don't be stupid," she said. "Those guys don't come close to comparing to you."

"But at the time, you thought you were truly interested in each one of them, right?"

"I don't know," she mumbled, looking down at her hands. "It doesn't matter, because it didn't work out with any of them. *They* don't matter. They never did."

"You say that, but I'm just as—if not *more*—off-limits than they ever were." He checked his watch, and Peyton's chest ached at the realization that he was leaving soon. "I held your interest for this long because I've told you no."

"You're wrong," she said. "But I don't know how I can make you see it…especially since you won't even add me on Facebook so we can keep in touch."

He raised an eyebrow. "Out of everything we've talked about tonight, your biggest concern is Facebook?"

"It's a good way to keep in touch." She shrugged. "If you want to."

He took out his phone and tapped on the screen a few times. "There," he said, sliding the phone back into his pocket. "Friend request accepted."

"Thanks," she said, although now she felt stupid for making such a big deal out of it. She rarely *used* Facebook. Her feelings for Jackson were turning her into a drama queen, and she hated it.

"By the way, congrats on applying to UNLV," he said.

She jerked her head, surprised by the change of subject. "How do you know about that?"

"Your dad mentioned it when we talked. I hope you get in."

"Whatever." She huffed. "I'm done with school. I'm not going."

"I always did see you as more of a gap-year type," he said, as if she should know what that meant. He studied her with so much intensity that her heart caught in her throat. The energy between them crackled, and she leaned forward, inviting him wordlessly to come join her on the bed. His eyes didn't leave hers, and for a moment she thought that this was it. He was finally going to kiss her again.

"I need to head out." He stood up and shoved the chair under her desk, ending whatever she thought she'd felt between them. "I don't want to miss my plane."

"Okay." She heard herself say it, but she felt numb. She couldn't move. She couldn't think. All she could do was sit there while he said goodbye and walked away.

The moment he left the condo, she locked her door, fell onto her bed, buried her face in her pillows and cried.

chapter 8: *Madison*

Madison walked into the Diamond Residences after school, her iPhone held up to her ear. As expected, the call went to voice mail. When was Oliver going to stop avoiding her and *talk* to her? It had been weeks since the accident, and all she'd gotten were a few text messages saying he was doing fine and that he would let her know when he was ready to talk. But it was now the beginning of February, and she was losing hope. Why didn't he want to see her? She was trying to be there for him, but she couldn't do that if he didn't let her in.

She was heading to the elevators when she spotted Damien in the Grand Café. She hadn't hung out with him one-on-one since the incident over the summer when she'd kissed him while drunk, but maybe he had a better idea of what was going on with Oliver. Despite her misgivings, she walked over to him.

He had a plate of the happy-hour meatballs and was doing something on his phone. He put it down when he saw her. A year ago, they would have already greeted each other and slipped into easy conversation. Now, his dark eyes watched her suspiciously. She missed the friendship they used to have.

"Hey." She smiled and forced herself to sound upbeat. "Mind if I join you?"

"Go ahead." He motioned for her to take the seat across from him, and she did. "Feel free to have a meatball."

The scent of the marinara and basil made her mouth water, but she ordered a freshly made "Green Machine" juice instead. "So, what's up?" she asked.

"Just grabbing a snack before hitting up the gym." He leaned back and studied her. "What about you?"

This was officially the most stilted conversation she'd ever had with Damien. Luckily, her drink arrived, and she swirled her straw around, taking a sip. She pursed her lips at the bitterness of the green juice.

Damien finally smiled. "Not a fan of green juice?"

"I'm getting used to it," she said. "According to the juice expert I follow online, pure green juice is the healthiest, but it doesn't taste as good because there's no sugar added from fruits." She took another sip, trying not to make a face this time.

"Well, good luck with that," he said.

"Thanks." She drank some water to chase away the taste. "Anyway, I saw you here and figured it would be a good time to ask—have you heard from Oliver lately? He doesn't pick up when I call, and when I do hear from him, it's just a vague text. I'm worried about him."

"It's been the same for me," Damien replied. "He told me that he's going through some stuff and that he needs space."

"But it's been over a month," Madison said. "He should be back in school. Or at least he should want to see his friends."

"Didn't you have a fight with him before he left Savannah's party?"

"Yeah." She looked down, unable to meet his eyes. She hadn't told anyone the details about the fight, and she didn't plan to. It was too humiliating. "But Oliver and I have been friends for years. One fight doesn't change that."

"Depends on what it was about."

"It doesn't matter," she lied. "It was stupid."

"If you say so." He popped another meatball in his mouth, looking off into the distance as he chewed. "But I'm worried about Oliver, too. I'd hoped he was at least talking to you."

"He's not." She sighed. "I hate this. I want to be there for him, but I can't if he won't even *talk* to me."

"I know what you mean," Damien agreed. "I think that if by the weekend he's still hiding out, we should go to his place and see what we can do."

"You mean go there and refuse to leave until he sees us?"

"Exactly," he said. "It'll be easiest if we do it together. As a team. Unless you have a better idea."

"If I had one, I would have told you already," she said. "That idea sounds as good as any. We might as well give it a shot."

"So we'll do it this weekend." He sipped his soda, watching her as if he was waiting for her to say something else. "Anyway, I'm glad you came over here. It's been a while since we've hung out."

"After what happened last summer, you told me that things couldn't go back to how they were between us," she said softly. "I assumed you meant it, so I gave you space. Isn't that what you wanted?"

"Come on, Mads." The use of the nickname made her heart ache. "I was angry at first, but you know me—I get over things fast. We've been friends for years, and while I used to want more, what you said to me in that hotel room was right—a relationship wouldn't work between us."

"I'm sorry," she said. "I know it came out mean when I said it. I've felt awful about it ever since."

"You definitely could have been nicer about it," he said. "But what you said got me thinking. You have your whole life figured out. You're ambitious, determined and independent. Which is all awesome...but me and you together would be a disaster. I want to be with someone who wants my help and support. Someone who still has ambitions of her own, but who looks up to me, and who I can be there for no matter what."

"You want someone who makes you feel needed."

"It sounds lame and old-fashioned when you put it that way, but yeah, pretty much," he said. "And you've never needed me—at least not like that."

Madison blinked, amazed that this was all coming from Damien. Despite how long they'd been friends, he'd never struck her as particularly insightful. "You'll find that person," she said. "I know you will. But I'm glad you're moving on."

"I've already moved on." He smirked. "I did months ago."

"Right," she said. "Of course you did." Sometimes she forgot that while she'd been in a haze these past few months, everyone else's lives had gone on without her. "So, who's the lucky girl? Is it Savannah? Or that redheaded friend of hers you were flirting with at her party?"

"I wasn't *flirting* with Evie." He ran his hand through his hair, exasperated. "Evie was in a corner alone, and she looked sad, so I went over to cheer her up because I felt bad for her. She took it the wrong way and threw herself at me. I tried letting her down easily, but Savannah saw us...and it turned into a mess."

"Sounds like you care a lot about what Savannah thinks." Madison leaned forward and rested her elbows on the table. "If I didn't know any better, I would think you were into her."

"Yeah, well, it doesn't matter." His eyes flashed with hurt. "She's into that douchebag from One Connection now. Perry whatever his name his. The one all the girls were screaming about and falling all over."

"Perry Myles," she said.

"Yep." His jaw hardened. "When the *Fabulous Sweet Sixteen* episode aired, there was a bit with Savannah and Perry flirting, and now they Tweet each other all the time." He stabbed one of his meatballs, shoved it into his mouth and swallowed it in a few bites. "They even have a 'celebrity couple name' online. 'Sarry.' How stupid is that?"

"Pretty stupid," Madison agreed. "But it's better than 'Pevannah.'"

"They both suck," he said. "This whole thing sucks. I had my chance with her last summer, and I blew it."

"Because of me." Madison bit her lip and sipped her juice. It wasn't tasting any better, so she opened a sugar packet and dumped the entire thing inside.

"You never could figure out how to like the taste of healthy food." Damien laughed and handed her another sugar packet, which she gladly emptied into the juice.

"Life would be much easier if I were one of those people who *loved* salad," she said, stirring the juice and taking another sip. It was only slightly better than before, so she gave up and ordered an extra thick chocolate milkshake. She'd been doing well with eating healthy all week, and times like these called for comfort food...right?

"That's more like it." Damien smiled when the milkshake arrived. "But about last summer...I don't blame you for it. Maybe I did at first, but I kissed you back when I knew Savannah would see. I barely knew her at the time. I just thought she was hot, and I was having fun over the summer."

"And now you regret it?"

"I tried making it up to her by helping her with her You-Tube," he said. "We spent a lot of time together last semester—as friends. She's an awesome girl. But now she's moved on to bigger and better things, and Perry's getting her a lot of publicity. Why should I get in the way of that?"

"I might be stating the obvious," she said. "But have you tried telling her how you feel?"

"And have her shoot me down because she wants Perry Myles instead of me?" he scoffed. "Hell no. I screwed up, and I lost my chance. It's done."

"I don't know…" Madison wished she had a better answer, but Damien knew Savannah a lot better than she did. Which was pretty sad, since Savannah was technically her sister. "You could try. After what happened with Oliver, it got me thinking—what if you never *have* another chance? You don't want to have any regrets."

"Maybe," he said. "But Savannah can make her own choice, so there's no point in talking about this anymore."

"All right," she said. "Then what *do* you want to talk about?"

"You."

She shifted uncomfortably, running her hands over her jeans. "What about me?"

"I saw how you shut everyone out last semester. I've been worried about you."

"You don't have to worry about me." She cringed at how robotic and unconvincing it sounded. "I'm fine."

"Don't pull that on me," he said. "We've been friends for years, and I can tell when something's bothering you. You know you can trust me, right?"

He looked so sincere, and she *wanted* to tell him the truth. But she'd already told Oliver. And Brianna. She couldn't tell Damien. Because with each person she told, there was a higher chance the Diamond sisters would find out before she could tell them herself. And she planned on telling them—she really did. But how? She couldn't just knock on their door and say, "I know it's unexpected, but we're sisters. Surprise!"

That would be a total disaster.

"I know I can trust you." She took a bite of her milkshake, savoring it. It was thick enough that she needed a spoon to eat it—like ice cream—which was the way that all milkshakes should be made. "And you're right—these past few months have been rough. But this thing I've been worried about involves other people, so I can't tell anyone without betraying their trust. Not even you."

"Okay." He sank back into the booth. "But you're hanging out with everyone again, so whatever happened is getting better, right?"

"Sort of," she said. "After everything with Oliver, I got… distracted. It's too much all at once, and I feel like I'm drowning in it, and I hate it. I just wish he would talk to me."

"We're seeing Oliver soon," Damien said, as if it were a fact. "But you also shouldn't let his issues stop you from taking care of yourself."

"I'm trying," she said. "It's just hard."

"Even though I don't know what's going on with you, I know you'll get through it," he said. "You're the most determined, stubborn person I know, and I mean that in only the best way. I'm here for you if you need a friend, all right?"

"Thanks." She blinked away tears. "Really—it means a lot."

"Anytime," he said. "And this weekend, we're breaking down the doors of the Prescott villa and we're talking to Oliver, whether he wants to see us or not."

"Sounds like a plan," she said. "So…can I have that last meatball?"

He motioned for her to take it, and she picked it up and popped it into her mouth, enjoying every bite.

★ ★ ★

A few hours later, Madison paced around the living room, and as always, the sound of the key in the front door echoed through the condo at 9:30 p.m. Her parents entered the foyer, still dressed in their scrubs from work. They stopped when they saw her.

"Hey," her mom said cautiously, hanging her jacket in the coat closet. "Is everything okay?"

"No." Madison shoved her hands into the back pockets of her jeans, forcing herself to stop pacing. "I need to talk to you guys."

"Is this about Oliver?" Her mom's brow crinkled. "I know you're worried about him, but like I've told you before, even though your dad and I work at the hospital, we can't find out information about his condition. I wish I could, but we can't break our confidentiality agreement. If anyone found out, we could get in serious trouble."

"I don't think this is about Oliver," her dad broke in. "Is it?"

"No." Madison took a deep breath—she might as well get this over with quickly. "It's about Adrian and the Diamond girls. They need to know the truth."

Her mom's face went from sad to worried in less than a second. "You know that the girls aren't emotionally ready yet after finding out about Britney," she said. "They're going through an extraordinarily tough time. Especially Courtney."

"But what about *me*?" Madison crossed her arms, determined to hold her ground. "I can't keep this secret anymore. I'm lying to everyone—even my closest friends. I hate it."

"You have us," her dad said. "I know you're angry at us, but I hope you know that we love you, and you can talk to us about anything."

"But I don't want to *talk* about it anymore," she said. "I'm done talking. I want to *do* something."

Her mom reached for her cell phone. "If you need to speak with a psychiatrist, I can get you an appointment as soon as possible. I'll even let you skip school tomorrow." She smiled, as if the offer were a real treat.

"No psychiatrists." Madison raised her voice, holding her gaze steady with her mom's. "I'm done keeping this secret. If Adrian won't tell Peyton, Courtney and Savannah the truth, then I'll just…tell them myself."

"You can't do that," her mom said, stepping forward. "Especially two months before he marries Rebecca. Do you really think that timing's wise?"

"It's even *more* of a reason to tell them now." It took all of Madison's strength to not rip her own hair out. "This wedding won't just be about Adrian and Rebecca. The Diamond girls will be in the wedding, and Brett will be in it, too. They're becoming a family. And I'll just be sitting there watching, as if I had no more connection to the people at the altar than the rest of the guests. And what do they always say during weddings… 'if anyone has a reason why these two people shouldn't be wed, speak now or forever hold your peace?' The husband keeping an illegitimate daughter secret from his wife-to-be and three daughters is a good reason to speak up, don't you think?"

"Well, Rebecca already knows," her dad said.

"What?" Madison dropped her arms to her sides and looked back and forth from her mom to her dad.

"Back when Rebecca was still with John Carmel—Brett's dad—and when Adrian was still with Donna—that's Peyton, Courtney and Savannah's mother—the six of us would do everything together," her mom explained. "We were best friends. So after your dad and I separated, and I ended up pregnant with you, Rebecca was the first person I confided in. She helped us come to the…arrangement we have today."

"And she's kept quiet for all these years?" Madison couldn't imagine how she was able to manage that.

"It wasn't her place to say anything," her dad said. "Rebecca would take a secret with her to her grave."

"Okay." Madison was caught off-guard, but she was determined to hold her ground. "So Rebecca knows. But the Diamond girls still need to know before the wedding, and I meant what I said. I don't need anyone's approval anymore— not yours, and not Adrian's. If I have to, I'll tell Peyton, Courtney and Savannah the truth myself."

"Let's not get to the point of threats," her mom said. "You do realize that Adrian Diamond is one of the most powerful men in America? Angering him probably isn't a good tactic."

"Well, he 'angered' me when I found out that he wanted nothing to do with me, and that he *still* wants nothing to do with me," Madison said. "I don't even *want* him to be my father—I hate him."

"You're acting rashly—"

"No, I'm not," she said. "Adrian doesn't want to be my father. I get it. And I don't care, because I already have a great dad, and I don't need another one. But Peyton, Courtney and Savannah should at least be given a *chance* to be my sisters."

"You're right," her dad said, pressing his fingers to the bridge of his nose.

Her mom glared at him. "You can't just say something like that without talking to me first."

"Yes, I can," he said. "Because we already talked about this. The day after Thanksgiving—remember? Then Adrian told us about the girls finding out about Britney, and everything got put on hold, but we've all been keeping this secret for far too long. It's going to come out, and it might as well be sooner rather than later."

"Really?" Madison asked, stunned.

"Really," he said. "I'll call Adrian tomorrow."

www.campusbuzz.com

High Schools > Nevada > Las Vegas > The Goodman School

Is Oliver EVER coming back to school????
Posted on Thursday 2/5 at 4:38 PM

Ok so I don't mean to be insensitive or anything, cause I know Oliver was in a bad car crash in December, but isn't it about time he came back to school? It's FEBRUARY, for crying out loud! People are saying he's recovering, but if he were REALLY doing better, wouldn't he be back? Something's totally up that we don't know about...

1: Posted on Thursday 2/5 at 4:59 PM

andddd now the rumors will start. What do you all think? Paralyzed? Disfigured? Brain damage? Would have died, but the Prescotts paid top dollar for an experimental process where they scan Oliver's brain and put him into a robot body that looks human??? It would take time for him to get used to the new body, which could explain his extended absence!!

2: Posted on Thursday 2/5 at 5:10 PM

this is real life, not a science fiction novel!

3: Posted on Thursday 2/5 at 5:27 PM

obviously oliver isn't a robot. but those other ideas arent impossible. it would explain why he hasn't come back to school yet.

4: Posted on Thursday 2/5 at 5:42 PM

this is OLIVER PRESCOTT! Party king of Goodman!! I'm gonna guess the accident didn't happen cause he was driving sober. Who knows what was in his system? My guess is that he's in REHAB!!!

5: Posted on Thursday 2/5 at 6:02 PM

ohhhh it sounds like you're onto something!

chapter 9: *Savannah*

"Nice scrimmage today, girls," Tegan, the senior volleyball captain, said as the team headed back to the locker room. Volleyball season was in the fall, but they were practicing two days each week after school to give them a shot at winning regionals next year. Everyone was doing well—except for Savannah. All she was thinking about were the texts she'd exchanged with Perry earlier. They'd been talking about seeing each other again, *and* he'd asked her when she had spring break. It had distracted her all through practice.

The moment she opened her bag, Savannah picked up her phone, her heart fluttering when she saw a new text from Perry.

So…since your spring break is during my time off from tour, it would be a perfect time for us to see each other again, don't you think? ;)

Was he serious? Of *course* she wanted to hang out! She was in the middle of replying when Tegan jumped onto the bench, holding her phone in the air.

"Harrison just texted me that his parents will be gone all weekend, so he's having a party!" she said. "Who's coming?"

A bunch of girls chimed in that they were going—Jackie, Brooke and Alyssa included. At the sound of their voices, Savannah placed her phone down.

"What about dinner at the Diamond?" she asked them. "We've had plans for days."

"Of course," Brooke said. "We'll get dinner, then head over to Harrison's when we're done. The party won't get good until later, anyway."

"Can we sleep over your place afterward?" Alyssa asked Savannah.

"And can your driver take us to the party?" Jackie—the only one of the four of them with her license—asked. "I don't want to be stuck as the DD."

"Sure," Savannah said, zipping her volleyball bag shut. "And we can definitely do a sleepover after the party."

"Are you sure?" Brooke asked. "You don't need to check with your dad or Rebecca first?"

"Are you kidding?" Savannah laughed. "My dad doesn't care about three of my friends sleeping over, and all Rebecca thinks about is planning the wedding. Speaking of, the brides-maids' dresses are arriving this afternoon, and she'll be *so mad* if I'm late to try them on. I'll see you girls at eight for dinner at Adagio, okay?"

They said bye, and Savannah rushed to the parking lot, waiting for her bodyguard—Carl—to pull around the car. She reached into her bag to finish replying to Perry's text, fumbling to find her phone. Where was it? It had to be in there somewhere. But as much as she dug through the mess of papers and random crap that had somehow ended up in there, she couldn't find it.

Courtney would tell her to think about when she'd seen

it last. Which was easy—it was when she'd seen Perry's text. She'd been in the middle of replying when she'd gotten distracted by her friends…and had put it down on the bench.

"I have to run back inside and grab my phone," she told Carl once he pulled up in the Range Rover. The car was technically hers, but since she only had her learner's permit, she could only drive when an adult was with her. "I'll be back in a second."

"All right," he said. "But I would recommend hurrying—you know how Rebecca gets with this wedding stuff."

"Trust me, I know." Savannah smiled and dashed back to the gym. She was wiped from volleyball practice—they'd gone hard that day, and the Vegas air was dry in the winter—so she stopped to grab a drink from the water fountain.

As she was drinking, the door to the locker room slammed open, echoing through the hall.

"I'm so sick of pretending that Savannah Diamond's the most amazing person on the planet," a loud voice that was unmistakably Jackie's said. "She expects us to worship her just because of who her father is. It's so annoying."

Savannah took a sharp breath, nearly choking on the water. She didn't expect anyone to *worship* her. Especially not because of Adrian.

"She's such a joke," Alyssa replied. "Thinking we'll like her because she invites us to dinner at that restaurant at the Diamond? She's been asking for so long that she pretty much forced us to say yes."

The footsteps came closer, and Savannah ducked around the corner into a nearby hall. She leaned against the wall, her palms pressed flat against it, keeping as still as she could. These girls were her teammates—they were supposed to be her *friends*. Where was this coming from? But as much as she wanted to ask, she couldn't. It was too humiliating. So she stayed there, hidden, keeping quiet as they got closer.

"Come on, you guys," a soft voice—Brooke's—said. "Savannah's been nothing but nice to us. Maybe tonight will be fun."

"Nice?" Alyssa's laugh filled the lobby. "She's materialistic, obsessed with herself and judging from the classes I've had with her, she's stupid, too. And her YouTube channel… what a joke."

"Omigod, I know!" Jackie joined in the laughter. "She makes the most ridiculous faces at the camera. Sometimes I'll pause at certain spots and take screenshots, and it's like, the funniest thing ever."

"The one you texted me yesterday was epic—let me find it," Alyssa said, and they paused, presumably so she could bring it up on her phone. "Look at this!" She and Jackie burst out laughing again. "I would totally Instagram it, but she would see it was from my account."

"You could make a fake account," Jackie suggested. "How funny would that be?"

"What would my username be?" Alyssa asked. "Savannah-DiamondSucks?"

"Something like that," Jackie said. "You *so* have to do it."

"Don't do that," Brooke said, and Alyssa and Jackie stopped laughing.

"Why not?" Jackie sounded genuinely confused. "No one will know it's us. And with all those people who follow her online, Savannah will never see it."

"When did you become Savannah's best friend?" Alyssa said. "Last year, it was all about the three of us. No Savannah. I liked it better that way."

"But we were all friends with her last semester," Brooke said. "What'd she do to make you hate her so much?"

"She tries too hard," Alyssa said. "It's annoying. She's only worth putting up with because her driver takes us anywhere, she gets us VIP passes and she'll let us stay at the Diamond."

"And she talks about Perry Myles like he's actually interested in her." Jackie laughed. "Yeah, right. Did you see that picture of him with Serena Lopez? It's all over the internet. They're totally together... He only flirted with Savannah at her party because her dad *paid* him to."

Savannah knew the picture. She'd asked Perry about it... He'd said his publicist asked him to get dinner with Serena since she had a new album coming out, and her last album didn't do well. They thought getting people talking about her would get them to buy her album. He'd even promised Savannah that while Serena was a good friend, she got crazy in relationships, so he would never date her.

"Savannah's just excited," Brooke said. "Wouldn't you be excited if Perry Myles was texting you?"

"*If* he's even texting her," Alyssa said. "She's probably making it up to get attention."

Heat rushed through Savannah's body, and she clenched her fists so tightly that her fingernails broke through skin.

"But we've seen the texts," Brooke said. "And we've seen his Tweets to her, too."

"Whatever," Jackie said. "He's probably playing her. Who knows how many girls he's saying the same exact shit to?"

"And not only does Savannah try too hard, but she's a self-absorbed bitch," Alyssa added. "She had the attention of Damien Sanders *and* Nick Gordon, and she played them for months. She acted all innocent about it, but *come on*. She was totally doing it on purpose and gloating in the attention. I saw how much she loved it on the first day of school."

Savannah tried to breathe steadily, tears pooling in her eyes. Whatever she'd had with Nick had fizzled out because he was too busy with school, football and work to have time to hang out. They were friends now. And she hadn't "played" anyone, especially not Damien. To do that, he would have had to have been interested in her as more than a Madison replacement. Now he saw her as only a friend—or worse, a little sister.

"If you both hate Savannah, why are you even coming tonight?" Brooke asked. "Why not pre-game at Tegan's and go to Harrison's party with the rest of them?"

"Because Tegan's staying at Harrison's, and if I stayed at Harrison's and my mom found out, she would flip out and ground me for a month," Alyssa said. "Savannah will charge our dinners on her dad's credit card, her driver will take us to and from the party and we can stay over her place, which my mom is totally cool with. I'll put up with her for all those perks."

"And she's decently pretty, she has great clothes and she's internet famous," Jackie added. "I get more Instagram followers whenever she posts pictures with us and tags us."

"You're talking about her like she's an accessory," Brooke said.

"Whatever," Alyssa said. "That's what she gets for thinking that being Adrian Diamond's daughter and a wannabe pop star is a good enough reason for people to want to be friends with her. If she wants to be used, then fine, I'll use her."

They left the gym, their conversation cut off when the door slammed shut behind them.

Once sure they were gone, Savannah crept out of her hiding spot and watched their backs as they walked to the parking lot. Her body shook as she replayed what she'd just heard. Why did they hate her so much? All she'd ever done was be nice to them, because they were on the volleyball team with her and they had some classes together. They sat together at lunch, went to Starbucks together after school and went to the same parties. Her Facebook cover photo was a picture of her, Alyssa, Brooke and Jackie with their arms around each other, smiling at her Sweet Sixteen party.

She'd thought they were best friends. But this entire time, they'd hated her. How had she been so clueless?

She hurried to the locker room and grabbed her phone. On her way back to the car, after letting Perry know that of course she wanted to see him over spring break, she opened a group text message to Alyssa, Brooke and Jackie.

Family stuff came up—I have to cancel tonight. Have fun at the party!

She pressed Send, shoved her phone into her bag and tossed it onto the back seat, not wanting to see their replies.

Savannah walked into the condo expecting to find her sisters, Rebecca and the wedding-planning entourage ready with the dresses. Her sisters were there—Courtney sitting on the couch with her laptop balanced on her thighs, and Peyton at the table eating a bowl of cereal—but there was no sign of Rebecca, or of the dresses.

"What's going on?" Savannah dropped her bag on the floor. "Aren't we supposed to be trying on the bridesmaid dresses?"

"Yep," Peyton said in between bites of cereal. "But Rebecca texted us saying something came up, and that we can't do the dresses today, but to wait at the condo because she and Adrian wanted to talk with us. Didn't you see it? I thought you were permanently attached to your phone."

At the mention of her phone, which she was avoiding so she wouldn't have to talk to Alyssa, Jackie and Brooke, Savannah stomped to the fridge and pulled out a Coke. It fizzed when she opened it, and she took a long, satisfying gulp.

"I thought you and your friends swore off non-diet soda for the New Year?" Peyton asked. "That lasted all of…five weeks. Not bad, actually. I thought you would have given in earlier."

"Screw my friends." Savannah slammed the refrigerator shut and took another delicious sip of regular soda.

"Whoa." Courtney moved her laptop off her legs. "What happened? Did you all get into a fight?"

"No. Not really a fight." Savannah's voice wavered, and she took another sip of her drink. Courtney motioned for her to join her on the couch, and she did, pulling her legs up to her chest and wrapping her arms around them. Peyton was sitting with them a second later, her cereal bowl balanced on her lap. "But I heard them talking about me in the gym after they thought I left."

She recounted everything up to the text she'd sent them to cancel their plans. Courtney listened quietly, while Peyton threw in occasional comments like "What a bitch" and "If I was there, I would have punched her in the face." By the end of the story, Savannah had cried so much that she'd gone through half a box of tissues, and judging from the black smudges on them, she had mascara all over her face.

"I don't know what I'm going to do when I see them at school on Monday." She sniffed, blew her nose and dropped the tissue on the couch next to her. "How am I supposed to act like nothing's changed? But if I don't sit with them in class and at lunch, they'll know something's up." She slumped against the couch, pressed her palms into her forehead and groaned. "This is awful."

"Back up a second." Peyton slammed her empty cereal bowl onto the coffee table. "You're not going to pretend this never happened and stay friends with them, are you?"

"I don't know," she said softly, not meeting her sister's eyes.

"If I stop being friends with them, they'll ask why. What am I supposed to say?"

"The truth?" Peyton looked at her like she'd lost her mind.

"That I was listening to their conversation?" Savannah shook her head. "No way. Then they'll make fun of me for that, and turn more people against me. You didn't hear them, but they were so…cruel."

"I believe it," Peyton said. "But you can't keep being friends with those bitches."

"Without them, who am I supposed to hang out with at school, or sit with during lunch?" She could barely choke each word out. "I have no one."

"Not true," Peyton said. "You have me and Courtney. Sit with us at lunch. Or with Damien or Nick… Didn't you sit with them last semester?"

"Nick's always at the library doing homework, and Damien's barely spoken to me since we got back from break." Savannah's throat tightened, and she blew her nose again. Did other people have this much trouble fitting in, or was it just her?

"Then you'll sit with me and Courtney." Peyton looked at Courtney, who hadn't gotten much of a word in yet. "Right?"

"You're always welcome to sit with me," Courtney said. "And I agree with Peyton that Alyssa and Jackie are *not* your friends. But what about Brooke? It sounds like she was trying to stand up for you."

"They didn't listen to her," Savannah said. "And then they all left together, discussing what they wanted to wear to the party tonight, as if they hadn't been talking about me seconds before."

"What bitches," Peyton said.

"Yeah," Savannah agreed. "If it had been Evie there instead, she wouldn't have let them get away with that."

"I thought you weren't talking to Evie after your fight at the party?" Courtney asked.

"Right." Savannah shrugged and looked down at her hands. "I guess I have no friends left."

"Yes, you do." Courtney scooted closer and wrapped an arm around her shoulders. "You have us. Never forget that, all right?"

"Thanks," Savannah said. "I love you guys."

"We love you, too."

They all hugged, and Savannah smiled, grateful that no matter what, they always had each other. How did people get through life without sisters?

Then the doorbell rang. Savannah wiped the tears off her cheeks, although she knew she was probably hopeless-looking by this point.

"That must be Adrian and Rebecca," Peyton said. "Anyone know what's going on?"

"I have no idea," Courtney said. "But we're about to find out."

chapter 10: *Courtney*

Adrian and Rebecca walked into the condo, their expressions serious. Courtney's stomach swooped, and she shut her laptop, placing it on the floor.

Rebecca glanced at the used tissues scattered around Savannah. "Are we interrupting something?" she asked.

"Nope." Savannah somehow managed to smile. "Just friend drama. I'm fine."

"Are you sure?" Rebecca's forehead creased, and she glanced worriedly at Adrian. "Maybe now isn't the best time?"

"We can't put it off any longer," he said. "It has to be done now."

"What's going on?" Courtney bit her lower lip, looking back and forth between Adrian and Rebecca. "Is everything okay between you two?"

"You're not calling off the wedding, right?" Peyton asked, resting her feet on the coffee table.

"No, nothing like that." Adrian waved that notion away.

"But we do need to talk with you about something important."

If it wasn't about the wedding, then what *was* it about? Had they done something wrong? Nothing came to Courtney's mind—they'd all been getting along well since their vacation to Italy. Unless…they hadn't found out about her and Brett seeing each other, had they?

That couldn't be it. If it were, they would have wanted to talk to Courtney alone. She relaxed slightly. Whatever this was, it had to do with all three of them.

"Does anyone want something to drink?" Rebecca asked, walking into the kitchen. "Water, soda, juice?"

Savannah was still working on her Coke, and as Rebecca grabbed a Diet Coke for herself and a regular for Peyton, Courtney got up to get an ice water. Adrian wanted water, too, so she brought one over for him. Finally they situated themselves in the living room, drinks in hand—Courtney, Peyton and Savannah on one couch, and Adrian and Rebecca sitting close together on the other. They were all fidgeting, except for Adrian, who kept completely still, his hands resting on his thighs.

"So, what's up?" Peyton was the first to speak.

"There's no easy way to say this." Adrian clasped his hands together and looked closely at each of them, as though searching for the right words. "Which is why I've been putting off telling you." He took a deep breath and said, "When Courtney found out about Britney, I promised there would be no more secrets. I promised we would be honest with each other from there on out, because I wanted to have relationships with you. And that's still something I want, and something that I think has been going well, with the Sundays we've spent together and our vacation over winter break."

"Okay…" Courtney's stomach twisted, feeling as if she wasn't going to like where he was headed with this.

"The Sundays have been going really well," Savannah added.

Adrian managed a tight-lipped smile, and he continued, "But there's something else you need to know. I didn't tell you originally because it involves other people. Now they're ready for you to know—they were actually ready weeks ago—but it was around the same time you found out about Britney." He directed that last part to Courtney. "I knew how hard that was on you—on all three of you—and I didn't want to drop anything else on you while you were grieving for your sister. But I'm not perfect. I've made mistakes, and keeping this from you is one of them."

"You mean there's something else you've been hiding?" Peyton rolled her eyes. "Why am I not surprised?"

"This is the last secret," he said. "I promise. It's not going to be easy to hear, but I want you to know that I've enjoyed spending time with you every Sunday, and I would like for you to continue giving me the chance to be your father."

With every sentence he spoke, the anticipation built on itself until Courtney felt like she might explode. "We can't promise how we'll react before knowing what's going on," she said.

"But I can't imagine it will change anything, since you're choosing to tell us," Savannah added.

Peyton just stared at him, waiting.

"Maybe you should start from the beginning?" Rebecca said to Adrian. "Girls, this will be hard for you to hear, but please listen to the whole story, and try to understand that none of the decisions made by anyone involved were easy."

"Okay, okay," Peyton said. "Just tell us already."

"It started right after Peyton was born," Adrian said. "Your mother changed a lot—I suspect it was postpartum depression—but she's always had a thing against psychiatrists, so she refused to get checked out. I tried to be there for her, but nothing I did made a difference. Seeing her so sad and hopeless made me feel…worthless. I didn't know what to do.

"At the time, a couple that your mother and I were friends with separated. It was a rough time in all of our lives, and the woman in the other couple and I ended up…spending a lot of time with each other."

"You slept together?" Leave it to Peyton to be blunt.

"Yes." Adrian nodded. "I'm not proud of it—especially since your mom was struggling—but it is what it is. I can't change the past."

Okay, so Adrian had had an affair years ago. It didn't shock Courtney, since Mom had said he hadn't been faithful. But why did this one affair matter more than the others?

"Then your mom found out she was pregnant again—with you this time, Courtney," he continued. "After what happened when Peyton was born, she agreed to see a psychiatrist. He worked with us, got her on the right medications, and everything was looking up. Not only for us—but for the woman I'd had the affair with, too. She'd gone back to her husband, and they were happy, so we agreed to never mention it again."

Peyton crossed her arms and narrowed her eyes. "But that woman got pregnant, didn't she?" she asked. Adrian flinched, and she continued without giving him a chance to respond. "Which means we have a *half sibling* we've never known about. Oh, wait, don't tell me—that half sibling was killed in another Vegas hotel-owner heist, right?" She leaned forward, resting her elbows on her knees. "Because if he or she *was* alive…that would be a really shitty thing to keep from us."

"It's more complicated than that," Rebecca said, jumping in. "But yes, she's alive."

"So it's true?" Courtney felt like the world had gone fuzzy, and she braced her hands on the edge of the sofa. "We have another sibling...who's around my age? And we've never known about her?"

"Yes," Adrian said. "It's true."

"And you thought we would be okay with this?" Peyton dropped her legs from the coffee table, her feet slamming onto the floor. "Because you're telling us before we found out ourselves?"

"Yes, I thought it would be better if I was the one who told you," he said. "Which is why I'm doing it now."

"It doesn't work like that," she said. "You promised last time that there were no more secrets. But you lied. I'll never trust you, or Mom, again...not like I ever did in the first place." She stood up and glared at him. "I can't even *look* at you. I'm going to my room."

Adrian's jaw hardened. "In your mother's defense, she never knew about this. She knew I was unfaithful to her, yes. But she never knew about the...results of that."

That stopped Peyton in her tracks. "Well, that makes it even more terrible than I thought, doesn't it? You kept this from us *and* from Mom. It's a miracle that Rebecca wants to marry you, knowing what a liar you are."

"You have a right to be unhappy with your father." Rebecca's voice was sharper than Courtney had ever heard it, and her hand rested on Adrian's knee. "But I've been there through all of this, and Adrian's always been honest with me. You have to remember that other people are involved in this, too—for instance, your half sister's parents."

"So what?" Peyton asked. "Her parents didn't want her being part of our family, and you were just okay with that?"

"Or have you been part of her life this whole time?" Courtney clenched her fists. She was angry at Adrian for keeping this from them, sad that she hadn't known about this sister until now and had missed all those years of getting to know her, and amazed that this *sister* was out there at all.

"No, I haven't been," Adrian said. "I *wanted* to be in your sister's life, and for her to be in yours. That was the original plan. But the moment that Britney was killed…everything changed."

"That's just an excuse," Peyton said. "Another cover-up for another lie." She spun around, her hair flying around her shoulders, and marched toward her room.

"Are you really going to lock yourself into your room without hearing the full story?" Adrian called to her, stopping her in her tracks. "Without knowing your sister's identity?"

"Another sister," Savannah repeated, breathless. "We have *another sister*. How could you not think we should know about her?"

"Once Peyton sits back down, I'll continue telling you everything."

Peyton glared at Adrian and crossed her arms.

"Come on, Peyton," Savannah said. "Don't be so stubborn that you stop us from hearing the whole story. Please?"

"I'm not being 'stubborn,'" she said. "I'm *pissed off*. Don't you realize that we're never going to hear the 'whole story' about *anything*? Everything we've ever known about our lives has been a lie. I'm done."

"I don't like this, either." Courtney's stomach swirled, and she sipped Savannah's soda to try and calm it. "But Savannah's right. We need to know more. Don't you at least want to know who this other sister is?"

"Fine," Peyton muttered, throwing her hands in the air and reclaiming her seat on the couch. "I'll listen, but it doesn't mean I'm not angry."

"Point taken," Adrian said. His calmness unnerved Courtney. It was as if by remaining calm, he could block off all emotion associated with what he was telling them.

The three of them watched him expectantly, waiting for him to continue.

"You were about to tell them about the girl's parents," Rebecca reminded him. "About them asking you to keep quiet about being her father."

"Yes." Adrian cleared his throat, and took a sip of water. "The situation was difficult for me and the girl's mother, Leena. You see, Leena comes from a deeply religious family. While she's more modern, she was afraid that if her parents knew she had a child with a man who wasn't her husband, her family would no longer respect her, and it would destroy her relationship with them."

"So you never told us about our half sister because…you were worried about her mother's relationship with her family?" Peyton raised an eyebrow. "That's not enough."

"There are more reasons," he said. "I'm just trying to help you girls understand how all this happened."

"All right." Courtney nodded. She might not *like* that this had been kept from her, but she wanted to understand why.

"Leena found out she was pregnant a few weeks after your mother did," he continued. "By that point, your mom and I were already on track to fix our marriage—the meds were kicking in, and she was back to being herself again. Leena and I had agreed to never speak of our affair to anyone. So when Leena first told me she was pregnant, I knew if your mom found out, it would shatter her. But then Leena said she didn't want anyone to know, and that her husband had agreed to raise the child as his own—that he was *happy* to raise the child as his own. She asked me if I would be the child's godfather, so I could be in her life, but still keep our families intact. The decision wasn't easy, but in the end, I agreed with her that it was for the best. Her daughter would be raised as practically your sister, and since she was my goddaughter, no one would question the trust fund I created in her name."

"And you seriously thought that plan was okay?" Courtney asked. "Raising her as 'practically' our sister wouldn't have been the same as knowing we're *actually* sisters."

"Looking back on it now, I would have handled it differently." He glanced down at his hands. "But everything else in my life seemed to be going well for the first time in nearly a year, and Leena's idea seemed like the best solution to keep it that way."

"You lied to us, you lied to Mom and you lied to this half sister of ours," Peyton said. "The only people it was a 'good solution' for were you and Leena."

"I didn't think your mother would be able to handle the truth," he said. "I was trying to keep her from having another breakdown. You should have seen her after she had you, Peyton. It was like all the life had been sucked out of her. I couldn't put her through that again."

"We've all seen her like that," Courtney said. "It's like she's not part of the world anymore. She's impossible to reach, and it's scary. It's why she started drinking."

"I hate when she gets like that." Savannah shuddered. "It's awful."

"So you know what I'm talking about," Adrian said, his palms up. "I couldn't help her. I tried, but I couldn't. I'm sorry."

"But when you were raising our half sister as your goddaughter, did you ever think about telling us the truth?" Courtney asked. "Or did you plan on keeping it a secret forever?"

Adrian shifted in his seat and cracked his knuckles. "If everything had continued on the path I thought we were headed,

I'm not sure what would have happened," he said. "Maybe raising you all so close would have been too hard, and we would have told you the truth. But then Britney was killed, and everything changed. Your mom took the three of you back to Fairfield, and I told Leena it wasn't worth risking our daughter's safety for me to be in her life, especially since she has a father who loves her as if she were his own. I was harsh about it—I was in a dark place after Britney's death—and didn't give her much say. She, her husband and our daughter moved across town. They never told her that I'm her biological father. So with all four daughters out of my life—and safe, until your mother spiraled out of control—I threw myself into what I do best—my work."

Courtney pressed her fingers against her temples, trying to get this all straight. "So we have a half sister, who's my age, living her life with no idea of our existence."

"Is she still in Vegas?" Savannah asked. "Have we *met* her?"

Courtney sucked in a sharp breath at the possibility. Had they met anyone who could be their sister? She, Savannah and Peyton all had various shades of blond hair, fair skin, blue eyes and tiny noses. They had their differences, too—Peyton had inherited Adrian's high cheekbones, whereas Savannah's face was round, like their mom's, and Courtney had Adrian's height. But despite those differences, anyone looking at them side by side could tell they were sisters.

Courtney had no idea what this Leena looked like. If their half sister looked more like her mom, Courtney might never be able to guess who she was.

"Yes, you do know her," Adrian said. "She also lives in the Diamond."

Courtney's hands dropped to her sides. She only knew one girl her age who lived here. "You mean that our half sister is...?"

"Madison Lockhart."

Courtney stared at him, as if waiting for him to take it back. How could this be true? Madison had hated them from day one; she'd gone out of her way to kiss Damien at a club to embarrass Savannah, she'd teased Courtney about her fling with Brett and she'd taken a picture of Peyton with her teacher at the bar and sent it to her friends. And they were *related*. Courtney shuddered at the thought.

"That bitch can't be our sister." Peyton slammed her soda can on the coffee table, drops of Coke splattering everywhere. "She's treated us like shit from the first day we got here."

"Yeah," Savannah chimed in. "She *hates* us. And none of us like her, either."

"Don't you think you're being too hard on her?" Rebecca asked.

"No," Courtney said. "We're not."

"Madison didn't know she was related to you until recently," Adrian said. "If she'd known, she might have been more welcoming when you moved here."

"Yeah, right," Peyton said. "She probably would have hated us more."

"You're wrong," he said. "Since finding out, she's been pushing for me to tell the three of you the truth, so she can get to know you. I was the one who held back—I thought you needed time to process what you learned about Britney before I threw something else at you."

"When did she find out?" Courtney asked. "She knew the week of Thanksgiving, didn't she?"

"That long?" Savannah gasped. "No way."

"It's possible," Courtney said. "Madison and I had a strange conversation in the tutoring center before Thanksgiving break. She asked me questions about my relationships with you and Peyton, and she asked about Adrian, too. It all seemed so random. But now it makes sense. Madison knew the truth at that point. Didn't she?"

"Yes." Adrian cleared his throat. "She did. Her mom—Leena—called me after Thanksgiving break to tell me that Madison knew."

"But she was at my birthday party, and she barely talked to us," Savannah said. "She acted like she didn't know us..."

Courtney's body went cold, and she could barely move. Because when Peyton had accused Madison of posting that picture of her and her teacher online—that had been after Thanksgiving, too. She and Peyton had talked to Madison in the Lobby Bar, right under the statue of Daphne turning into a tree, and Madison had acted like she barely knew them. Like she didn't know she was their *sister.*

"How could she have known for that long and not told us?" she asked. "Why would she do that?"

"Madison found out early in the school year—around late September," Adrian said. "Her parents convinced her not to say anything, but apparently it was tearing Madison apart so much that they couldn't force her to keep the secret anymore. They called me and told me it was time for us to tell you the truth, but it was right after you'd found out about Britney. Like I said earlier, I couldn't imagine telling you something this huge while you were still grieving for her. So Madison's parents explained it to her, and told her that I would break the news to you when I felt you were ready."

"It wasn't up to you to decide when you 'thought we were ready,'" Peyton said. "You should have told us the moment we moved here, when we were at dinner that first night. You shouldn't have *kept* this from us in the first place! How could you think it was okay to never tell us that we *have another sister*?"

"I've already explained all of that." Adrian somehow remained calm, despite Peyton's yelling at him. "Looking back on it now, there's a lot I would have done differently. The guilt I felt after Britney was killed was more painful than anything I've ever experienced—it felt like I'd killed her myself. I couldn't think clearly for years. Not one day passes when I don't look back and wonder if I could have prevented what happened, so she would still be alive today. Seeing the three of you again reminded me of how I failed as a parent." His voice wavered, and Rebecca took his hand in hers, which seemed to give him the strength to continue. "I rationalized my decision by making myself believe that keeping all of you—including Madison—away from me was the best way to keep you safe. But pushing you out of my life was just as bad. Maybe even worse. Because I should have been in your lives, I should have told you about Britney and you should have been raised knowing Madison was your sister."

"But that's not what happened," Courtney said.

"No." He shook his head sadly. "It was a mistake. But I can't change the past. And we were on such a great track after winter break, and it's gotten better with all the Sundays we've been spending together. Didn't the three of you have fun riding horses through the mountains last week?"

"Yeah," Courtney admitted. Sure, Peyton hadn't layered her clothes enough for the cold weather and had to wrap herself in the tour guide's dirty blanket, Savannah had almost fallen off her horse while taking a selfie and they were all sore for days afterward. But they'd had fun, especially when Adrian had surprised them by showing off how he could stay on a cantering horse while throwing a hand up, rodeo style. At the end of the day, the tour guide had taken a picture of the four of them together, and no one looking at it would have been able to guess that they'd first met their father months ago.

"When you told us about Britney, you *promised* us it was the last secret," Peyton said.

"I know," Adrian said. "That was before Madison's parents told me she'd found out the truth."

"How did she find out?" Courtney asked.

"They did blood testing in one of her science classes," he said. "Apparently her father had mentioned his blood type before, and when Madison tested hers, she realized the results were impossible. She approached her parents about it, and they had no choice but to tell her the truth."

"Interesting." Courtney might not like Madison, but after spending time with her in the tutoring center, she knew she worked hard and was smart. She did respect her for that.

"So you're only telling us because Madison found out on her own?" Peyton asked, glaring at Adrian. "If she hadn't found out, you would have kept it secret forever?"

"I'd considered telling you before," Adrian said. "But yes, Madison finding out was what pushed me to tell you now. I know you might not be able to immediately accept it. But I hope that over time, we'll be able to overcome it and be a family."

"That is such a load of shit." Peyton stood up with so much force that the couch moved backward. "I can't deal with this anymore."

She stomped to her room and slammed the door, leaving them all staring in her wake.

"Well, that went better than expected," Adrian said, breaking the silence. "What about the two of you? What are your thoughts?"

Courtney glanced at Savannah, who had been alarmingly silent through the majority of this conversation. Her younger sister's eyes were glazed over, and she was running her fingers over the hem of her shirt.

"It's probably best if you give us some space." Courtney barely realized that she was speaking—it was like she was watching herself in a play or movie instead of it being real life. "This is a lot to process."

"All right." Adrian cleared his throat and finished his water. "I can respect that. I know that Madison and her parents are hoping to talk to you—Madison wanted to do it tonight—but they'll understand if you want to wait a day or two."

"But we don't think you should wait past Sunday," Rebecca added. "It's best for you to speak with her before seeing her in school on Monday. That's why we wanted to tell you first thing after school."

"As long as Peyton agrees, we'll do it on Sunday," Courtney said. Sunday was their usual "father/daughters" day, but there was no way they would be in the mood for that after what they'd just learned.

"We'll leave the three of you to talk." Adrian stood up and straightened his jacket. "I really do hope we'll be able to find a way to work through this."

"And remember that we're right down the hall if you need anything," Rebecca said.

"Thanks," Courtney said, the word feeling hollow. "But I think we need space right now."

"We'll be there if you change your mind." Rebecca placed her hand gently on Adrian's arm. They said they would see them Sunday, reminded them again to come by if they needed anything and left.

The door shut, and the living room was silent.

"How can Madison be our sister?" Savannah asked, her voice small. "She *hates* us."

"She didn't know we were sisters when she first met us." Courtney tried to rationalize the situation, even though it made no sense to her, either. Sisters or not, she couldn't forget about the way Madison had acted toward them when they first got to town. "Although it would be nice to think that she would have felt something. Some kind of sisterly connection. But Madison is just so…"

"Hateful?" Peyton's voice echoed from the hall, and she joined them in the living room. "Bitchy? Smug? Catty? And a million other terrible words. I wonder what she'll have to say for herself on Sunday. Because *nothing* will make me change my mind about her."

"You were listening from your room?" Courtney asked.

"Obviously." Peyton rolled her eyes. "I didn't want to be around Adrian anymore, but I wanted to know what was going on. Add it to the list of things he's lied to us about. Madison Lockhart is our half sister? Yuck."

"I know," Courtney said. "But since she's found out—which Adrian said happened around the end of September—can either of you think of anything blatantly mean she's done to us?"

They were silent for a few seconds, thinking.

"She didn't tell us she was our sister," Peyton said. "She's known since September, and she didn't say anything. That's messed up."

"What if she didn't say anything because she doesn't *want* to be our sister?" Savannah asked.

"Adrian said Madison wanted us to know the truth," Courtney said. "Her parents lied to her, just like ours lied to us. We might not have much in common with her, but we do have that."

"So you're going to trust her and forget about what a bitch she's been to us, just because she shares DNA with us?" Peyton asked.

"I never said I would forget how she treated us," Courtney said. "But it might not hurt to give her a chance."

chapter 11: *Peyton*

It wasn't long before Sunday morning came, and while Peyton had no interest in impressing Madison and her family, she did take extra time getting ready. Black leather pants, ankle boots, a leather jacket, smoky eyeliner, and she was ready to go. She wanted Adrian to *see* how angry she was. To know she wouldn't forgive him.

If only her insides didn't feel like a trembling mess.

She walked over to her desk, uncapped the Sharpie lying next to the calendar, and Xed out February 8—yesterday—which had the number 112 written on it. Which meant as of today, there were 111 days until graduation, when she would be out of here and free to do whatever she wanted. And despite letting Courtney send in that application, it *wasn't* going to be college.

What was it that Jackson had said when she'd told him she wasn't going to college? That she'd always struck him as more of a "gap year" type.

She still had no idea what that meant, so she opened her laptop and typed *gap year* into the search bar.

A gap year seemed to be what it sounded like: A year off between high school and college. One of the reasons listed for taking one was because of being "burned out of classroom education."

That was *exactly* how Peyton felt.

She read more about gap years, but then someone knocked on her door, and she closed out of the browser.

"Peyton," Courtney said, opening the door a crack. "They'll all be here soon. Are you up?" She came inside and did a double take when she saw that Peyton was awake. "Wow," she said. "I was expecting to have to drag you out of bed. Not to find you up and dressed."

"It's not every day that we find out the bitchiest girl in school is our half sister," Peyton said, pushing her laptop away. "I wanted to be armed and ready. And this—" she motioned to her all-black leather outfit "—is my armor."

"I don't think I'll ever be ready." Courtney yawned, and Peyton noticed the dark, baggy circles under her eyes—she must not have been able to sleep last night. "I just can't picture Madison as our sister. Me, you and Savannah—we've been through so much together. All Madison has done is give us trouble."

"You were the one who thought we should give her a chance," Peyton reminded her.

"I still think that," Courtney said. "But that doesn't make this any less nerve-racking."

"There's three of us and one of her," Peyton said. "We've got this."

They walked into the living room, where Savannah was sitting at the table, finishing up a plate of pancakes. It was too early for Peyton to be hungry, so she made a cup of coffee.

At ten o'clock on the dot, Adrian and Rebecca entered the condo. Before the door shut, Peyton glimpsed someone with dark hair in the hall—Madison. Peyton's hands shook, and she gripped her coffee mug tighter.

"Good morning," Adrian said, running his fingers over the table in the foyer. "I'm glad you're all up and ready."

"The pancakes smell amazing." Rebecca took a deep breath and smiled.

"I couldn't touch my French toast, so it's there if you want some," Courtney offered.

"I would, but French toast isn't on my prewedding diet." Rebecca stood straighter and sucked in her stomach. "It was egg whites and fruit for me this morning."

"You don't need to lose weight," Savannah said. "You're already super tiny."

"Thanks," she said. "But I'm hoping to *stay* that way through April."

Peyton looked back and forth between the two of them. How were they talking about *wedding* stuff right now? "Let's cut it with the niceties," she said. "We all know what's about to happen, so let's get it over with. Bring her in."

"Since Brett's at his dad's for the day, we were hoping to all talk in his condo," Rebecca said. "Madison and her parents are waiting there now."

"We thought everyone should be on neutral territory," Adrian added.

"I would rather them come here." Peyton crossed her arms, staying firmly in place.

"Me, too," Savannah chimed in.

Adrian took a deep breath and clasped his hands behind his back. "Madison's nervous enough as it is," he said. "I don't think this is asking too much."

"You don't think you're *asking too much*?" Peyton repeated, her eyes wide. "You had nothing to do with us until last summer. You didn't tell us about Britney until Thanksgiving, and you didn't mention that we have another sister until two days ago. So yeah, I think you're asking too much. If we want Madison and her parents to come over here, then they're coming over here."

"They're already in Brett's condo…" Rebecca glanced worriedly at Adrian.

"Then they can get up and come over here," Peyton said. "They're capable of that, right?"

"Come on, Peyton," Courtney said, her eyes welling up "Let's not start fighting before we even see them? Please?"

"Fine." Peyton gave in, not wanting her sister to cry before this even began. "Brett's condo it is. Let's get this over with."

Adrian opened the door to the condo, and as he and Rebecca led the way inside, Madison and her parents stood up from the couch. It reminded Peyton of those historical movies that Courtney liked, when people stood whenever royalty entered. Madison's eyes darted around—focusing everywhere but on Peyton and her sisters.

"You girls know Madison." Adrian cleared his throat and walked to the center of the room. "These are her parents, Dr. John Lockhart and Dr. Leena Lockhart."

Peyton studied Madison's parents while Courtney said the obligatory "Nice to meet you." Madison's dad was on the shorter side, with a large nose, thick brown hair and kind eyes. Her mom had olive skin, shiny black hair and stunning green eyes. Madison's dark hair and naturally tan skin were clearly from her mom. But she had deep blue eyes—the same as Adrian, Peyton, Courtney and Savannah. And while Savannah and Courtney had softer facial features, like their mother's, Madison had the same defined bone structure as Adrian...and as Peyton.

How could they have missed the resemblance? Sure, Peyton had noticed that Madison's eyes were a similar color to hers and her sisters', but she'd chalked it up to coincidence. She'd certainly never thought that they could be *sisters.*

"Why don't we sit down?" Rebecca said, somehow managing to smile despite the ridiculous amount of tension in the air.

Madison and her parents had already claimed a couch, with Madison between them, as if they were protecting her. Peyton and her sisters took the couch across from them, with Courtney naturally in the middle. Rebecca and Adrian happily sat in the chairs.

"At this point, everyone is up to date on the situation," Adrian said. "No one knows more than anyone else."

"So what are we supposed to do now?" Peyton leaned back and crossed her arms, purposefully avoiding Madison's gaze. "Hug each other and become one big, happy family?"

"We know there's been some tension between you girls." Rebecca twisted her gigantic engagement ring around her finger. "Adrian and I—and John and Leena—were hoping you would talk with us about it so we can help you work through it."

Peyton bit the inside of her cheek to stop from laughing. No way would they tell the parents about how Madison had kissed Damien to hurt Savannah, given Courtney a hard time about her summer fling with Brett and taken the picture of Peyton and her teacher at the bar. And they *definitely* weren't going to talk about how they'd been convinced that Madison had written that post about them on campusbuzz, so Peyton and Savannah had blackmailed Oliver into trying to take Madison's virginity, only for Peyton to tell Madison the truth at the party, which had resulted in the fight that had left Oliver storming out of there drunk and totaling his Maserati.

Madison had her arms crossed and an eyebrow raised—she must also be thinking there was no way in hell she would talk to their parents about their drama. At least they were on the same page about *something*.

"We just have different groups we hang out with in school." Courtney spoke calmly and slowly, which Peyton knew meant she was choosing her words carefully. "We don't know each other well. It's all very…awkward."

"Imagine finding out months ago and having to keep quiet about it until now." Madison finally spoke for the first time since they'd entered the condo.

"I can't imagine that," Peyton said. "Because if I'd found out, I would have said something—no matter what."

"Why *did* you stay quiet about it for all that time?" Courtney asked Madison.

"A few reasons." She glanced at her parents, and they nodded for her to continue. "Mainly because when my parents first told me that Adrian's my biological father, I thought he wanted nothing to do with me."

"Which isn't true," Adrian said.

"Right." She crossed and uncrossed her legs, not looking at him. "But it was what I thought, and it hurt. So I did what my parents wanted and stayed quiet. Plus, I doubted that you all would even *want* me as a sister. But I kept seeing the three of you around school, and I couldn't keep it secret anymore. I talked to my parents, and my mom called Adrian to let him know that we wanted to tell you all the truth. But that was right after you found out about Britney, so Adrian didn't want to drop something else on you." She lowered her eyes. "I'm sorry about what happened to her."

"Thanks." Courtney's voice wobbled, and Peyton squeezed her hand for support.

"Anyway," Madison said. "If I'd known from the beginning that we were sisters, I would have reached out. I'm sorry for anything that might have been taken the wrong way since you all moved here. I never meant to hurt any of your feelings."

Peyton stared at Madison, waiting for a punch line. Then she laughed.

"Is there something you want to say?" Rebecca asked, her expression calm.

"Nope," Peyton managed to say. "Since everything she says is bullshit."

"No, it's not," Madison said. "I'm trying to apologize."

"If that's the best you've got, then you should just give up now."

"Is that really fair?" Madison's mom—Leena—said. "I know you girls have been through a lot, but so has Madison."

"This is just a lot to process all at once," Courtney jumped in. "I don't think any of us know what to do."

"What do you mean?" Adrian asked.

"Savannah, Peyton and I—*we're* sisters," she explained. "We've gone through everything together, and we know everything about each other. I'm not sure that anyone could have the same bond with us that we do with each other."

"I know that." Madison scuffed at the floor with her feet, her hands clenched on her lap. "And I don't expect to suddenly have a magical sisterly bond with you. But I was hoping we could get to know each other. Try being friends."

"And how do you think we should do that?" Peyton asked. "Get a table at Myst and party all night? That *might* be okay for a few minutes…until you started throwing yourself at whatever guy we each were interested in, and taking pictures of us that we don't want taken and sending them to your friends, so that they can post them online and ruin our lives."

Madison's lip curled—*there* was the bitch hiding behind her trying-to-be-friendly exterior. "You have no idea what you're talking about," she said.

"Seriously?" Peyton leaned forward, narrowing her eyes. "You want to go there?"

"Girls!" Madison's mom clapped her hands, silencing them. "What's going on here? This sounds like more than a 'few misunderstandings.'"

"It's nothing." Madison shot Peyton a look, clearly telling her to shut up.

"Nothing?" Peyton snorted. She didn't care if their parents were there or not—she was *not* letting Madison bully them. "Is that what we're calling it when you made Savannah cry in front of all your friends the first week we were here?"

"Is this true?" Rebecca asked Savannah, her eyes full of concern. Savannah glanced down at her hands. "Why didn't you say anything to us?"

"Of course it's true," Peyton said. "I wouldn't have said it if it wasn't—"

"I can speak for myself," Savannah interrupted, surprising Peyton enough to make her stop talking midsentence. She took a deep breath, looking each one of them in the eyes. "Yes, something happened this summer, and yes, it upset me. But it happened forever ago. It's done with now. So let's drop it, okay?"

"I'm still sorry about it," Madison said.

Peyton just sighed and rolled her eyes.

"For the past few months, Madison's been under so much stress that she stopped going out with her friends," Madison's mom said. "Then after what happened to Oliver...this has been an extremely difficult time for her. I was hoping—we were *all* hoping—that the four of you could have a fresh start."

"And we have just the idea for how that can happen," Adrian continued. "Spring break is next week, and Rebecca and I want to take you to the house in Aspen."

"All of us?" Peyton asked. "Meaning Madison's parents, too?"

"No." Rebecca smiled. "Although we have discussed it with them, and we all agree that this will be a great opportunity for the four of you girls to get to know each other. Brett will be coming, too, and the house is big enough that you can bring friends."

"Aspen…" Savannah repeated. "Isn't that a ski town?"

"Aspen's more than just any old ski town." Madison sat straighter and flipped her hair over her shoulder. "It's the best place to ski in the world. Tons of movie stars and celebrities vacation there."

"Sounds exciting," Peyton said, completely void of emotion. "Except that I'm not going."

"Yes, you are," Adrian said. "This trip isn't an option. You can stay in the house the entire time, but you're coming to Aspen."

"Whatever." Peyton sat back and crossed her arms. What were they going to do—have her bodyguard force her onto the plane?

"What about the two of you?" Adrian asked, looking at Savannah and Courtney. "What do you think about this plan?"

"You said that celebrities go there?" Savannah asked.

"I'm sure you'll come across one or two," he said with a knowing smile.

"It sounds fun." She bounced her legs, as if she suddenly couldn't wait for this trip that they'd learned about all of five minutes ago. Peyton rolled her eyes, because it was so typically *Savannah*. One mention of celebrities, and everything else was forgotten.

"We're forgetting one big thing," Courtney said, and every head in the room turned to look at her. "We don't know how to ski."

"That's not a problem at all," Adrian said. "You'll have a private ski instructor, and you'll learn fast. The point is for us to spend time together."

"Great," Peyton said in a tone that made it obvious that she thought it was anything but. She mainly just said it to shut them up, because clearly nothing important was going to be said with the adults in the room. "But do you all think that my sisters and I can talk to Madison? Alone?"

"Is that all right with you?" Madison's mom asked her.

"Yeah," Madison said. "It's fine."

"Well, then," Rebecca said brightly. "We'll do that. I'm sure you have a lot to discuss. Remember that we're down the hall if you need anything, okay?"

The adults left within minutes, leaving the four of them in the condo.

"Even though you don't believe me, I really am sorry." Madison crossed her legs, balancing her hands on her knees. "I've changed a lot since last summer. I know I wasn't the nicest when you first moved here—"

"Understatement of the century," Peyton said. "You were a total bitch."

"I was," she said. "Then I found out that my entire life was a lie. These last few months have been hell. I wish I could take back the things I did this summer, but I can't, and I don't know what to do to make you all realize that I want to make things right between us."

"I just don't get it," Savannah said. "This summer, you knew I was interested in Damien. Then you made out with him in front of everyone—and you were just using him to embarrass me. I don't understand why you hated me so much when you didn't even know me."

Madison took a deep breath, pressing her hands together. "I was jealous, okay?" she finally said. "Damien had always had a thing for me, and I thought it meant that he would always be there for me. Then when I saw him with you, I worried that I'd made a mistake. I was afraid I would lose him. I wondered if I *did* have feelings for him. So I kissed him. And all it did was made him hate me."

"At least we know that Damien has some sense," Peyton muttered.

Madison flinched, her eyes flashing with hurt. "I was wrong," she said. "I know that. I can't take it back, but Savannah—I really think you still have a chance with him."

Savannah sat up straighter, her eyes bright. "Really?"

"I wouldn't say it if I didn't mean it."

"Don't fall for it," Peyton warned Savannah. She turned back to Madison, and asked, "Why should we trust anything you say?"

"Because I want to be your sister," she said. "And remember— you're not exactly a perfect angel, either. You tried to blackmail Oliver into sleeping with me. Shouldn't that be enough to consider us even?"

"I called it off before he could go through with it," Peyton said. "And believe what you want, but I'm glad that I did."

"You certainly enjoyed gloating about it at Savannah's party," she said. "Which, by the way, was the reason Oliver took off and got in that accident. I hope you're proud of yourself for that."

"Oliver got in that accident because he drove when he was drunk." Peyton leaned forward, narrowing her eyes at Madison. "*Not* because of what I said at the party."

"Well, it was a crappy time to suddenly decide to tell me the truth."

"He was flirting with you so much that I thought he was still trying to go through with the bet," Peyton said. "I was doing you a favor."

"How do you not feel guilty about what happened to him?" Tears glinted in Madison's eyes, and her voice wavered. "If you hadn't called him out that night, he wouldn't have left the party, and the accident never would have happened."

"Oliver made his own decision," Peyton repeated, clenching her hands into fists. "No one forced him to drive that night."

"But I should have done more to stop him," Madison said. "I would have been able to stop him, if I hadn't been so upset."

"You can't blame yourself for that," Savannah said. "It wasn't your fault."

"She's right," Courtney said. "And I've been wanting to ask—how's he doing? I heard he's recovering, but he hasn't been in school…"

"I don't know," Madison said. "He hasn't seen anyone besides his family."

"Isn't he one of your 'best friends'?" Peyton asked. "I thought you would have seen him by now."

"Well, I haven't," she snapped. "I've tried, but he hasn't wanted to see me, or any of his friends. It sucks, and I don't want to talk about it."

"Fine with me." Peyton chipped at her nail polish and leaned back in the couch. Neither of them looked at each other.

Courtney broke the silence. "I still can't understand how you knew we were your sisters for *months* and you didn't say anything," she said. "How could you see us every day—you even talked to us a few times—and never say anything?"

"I hated every second of it," Madison said. "I was so stressed that I stopped going out, and I gained ten pounds in less than a month. I know you still probably don't like me very much… but I'm glad you finally know the truth."

As much as Peyton hated it, she was glad to know the truth, too.

But that didn't mean she would ever *truly* feel like Madison was her sister.

chapter 12: *Madison*

On Sunday evening, Madison waited with Damien in the lobby of the Villas at the Gates, pacing around the marble floor. The man working the front desk kept his eyes on her—maybe he thought it strange that she wasn't sitting down on the red velvet sofas that looked fit for a palace—but she had too much energy to sit.

"Are you sure you're okay doing this now?" Damien asked again, his dark eyes flashing with concern.

Before they'd come to the Gates, she'd told him everything that had happened over the past few months: from her blood-type test not giving the results she expected, to her confrontation with her parents, to the "meeting" with Adrian, Rebecca, her parents and the Diamond girls that morning. It was going to come out eventually, and now that their friendship was finally on the mend, she wanted him to hear it from her before anyone else. He was taking it in stride.

Or maybe it was such a convoluted story that he was having trouble taking it in at all.

"It's too late to turn back now," she said. "Ellen Prescott's already on her way out here to talk to us."

Damien checked his watch. "What's taking her so long?"

"Hopefully she's talking to Oliver," Madison said. "Trying to convince him to see us."

Fifteen minutes later, Ellen walked into the lobby. As usual, she looked completely put together—a knee-length pencil skirt, purple blouse and her short hair sprayed into place.

"Good evening," she said as she approached them.

Madison stood straighter and repeated the greeting. Damien also took on better posture. Being in Ellen Prescott's presence tended to do that to people.

"I apologize for having you wait out here all this time," she said. "I just finished talking with Oliver. It took quite a bit of convincing, but he's ready to see you. You can come inside."

"Really?" Madison's eyes widened.

"Yes, really," Ellen said. "That is what you wanted, correct?"

"Of course," she said quickly. "It's just that after all this time, we weren't expecting it to be so easy."

"Oh, it was anything but easy." Ellen shook her head and buzzed them into the hall that led to the Villas. "I've been trying to convince Oliver to see his friends for weeks. You're the first two who've stopped by unannounced. People dropped by when he was still at the hospital, but he only wanted to see family while there, and once he came back home, everyone gave up. He's barely left his room. I hope seeing his friends will get him out of this funk."

Damien walked right next to Madison, and whispered, "If he's barely left his room, what's he been *doing* all day?"

"Logan and I hired a tutor to make sure Oliver stays on top of his classes," Ellen said casually over her shoulder. "He also works with him on his SAT prep. This is the most focused he's ever been on his studies."

"So he's been studying all the time?" Damien didn't sound convinced.

"He's also been doing physical therapy." Ellen stopped in front of the grand two-door entrance to the Prescotts' villa, straightened her skirt, and eyed both of them up and down. "He's waiting in his room. You know where it is."

"Wait." Damien stopped her before she opened the door. "There's nothing we need to be warned about, right? He didn't get some severe disfiguration in the accident or anything?"

Madison pressed her lips together at how insensitive that sounded—but she was glad he'd asked. Better to be prepared for something like that.

"His knee took the worst of it," Ellen said softly, as if Oliver could be listening from inside the villa. "He had surgery to get it reconstructed, and he's off his crutches, but it'll be about five months until he can resume normal activity. He has a few scars from the glass shattering, but other than that, he's physically okay."

"Thanks again for letting us see him, Mrs. Prescott," Madison said. "We—and all his other friends at school—have been really worried."

"I'm glad you're here," she said. "He needs to see his friends. But try to act normal, all right? He hates when people treat him differently because of what happened."

With that, she opened the door and let them inside.

Oliver was lying in his king-size bed, watching snowboarding on ESPN. If it hadn't been for the crutches leaning against the wall near the window, the bottles of prescription medications on his nightstand and the well-worn SAT book on the other side of the bed, Madison would have thought this was no different from the many times in the past that she'd stopped by to hang out.

He picked up the remote and muted the volume. "Hey," he said, his gaze meeting Madison's. She stopped in place, surprised by how different he looked. Normally his deep brown eyes were full of life and enjoyment. Now, they looked dull and…lifeless. It was like a stranger had taken over his body.

"Hey, man." Damien strolled over to Oliver's desk and made himself comfortable in the chair. "How's it going?"

Oliver stayed focused on Madison, as if Damien hadn't spoken. "You don't have to stand there in the doorway looking at me like that," he said. "Like you think I'm about to break."

"Sorry." Madison shook herself out of it. "It's just been such a long time since I've seen you. I missed you."

"Really?" He tilted his head. "Because after Savannah's party, I thought you hated me."

Damien looked back and forth between the two of them and stood up. "I'm going to grab some drinks from the kitchen," he said. "Do you guys want anything?"

"Sprite for me," Oliver said.

"I'll have a Diet Coke." Madison shot Damien a grateful look, glad he was giving her and Oliver time alone.

She kicked off her boots and sat on Oliver's bed, leaving a friendly amount of space between them. She'd sat with him like this so many times before. So why could she think only about when they'd been on this bed together over Thanksgiving break—the way his lips felt on hers, her body pressed against his, and how they couldn't get enough of each other?

But he'd been with her only because of that bet with Peyton. Madison had been an idiot to fall for it. And before all that, they were best friends. She couldn't desert him now, when he needed her…even if seeing him made her stomach flutter with unwanted butterflies.

"I could never hate you," she said, wrapping her arms around herself. "Yes, I was angry about what Peyton told me

at Savannah's party. But after what happened that night…"
Her eyes filled with tears, and she swallowed to compose herself. Ellen had asked her not to mention the accident, and to
act like everything was normal. But everything *wasn't* normal.
And Madison couldn't pretend otherwise. "I had no idea if
you were going to make it or not. Do you have any idea how
terrifying that was? I couldn't focus on anything but worrying
about you. And you didn't even want to talk to me."

"I don't need anyone to worry about me," he said. "I'm
fine."

She studied him, noticing the tiny scars near his temple.
They were new—they must have been from glass during the
crash. "I care about you." She reached for him, but stopped
herself. "Of course I worried about you. I had no idea what
was going on with you, besides Brianna telling me that you
would be okay. But it wasn't the same as seeing you."

His eyes darkened. "I told Brianna not to tell anyone anything."

"That's all she said." Madison didn't want Brianna getting
in trouble with Oliver. "That you needed physical therapy,
but that you would be fine and would talk to everyone when
you were ready."

"I *am* fine," he said. "I'm talking to you now, aren't I?"

"Yeah, you are." Madison ran a hand through her hair,
not wanting to push this. She couldn't drive him away when
she'd gotten this far. "So what's been going on? Your mom
said you've been able to walk, and you look much better than
I imagined you would."

"My knee hurts like a bitch, but the doctors are impressed
by my progress," he said. "The mental-health-care shit my parents have been making me go through…that's another story."

"Oh." Madison picked at a hole in her sock and glanced at
the pill bottles on his nightstand. Three of them total. She'd

assumed they were pain meds for his knee…but why would he need *three* different types of pain pills? She noted the prescriptions on the labels so she could look them up later. After all, if he hadn't wanted her to see them, he would have hidden them. "What kind of mental health stuff?"

"Why do you care?" he asked.

"How could I *not* care?"

"Forget about it." His eyes were so empty that it gave Madison chills.

"I can't do that," she said. "But you don't have to tell me now if you don't want to."

"Fine," he said. "This conversation is *over* the minute Damien comes back in, but since I know you won't give up until you get your way, here are the basics. My blood-alcohol level was over the legal limit when I got in that accident. When they brought me into the hospital, the doctors found the coke I'd had on me to bring to the party. My parents paid enough to make any legal problems go away, but since then I've had more psychiatric appointments than I can keep track of."

"For outpatient treatment?" Madison hoped he was getting help, but she kept her voice steady and neutral, since he'd probably had enough judgment from his parents.

"That and some other shit." He ran his hands through his hair, which was longer than usual. He must not have had a haircut since the accident.

"What 'other shit'?" She didn't want to push him, but she also wanted to know. And she couldn't know if she didn't ask.

"This is the part I haven't wanted to tell anyone—it's why I've been avoiding everybody," he said. "My doctors told me I don't have to tell anyone if I don't want to. But you're staring at my pill bottles, and knowing you, you've already memorized what's on them and will look up what they're for the moment you get home. So I guess you can know."

Madison nodded three times—she'd read in a medical article that that clued someone in that you were listening—and waited.

"I have all these mental issues." Oliver let out a short laugh, even though it wasn't funny. "My mind's all fucked up. You already know I have ADHD—I've known about that for years. And it's no big deal, because everyone knows people with ADHD aren't crazy. But apparently I have bipolar disorder, too. Fucking *bipolar* disorder. Can you believe it?"

"Wow." Madison leaned back into the pillows, curling up in the bed and facing Oliver. She'd had an interest in anything medical for as long as she could remember, so she knew a little about bipolar disorder, and honestly—yes, she could believe it. The way that Oliver's drinking, partying and gambling had been out of control over the summer and all of first semester, and then how he'd locked himself away and refused to talk to his friends for weeks after the accident...it all fit together.

"You think I'm crazy, right?" he asked.

"No," she said. "I just wish you'd told me earlier, so I could be there for you, like you were there for me after I found out the truth about Adrian." She glanced down after saying it, because *had* he been there for her? Or had it been part of Peyton's dare? Her heart panged at the reminder of his betrayal. But this visit was about him, and he'd just confessed something huge to her, so she asked, "How're you holding up?"

"Well, I've spent the past few weeks avoiding school. The idea of going back..." He sucked in a deep breath and shook his head. "I would be fine if I never had to go back. I don't trust anyone anymore."

Madison scooted closer, leaving only inches between them, and he watched her with so much intensity that her cheeks heated. "You have to come back eventually," she said. "School sucks without you. I miss you."

"Do you, though?"

She reached for his hand, her fingers intertwining with his. The air buzzed between them, her heart feeling like it was being pulled toward his, and she wanted to lean forward and kiss him so he would know how much she cared about him.

She wasn't supposed to have these feelings for him…not after finding out about the bet. But he'd promised Madison that his feelings for her went beyond the bet—that while it started out that way, it had turned into more than that. Now he watched her with so much intensity, as if he truly cared about her and could see all the way into her soul.

Then there was a knock on the door, and Damien came inside, carrying three drinks in one arm. Madison yanked her hand out of Oliver's, the spell between them broken.

"It took you fifteen minutes to figure out how to bring three glasses in at once?" Oliver asked.

"Your mom was in the kitchen, and I talked to her for a bit," he said. "You guys look cozy. What's been going on while I've been gone?"

"I'm trying to convince Oliver to come back to school," Madison said, since she didn't want to break Oliver's trust and tell Damien what they'd *really* been talking about.

"Yeah, man." Damien settled back into the chair. "What's taking so long? You look ready to come back to me. You're walking fine now, right?"

"The knee still hurts sometimes, but I'm off the crutches," he said. "My doctors say I should go back to school in the next week or so."

"Don't sound *too* excited," Damien joked. "But I can't blame you. You've been getting to sleep in, while the rest of us have been waking up at dawn."

"I wish," Oliver said. "My parents are making me work with a tutor to keep up with my classes, and they're forcing me to wake up at the same time I would for school. And working with a tutor is *harder* than being in class. In class I can zone out. That doesn't fly with a tutor. I actually have to do shit."

"So come back," Damien said. "Everyone's wondering where you've been."

"Really?" Oliver asked. "What've they been saying?"

"The biggest rumor is that you got disfigured in the accident and you're afraid to face everyone," Madison said. "Which is clearly wrong. You look great. You look…" She searched for the right word. "Rested." And it was true—the circles that had been under Oliver's eyes last semester from the partying, drinking and barely sleeping were gone. He looked better now than he had before. Except now that he'd pulled away again, the distant look had returned to his eyes. Even though he'd opened up to her earlier, she still felt like he was holding something back.

"Don't worry about convincing me, because I'm being forced to go back this month," he said. "So, what've I missed while I've been gone?"

Madison launched into the story of what had happened recently—most important, about what had happened this past weekend with the Diamonds. It was hard to imagine that it was only that morning that she'd sat in the condo talking to Peyton, Courtney and Savannah as sisters for the first time. And as she'd expected, it hadn't gone well. Peyton hated her, Savannah didn't trust her and Courtney seemed hesitant to let her in. None of them could understand why she hadn't told them immediately. But they didn't know what those few months had been like for her—how much she'd *wanted* to tell them the truth. It just hadn't been that simple.

And while she planned on telling only her close friends, with a secret this big, it wouldn't be long until their whole school—and the rest of the world—knew, too.

www.campusbuzz.com

MADISON'S A DIAMOND?!?!?!
Posted on Wednesday 2/11 at 6:11 PM
the title says it all! SOOO many people are talking about this around school. Is it true???

1: Posted on Wednesday 2/11 at 6:35 PM
hell yeah it's true!!! Apparently she's known for MONTHS and the Diamond girls just found out last weekend!!!

2: Posted on Wednesday 2/11 at 6:42 PM
So she found out months ago and didn't tell anyone until now? THAT explains why she was acting so weird last semester...

3: Posted on Wednesday 2/11 at 7:11 PM
HAHAAHAHA is this for real? Madison HATES those girls!

4: Posted on Wednesday 2/11 at 7:39 PM
YES it's true. Over the past day, articles have been popping up about it all over the online tabloids. Madison didn't even tell her close friends until early this week. I would be so pissed if one of my best friends kept something like that from me.

5: Posted on Wednesday 2/11 at 8:02 PM
You would be pissed if you were one of her best friends?

I would be pissed if I were Peyton, Courtney, or Savannah! If what you're all saying is true (and from what I've heard around school, it is) then Madison knew she was their half sister for MONTHS and didn't tell them. Seriously, how messed up is that?

chapter 13: *Savannah*

For the past week, Savannah had been teaming up with You-Tube star (and agent-sister) Emily Nicole on a professional video, and it had been a complete whirlwind. Every day after school she'd rushed to wherever they needed to go to film, and they'd worked until late at night. All it had taken was an offer from Adrian to produce the video, and Emily was on board.

In the beginning of the week they'd gone to the studio at the Palms to record the vocals, where they had professional musicians playing with them and everything. Once the music was recorded, they moved on to the video. During the week they could only record at night, which was fine because they were using Vegas as a backdrop and Vegas looked the best at night, anyway. There was a *lot* of waiting around between shots—more than Savannah had expected—but there were fun parts where they got to play around in the arcade in New York, New York, ride the roller coaster and bungee jump off the Stratosphere. Everyone walking by stopped to watch what they were doing, and a few people recognized them and asked for autographs.

Between volleyball practice and filming, Savannah hadn't had time to do homework, but her grades would recover. And at least all the busyness was an excuse not to hang out with Jackie, Alyssa and Brooke, and it distracted her from the revelation that Madison was her sister. She'd barely spoken to *any* of those girls this past week, which was fine by her.

Friday after school, she slammed the volleyball over the net and checked her watch to see how much longer it would be until practice ended. Ten minutes. Then she would run straight from practice to the car, get home, and rush to get showered and ready to meet up with Emily Nicole for filming. The entire process was positively exhilarating—and exhausting.

Except that as she was packing up her bags in the locker room, Jackie, Brooke and Alyssa surrounded her. Jackie smiled as if they were best friends, Alyssa flipped her hair over her shoulder and Brooke stood behind them, her arms crossed. Savannah's stomach dropped. This couldn't be good. But whatever they wanted, Savannah would do what she'd been doing for the past week—pretend like she was too busy to speak to them. It wasn't even pretending. She actually *was* too busy to stand around chatting.

"Hey, girl," Alyssa said. "Are you coming to Tegan's party tonight?"

"Nope." Savannah yanked the zipper of her bag shut.

"Really?" Jackie raised an eyebrow. "It's been *so long* since you've hung out with us. And it's Friday night! You have to come out."

"Can't." Savannah breathed deeply, trying to keep her cool. "I'm finishing up that video with Emily Nicole."

"Of course you are." Alyssa rolled her eyes. "You're always too busy to hang out with us now."

"Sorry." Savannah shrugged, not meeting their gazes. "Maybe another time."

Part of her wanted to say something to them—to let them know she'd heard them talking about her, and that they weren't actually her true friends. But just the thought of conflict made her tense up. So instead, she grabbed her bag and hurried past them, avoiding glancing over her shoulder as she made her way to the parking lot.

The filming went well on Friday, and by Saturday, Savannah, Emily Nicole and the rest of the team were finishing the daytime scenes to wrap up the video. They'd started at the tennis courts that morning, where they did a choreographed dance with tennis rackets while wearing tennis gear. Now they were at the rooftop pool at the Diamond, shooting the summer party scene, complete with inflatable tubes, colorful sunglasses and teen models dancing behind them as extras.

"You're all partying at the pool and having the best time of your *life!*" their director shouted from behind the camera. "Jump, jump, jump, throw your hands in the air, dance to the imaginary music that's not playing right now but will be in the video, smile, laugh—it's a beautiful, hot day and you're all having a blast!"

This would be easier to believe if they weren't wearing bikinis in windy, sixty-degree weather. It was the third time they'd tried this scene, because apparently Savannah's energy wasn't high enough, and it was coming through to the camera that she was freezing cold, and they were running out of time before the sun set. She *had* to get it right this time.

So she tried to ignore how freezing she was and jumped and partied and pumped her fists in the air as if it was a hot summer day, smiling and laughing with her heart-shaped sunglasses on as if this were the best summer party ever. She even hip-bumped one of the sexy male models, flipping her hair over her shoulder and shooting him a flirtatious smile.

"And...that's a wrap!" The director pushed the button to stop recording. "Everyone can get some clothes on now and warm up!"

Savannah rushed to the back corner where they'd left their clothes in a pile. Why hadn't she brought a comfy sweatshirt instead of her zip-up hoodie?

"Before we get dressed, let's take a behind-the-scenes picture for Instagram," Emily Nicole said, handing her phone to one of the extras. She and Savannah posed for a few shots—first for Emily Nicole's phone, then for Savannah's. The moment they were finished, Savannah pulled her clothes on. Then she picked her favorite photo and posted it on her Instagram, which was also linked to her Twitter, Facebook and Tumblr.

Had the best day EVER shooting a new video with @EmilyNicoleMusic! Can't wait for you all to see it! xoxo <3 <3 #Vegas #YouTube #MusicVideo #SavannahDiamond #EmilyNicole #Fun #Happy #Love #PoolParty #Summer #EvenThoItsFeb. She added summer-themed emoticons at the end and clicked Share.

Once the photo was online, and she was finally warming up, she and Emily Nicole walked over to the director.

"Thank you so much for everything," Savannah said to him, still breathless from jumping at the "pool party." "I had a blast."

"I'll have the edited video to you soon," he said, pushing at the bridge of his hipster glasses. "I have a feeling that this one will be a hit."

"I hope so!" Emily Nicole beamed and turned to Savannah. "It was so awesome of you to ask me to do this video with you. I can't wait to see how it turns out."

"Me, too," Savannah said. "And thank *you* for agreeing to do the video with me! I know I've already told you, but I've been a fan of your channel since you started, so recording with you is so amazing."

They said thanks to the extras, the microphone guys and everyone else they'd been working with for the past week. By the time the goodbyes were said, the sun had set and it was getting colder, so everyone was clearing out.

"Want to get hot chocolate and warm up?" Savannah asked Emily Nicole.

"Hell yes," she said, and they headed down to the Diamond Café. The coffeehouse was packed, but they eventually managed to get their drinks—a Diamond Signature Hot Chocolate for Savannah, and a pumpkin-spice latte for Emily. When Courtney had worked at Starbucks, she'd made fun of the people who ordered pumpkin drinks when it was past fall, and Savannah smiled to herself at the memory when Emily ordered it. She put the drinks on her dad's card and they snagged a table in the corner.

"So," Emily said, blowing into her drink. "There's been talk all over the internet, and I've been dying to ask—what's going on with you and Perry Myles?"

Savannah's cheeks heated, and she ate a whipped-cream-filled spoonful of hot chocolate. "We've been texting since my party in December," she said. "He's on his world tour, so I haven't seen him. But he does want to see me over spring break, and my dad's letting my sisters and I bring friends to his house in Aspen, so I think I might invite him…"

"On a family trip?" Emily asked.

"It was *supposed* to be," Savannah said. "But yesterday my dad said he had to go to China that week for business, and

Rebecca's staying in Vegas to do wedding-planning stuff. I guess Adrian felt guilty for having to cancel, because he said my sisters and I should all go anyway, and that we can invite friends. Courtney, Peyton and Brett don't want to invite anyone, so they told me that I can have all their invites."

"Let me get this straight," Emily said. "You have a house in Aspen over spring break to yourself with you and your sisters?"

"And Brett and our bodyguards," Savannah said. "Adrian made sure we knew that our bodyguards would be there the whole time, making sure nothing got out of control."

"Still, that's awesome," she said. "Why haven't you invited Perry yet?"

"I want to," Savannah said. "But I don't know. He's so famous. What if he thinks that spring break with me and my sisters is lame?"

"Savannah Diamond." Emily placed both hands on the table and smiled. "You're not some nobody inviting him to go camping in the middle-of-nowhere Montana. Aspen is for the rich and the famous. He's famous, and you're rich—on your way to becoming famous, too."

"You think so?"

"I *know* so." Her eyes sparkled. "And he said that he wants to see you. You *have* to invite him. I don't know what you're waiting for."

"You think I should text him right now?" Her stomach fluttered.

"Hell yeah." Emily nodded. "I want to see what he says!"

Savannah took out her phone and composed the text.

Hey there ;) Over spring break me, my sisters, and some friends are going to my dad's house in Aspen—do you wanna come?? March 7–15 <3

She showed it to Emily.

"Perfect," Emily said. "Send it!"

Savannah's thumb hovered over the send button.

"If you don't do it, I will…" Emily's hand crept toward the cell phone.

Savannah pressed Send and laid the phone on the table. "Done." Her heart raced, and she took a deep breath to try to calm it. "It's late in Europe right now—where he's touring—so he should be finished with his show."

They chatted about YouTube stuff—Emily gave Savannah a few helpful hints—but the whole time, Savannah fidgeted and glanced at her phone. Would Perry text her back? Maybe he'd seen the text, didn't want to go to Aspen and was trying to think of a good excuse. Or maybe he was already bored of her—he probably met tons of girls on the road. And if he *did* text her back, should she text back immediately? Or wait and play it cool? Sometimes it was a few hours—or even *days*—before she heard back from him. Then she would stare at her phone wondering what she'd said wrong, and contemplate sending him another text to restart the conversation. Her sisters would stop her, and that was usually when she would hear from him again.

But as much as she wanted to hear back from him *now*, she refused to do the double-text. So she needed to distract herself.

"How do you deal with the mean comments people post online?" she asked Emily, twirling her spoon in her hot chocolate. "I know I should brush it off, and I tried at first. But it's so hard to just ignore it…"

Emily's eyes softened, and she sat forward. "When you put yourself out there, people are going to talk shit about you online," she said. "You know why I switched from regular school to homeschooling, right?"

"Nope." Was this something Savannah *should* have known?

"When I started on YouTube, I uploaded a few covers, but most of the songs I recorded were originals." She sat back, her eyes far off. "The songs were really personal. I didn't mention specific names, but I referred to stuff that had been going on in my life—guys I was interested in, unrequited love, hoping to reach my dreams, that kind of stuff."

"But you only record covers," Savannah said. "I've never seen one of your originals. I didn't even know you *had* originals."

"I took them down," she said. "Strangers who watched the videos had nice things to say, but my classmates?" Emily chuckled, although it sounded forced. "Not so much. I would walk through the halls at school, and they would laugh about my lyrics, trying to guess who I was referring to. They made fun of how I go by 'Emily Nicole' online instead of just 'Emily,' which was what everyone called me in school. I deleted my original songs and only posted covers after that, but it didn't stop them from torturing me about everything I did online. I came home crying more days than I didn't. But I kept pushing, and after months of feeling like it might all be for nothing, eventually my channel took off. So my mom and I agreed to switch to homeschooling so I could focus on my career."

"Wow," Savannah said. "That sounds awful...but like a good choice. Maybe I should switch to homeschooling, too."

"Why would you do that?" Emily scrunched her eyebrows. "You have the perfect life."

"Far from it." Savannah shook her head, and told her about what happened with Alyssa, Jackie and Brooke. "I've been avoiding them ever since. Yesterday after practice they invited me to a party, and I almost said something to them, but I didn't want to cause a scene, you know?"

"They sound like bitches," she said. "After I started homeschooling, some of the girls who were mean to me started reaching out to me again, trying to get me to give them shout-outs online and stuff like that…but they were using me. Like how your 'friends' are using you. You should have told them off."

"I know." She looked down at the table and bit her lip. "But I hate fighting with people."

"I get that," Emily said. "But you wouldn't be fighting with them—you would be standing up for yourself. There's a difference."

Before Savannah could respond, her phone buzzed with a text.

Emily sat straighter. "Is it Perry?"

"Yeah." Savannah's heart thudded. "He says he would love to come to Aspen, and asked if he can bring Noel, too!"

"Two One Connection boys." Emily raised an eyebrow. "How many people are you allowed to invite?"

"Technically, only three," Savannah said as she wrote a text to Perry.

Can't wait to see you!! I'll give you the details later ☺

She pressed Send, and placed her phone back down.

"'Technically'?" Emily raised an eyebrow. "Does that mean you can actually invite more than three?"

"Yeah," Savannah said. "Courtney doesn't care about inviting anyone, since our stepbrother Brett will be there—long story—and Peyton doesn't want to invite anyone 'cause she wants to meet new people around town. I think she's trying to get over Jackson—*another* long story—but I'm not sure if it'll work. But anyway, since none of them are using their invites, I get to invite more people."

"I have an idea." Emily smiled and finished the last of her

drink. "The video we made this week is going to help both of us with publicity, because we'll bring our fans to each other's channels, right?"

"Yeah…" Savannah stirred the bottom of her hot chocolate.

"What if we took it further, and both of us were in Aspen with Perry and Noel, and we took some pictures and videos together, and maybe with them, too? Can you *imagine* how much publicity that would get us? Lynda would love it."

Savannah tilted her head, realizing what Emily meant. "Is this your way of asking if you can come to Aspen?"

"Well…yeah." She shrugged. "But it really will help both of us. And you don't plan on inviting those 'friends' who were being bitches behind your back, do you?"

"No," she said. "Of course you can come."

"Great!" Emily beamed. "This is going to be *so awesome.* We can make a video blog while we're there and everything. Can you imagine how many views that'll get—a video blog of our trip to Aspen with two guys from One Connection? Our channels will explode!"

"They will, won't they?" Savannah liked this idea more and more by the second. Not only would it help her You-Tube channel, but it also sounded like she had a new friend in Emily. A friend who understood her better than the volleyball girls at Goodman ever could.

She glanced around the Diamond Café—hopefully no one was listening in on their conversation—and spotted Damien stepping into line for a drink. He wore jeans and a gray, long-sleeved shirt that showed off his perfect body. His dark eyes stopped when they met hers, looking at her almost in question.

He flashed her a smile and waved. Not wanting to look like she was overthinking anything, she smiled and waved back, even though every time she saw him was a reminder that he saw her only as a friend, and it hurt.

But all of that felt too personal to share with Emily Nicole, so she glanced away from Damien, hoping she looked unaffected. After all, why should she be upset about him when she had *Perry Myles* texting her?

"Don't even try not telling me about the gorgeous guy who just waved to you." Emily scooted her chair closer. "Are you friends with him?"

"Yeah," she said quickly, focusing on Emily Nicole so she wouldn't accidentally look like she was staring at Damien. "He lives here and we go to the same school, so we see each other around."

Emily raised an eyebrow. "Well, it looks like I'm about to meet him, because he's coming over here now."

Savannah's chest tightened, and as she looked up to see Damien strolling toward them, she reminded herself to breathe.

"Savannah Diamond," Damien said when he reached their table. Just hearing him say her name made her heart warm. "And you're Emily Nicole, right?"

"Yeah, I am." Emily smiled and ran her fingers through her hair. "How did you know that?"

He pulled a chair up and sat down, placing his drink on the table. "I helped Savannah with her YouTube channel when she first started it, so I still check up on it every once in a while," he said. "She Tweeted about how excited she is to be filming this new video with you, so I had to check out your channel. Your videos are great. It's easy to see why you have so many subscribers."

"Thanks." Emily blushed a perfect shade of pink, and Savannah curled her fingers into fists under the table. Damien wasn't hitting on Emily, was he?

She shouldn't be surprised. He always hit on everyone *but* her. First Madison, then Evie and now Emily. And even though she should expect it by now, it didn't make it hurt any less.

"If you and Savannah are close enough that you helped her start her YouTube channel, I guess that means you'll be coming to Aspen with us over spring break, too?" Emily asked.

Savannah's mouth nearly dropped open. Emily had *not* just invited Damien without asking her. Except that she had.

But as far as Emily knew, Savannah was interested in Perry. Savannah had never *mentioned* Damien to Emily. So Emily hadn't realized that by inviting Damien, she might be creating a colossal mess.

"This is the first time I've heard about spring break in Aspen," Damien said. "Your dad has a house there, right, Savannah?"

"Yeah." She fidgeted with her empty drink. It wasn't that she *didn't* want to invite Damien—of course she wanted him there. She just didn't want him being there with Perry. And now that she'd invited Perry, Perry would be there as her date. Which shouldn't be a problem, since he was one of the hottest celebrities in the world…but Savannah would choose Damien over Perry, if he were interested.

Which he wasn't. And his seeing her there with Perry would make him even less interested. Her stomach twisted, because now she had no choice but to invite him. There was no way this could end well.

"Adrian and Rebecca will be busy over break, but Adrian's letting me and my sisters go to the house in Aspen with some friends," Savannah said, each word coming fast. "I was going to invite you, but it was so last-minute that I assumed you already had plans."

"The only plans I have are to go with my parents to Laguna Beach to visit my grandparents," he said. "They won't mind if I do something else, and Aspen sounds more fun—I haven't been skiing in two years."

"You have to come!" Emily said, clapping her hands together. "I'm a skier, too. Savannah said this will be the first time she and her sisters ski, so I need someone to hit the slopes with."

Damien leaned forward, his eyes flashing with challenge. "If you can keep up on Ajax Mountain, then sure."

"What's Ajax Mountain?" Emily asked.

"The hardest mountain around Aspen," Damien said, as if it were obvious. "Mostly blacks and double-blacks, and there are no greens. Think you can handle it?"

"I don't need greens." Emily laughed and flipped her hair. "I warm up on a blue, and then ski the blacks all day. I've even been known to do a double-black now and then."

Savannah dug her fingernails into her palms, her chest heating as she looked back and forth between Emily and Damien. What on earth were they talking about? Blues, blacks, greens? This was a different language. And did Emily need to flirt with him so blatantly?

"This ski trip is sounding a lot better than Laguna Beach," Damien said. "So Savannah, if you meant it that you were going to invite me, then I'm in."

"Yeah, sure," she mumbled. "It'll be fun."

"Can't wait," Emily said. "And with Perry and Noel from One Connection there, too, it'll be extra fun." She checked her phone and made a face. "My mom wants me to come back to the room to get ready for dinner. I'll see you soon?"

"Yep." Savannah reached for her bag. "I should probably get ready, too."

"Wait." Damien was watching her so closely that she forgot to breathe. "Stay for a few more minutes? I want to talk with you about something."

"Okay." With the way he was looking at her, did she really have an option?

Neither of them said anything as Emily Nicole headed out of the café and turned the corner.

"So…" Damien said once she was gone. "Perry Myles is coming to Aspen, too?"

"Apparently," Savannah said. "He texted me back a bit ago saying he can come, and we haven't worked out the details yet, but yeah, it seems like he's in. Noel, too."

"And you like this guy?"

"I guess." Savannah swallowed. "We're friends. And his being there will be good for my YouTube channel."

"Well, watch out around him," Damien said. "He's known for being a douchebag."

She sat back and crossed her arms. "You asked me to stay here so you could warn me about Perry?"

"No," he said, his gaze not leaving hers. "I asked you to stay because I wanted to talk about Madison."

"Oh." Savannah's stomach dropped. "I guess everyone knows about us being sisters by now."

"Adrian's PR people are doing a good job keeping it quiet, but yeah, I know," he said. "Madison told me."

"The two of you are hanging out again?"

"We're friends." He nodded. "Things were rough between us for a few months, but we're past it."

"Well, that's good, I guess." Savannah fidgeted with her hands. She wanted so badly to ask if he still had feelings for Madison, but she pressed her lips together, not letting herself do it. Because if his answer was yes, she didn't want to hear it.

"How've you been holding up?" he asked.

"It's just so weird," she said. "First I found out about Adrian being my father, then about Britney and now about Madison. And even though we're sisters, I have no idea what to say to her. Especially because we weren't exactly friends before all of this. She claims she's sorry…but even though I want to believe her, I can't."

"If it helps, I don't think she knows what to do, either," he said.

"Madison Lockhart doesn't know what to do?" Savannah chuckled. "I have a hard time believing that."

"She's had a rough few months," he said. "Give her a chance."

"I'll do my best."

Neither of them said anything for a few seconds, and he tapped his fingers on the table. "So…Aspen," he said, his gaze straight on her. "Are you sure it's cool that I come?"

"Of course." What else *could* she say when he was looking at her in that way that made her heart feel like it was about to explode? "It'll be fun."

"With Perry and Noel there, I'm sure it will be."

"I need to get ready for that dinner." She stood up so quickly that she nearly toppled over her chair. "I'll see you soon."

"See you, Savannah," he said.

She tried not to glance back at him, but it was impossible to resist. Their eyes met one last time, and her cheeks flushed as she looked away and turned the corner.

Earlier today, she'd been looking forward to Aspen.

Now she worried that it was going to turn into a complete disaster.

chapter 14: *Courtney*

Courtney and Madison walked silently to the parking lot after finishing up their student tutoring. Madison's car was stuck in the shop, which meant she'd had to catch a ride to school with Courtney and her sisters. That morning in the limo hadn't been awful, because it had been all four of them, but since Madison and Courtney were the only two who stayed late to be student tutors, they were riding back home together. And Courtney was positively dreading it.

She adjusted her backpack and glanced over at Madison, not sure what to say to her. Maybe she could claim to be tired from staying up late last night doing homework and pretend to fall sleep.

"Is it strange to have a driver take you everywhere you go?" Madison asked as they approached the Range Rover, where Teddy—Courtney's bodyguard—waited in the driver's seat.

"At first it was," Courtney said. "But Teddy would have to be in the car with me or following me anyway, and I don't actually like driving, so it's nice not having to worry about it."

They situated themselves in the backseat and fastened their seat belts. Teddy had Courtney's favorite Sirius XM station playing softly—the Broadway station. She expected Madison to ask if they could change it, but she said nothing, which surprised Courtney. Peyton and Savannah never tolerated listening to show tunes.

"So," Courtney said. "Do you know who you're bringing to Aspen?"

"I don't know." Madison sighed and rested an elbow on the armrest. "I want to invite Oliver, but I don't know if I should."

"Oliver?" Courtney gasped. If there was one person she *didn't* want in that house with them, it was Oliver. "Isn't he still recovering from his accident?"

"He is, so he won't be able to ski, but there are lots of other things to do in Aspen," Madison said. "And I think he'll be happy to hang out with everyone again."

"I don't know." Courtney shrugged. "He ate lunch outside by himself near where Brett and I eat. He looked like he wanted to be left alone."

"So *that's* where he was," Madison said. "It was his first day back, so I texted him to try to find him when he wasn't in the dining hall, but he didn't reply. I'll track him down and sit with him tomorrow."

Courtney sat back and looked out the window. "After what happened between you and Oliver, why do you want to invite him to Aspen?" she asked. "How can you forgive him so easily?"

"Oliver was the only person who was there for me last semester," Madison said. "He wouldn't have gone through with Peyton's dare without telling me the truth. And he's going through a tough time right now. I want to be there for him. I just wish he would let me."

"Would he be there for you?" Courtney asked. "If the situation were reversed?"

"Yes." Madison nodded. "He would."

Courtney ran her hands through her hair, saying nothing. The Oliver that Madison knew and the Oliver that Courtney had met might as well be two completely different people. And Courtney didn't trust Oliver for a second.

"I'm going to invite him," Madison said. "He might not come, but I have to try."

"He was a huge jerk to me and my sisters from the day we moved here," Courtney said, biting her lip. "If you want me to say that I'm okay with him coming to Aspen, I can't do that. It would be a lie, and I'm sick of all these lies everyone's been telling recently."

"Me, too," Madison said. "But you have to understand… these past few months have been rough for all of us. You have no idea how scared I was when Oliver's parents told me he was in the hospital…" She stared out the window, tracing her fingers along the glass. "I don't know what I would have done if he hadn't been okay."

Madison seemed so vulnerable in that moment, and for the first time since meeting her, Courtney felt bad for her.

Then Courtney realized—Madison loved Oliver. She wasn't sure if Madison had realized it yet, but Courtney could see it. Because she suspected she looked the exact same way when she was talking about Brett.

"If you invite Oliver, and he wants to come… I suppose I'll figure out how to tolerate him for a few days," she finally said.

"Thank you." Madison smiled. "And I'm glad you brought it up, because I did want to talk to you about it. Anyway, are you still set on not bringing anyone? It seems like Savannah's taking all of your invites."

"You mean with those One Connection guys?" Courtney asked, and Madison nodded. "I don't know what Perry's doing with Savannah, but it seems like he's leading her on, and I don't like it. I'm worried about her."

"At least Damien will be there," Madison said. "From what he's said to me, he really cares about Savannah."

"You trust him?"

"Yeah." Madison didn't miss a beat. "I do."

Courtney nodded, because while hearing that about Damien was unexpected, Madison seemed to believe it. And Damien *had* helped Savannah with her YouTube channel. Compared to Perry, he might actually be good for her sister.

It was crazy how much had changed since last summer.

"I'm not bringing anyone," Courtney said, answering Madison's earlier question. "All the people I want to spend time with are already there. My sisters and Brett."

When she said "her sisters," she meant Peyton and Savannah. Madison might be related by blood...but sisterhood meant more than that. It was about shared experiences, trust, knowing you had people who would be there for you and would listen to you no matter what, and who could always tell if there was something wrong. They were the ones who, with a single look, knew if you were about to burst into giggles or into tears and why, and who knew when you needed to get out of the house for a midnight trip to In-N-Out Burger to gorge on a milkshake and animal-style fries. They were the ones you could be raging angry with one moment, and completely forgive ten minutes later. She would always be there for her sisters, and they would always be there for her, because they loved each other no matter what.

And no matter what blood might say, Madison Lockhart didn't feel like Courtney's sister.

"I think I know what's going on." Madison smiled conspiringly. "You and Brett must be together in secret after that kiss over the summer, and you want to spend vacation together. I'm totally over him—what happened between us over the summer was a one-time thing and I've been over him for months—so you can be honest with me. I won't tell anyone."

"Brett and I aren't together," Courtney said—it had become automatic for her over the past few weeks of covering up their relationship. "We have a lot in common, so we're friends and we hang out a lot, but that's all it is."

She glanced down at her lap after speaking. Hadn't she just told Madison that she was done with the lies? And then she'd gone ahead and said that.

She was officially the biggest hypocrite ever.

But if she told Madison the truth, then Madison might tell someone else, and she couldn't risk that. She was doing what she had to do for her and Brett.

"Ooookay." Madison elongated the word, clearly not buying it. "Then what about your friends from school? There has to be someone else you want to invite to Aspen. Or from your old school in California?"

"Not really." Courtney shrugged and checked her watch. Five minutes until they were back to the Diamond. And in those five minutes, Courtney did not plan on telling Madison the pathetic truth about why she wasn't using her invites: because she didn't *have* any friends to bring along.

In California, once she was old enough to get a job she'd been so busy that she'd lost any friends she'd had. Here in Las Vegas, the acquaintances she had at school barely knew her. They would find it strange if she invited them on a vacation. Sure, on her first day at Goodman a few people had tried to reach out to her, but they'd all seemed disappointed when she wasn't a free-spirited, party-girl hotel heiress. It didn't take long for them to stop trying.

When she wasn't studying, Courtney had been spending

all her time with her sisters and with Brett, and she was perfectly fine with that.

At least that was what she'd been trying to tell herself.

chapter 15: *Peyton*

Dear Peyton,
Congratulations! You've been accepted to the University of
Nevada, Las Vegas (UNLV).

The email continued on to say how the acceptance was offered
with the expectations that her grades would stay where they
were and that she would graduate high school in the spring.
They gave her a student number to log into the website and
accept the offer—which, of course, she hadn't done.

It had arrived in her inbox a few days ago, with fireworks
in the background and everything. She'd stared at it every day
since. It also said that a formal letter of acceptance would be
arriving in the mail soon.

Which was why, every afternoon, Peyton had been making sure she was the first person to go through the pile of mail
the housekeeper left in the foyer. The official letter hadn't
arrived yet, but Courtney was bound to ask Peyton if she'd

heard from UNLV soon. And then Peyton would have to tell her the truth—that she'd gotten in.

She closed out of the email and went to Facebook to check on Jackson. He didn't post many pictures, except for some of his new apartment, which had so much snow piled up outside that it reached the hoods of the cars. It looked cold and miserable.

Her fingers hovered over the keyboard, wanting more than anything to send him a Facebook message asking how he was doing. But she stopped herself. If he'd wanted to contact her, he would have. And sending him a message and having him ignore it would only make her feel worse.

So she took a deep breath and closed out of his page. She had to stop checking up on him like this. She had to get over him. He didn't want to be with her, and since she couldn't force him to want her, she didn't have a choice.

Instead, she looked up the gap-year programs again. There were so many companies who offered them, and they went to places all over the world. Cities in remote areas that Peyton used to think she had a better chance of going to Mars than visiting. The photos were cheesy, of people her age smiling with their arms around each other, but Peyton wondered: what would it be like to do something like that? To travel the world for months, not worrying about school, or family drama, or anything else?

It sounded…freeing.

It would also mean leaving her sisters.

Would she be able to do that? Would she *want* to do that?

She couldn't remember a time in her life when she hadn't shared a home with her sisters. She'd never imagined a life where she didn't see them every day.

Before she could think it through, there was a knock on the door.

"Come in," she said, closing out the browser and shutting her laptop.

Adrian and Rebecca walked inside, and Adrian had a thick envelope in his hand. Peyton frowned at the sight of it. If it was what she suspected… Why had it gone to Adrian's condo instead of hers?

"What's that?" she asked, glaring at the envelope.

"A large packet from UNLV," Adrian said, as if it were something he received in the mail every day. He and Rebecca joined Peyton on the bed, and while it was a queen and had enough space for the three of them, it still felt cramped. He placed the overstuffed envelope in front of her. "It has your name on it, so we thought it was best that you open it."

"I know what it says." Peyton stared at it blankly. "I got in."

"They say a big packet is a better sign than a small letter, but you can't *know* until you open it and see for yourself," Rebecca said.

"I do know." Peyton gathered her hair over her shoulder and sighed. "They sent me an email a few days ago. I thought the actual letter would come here, but I guess Courtney put your address on the application instead of ours. I should have looked it over before she sent it."

"Courtney filled out your application?" Adrian asked.

"Yep," she said. "Do you think I would have applied otherwise?"

"It did seem rather…out of the blue," he said. "Especially since I thought you didn't want to go to college."

"I don't," she said. "I'm not going."

"Then why send the application at all?"

Since he and Rebecca clearly weren't going to budge until getting an answer, Peyton gave him a rundown of the deal she'd made with Courtney.

"So I told her that she could send in the application for fun to see if she could get me in," she finished. "And she did. I'm not surprised I got in. The essay she wrote was killer."

"She doesn't know yet that you were accepted?" Adrian asked.

"No." Peyton held his gaze. "I haven't told anyone."

"Interesting…" He stroked his chin, as if he thought she was considering going. Which was stupid. Hadn't she already been clear on her feelings about college?

"Since you've known for a few days now, have you already told them your decision?" Rebecca asked.

Peyton crossed her legs and looked down at her bedspread, where the package was still waiting to be opened. "No," she said. "I have a few weeks before I have to let them know, so I haven't bothered with it yet. But you already know I'm not going."

"If you have a few weeks, then there's no rush to tell them no." Adrian gestured to the envelope. "Are you going to open it, or should I?"

"I'll do it." Peyton grabbed the envelope and ripped it open, pulling the congratulations letter out from amongst the welcome pamphlets.

"Well?" he said.

She thrust the letter at him. "Like I said, I got in. Well… Courtney got me in."

Rebecca glanced at the door. "Do you think you should let Courtney know?" she asked. "She'll be so excited to hear the good news."

Peyton got out of the bed, walked over to her door and opened it. Sure enough, Courtney was there, standing close enough to have been listening to the entire conversation.

"When Rebecca looked over here, I figured that you were listening." Peyton moved aside and opened the door wide. "Come on… I know you're coming in no matter what."

Courtney rushed inside, jumped onto Peyton's bed and grabbed the acceptance letter. "You got in!" she squealed, beaming at the letter like it was the most valuable piece of paper on earth. "I knew I could get you in."

"And apparently you knew to put Adrian's condo as our address so I couldn't hide it from him." Peyton rolled her eyes. "But congratulations. You now know that you can write a college essay for the most challenging applicant ever and still get them in."

Courtney picked up the welcome pamphlet, which had happy students on the cover carrying backpacks, smiling at each other as they walked around campus. "You haven't said no yet, right?"

"No," Peyton said. "But I haven't said yes. And I'm not going to. You know that."

"Luckily this isn't a decision that needs to be made immediately," Rebecca chimed in. "You have a few weeks to get back to them."

"So during that time, I can do what?" Peyton asked. "Change my mind? *That* isn't happening. I'm not going to college next year—not UNLV, or anywhere else."

"You've made that quite clear," Adrian said. "But you have time to consider your options, so you might as well take it."

"I don't get all this fuss about college." Peyton sighed and leaned against the headboard. "At Fairfield High, people were proud of themselves for graduating at all, because not everyone did. If you said you didn't want to go to college, that was it. End of discussion. But here, whenever I say I don't want to go to college, people look at me like I admitted to committing a felony. It's stupid. Why *should* I go to college? College is for people who want to study something. I don't. So it would be a waste of time and a waste of money."

"But surely you've been thinking about what you want to

do after graduating high school?" Rebecca asked. "It's getting so close to the end of the school year."

"I'll get a job somewhere," Peyton said. "Once I graduate I'll figure it out. A lot of people who graduate college don't end up doing anything that has to do with their degrees, anyway. So why bother?"

"Get a 'job somewhere'?" Adrian looked skeptical. "That doesn't sound like a very well-thought-out plan."

She shrugged. "It'll work itself out."

Courtney played with the acceptance letter, biting her lower lip. Peyton already knew her sister thought she should take general requirement classes at college to figure out what she was interested in, so she wasn't going to bother asking what she was thinking.

"Well, you have a few weeks to get back to the school, so why don't you consider it a bit longer?" Rebecca took the letter from Courtney and placed it back inside the envelope, along with the pamphlet of the overly happy students. "At least you know it's an option. Anyway, while the letter's exciting, that's actually not the main reason we came in here right now."

"It isn't?" Peyton glanced at Courtney, who shrugged.

"Nope." Rebecca smiled and stood up from the bed. "I have something I need to ask you. Why don't we go into Savannah's room? She's in there now, right?"

"Yep," Peyton said. When Savannah wasn't out, she was on her computer, doing whatever the hell she did online. They went into her room, and sure enough, Savannah was lying in her bed, her MacBook Pro propped on her lap as she furiously typed on the keyboard.

"Hey," she said, not looking away from the screen. "What's up?"

Adrian walked to the center of the room. "Rebecca and I wanted to talk with you about something."

Savannah lowered her laptop screen and raised her eyebrows at Courtney and Peyton. Peyton shrugged to let Savannah know that they were as clueless as she was.

"Okay…" Savannah said, pushing her laptop to the side.

"It's about the wedding." Rebecca twisted her engagement ring around her finger. "The three of you already know how happy I am that you agreed to be bridesmaids."

"Yeah," Peyton said, dreading whatever new wedding thing Rebecca was going to ask them to do next. She'd already agreed to that boring photo shoot with some high-society magazine, and to sit around when Rebecca was interviewed about her dress, only to have one question asked of her that didn't even make the article. All of these details were so stupid. The wedding was still a month away, and it all seemed like a hell of a lot of stress for one event that would only take up one weekend.

"Well…" Rebecca paced in a circle, and Peyton sat down on Savannah's bed, not wanting to get dizzy from looking at her. "Adrian and I see this wedding as not only representing a union between the two of us, but of *all* of us—including the three of you and Brett—becoming a family. And now that you know about Madison…"

"We would like to ask her to be a bridesmaid, as well." Adrian took Rebecca's hand in his, which stopped her from pacing. She smiled gratefully, and he continued, "We know that things are still shaky between the four of you girls, and that it's going to take time for you to get to know each other. But the Lockharts are already on the guest list. Madison feels separate from our family as it is, and her grandparents are having a rough time with the news, so we think this would show her that she has a place in our family. That she's going to be a part of our future."

"Seriously?" Peyton rolled her eyes. "That sounds so corny."

"Does Madison know about this?" Savannah asked.

"Not yet," Rebecca said. "We wanted to run it by the three of you first."

"Are you *really* giving us a choice?" Peyton asked. "Or just pretending like you are so that when you ask Madison to be a bridesmaid, we don't get pissed because you didn't include us in making the decision?"

"Neither of us phrased it as a choice," Adrian said, unmoved by Peyton's outburst. She clenched her jaw—the things she said that would have pissed off her mom or grandma slid right past Adrian. It was so frustrating. "But we are giving you a heads-up, so you're aware of what's going on before we ask her."

"What if we don't want Madison to be a bridesmaid?"

Adrian paused, looking at Peyton as if he was truly shocked that she'd said it. Finally—a reaction from him. "Does that also mean you don't want Madison to be your sister?" he asked.

"As if I have a choice," Peyton scoffed. "But now that you're asking, if I *did* have a choice, then no, I wouldn't want her to be our sister. These are my sisters." She motioned to Courtney and Savannah. "Right here. Madison might technically be related to us, but that doesn't make her family."

Courtney and Savannah said nothing—Courtney played with her hands and Savannah looked down at her bedspread—which was as good as them agreeing with her.

"I'm sorry you feel that way," Adrian said. "But I can't help but feel that you're being unfair to Madison."

"No, we're not," Peyton said. "Because trust me—we're the *last* people Madison would want as sisters."

"We don't need to ask her today," Rebecca chimed in, grabbing Adrian's hand and pulling him back. "We can give you girls time to take it in and talk it over privately first. We can even wait until after Aspen, if you'd like. That way you'll have had more time to get to know her."

"Good plan." Adrian paused and took a deep breath, watching Peyton as if he thought she might change her mind. But she crossed her arms over her chest, standing firm. He must have realized that she wasn't going to budge, because he made a mention about wanting to take the three of them shopping for ski gear that week, and then he and Rebecca left the condo.

"Maybe it won't be such a bad thing for Madison to be a bridesmaid," Savannah said once Adrian and Rebecca were gone.

"Yes, it would be," Peyton said, pushing her fingers through her hair. She didn't want to talk about Madison, and she didn't want to talk about UNLV. What she wanted was to see Jackson. She wanted to ask for his advice, to cry and have him hold her and kiss her and tell her that everything would be all right. But that was impossible.

So she stomped to her room, locked the door and listened to music until she was finally able to fall asleep.

chapter 16: *Madison*

Since it was the end of February, it was chilly outside, so almost everyone was eating lunch inside. But Courtney had mentioned yesterday that Oliver had been eating outside, so Madison had put on warm clothing that morning to brave the weather. She was joining Oliver for lunch—whether he was happy about it or not.

He was sitting at a table by himself, near the lake, as far away from the other tables as possible. He had his Ray-Ban sunglasses on, his hood pulled over his head, and he was playing on his phone while eating. Clearly he didn't want company. But determination surged through Madison's veins, and she marched over to the table, plopping down next to him.

He looked up from his phone. What she could see of his expression around his sunglasses was blank. "You never eat this far away from the dining hall," he said.

"I heard you've been eating out here and wanted to join you." She opened her Diet Coke and took a sip.

"Without your entourage?" he asked. "Won't they wonder where you are?"

"I told them I had an emergency student-tutoring session that I was getting extra credit for."

"That sounds like you," he said, placing his phone on the table. "But how did you know I was out here?"

"Courtney told me." She motioned a few tables away, where Courtney sat with Brett under a tree. They had note cards out and were quizzing each other, their heads bent close together, looking at each other in complete adoration. They were totally together. Madison would have to be oblivious not to see it.

"I thought you and Courtney weren't close," Oliver said.

"We're not," Madison said. "But I had to ride home with her after school yesterday, and she told me she saw you sitting out here alone during lunch."

"I'm surprised she bothered to say anything." He laughed. "She hates me."

"After what happened this summer, can you blame her? You made a bet about her and her sisters and tried to play her. Of course she doesn't like you."

Oliver pulled away, took a sip of water and gazed out at the lake.

"Sorry," she said, wishing she could take it back. It had come out so much more harshly than she'd intended. Probably because she still wasn't over how Oliver had tried to play her, too. "I shouldn't have brought that up."

"Whatever." He shrugged. "You're right. And I don't know why you came out here, but if you want to get me to eat with everyone in the cafeteria like I used to, it's not going to work. They're going to expect me to be like I was before. I don't have the energy for that."

"I didn't come out here to try to convince you to come back to our table."

He raised an eyebrow. "Then why are you here?"

"I'm here because I care about you," she said. How could he be so blind to this?

"Or you just feel bad for me since I told you about my problem."

"I'm not here out of pity." She leveled her gaze with his. "No matter what diagnosis the doctors gave you, you're still the same person I've known for years. I won't let you sulk out here alone. And truthfully..." She bit her lip and looked down at her sandwich. "I need you."

"Need me?" He leaned forward, pushing his hood off so it fell around his shoulders. "Why?"

"Because you're the only person who really sees me," she said. "These past few days have been terrible. I told you about how it went when my parents, Adrian and I sat down to tell the Diamond girls the truth."

"Not good," he said. "But you also said you knew to expect that, since you weren't the nicest to them when they got here."

"I know," she said. "But I don't want them to hate me."

"Just act the same around them that you do around me. Then they'll have no choice but to love you."

"Thanks." She swallowed and sipped her soda. He didn't mean that *he* loved her, did he? The thought made her smile... but she had to push it away. Because that couldn't be what he meant. They said stuff like that to each other all the time. They loved each other as friends. That was all.

But he was watching her so closely that her cheeks heated, and she searched for a way to change the subject. "Anyway," she said, hoping she sounded casual. "Adrian's letting us spend spring break at his house in Aspen."

"That should be fun," he said. "You love skiing."

"Yeah." She took a deep breath and fiddled with her sandwich, although her stomach was doing too many somersaults for her to eat another bite. "He's letting us invite friends. I was hoping you might come."

"No way." His features hardened, and he shook his head. "My knee's messed up from the accident—you know I only started *walking* on it again a few weeks ago. There's no way I'll be able to ski in two weeks."

"There's more to Aspen than skiing," she said, determined to make him change his mind. "If you don't come, it's going to be me, the Diamond girls, Brett, those two guys from One Connection who are probably douchebags, a random girl Savannah knows from YouTube and Damien. The Diamonds hate that I'm their sister. The only reason I'm invited to Aspen is because of Adrian, and I have to go—if I don't, it'll seem like I don't care about getting to know them. But they're going to be one big group, and I'll be all alone." She leaned forward, begging him now. "I promise to take off days from skiing to hang with you in the house and around town. I would even skip skiing entirely if it meant you would be there with me. Please come?"

"I wouldn't want to keep you from the slopes," he said. "And Damien's your friend. He'll be there for you."

"Damien's been pouting over Savannah since Perry Myles flirted with her at her party," she said. "He's got it bad for her. He'll probably be fighting Perry for her attention the entire time. And I have nothing against Damien and Savannah together—weirdly enough, I actually like them together—but Damien's going because *Savannah* invited him. I need a friend on this trip. Someone there just for me."

"You have a lot of friends," he said. "And with the mood I've been in these past few weeks, I'll just bring you down. Why not invite Larissa, or Kaitlin, or Tiffany? You'll have more fun with one of them."

"Because *you're* the one I want there," she said. "After the accident, you have no idea how worried I was about you…" Her voice wavered, and she stopped herself, not wanting to think about what *could* have happened if one small thing had gone differently that night. If Oliver hadn't made it, the last time she'd have seen him would have been that fight they'd had at the party.

Ever since then, something between them had been broken. And she needed to fix it.

"I want you to come because I've missed you these past few weeks, and I want to spend time with you. Is that so hard for you to believe?"

Oliver took a deep breath, but still said nothing. He was watching her in that way of his again—the way that made her forget to breathe.

"Please?" Madison asked, softer now.

"I'll tell you what." He sounded confident, as if he'd made his decision. "I promised Brianna I would spend time with her over spring break. So if Brianna can also come to Aspen, then I'm in, too."

"Yes!" Madison smiled, feeling lighter than she had for days. For weeks. "There's definitely space for your sister."

"Don't get too excited yet," he said. "Brianna's been *really* excited about coming to Vegas over spring break. It's all she's talked about since getting back to school."

"Tell her that the guys from One Connection will be in Aspen with us," Madison said. "There's no way she'll be able to say no."

"She does love them," Oliver agreed.

They shared a smile, and she knew this was happening. He was coming with her to Aspen.

"Thank you, Oliver." She reached for his hand, but pulled back, still not sure where everything stood between them.

"It'll be so much easier to get through the week with you there."

"You have more confidence in me than you should," he said. "But since I haven't been away from Vegas since the accident, going to Aspen might not be such a bad idea."

"I'll look up everything there is to do besides skiing." She took out her phone to set a reminder to do that when she got home. "We'll have fun—I promise."

"Hold on." He reached out to stop her, his hand sending waves of heat up her arm. "You can't skip skiing because of me."

"I already told you I don't mind…"

"I never agreed to that part." He crossed his arms, and she slid her hands inside the pockets of her jacket, her skin still buzzing where he'd touched her. "I want to make a compromise. You can only skip skiing to hang out with me for half of the days. Brianna will take the other half. Deal?"

She smiled, because while she *would* have skipped skiing for the entire trip if it meant Oliver would come to Aspen, she was glad she wouldn't have to. "Deal."

www.campusbuzz.com

finally spring break!!!!
Posted on Wednesday 3/5 at 7:31 PM
Two days to go, and then we'll FINALLY be free for spring break! I'm so sick of homework, school, papers, and tests, that I can't wait to get away from it all. I'll be skiing with my family (not saying where, of course, cause then it would be too obvious to figure out who I am), but I can tell you that it's NOT Aspen, and I'm wishing it were! Because Adrian Diamond is letting Peyton, Courtney, Savannah, Brett, and Madison go to his house there and bring friends, and Savannah is bringing Perry and Noel from One Connection. So jealous!

1: Posted on Wednesday 3/5 at 7:59 PM
whats so great about aspen? (besides that crew partying there over break?)

2: Posted on Wednesday 3/5 at 8:15 PM
ummmm aspen's only the most exclusive place to go skiing in the entire country. It takes forever to get to unless you have a private plane. Tons of celebs hang out there (leo dicaprio, kate hudson, paris hilton, blake lively, and more), and its where Christian took Ana in the 50 shades books (they went to cardinal club!!)

3: Posted on Wednesday 3/5 at 8:29 PM

Isn't Adrian's house on Red Mountain, AKA billionaire mountain? I would love to see that!

4: Posted on Wednesday 3/5 at 8:45 PM
yeah and they're going without parents, too. I'm so jealous! My parents would never let me go away like that, unless it was an official teen program. lucky bitches.

chapter 17: *Savannah*

Savannah had fallen seriously behind on her homework because of all the time she'd been spending on YouTube and her other social media accounts, so she'd been spending every lunch period the week before spring break in the library. At least the library was pretty and peaceful—two stories tall, with warm golden carpeting, wooden walls and natural light flooding in from the large windows overhead. It was also nearly empty, so she had one of the second-floor study rooms to herself.

She'd finished her homework and was heading out when she spotted Nick by himself in a corner study room, typing away at his laptop. He was so focused on his work, and she didn't want to interrupt him…but it had been forever since she'd talked to Nick. And although whatever had been between them had fizzled out, she missed his friendship. When she'd been crying last summer over Damien and ran into Nick on her way out of the club, he'd brightened her night. That was a kindness she would never forget.

She knocked on the door and he jumped, his hands flying off the keyboard. His eyes met hers, and she gave him a small wave. He smiled and motioned for her to come inside.

"Hey," she said, closing the door behind her.

"Hey." He leaned back in his chair, and she noticed that he had more scruff on his face than usual. He must be really busy trying to get everything done before break. "Were you looking for someone, or is the library a new hangout for you? Because I don't think I've seen you here...ever."

"I was getting homework done." She shifted her tote on her shoulder, and feeling awkward standing, took the seat next to him. "Is this where you've been during lunch this semester? I barely see you in the dining hall anymore."

"Between school, sports practice and my job, my grades fell last semester," he said. "I was tired at night when I was trying to get my homework done. So since we have such a long lunch block, I've been using the time to work. It sucks to miss out on the time with my friends, but my grades have been getting better."

"That's good." Savannah paused, not knowing if she should bring up what she wanted to ask him. But if she didn't, she would always wonder. Best to live with no regrets, right? "I know I already texted you about it and you said no, but since you're here in person now, I wanted to make sure you didn't want to come to Aspen for break," she said. "I know you love skiing, and the flight and house and everything is all covered."

"I wish I could." He glanced at his laptop and ran his hands through his hair. "But I can't take off work. I'm actually taking on *more* hours over break. And I know how you and everyone else in that group vacations—after all, I used to be one of you. I wouldn't be able to keep up with the expensive dinners and nights out."

"I could take care of all of that." Savannah glanced down

at her hands, her face heating. She didn't want him to think she was giving him charity. She understood what it was like to barely be able to afford anything, and she *wanted* to help him out.

"I can't go." His voice was firm. "But thanks for the offer. Really. I wish I could go—I miss skiing—but I can't give up the chance to get in some more hours of work."

"Anytime." Savannah glanced at his laptop. "Anyway, how's everything been with you? We haven't had a chance to talk in a while, and I know things have been rough for you and your family."

Nick sighed and ran his hand through his hair. "Well, my dad won't be going to jail, so it's a start in the right direction," he said. "And my parents moved back in together."

"That's amazing news!" Savannah sat up straighter and smiled, but he only gave her a half smile in return. "Why don't you seem happier about it?"

"Because my dad's company is shot," he said. "After ignoring those building codes, he lost all the money in a class-action lawsuit, and they're going out of business. Our condo on the Strip is up for sale so we can move to the suburbs, but the market sucks right now. No one's buying."

"It'll sell eventually," Savannah said, even though she knew nothing about real estate. "If your dad's anything like you, he has to be smart. He'll find another job."

"I hope so," he said. "I've been working every hour I'm awake to pay for this year at Goodman in the hope that next year, my dad's business would be back on track so we could afford my senior year. But it's looking like that's not going to happen, so I'll probably be spending my senior year in public school."

"Wow." Savannah toyed with the ends of her hair. "But according to Brett, there are a lot of great public schools in this area. They don't sound anything like the school I went to in Fairfield. And your parents are back together, so that's a good thing, right?"

"I guess." Nick shrugged. "But I have my friends here, I used to have great grades and I'm the quarterback of the football team. Coach has been talking me up to the scouts, and he told me they already have their eye on me for playing in college."

"You're going to be amazing at football, whether you're playing at Goodman or at a public school," Savannah said softly. "And won't you feel a lot better next year, not having to worry about paying all the money for Goodman?"

"Yeah," he said. "You're probably right. But enough about me. You're the one who recently found out that *Madison Lockhart* is your half sister. I was going to text you when I heard, but I got caught up with work… How's everything going with her?"

"It's weird," Savannah started. "It hasn't really been 'going' anywhere. I have no idea what to say to her. Since we're all going to Aspen over break, I guess we'll deal with it then? I have no idea. It's the most awkward thing ever. I know she's technically our sister now and all, but it doesn't really seem like she wants to get to know us."

"She probably does," Nick said. "I know you all haven't seen the best side of her since you've met her, but remember, I did date her last year. She acts tough—and admittedly, kind of bitchy—when she feels threatened. But there's more to her than that. She understands people, and she's easy to talk to."

"Except that Madison wasn't 'threatened' by me or my sisters," Savannah said. "She just decided she hated us the second we arrived."

"Are you so sure about that?" Nick picked up a pen and twirled it with his fingers. "At the start of last summer, Madison had been dating me, thought she had a thing for Brett, Damien followed her around like a lovesick puppy, and who knows what was going on with her and Oliver. Then you and your sisters arrived. Suddenly Brett was with Courtney all the time, Damien asked you out, Oliver hooked up with Peyton, and I reached out to you. In Madison's mind, that would make her feel *extremely* threatened."

"You're sticking up for her a lot, considering that I thought you hated her after last summer," Savannah said. "Are you sure you're over her?"

"Trust me, I'm sure." He chuckled. "She's not the girl for me. But she's your sister, and I think she would be a good one, if you let her try."

"Maybe." Savannah shrugged. "But I already *have* two sisters. I never asked for another."

"All I'm saying is that it might not hurt to give Madison a chance. She might surprise you." Nick glanced at his watch. "Anyway, I need to finish up this paper. Have fun in Aspen, and let me know how it goes with Madison, all right?"

"I will," she promised, although she doubted it would go well.

She was heading out of the library when she saw someone she hadn't thought about in a while—Wendy, the girl who had been nice to her on her first day of school when she'd been crying. Wendy sat in one of the cubicles downstairs, hunched over a notebook, her hair pulled back into the same thick bun that she'd been wearing on the first day of school. Savannah hadn't spoken to her since that day—when she'd ditched Wendy's lunch invitation to sit with Damien and Alyssa. At the time, she'd figured she and Wendy had nothing in common, and she was happy to have an in with the girls on the volleyball team.

But those girls had turned on her, if they ever truly liked

her. And while Savannah didn't know Wendy well, she had a gut feeling that Wendy wasn't the type of person to go behind the back of someone she called a friend.

She stood there, staring at Wendy's back for a few seconds. Wendy had no idea she was there. She could leave, and no one would know any differently.

But she didn't want to do that.

So she gathered her courage and walked over to where Wendy sat.

"Wendy?" she said softly, playing with the strap of her bag.

Wendy turned around, looking at Savannah from behind the rims of her thick black glasses. She still held onto her pencil, and the side of her hand was smudged with lead. "Hey, Savannah," she said. "What's up?"

She was so casual—as if Savannah hadn't ditched her at lunch on that first day. Was it truly possible for someone to be that nice?

Yes, Savannah knew. Because it was something that Courtney would do, also.

"Is it okay if I sit?" Savannah glanced at the chair next to Wendy.

"Sure."

Savannah situated herself in the chair, aware of Wendy watching her the entire time. It was going to be up to her to speak first—she knew that. If only she knew what to say.

"I was in the library doing homework, and saw you sitting here, and even though it's been a while, I figured I would come over and say hi," she started. Wendy scrunched her forehead, and Savannah fidgeted, her legs bouncing. She was babbling, and wasting Wendy's time while she was clearly working. She needed to get to the point. "I shouldn't have left you on the first day at lunch. I'm sorry."

"No worries." Wendy shrugged. "It's cool."

"No," Savannah said. "It's not. You were the first person who was nice to me here. When I was crying in the bathroom, you talked to me and invited me to sit with you. Then I blew you off. I feel awful about it."

"It's okay," Wendy said. "I didn't take it personally."

"Really?" Savannah asked. If she were Wendy, she definitely would have taken it personally. "Why not?"

"Because I have my friends, and they're awesome," she said, as if it were obvious. "If you wanted to sit with the seniors or the volleyball team, that was your call. Although I always wondered how, in the few minutes it took for you to buy a sandwich, you went from crying by yourself in the bathroom to sitting with the most popular kids at school."

"It happened when I was waiting in line," Savannah said. "Damien Sanders said hi to me—I knew him from over the summer—and Alyssa saw. She hadn't wanted to talk to me in first period, but then I guess she figured that since Damien and I knew each other, she would be nice to me. He invited us to sit with him and his friends, and that was that. I made the volleyball team that week, and thought Alyssa and all them were my friends. But they're not—they never were. They're fake and they talk about people behind their backs, and I feel like an idiot for not seeing it sooner." She sniffed, not realizing that a tear had escaped until it was halfway down her cheek. She wiped it away quickly, embarrassed for spilling her guts out like that.

Wendy reached into her bag and pulled out a pack of tissues. "Here," she said, handing one to Savannah.

"Thanks." Savannah blew her nose lightly.

"Anytime," Wendy said. "I always knew those girls were fake. I've known them since I transferred to Goodman in middle school, but I figured that either you were just like them, or that you would realize it on your own time."

"I'm not like them," Savannah said. "I would never treat a friend like they treated me."

Her throat tightened, because even though she meant it, was it true? Besides her sisters, Evie was the only person in her life that she'd ever called a true best friend. Then she and Evie had fought at her sixteenth birthday party, and Savannah had shut her out. She'd ignored her calls, her texts, her Snapchats…everything. It was so easy to tell herself that because Alyssa, Jackie and Brooke had been fake friends, that Evie was a fake friend, too. But she knew Evie better than that. And she'd been no better to Evie than Jackie, Alyssa and Brooke had been to her.

Her eyes filled with tears again, and she wiped them away, the tissue smeared with mascara.

"Do you want to go upstairs?" Wendy closed her notebook. "It's more private up there. We don't have long until next period, but it seems like you need to talk to someone."

"You're right." Savannah sniffed and swallowed away the tears. "There is someone I need to talk to. Someone I need to call. I should do that now. But…thank you for listening to me. And for not hating me."

"I can't hate you." Wendy laughed. "I don't really know you."

"True," Savannah agreed. "But it means a lot."

"I'm gonna get back to work," Wendy said. "I'll see you around?"

"Yeah," Savannah said. "See you around." She smiled at Wendy and hurried out of the library. Once she found an empty bench outside, she took out her cell and called Evie. Her heart raced, but she took a deep breath, waiting for Evie to pick up.

It rang five times, and went to voice mail. What was Savannah thinking by calling during the school day? Sure, she had a long lunch at Goodman, but Evie was probably in class.

She was about to put her phone away and head to her next class when it buzzed with a text.

Saw you called...in class and can't talk. What's up?

From Evie. Although they technically weren't allowed to use their phones during class, it never stopped them from texting. Savannah replied quickly, wanting to get it out before she could overthink it.

I'm sorry for being such a bitch these past few months. You're my best friend and I miss you and I want to make it up to you. I know we have the same week off for spring break... want to come to Aspen? Perry and Noel from One Connection will be there :P

Her phone rang a minute later.

"How are you using your phone during class?" Savannah asked.

"I got a bathroom pass," Evie said, breathless. "But that's not the point. Of *course* I want to come to Aspen!"

Savannah grinned. Just like that, all the months of fighting and not talking were forgotten, as if they'd never existed at all.

chapter 18: *Courtney*

For the sixth time in her life, Courtney was sitting inside a private jet—and not just any private jet, but the *Diamond* jet, which could easily hold fifteen people. Adrian had chartered a jet to China and let them have the Diamond jet for Aspen, probably because he felt bad for not being able to come on the trip.

Right now, thirteen of them sat inside the roomy interior that looked more like a living room than an aircraft—Courtney, her sisters, Madison (who was technically a sister, but Courtney wasn't counting her as one yet), Brett, Oliver, Brianna, Damien, Evie, Emily Nicole and their bodyguards. Perry and Noel had their own jet and would be meeting up with them in Aspen.

Courtney had naturally rushed to the frontmost seat, and Brett had settled across from her. Oliver was sleeping in a fully reclined seat on the opposite side of the plane, and Peyton was across the aisle from him, her earbuds plugged in as she stared out the window. The three bodyguards were in the back. Everyone else was in the center.

"Now it's time for a toast!" Madison held up her flute of champagne, and everyone around her—Savannah, Evie, Emily Nicole, Brianna and Damien—raised theirs and watched her expectantly. How did Madison get onboard the jet for the first time and command everyone's attention, looking so at home?

"To what's sure to be an incredible week in Aspen," Madison said. "Some of us already know each other well, and others will be getting to know each other for the first time. What better place to do that than in the most glamorous ski town in the world, with a house all to ourselves?"

"To a kick-ass week!" Damien held his glass high. "Aspen won't know what hit it."

They clinked glasses and launched into chitchat about what they were most looking forward to in Aspen, what they'd packed, advice on skiing, which celebrities they were hoping to spot and more. It was like they'd all known each other forever. Even Savannah and Madison were getting along. Courtney curled up in her seat, feeling like an outsider as she watched them. With all the years she'd spent dedicated to her work and only having time for her sisters, had she missed out on having a fun group of friends?

"Is everything okay?" Brett asked, nudging Courtney's leg with his foot. Just the small contact made her heart speed up. She wanted to feel his arms around her so badly right now— probably more so because they had to keep a friendly distance. There were people around who didn't know about their relationship. "You spaced out there for a minute."

"Yeah." She blinked and forced herself to focus. "I guess I just find all of this so strange."

"You mean how random this group is, and knowing that we're all going to be cooped up in one house for a week, along with two international pop stars? Because if that's what you're referring to, then yeah, I know exactly how you're feeling."

"It's more than that," she said. "Look at them…most of them barely know each other, but they're so happy and natural, chatting away about nothing in particular."

"That's Madison for you," he said. "I don't always have the best things to say about her, but she knows how to bring people together. Damien's like that, too."

"When Madison and I rode home in the car together last week, she made an effort to talk," Courtney said. "But it's so awkward between us. I'm not sure what to say to her, or how to relate to her."

"She's grown up inside a bubble, and I don't think she's looked outside it much, but she's not always so bad," Brett said. "And who knows…maybe the last few months *have* changed her."

"Maybe," Courtney said. "I know I should give her a chance. I think that this week, I'm going to try."

"That sounds like a good plan," he said.

She sat back, her eyes still on the group. Everyone was excitedly talking over each other in a way that made her head spin and the conversation blur. How did people tolerate fighting to be heard like that? Just watching it was exhausting. But they all seemed to be enjoying it, as if it energized them.

"Do you want to go over and join them?" Brett asked. "There's room for two more."

If Courtney went over there, she knew what would happen: she would be stuck on the edge of the couch, listening to them going back and forth. When she had something to say, they would have moved on and her thought wouldn't matter anymore. She was fine when one-on-one with a person, or even in groups of two or three, but *six* people, who were all outgoing and loud? They would drown her out.

She watched them for a few seconds more. Emily Nicole stood up and did a booty dance, Evie squealed as if it were the funniest thing in the world and Brianna threw a pillow at Emily Nicole's butt. That was enough to solidify Courtney's decision.

"I'm happy here," she said, and Brett relaxed. He must not have wanted to join the big group conversation, either. "There's a book I wanted to read on the flight. I'm sure we'll get busy once we're in Aspen, seeing the town and everything, so I might as well get some reading done now."

"And I've got some TV shows on my iPad." He smiled, then lowered his voice. "Although I wish I was watching something with you in my condo, just the two of us. You're gonna drive me crazy this week, you know that?"

Courtney blushed and looked at the group to make sure they hadn't heard. Luckily they were too involved in their conversation to have caught a thing.

She took out her Kindle and tried to read. But everyone was talking so loudly that it was impossible to concentrate on the words. They sounded like they were all having so much *fun*.

She wished she could let loose and be a part of that, too.

The flight to Aspen was short—only an hour and a half— and as they began their descent, Courtney pulled her eyes away from her Kindle to watch as they landed.

The Rocky Mountains were one of the most beautiful sights she had ever seen. They seemed to go on forever, as if the ground would never flatten out again. As the wheels touched the runway, Courtney kept her forehead pressed against the window, tilting her head so she could take it all in. The mountains towered majestically over everything, shooting up into the clouds, blanketed in layers of untouched snow that sparkled under the sun. The tiny airport was a speck in a crevice of the summits surrounding them.

She paused when she exited the plane and rested her fingers on the rail, taking in a deep breath of the snow-scented air. It was a fantasy world, like Narnia when the White Witch reigned.

"It's beautiful, isn't it?" Brett whispered in her ear, his hand brushing against her waist.

"Yes," she breathed. "The Rockies were never on my list of places to visit. Now I wonder why not…and how many other beautiful places are out there that I haven't thought to explore."

"You'll see them all," he said. "We'll write down a list of all the places you want to go, so you'll never forget them."

"Are you guys coming?" Madison yelled from the tarmac, where a gigantic limo-truck waited. It looked like someone had taken an Escalade, chopped it in half, added pieces to the center and welded it all together.

"Yeah," she said, scrambling down the steps. "Sorry."

"We've never seen the Rockies before," Savannah explained to everyone as Courtney climbed into the limo.

Courtney was last inside—she couldn't tear her eyes away from the mountains—and she took the back right window seat. It was her favorite seat because it had the best view, looking out to the scenery instead of the opposing side of the road.

She'd expected Aspen to be over-the-top and glitzy. But as they drove through the town, it was surprisingly quaint, with rows of two- and three-story wooden buildings with thatched roofs that belonged in a Christmas snow globe. The town sat in a valley between two mountains—one of them gigantic, covered in trails of fresh snow between the pines, and a smaller one without as much snow, dotted with houses up the base. The limo traveled down Main Street, which was lined with Victorian houses that looked like they'd been transported here from a hundred years ago, and continued toward the mountain.

"Is your dad's house on *Red Mountain*?" Emily Nicole asked, her eyes wide.

"I don't know." Savannah shrugged. She looked at Peyton and Courtney, as if they had the answer. But Courtney had never asked *where* in Aspen Adrian lived.

"Yes, it's on Red Mountain," Oliver answered for her. "Where else would Adrian Diamond's house be?"

The drive up Red Mountain was full of twists and turns, past mansions of different styles—some wooden mountain homes, and others full-out modern. They were the biggest houses Courtney had ever seen. They were all built into the side of the mountain, and she couldn't imagine what they looked like inside. Finally, the limo pulled into the driveway of a sprawling three-story modern house, with light-colored wood and brick siding and floor-to-ceiling windows.

They hurried inside, and all Courtney could focus on was that within the two-story cavernous living room was a *pool and hot tub*. A stairway curved above the pool and into a room beyond, and behind the pool, a wall of windows overlooked the snow-capped mountains.

"Well, this is going to be fun." Damien knelt next to the pool and stuck his hand in the water. "Warm as a bath. Who wants to jump in?"

"We don't have time!" Savannah glanced at her watch. "Perry and Noel will be here soon, and Adrian made us those reservations at that club for dinner. We have to get ready."

"Come on, I know someone's up for a little fun." He zeroed in on Emily Nicole, who had already taken off her shoes and jacket. She gave him a small smile, which was apparently enough incentive for him to pick her up and toss her into the pool with her clothes still on. She squealed as she hit the water, laughing as she surfaced and shaking out her hair. He jumped in after her.

Savannah glared at them, her hands clenched into fists. "The One Connection boys will be here any minute, and you guys are going to be soaking wet when you meet them!" she said, stomping her foot on the floor.

"Oh, well." Emily Nicole laughed and spun around, her arms spread wide. "If anything, they'll certainly find us interesting. Come on, you guys. Jump in!"

Courtney shook her head no, sliding her hands into the back pockets of her favorite jeans. She wasn't going to ruin them. "I'm picking a room and getting ready for dinner," she said, wanting to make sure she got a room as far away from the craziness as possible. She glanced at Peyton, since they would be roommates. "You want to help me choose?"

"Sure," Peyton said.

They ventured through the house, which was sleek and modern—it fit Adrian's personality perfectly. The floors were all light-colored wood, the furniture a mix of white and gray, and every room had huge windows letting in tons of sunlight and providing out-of-this-world views of the mountains. There were three bedrooms down the hall from the pool— where, judging from just now, most of the partying would take place—and Courtney continued exploring. On the other side of the house was the master bedroom, which Savannah had claimed for herself and Evie. Upstairs were two rooms that opened to below, and the bodyguards would be staying in the basement.

Finally, Courtney found a room on the first floor that she'd missed earlier. It was larger than the others, and it was set apart in its own section in the front corner of the house.

"This is our room," she declared, tossing her bag onto the king-size bed.

"Whatever you say," Peyton said. "I'll only be in here to sleep, anyway."

"Cool," Courtney said, since that meant more quiet time for her. It was exactly why she'd wanted to room with Peyton. "I think I'll take a shower now."

"You mean you don't want to be around when the One Connection boys get here?" Peyton's tone dripped with sarcasm.

"Between Savannah, Evie, Emily Nicole and Brianna, they'll have enough fangirls to handle," she said, unpacking her stuff she'd need for tonight. "I think I'll survive."

But then Savannah burst into their room. Her cheeks were pink, and there were droplets of water all over her clothes—they must have gotten into some sort of splashing fight in the pool.

"You know that shirt is silk, right?" Courtney asked. "You shouldn't get it wet."

"Whatever." She straightened the top. "It'll be fine. At least I didn't jump in the pool with it on."

"Right," Courtney agreed. "Anyway, I'm about to take a shower. Remember that we have to leave for dinner at Cardinal Club in an hour."

"You can't shower now!" Savannah widened her eyes. "Perry and Noel are getting here any second. He literally just texted me that they're at the base of Red Mountain." She held up her cell phone as proof. "That's why I came in here—to get you and Peyton. You *have* to be there when they get here. Please?"

Courtney blew out a breath and looked up at the ceiling. She'd wanted some time to herself before what was sure to be a busy night, but how was she supposed to say no when her sister looked so nervous? "Fine," she said. "Just don't throw me in the pool, okay?"

"I would never!" Savannah smiled.

"At least Noel's cute," Peyton said, fixing her hair and checking herself out in the full-length mirror. She turned to the side and posed, making a "come hither" look with her eyes.

"No." Savannah's mouth dropped open. "You *cannot* go for the bandmate of the guy I like. He and Perry are practically brothers. That would be too weird."

"Chill out." Peyton laughed. "I was kidding. Boy-band pop stars are *not* my type."

Savannah's phone buzzed, and when she checked it, her eyes bulged so much they looked like they were about to pop out of her face. "They're here!" she said, bouncing to the door. "Come on!"

They followed Savannah to the living room, where everyone was still hanging out. Damien and Emily Nicole were still the only ones in the pool, and they were splashing anyone who dared to get too close. Brett had been talking with Evie—it was nice of him not to leave Savannah's friend alone—but his eyes lit up when Courtney walked into the room. She smiled back at him, glad to have come back, if only to see the way he looked at her.

Madison, Oliver and Brianna were sitting on the sofas, listening as Brianna animatedly talked about something that clearly excited her. Oliver listened to his sister—his *half sister*—so closely, as if everything she said was fascinating. It was clear from looking at them that he loved her.

Madison was related to Courtney the same way that Brianna was related to Oliver. But they hadn't grown up together. How was Courtney supposed to feel the same bond of sisterhood with Madison that she felt with Savannah and Peyton?

She didn't have time to think about it, because there was a knock on the door, and everyone quieted.

"They're here!" Emily Nicole squealed from the pool. "Perry and Noel are *here!*"

Savannah stared at the door as if she didn't know how to open it, Evie clutched Savannah's hand so tightly that it turned white and Brianna bounced her legs, her hands clasped to her mouth as if she might scream if she removed them.

"Everyone try not to fangirl," Madison said. She was totally calm, as if pop stars knocked on her door every day. "Perry and Noel might be famous, but they're still people. They're here to take a vacation and chill out. They won't be able to do that if you're all running around like chickens with your heads cut off."

Courtney nodded at Madison. As much as she wouldn't admit it out loud, Madison was right.

Peyton marched toward the door, the heels of her boots pounding against the wood. "Since none of you seem to be capable of opening a door, it looks like I'll have to do it myself." She flung the door open, and standing on the steps were none other than Perry and Noel from One Connection. Which wasn't surprising, since who else would be there? But it was strange, since Courtney had seen them on posters on Savannah's walls, and now here they were, in the flesh.

Even though she'd met them at Savannah's birthday, the first thing she was struck with was how much smaller they were in person than they looked in photographs or on TV. She joined Brett next to the wall, leaning against it. Even though Savannah had wanted her to be there when the guys arrived, her sister wouldn't notice if she stood off to the side.

"Who's ready for a kick-ass week?" Perry yelled, holding a bottle of champagne up in the air. He rushed over to Savannah, scooped her up into a huge hug and spun her around in a circle. Savannah's eyes were squeezed shut, her arms wrapped tightly around his neck as if she never wanted to let go. Noel had followed him inside, and was standing awkwardly next to Evie.

"Hi," he introduced himself, holding out a hand. "I'm Noel."

"I know." Evie blushed as she shook his hand. "I mean, of course I know who you are. I'm a huge fan. Except…I'm not supposed to fangirl. Not that I'm a fangirl. I just love your music." It all came out in a complete jumble. She looked away from him, took a deep breath, and focused on him again. "That was really awkward," she said, calmer this time. "Can we try that again?"

"Sure." He smiled, his hand not leaving hers. "Hi, there. I'm Noel."

"I'm Evie," she said. "It's nice to meet you."

"It's nice to meet you, too."

From the way they were looking at each other, it was hard to say which one of them was more starstruck.

Perry placed Savannah back down and popped the cork of the champagne, sending it flying across the room. Foam leaked out of the top and spilled onto the floor. Savannah had a huge smile on her face, her eyes worshipping him. Emily Nicole cheered from the pool, Evie and Noel had stopped shaking hands but were still sneaking glances at each other and Peyton rushed to the bar to grab some champagne flutes.

"That better not stain the wood," Courtney mumbled to Brett. "If they trash the house, Adrian won't be happy."

"It won't stain the wood." Brett gave her hand a squeeze. "And don't worry—I won't let anyone trash the house. But it's spring break. Don't let a little spilled champagne stop you from having fun."

Courtney stilled at his words. Was she not fun? She looked around as everyone filled up glasses of champagne, and naturally turned down a glass when Brianna tried to hand one to her. Everyone was smiling, laughing and enjoying themselves.

And she was standing to the side, watching.

She imagined what it would be like to join in. To introduce herself to Perry and Noel and slip easily into the conversation. Madison and Oliver had done that—even Peyton had done that. Now they were all hanging around like old friends. Brianna jumped into the pool and started a splash war with Damien, shrieking as he captured her and held her over his shoulder. They were all so relaxed and carefree.

Courtney wished she could be that way, too.

Instead, she mumbled something to Brett about needing to take a shower before dinner, and scurried back to her room.

chapter 19: *Peyton*

The limo dropped their group off in front of an unmarked building, and Peyton followed everyone into an indoor hallway that held no signs of leading to one of the most exclusive clubs in Aspen—the Cardinal Club. Adrian was a member, and he'd insisted on making a reservation for them the first night they arrived, to give them their "first taste of Aspen." So far it didn't seem like anything special, especially compared to the clubs in Las Vegas.

"Are you sure this is the right place?" Peyton said.

"Yep." Oliver strolled ahead, since he and Brianna were the only two who had been there before. "Here it is." He gestured to a plain wooden door with the numbers 411 on the top, and PRIVATE written in capital letters in the center. The only sign that it led to the mysterious Cardinal Club were the two interwoven Cs on the wooden panels.

He opened the door and motioned for the girls to go first.

"They must not want people to find this place," Peyton said as she walked through. The entranceway was a small room with a Persian rug, a wooden balustrade and wide winding steps leading down below. No one was there to greet them. "I guess it's down this way," she said, pointing down the stairs.

They made their way downstairs, where they were greeted by the host and instructed to check their coats. Then they were led into a lounge room that felt like a hunting lodge, complete with patterned carpet, green walls, wood trim and red couches and chairs that surrounded low tables. They chose their seats, and a waiter quickly appeared to take their drink orders.

The atmosphere was so different from Vegas. It wasn't nearly as flashy, although the designer outfits and jewelry worn by the people inside made it clear that everyone came from money. Their group was the youngest there—most everyone else appeared to be in their 30s or 40s. And there were no windows anywhere, since the club was in a basement. Peyton imagined this was what those speakeasies in the twenties were like.

They settled in with their drinks—Perry and Noel in the center—and chatted about how the One Connection world tour was going. Savannah kept smiling at Perry, Damien kept glancing at Savannah, Brianna was focused on Damien, Courtney and Brett had their pinkies intertwined and were pretending to be inconspicuous, Madison and Oliver couldn't take their eyes off each other, and Noel and Evie's legs kept grazing each other's. Peyton couldn't help being amused by the dynamics. Things were sure to get…interesting on this trip.

And of course she would be left alone. Not for the first time since she arrived, she wished Jackson were here. But that wasn't going to happen. Feeling like this for the rest of the trip would suck. Sometimes it felt like no one was ever there for her. Everyone thought she was so strong. And she was, for the most part. But that didn't mean she never needed anyone to lean on.

"I'm going to the bathroom," she said, standing up from the couch. "Be back in a few."

There were no obvious restroom signs, and after asking the host, she found it around the corner and down a hallway near the entrance, right past the coat check. On her way back, she paused next to a mirror in the hall, staring at her reflection. She'd tried so hard not to let the past few months change her, but she could see the difference in herself. Her eyes no longer had circles under them, because she was getting better sleep now that she had a room to herself. Her skin glowed with a healthy tan from her time spent at the pool. Her hair still had her trademark blue steaks on the undersides, although it was fuller and healthier now that she was getting regular trims at the salon.

But the biggest difference wasn't on the outside—it was on the inside. Peyton had been insistent since she moved here that she wasn't going to college, and she'd refused to budge, because changing her mind would mean giving in to the mold everyone else was trying to shape her into. But those gap-year programs she'd been researching required that you *defer* college acceptance, not decline. The programs were meant to be something you did between high school and college. And she wanted to do one. Technically, she supposed she could jet around the world by herself for a few months, but she didn't want to go alone. Traveling with a group of people her own age, all of them working together in different countries around the world, really did sound like fun.

But that would mean that she wouldn't be able to decline her acceptance to UNLV, like she'd been telling everyone she was going to do. If she did that, they might think she was weak, and didn't know her own mind. It would be humiliating.

If Jackson hadn't mentioned the gap year, none of this would be an issue. But she was glad he had. And if he were here, he would tell her to go for it.

She wished she could ask him. But he'd made it clear enough that he didn't want to be with her. That he *couldn't* be with her. She kept waiting for him to change his mind, but waiting around for him—hoping that every time her phone buzzed it would be him—was driving her crazy. Maybe he never wanted to talk to her again. She wrapped her arms around herself and sighed. She might finally have to accept that he was gone from her life forever.

"Ms. Diamond?" a low voice asked from nearby. "Is everything all right?"

Peyton glanced over her shoulder, her eyes meeting those of Courtney's bodyguard, Teddy. She'd always liked Teddy. Out of the bodyguards, he was the oldest. He wasn't quite old enough to be a grandfather—and while she'd never gotten a chance to know either of her grandfathers—she'd imagined that she would want them to be like Teddy.

"Yes," she said. "Well, sort of. I don't know. I just have a bunch of stuff on my mind."

"Anything you want to talk about?" he asked. "Or should I say any*one*?"

She pushed her hair behind her ears and checked around to make sure no one was listening. "What do you mean?"

"One of the most important qualities of being a good bodyguard is to be observant." He chuckled, as if he knew something she didn't. "I've been around a few years—I know what heartbreak looks like when I see it."

"I'm not heartbroken," she lied. "I'm just bored."

His brow crinkled, and he smiled—it was that knowing smile again, as if he didn't believe her. "Which means that you've been 'bored' since Jackson was dismissed?"

"Yes." Her voice shook, and he raised an eyebrow. "Well… no. But I guess you already know that."

He nodded. "I do. And I've been debating whether to say something for weeks now. I haven't wanted to overstep any professional lines, but I've seen how this is tearing you up inside. So I want you to listen to me, and trust me on this—Jackson cares about you. The way he looked at you—well, I don't want to scare you, but it's the way I must have looked at my wife the first moment I laid eyes on her."

Peyton's heart leaped, and she wished that what Teddy was saying was true. But she'd been let down enough times to know not to believe in fairy tales.

She shook her head. "He doesn't even want to *talk* to me."

"I'm not sure it's quite that simple."

"Yes, it is," she said. "He left to go across the country without caring that he wouldn't see me again. I texted him. He didn't reply. I think his message is clear—he doesn't want anything to do with me."

"Perhaps." Teddy took a deep breath, his eyes darting sideways, then refocused on Peyton. "And you'll have to forgive me if what I say next is stepping out of line, because this probably isn't what you want to hear."

"Go ahead." Peyton motioned him to continue. "It's hard to say anything that offends me. But you're welcome to try your best."

"All right," he said. "Like I said, I apologize in advance, but it's possible that you might be making this all about you, and not taking the time to see this situation from Jackson's perspective."

Peyton took a sharp breath. "He moved across the country and hasn't tried to reach out to me since," she said. "I'm trying to accept that he just isn't that into me and move on. What else am I supposed to do?"

"Jackson's been put in a very precarious position," Teddy said. "He's twenty-three, and you're a minor—not only a minor, but the daughter of a well-known hotel owner. In certain states, including your home state of California, he could be convicted of a felony by being involved with you. The punishment for that is jail time. It would be on his record forever."

"No one would *actually* convict him of anything," she said, shaking her head in disbelief. "Would they?"

"Most likely not," he said. "But if you truly do care for him like I think you do, would you want to put him at such a risk?"

"No." Despite how much she missed him, she didn't have to think twice about her answer. "But I'm turning eighteen at the end of the month."

"Precisely," he said. "Jackson may contact you after your birthday, or he may not. Give him time. But until then, pining for him isn't doing you any good."

Was that what she had been doing? *Pining?* When said that way it sounded so...pathetic. But it was true. Ever since Jackson had left, she'd been spending more time than ever by herself, zoning out in front of the computer or the television, waiting for him to show up at her doorstep like he had a few weeks ago. Even here in Aspen, amongst her sisters and friends, she'd been so distracted by the thought of Jackson that she was disappearing into the shadows. That wasn't *her.* She didn't sit back and wait for life to come to her. She threw herself into it for all it was worth.

"You're right." Peyton straightened. "Pining sucks. I'm here now, and I should enjoy myself."

"That's the spirit," he said. "May I recommend you start by rejoining your sisters and friends?"

"Good idea," she agreed. "Thank you, Teddy."

"Anytime."

She sat back down with her group—who were now asking

Perry and Noel about British slang—and looked around the lounge. It didn't take long for her eyes to lock with those of a gorgeous bartender. He had dark hair, a few days of scruff on his face, and he was checking her out, too.

What would Jackson think if he saw the way the bartender was looking at her? Would he get jealous? Or was he eyeing up bartenders himself during his hours off in New York? She sat back, the thought of Jackson moving on from her so easily causing a dark cloud to settle over her thoughts.

But what was it that she'd said a few minutes ago—that she was going to stop pining and start living her life again?

Maybe this hot bartender would be the perfect way to do that.

She gave him a closed-lip smile long enough to get a smile in return, and then broke eye contact, laughing at something Noel had said. She wasn't quite sure *what* he'd said, but Evie was laughing and looking at him like he was the most entertaining person ever, so Peyton figured it must have been somewhat funny. A few minutes of conversation in, she snuck another glance at the bartender, happy to see that she was still on his radar. But before she could get up to talk to him, a hostess escorted them to the dining room for their dinner reservation. Apparently, cute bartender would have to wait.

The dining room was fit for royalty with parquet floors, red walls and tables with white tablecloths that hit the floor. They had a long banquet table set up, big enough for all twelve of them. Their bodyguards sat with Perry and Noel's bodyguards at a round table nearby.

The food at Cardinal Club was amazing. Peyton had creamy tomato soup with cheesy bread (it was a fancy version of tomato soup and grilled cheese) and a bacon-wrapped filet that was out of this world. She inhaled the entire thing. She normally didn't worry too much about what she ate (as opposed to Madison, who dutifully ordered salad with fat-free dressing as her appetizer and grilled fish and vegetables for her main course), but she liked wearing crop tops, so she couldn't eat like this for the entire trip. But skiing burned calories, right?

After the meal was cleared, three dessert trays were brought to their table.

"Complimentary dessert trays, for Adrian Diamond's daughters and their guests," their main waiter explained. He pointed to each item on the tray. "Cinnamon ice cream, macarons, chocolates, cheesecake and sauces for extra flavor." There was one of each for everyone—luckily in bite-sized portions, since Peyton was so full she couldn't imagine eating more than that.

Perry Myles insisted on taking the check, and they all made their way to the bar, which had filled up since they'd arrived. Some people pointed and whispered to friends when they saw Perry and Noel, but no one bothered them. Oliver situated himself at a single blackjack table in the back corner of the lounge. Madison went over to watch him play, and Courtney and Brett made themselves comfortable on a couch. Perry, Savannah, Emily Nicole, Noel and Evie were chatting away in a circle, and Damien and Brianna had broken away from the group to talk near the wall.

After Peyton's conversation with Teddy, she didn't want to stand off by herself, getting sad about Jackson. She could go join the group. But what would she have done *before* she knew Jackson?

Easy—she would have approached that hot bartender she'd spotted earlier.

She took a deep breath, ran a hand through her hair and cleared her mind of Jackson. Her hand itched to grab her phone to see if he'd posted anything on Facebook recently (or to see if there was the slight chance that he'd texted her), but she stopped herself. She'd had a life before Jackson, and she would have a life now.

So she reapplied her lip gloss and strutted over to the bar. The bartender's dark eyes connected with hers, and the corner of his mouth lifted into a knowing smirk. But she didn't say a word—she wanted *him* to start the conversation.

He cleared away an empty glass, his eyes not leaving hers. "I'm going to need to see some ID," he said, as if it were a challenge.

Peyton found her fake ID and handed it to him.

"Peyton Diamond from Owings Mills, Maryland," he repeated the fake information on the ID. "Funny—my manager mentioned that Peyton Diamond, teen daughter of Cardinal member Adrian Diamond, would be here with her sisters and some friends this evening. But that Peyton Diamond lives in Las Vegas, not Maryland."

"What a coincidence." Peyton shot him a frosty smile. Was he going to serve her or not? These members-only clubs usually didn't care about underage drinking—they just needed to go through the motions of checking the ID of anyone under thirty for appearance's sake.

"Sure is." He handed the ID back to her. "What'll it be?"

"An Absolut martini with no vermouth," she said, even though her head still buzzed from the champagne she'd had at dinner. What was going on with her? She knew her tolerance level. Dinner had lasted over two hours—she should *not* still be feeling the alcohol from one glass of champagne.

The bartender prepared her drink, and she realized he still hadn't introduced himself.

"What's your name?" she asked.

"I'm Zack." He poured her drink and handed it to her. "So, Peyton Diamond, what brings you to Aspen?"

"Family trip." She took a sip of her drink. "What about you? Are you from here?"

"Nope," he said. "Born and raised in Michigan. Went to college there for two years, but it wasn't the life for me, so much to my parents' disappointment, I moved out here to become a ski bum."

"And has it been worth it?"

"It was the best decision of my life."

"Good for you." Peyton toasted him with her martini glass and smiled. "That's cool that you found something you love and are living it."

"Yeah, it is," he said. "Are you a skier? Or just here for the Aspen social scene?" He gestured at the crowd in the bar.

"I've never skied before," she confessed.

His mouth dropped open. "*Twenty-two* years old and never skied?"

She smiled, since he must know that wasn't her actual age. "You say it like it's the craziest thing you've ever heard," she said. "But don't fret—I'll be hitting the slopes for the first time tomorrow. Think I'll get the hang of it quickly?"

He leaned forward and rested his elbows on the bar, so there were only inches between them. Now that he was closer, she saw that his eyes weren't brown—they were hazel. Like Jackson's. "You will if I'm teaching you," he said confidently.

She laughed and raised an eyebrow, even though her heart panged at the thought of Jackson. She took another sip of her drink, trying to swallow her feelings away. Zack was hot and easy to talk to. She should focus on him, since he was the one here with her *now*.

"You're a bartender, a ski bum *and* an instructor?" she asked.

"Aspen's not a cheap town," he said. "Gotta find some way to make extra money. Why not enjoy myself while doing it?"

"True." She nodded. Adrian had arranged for her and her

sisters to have a private lesson tomorrow…but Savannah and Courtney would understand if she wanted a one-on-one lesson with Zack instead. Or at least she thought they would. She was more inclined to agree to it right now, with the warmth from the alcohol traveling through her body, making her tingly all over, and her brain fuzzy. "What do you all put in your drinks in Aspen?" she asked. "I'm such a lightweight here."

"When did you get here?" he asked.

"A few hours ago."

"Ahhh." He nodded, as if that explained everything. "Your body hasn't adjusted to the altitude yet. Alcohol affects some people twice as much here—at eight thousand feet up—than at sea level. You'll get used to it in a few days. I've built up my tolerance so much that when I visit friends in California, I can drink them all under the table."

"That explains it." Peyton placed her drink down—she would have to slow down if she wanted to make it through the night. "Have you ever taught someone who's never skied before?"

"Of course," he said. "They were all under ten years old, but I know what I'm doing. You'll be in good hands. So, what do you say?"

Peyton stirred her drink, thinking about it. Even if she let Zack teach her to ski and she had a good time with him, he lived in Aspen and she lived in Las Vegas. It would be yet another fling. And then wouldn't she just be proving Jackson right about how he thought she only went for guys who were off-limits?

There she went again, thinking about Jackson.

"All right." She straightened her shoulders and locked her gaze with Zack's. "Let's do it."

chapter 20: *Madison*

The next morning, everyone except for Madison and Oliver had left the house for a day of skiing. They'd stayed at Cardinal Club until it closed last night—the dance floor had gotten fun after midnight—but unlike Oliver, Madison had woken up early to eat breakfast with the group. She was jealous of everyone in their ski gear, but she would be on the slopes tomorrow.

Right now, she had to get Oliver out of bed.

She entered his room without knocking. "Time to wake up," she said, prancing over to the window and opening the blinds.

He glanced at his watch, groaned and buried his face in the pillow. "Two more hours?" he mumbled.

Madison had expected this. Luckily, she needed more time to get ready, and she'd brought her science textbook on the trip so she could read ahead on the next unit. "One hour," she said. "Then I'm dragging you out of bed, and we're heading into town."

"You know my knee's still healing, right?" He rolled over and threw his arm over his eyes to protect them from the light. "Town's gonna be a drag if I'm slowing you down. Why don't we just chill here?"

"We're in Aspen, and we're going to enjoy it," she said. "You're *not* moping around the house all day. I know your knee's still healing—but lucky for you, we have a driver. I'll be back in an hour to make sure you're up."

She left the room and shut the door, not giving him time to say no.

Madison let Oliver have an extra thirty minutes of sleep, since the chapter she was reading in the science book was really interesting, and she wanted to finish it. Then she bundled up and met him in the entrance hall.

He gave her outfit a once-over and smiled. It was one of her favorites for walking around a ski town—white pants, white boots with fur lining, her favorite white Blumarine puffy jacket and a white knitted hat with a puffball on the top.

"Don't you look the part of a perfect little snow bunny?" he said.

"Thank you." She placed a hand on her hip, striking a pose. "Although if we don't get out of here soon, I think I'm going to overheat."

"Since you're determined to explore town, where do you want to go?"

"Are you hungry?" She assumed he was, and she was ready for lunch. The fruit she'd had that morning while everyone else was eating pancakes wasn't very filling.

"Yeah," he said. "I could always eat. Where did you have in mind?"

"Ajax Tavern?"

He frowned. "Out of all the places in Aspen, you choose

the one where we'll be watching people skiing, when you know I can't ski for the entire trip?"

"They have great food," she said. "And I thought it would be nice to eat outside, on the base of the mountain. But if you don't want to watch the skiers, we could eat inside. Unless you have another idea?"

"I do love their burgers," he said. "Fine. Ajax Tavern it is."

Thirty minutes later, they had a table on the deck of Ajax Tavern, under a heat lamp, watching the skiers fly down the mountain. The deck was packed, mostly with people in ski gear who were enjoying their lunches of fondue, burgers, truffle fries and more.

It all looked so deliciously tempting. Madison studied the menu, estimating how many calories were in each dish, categorizing each option into "acceptable" and "unacceptable." The ten pounds she'd put on a few months ago and worked her butt off to lose had reminded her why she never wanted to get to that point again. She hated feeling like she had to use her clothes to *hide* her body instead of accentuate it.

When the waitress came over, she placed a freshly baked roll and bean dip in front of them. Looking at it made Madison's mouth water. She wanted to get something greasy and delicious—like a cheeseburger, mac and cheese, grilled cheese or cheese fondue—but she resisted and ordered a salad with grilled chicken. Oliver ordered a cheeseburger and truffle fries.

He could eat whatever he wanted and never get fat. It was so annoyingly frustrating.

"There's a few hours left until the chairlifts close," he said once the waitress walked away. "After we eat, if you want to go back to the house, get your ski stuff and join everyone on the slopes, I wouldn't blame you."

Madison sighed—this was the second time he'd said something like that this morning. "No." She placed her hands on the table and looked at him straight-on. "I *want* to be here with you. I invited you on this trip knowing you wouldn't be able to ski, and knowing that I wouldn't ski as much because I would be spending time with you. So stop letting it bother you that I'm not skiing today and let's enjoy ourselves."

"You invited me because you felt sorry for me," he said bitterly. "And you're here with me right now because you feel sorry for me, too."

"That's not true," she insisted. "I invited you because you've locked yourself away since December, and I *miss* you. Don't you get it, Oliver? I care about you, and I want to spend time with you. Why is that so hard for you to believe?"

He looked away and took a deep breath. Then he refocused on her and said, "Because I saw the way you looked at me at Savannah's party after Peyton told you about the dare. Like you hated me and never wanted to talk to me again. So I don't get why you're here with me now, or why you invited me on this trip, or why you cared about coming to see me when I was out of school for all those weeks."

Madison stared at him, shocked that he truly didn't get it. "Do you really think I *hate* you?" she asked, her voice cracking.

"You should," he said. "I wouldn't blame you if you did."

"Well, I don't." She clenched her hands, wishing he would believe her. "We've been friends forever. You saw me through my awkward ugly/fat phase, through the first time I was heartbroken, through when I broke up with Nick and hated myself for it and through finding out Adrian's my biological father. I've gotten annoyed with you, yes, and after what Peyton told me at Savannah's party, I was hurt and angry. But no one's *ever* been there for me as much as you. After the accident…" Her throat tightened, because she hated thinking about that time, but she swallowed back the tears and forced herself to continue. "After the accident, I thought I might lose you forever. That terrified me. So please, trust me, Oliver—I don't hate you. I could *never* hate you. I just wish you would believe me."

He held her gaze, frozen, as if he didn't know where to start. As if she'd left him speechless. Could she have finally broken through? Her heart raced at the possibility.

But then the waitress delivered their food, ruining the moment.

"Want some fries?" Oliver asked, motioning to them.

"Seriously?" She glared at him. "After everything I just told you, you're asking me if I *want some fries*?" She wanted to take a handful of fries and throw them at his face. Instead, she stabbed a piece of grilled chicken and ate it, trying to convince herself that it tasted just as delicious as the cheeseburger sitting in front of Oliver.

"I remember everything you said on the night of Savannah's party," he said, and she stopped eating, waiting for him to continue. "You thought I was playing you because of Peyton's bet. I'd told you that she'd called the bet off, and she said it was true, and I promised I was there with you that night because I wanted to be. But you didn't believe me. You said you didn't think I cared about you—that all I cared about was getting what I wanted."

"That's not true…" Madison bit her lip and watched the skiers flying down the mountain, knowing it was a lie. She *had* said those things to him. "Well, I might have said all of that in the moment, but I wasn't thinking straight. I didn't *mean* it."

"You said you never should have trusted me," he continued, gazing off at the mountain. "And then you let me get into my car. You *knew* I'd been drinking, and that there was no way in hell I should have been driving, but you let me get behind the wheel, anyway."

"I told you not to drive," she reminded him. "I tried to wrangle the valet slip from your hand, and you pulled it away from me."

"You didn't try hard enough." He turned to her again, and she was glad his sunglasses were on, because if his eyes were as angry as he sounded, she might break down on the spot. "If you had, I wouldn't have been driving that night, and the accident never would have happened."

"What are you trying to say?" She placed her fork down, her appetite gone. "Are you blaming *me* for your accident?"

"You saw I shouldn't have been driving, and you let me leave, anyway," he said. "If you'd cared enough, you would have stopped me."

"You've got to be kidding me," she exclaimed. "I *tried* to stop you. You know I did. But it was *your* decision. If I could go back and do more to stop you from getting in that car, I would. Do you think I haven't wished every day since finding out that you were in the hospital that I could go back and change what happened that night? But I can't do that. No one can. And blaming me for what *you* chose to do is total crap."

Oliver flinched, as if her words had physically hurt him. Had she been too harsh? After all, he'd had a rough past few weeks. But she'd meant it, and she couldn't take it back now, even if she'd wanted to.

"You're right," he finally said. "I should have known better. It was my own stupid fault."

She watched him closely, making sure he meant it. His gaze stayed locked on hers, and her heart rose into her throat. She knew in that moment that he meant every word.

"Thanks," she said softly. "And I really am sorry for what I said that night. Our friendship is important to me. I don't want to lose it."

"I know," he said. "You wouldn't have been blowing up

my phone these past few weeks and coming to my place otherwise. I'm glad you forced yourself back into my life, Mads."

"Good." She smiled and grabbed a handful of his fries. "Because I'm not going anywhere."

She wanted to say so much more—she wanted to ask how
much of what had been between them had been because of
the dare, and how much had been his true feelings? But she
couldn't do it. Because she finally had her friend back, and
if his answer wasn't what she wanted to hear, she feared she
would lose him forever.

www.campusbuzz.com

High Schools > Nevada > Las Vegas > The Goodman School

Perry Myles and Savannah Diamond getting hot on the slopes!!
Posted on Wednesday 3/11 at 2:15 PM
Who else has seen the pics of Savannah and Perry Myles on the slopes of Aspen?!?! Or, even better, on the chair-lifts?! If you haven't *CLICK HERE*. I gotta admit, I'm kinda jealous. What girl DOESN'T want to make out with Perry Myles on a chairlift?! They actually look really cute to-gether <3

1: Posted on Wednesday 3/11 at 3:49 PM
as if perry myles is ACTUALLY interested in Savannah! He's a total manwhore. And who wouldn't be, with that much fame? The pathetic part is that Savannah probably thinks he's interested in her. That girl is so desperate for attention it's ridiculous.

2: Posted on Wednesday 3/11 at 4:03 PM
the pathetic part isn't that Savannah thinks Perry is in-terested in her—it's that she actually thinks she's gonna make something of herself by being a "youtube celebrity." Ummm, wtf? It's YOUTUBE, not a record deal.

3: Posted on Wednesday 3/11 at 5:16 PM
the only way savannah diamond would get a record deal would be if her dad bought the label. which I wouldn't put past him...

4: Posted on Wednesday 3/11 at 5:56 PM

w-o-w, someone's a jealous bitch who obviously hasn't listened to any of savannah's videos. she's actually an amazing singer!

5: Posted on Wednesday 3/11 at 6:10 PM

whatever. We all know Perry Myles is gonna find someone else to hook up with after his spring fling with Savannah in Aspen is over! She's gonna be SUCH A WRECK when that happens haha it's gonna be so funny. Almost as funny as when she cried in front of everyone at Luxe when Damien kissed Madison! I wish I'd recorded THAT to put on YouTube.

6: Posted on Wednesday 3/11 at 6:32 PM

ummmm that thing with Damien happened LAST SUMMER. You're probably the only person who still cares. Anyway, Savannah and Damien are friends now. They're over it, so you probably should be, too.

chapter 21: *Savannah*

Skiing was pretty fun—once Savannah figured out how to stand, stop and get down the bunny slope without falling. Now it was day two, and Perry was even spending time with her—he was doing the easy "green circle" runs with her and her instructor in the morning, and then doing the harder runs with the experienced skiers in their group in the afternoon.

As they stood in line together for the two-seat chairlift, Savannah couldn't stop fidgeting with her ski poles. Her instructor got on first, then Evie and Noel took a chairlift—it was nice of Noel to be so friendly to Evie to make sure she didn't feel left out—and Peyton got on with her instructor, Zack. Courtney and Brett had taken a break for the day to explore Aspen, so Savannah and Perry were the only ones left, besides their bodyguards, who would be getting on after everyone else.

They situated themselves on the chair, which lifted into the air to bring them to the top of Buttermilk Mountain. Savannah's stomach swooped—not from the chairlift, but from the reminder that she was on a chairlift with *Perry Myles*. His trademark dark hair peeked out from underneath his beanie, his perfect face exactly the same as it looked in the magazines she and Evie used to browse together during their sleepovers. How was this her life?

But while she'd been hanging out with him and the rest of the group since they got to Aspen, she hadn't had any one-on-one time with him. Now that they were alone, what was she supposed to *say*? She wanted to take out her iPhone to snap a selfie of them together so she would never forget this moment, but she didn't want to annoy him by seeming like a wide-eyed fangirl.

"So, Savannah," Perry said in his gorgeous, perfect British accent. He made her name sound beautiful, and she wanted to ask him to say it over and over again. "Have you thought yet about the next step in your music career?"

"Emily Nicole and I just put the music video we made in Vegas up on YouTube, and it's getting lots of hits." She swung her skis, using her poles to scrape the snow off the top of them. With anyone else, she would be proud about how her music was progressing, but Perry was an international pop star. What she was doing must sound so amateur to him. "Now my agent's looking for a songwriter for me to work with so I can record a demo and try to attract the attention of major labels."

"Cool." He nodded, and Savannah glanced back down at her skis, unable to help feeling like it wasn't that cool at all. "I wasn't sure if you were going to go for a label, or have your dad produce an album for you, or if you were happy with just recording covers for YouTube."

"I love how many hits my YouTube channel's gotten," she said quickly. "I never could have gotten so many without your help at my party, and the feature on *My Fabulous Sweet Sixteen* got me a ton of subscribers."

"But you want more." His eyes locked on hers, and her head went fuzzy. It took a second to remember that she had to respond.

"Yes," she said.

"Like what?"

"I want to work with songwriters and learn how to write songs of my own," she said. "I want to get a record deal, record an album, and then see it in stores and on iTunes. My dad's offered to hire people to produce everything for me, but I would feel more legit if I had a label behind me. Because most of all, I want to have professionals in the industry work with me and invest in me—not because of who my father is, but because they think I have talent and believe in me."

"That's the attitude I like to hear." Perry leaned back and smiled his famous megawatt, genuine smile that made girls everywhere crazy for him. "Getting out a demo might work, but as you know, the competition's rough, even for the most talented people. So I had another thought that you might want to consider."

"Okay..." Savannah couldn't breathe as she waited to hear it. Could he want to feature her as a guest star in a song in One Connection's upcoming album? She'd been secretly dreaming about that for months.

"Have you heard of the show *American StarMaker*?"

It wasn't what she'd been hoping he would say, and her heart sank at the lost dream of being featured on a One Connection album. But she smiled, not wanting him to see her disappointment. "Of course," she said. Because who *hadn't* heard of *American StarMaker*? It was the greatest reality show out there—it wasn't about who had the best voice, but about who would be the best *star*. Four celebrity judges, and one guest celebrity judge per episode, sat on a panel. Fifteen people were chosen to move into a house in LA for three months and get "trained to be a star." Every week was a different competition—interviews, modeling, music videos, stage presence, etc. The judges eliminated one contestant each week, until the final week, when they crowned America's Next Superstar.

The winner received a record deal, an interview in *Rolling Rock* magazine and more. There were two "cycles" per year—the winter was the adult version, and in the summer, it was *Teen American StarMaker*, to discover the next teen star.

A year ago they'd held auditions in San Francisco for the teen version. Courtney had said Savannah should try out, and Peyton had offered to drive. But Savannah had brushed it off, too terrified at the prospect of getting on that stage and getting rejected by the celebrities she loved.

What would have happened if she'd given it a shot?

"I have an in with one of the judges," Perry said. "Alan Levy—he played a big part in getting me and the boys off the ground. If you want to try out for the show, I'll put in a good word for you. I can't *promise* he'll let you on, but you'll have a better chance of it happening than if you went in for a blind audition."

"So you can talk to him, and then I might have a shot of getting on national TV?" It sounded too good to be true.

"Yep," he said. "With your talent, looks, YouTube following and your life story of how you came from nothing only to discover that your father is Adrian Diamond, I wouldn't be surprised if you were a no-brainer to let on the show. And my personal opinion is that you have a great chance to win it, too."

"Which means…a record deal," she said, breathless.

"And more," he said. "The LA auditions are the last weekend of the month. Think you'll be able to make it?"

That was the weekend before Adrian and Rebecca's wedding. They would be busy, and Rebecca wouldn't be able to go with her, but Peyton would be eighteen by then, and Savannah had her bodyguard. She couldn't imagine why she wouldn't be able to go.

"Of course I'll be there," she said. She would *make* it happen. "But I can't help wondering…why are you doing all of this for me?"

"Isn't it obvious?" He looked at her like she was the center of his universe, which sent her heart racing. "I like you, Savannah."

Then he leaned forward and kissed her, his lips warm, and Savannah's head spun as she kissed him back. Was *Perry Myles* actually *kissing* her right now? It was unbelievable, and totally surreal, but true. She couldn't believe it. Out of all the girls in the world, Perry Myles liked *her*. He actually *liked* her. He deepened the kiss, his tongue brushing hers, and fireworks exploded in her chest. She wanted this moment to last forever.

She leaned closer into him and felt something fall from her hand, *ploofing* into the snow below.

Perry laughed and glanced down at the mountain. "There goes your ski pole," he said, his eyes dancing. "And I'm pretty sure the trail below us is a blue. Think you're up for trying an intermediate run with me, or do you want me to get it for you and we'll meet back up at the bottom of the mountain?"

"I'll go with you," Savannah said, smiling. "I'm feeling up for an adventure."

He kissed her again, and in that moment, everything was perfect.

After the last run of the day, the group met up at a bar called 39 Degrees in the Sky Hotel for what skiers called "après-ski." It was basically a fancy word for happy hour. 39 Degrees was a sleek bar with a lodge-like flair, overlooking the hotel pool and Aspen Mountain, and it was *packed* with skiers relaxing after a long day on the slopes. Luckily, a group hanging out in the couches near the fireplace was leaving, and Savannah and the rest of her group snatched the prime seating area. Perry and Noel kept their hats and sunglasses on, but it didn't stop people from staring and snapping photos on their phones. People might not mob celebrities in Aspen, but that didn't mean they went unnoticed.

They saved seats for Courtney and Brett, who were making their way to the lounge after their adventures around town, and Brianna and Oliver, who had gone dogsledding. It didn't take long for the four of them to arrive, and they were all so hungry that they ordered pretty much every appetizer on the menu. A day of skiing made you work up an appetite.

"I'm sore in muscles that I didn't know existed," Savannah groaned as she sipped her hot chocolate. Nothing tasted better after a long day on the slopes.

"And you're the athlete of the family," Courtney said. "Imagine how I feel. I literally can't move. I'm just glad Brett agreed to take the day off from skiing to walk around town."

"What'd you all do all day?" Brianna asked Courtney. She crossed her legs, her foot brushing Damien's, and left it there. Savannah's chest heated, and she glared at Brianna's foot, as if that was enough to get her to stop touching him. But why should she care? She'd spent the morning kissing *Perry Myles* on ski lifts.

She crossed her own legs, letting her foot brush against Perry's. Damien glanced at their contact. He raised an eyebrow, but said nothing, and she smiled in victory.

"We walked around with no map, figuring it would be the best way to discover cool places," Courtney said. "And it was. We stumbled upon a great indie bookstore with a cozy coffee shop in the second floor attic, and hung out there all afternoon."

"Don't tell me you bought more books?" Peyton asked. "Because you don't need any more books. Your bookshelf is overflowing."

"I found two that I just had to have," Courtney admitted. "After staying for so long, I couldn't leave without supporting the store! Plus, they were books I'd been eyeing up for a while."

Courtney said that about *every* book, but whatever.

"While you two were at the bookstore, you missed a Leonardo DiCaprio spotting at lunch." Evie grabbed her phone, scrolled to the picture and pushed it in Courtney's face. "He was eating at that special lunch club while we were there."

"You didn't just refer to the Aspen Mountain Club as 'that special lunch club,' did you?" Noel looked shocked, although Savannah could tell from the way his eyes twinkled that he was amused.

"Yeah, that's what it's called," Evie said. "It had a private door, like Cardinal Club, and the lady who worked there couldn't stop raving about how much she loved the Diamond Hotel and was looking forward to staying there again the next time she goes to Vegas."

"How'd you even get up there?" Oliver asked. "It's on top of Aspen Mountain. I thought you'd never skied before and were sticking to the greens on Buttermilk."

"We took that thingie up and down." She looked at Savannah for help. "The chairlift that was actually a room for a bunch of people. What was it called?"

Madison looked at Evie as if she were missing brain cells. "The gondola?"

"That's it!" Evie snapped her fingers, and Noel chuckled, draping his arm around the couch so it was almost around Evie's shoulders. "It was fun. There was an iPod dock inside it, so we could have a party. But anyway, I can't believe we saw Leonardo DiCaprio."

"She's had the biggest crush on him since fifth grade, when we stayed up all night watching every movie he was in," Savannah added.

"*Titanic*'s the best, hands down," Madison said.

Savannah stopped drinking her hot chocolate to stare at Madison. *Titanic* was her favorite Leo movie, too. And Savannah hadn't imagined Madison to be a romantic...or that she and Madison had anything in common.

"Surely I'm hotter than Leo," Perry joked. "I respect his acting and all, but isn't he like 40 now?"

"I don't care how old he is," Evie said. "He's gorgeous!"

"But definitely too old for us," Emily Nicole added, smiling flirtatiously at Perry. "I would choose you over Leonardo DiCaprio any day."

A twinge of jealousy passed through Savannah's stomach, but Emily Nicole flirted with everyone. She didn't mean anything by it. Besides, Perry had made it clear on the chairlift this morning that he was interested in *her*. He wanted to get *her* on *American StarMaker*, not Emily Nicole.

She was glad when Evie changed the subject by asking Noel and Perry about what it was like growing up in England.

The entire time they were talking, Peyton kept fidgeting and glancing at her watch. Then she picked up her phone, smiled and texted someone.

"Are we keeping you here?" Oliver asked, although he didn't sound like he cared.

"Zack's picking me up at the house later to take me out," she said. "He wants to show me Aspen from a local's point of view. So I need to head back to shower and get ready."

"I'm glad you've both been skiing with us," Savannah said. Because when Peyton had first broken the news that she'd met a bartender at Cardinal Club who was going to teach her to ski, Savannah had been bummed that Peyton wouldn't be skiing with her and Courtney. It hadn't taken long for Peyton to give in and say she still wanted Zack to teach her, but they would stick with the group.

Once Savannah had seen Zack, she'd understood why Peyton had wanted him to be her instructor. He was gorgeous in that rugged, outdoorsy way that made you think that if you were stuck on a deserted island with him, he would know how to build a fire and hunt for his own food. He wasn't *Savannah's* type, but she could see why Peyton liked him.

"Where's he taking you?" Brianna asked.

"We're starting at a place called White Onion," Peyton said. "He said the rest of the night will be a surprise." Her phone buzzed again, and she read the text. "My driver's waiting for me outside." She gathered her jacket, gloves and hat, and bundled back up. "Have fun tonight, and don't wait up for me."

They all said bye, and she hurried out.

Oliver smirked at Damien. "What do you want to bet that she hooks up with him?"

"No more bets." Madison crossed her arms and glared at Oliver. Her tone was so harsh that everyone stopped chatting to stare at them.

"Sorry," he said, which surprised Savannah so much that her mouth dropped open. "It was just a figure of speech. No more bets, I promise."

No one said anything for a few seconds. Savannah yawned and stirred her hot chocolate—after a late night last night and two full days of skiing, her eyes felt so tired and the couch was so comfy that she could fall asleep right here.

"So," Damien said, bringing his hands together. "Now that this place is calming down, what did you all have in mind for the rest of the night?"

"Escobar was cool last night, but I don't want to go to the same place two nights in a row," Emily Nicole said. "What about that other club we heard about—The Regal?"

"That could be fun," Brianna said slowly, although her wind-burned cheeks and the circles under her eyes said otherwise. She rested her head on Damien's shoulder, and Savannah chugged her hot chocolate, trying to keep herself from staring at them. Luckily, Damien leaned forward to finish off the rest of the cheese platter, which forced Brianna to sit up.

"Maybe." Perry leaned back into the couch, not as upbeat as usual, either. "If you all want to go, I'll tell my assistant to get us a table."

Madison, Noel, Evie, Oliver and Damien gave noncommittal shrugs and nods.

"I'm pretty tired from skiing yesterday and going out last night," Courtney said.

"You didn't even stay out," Madison pointed out. "You left the club after thirty minutes."

"I know," Courtney said. "But I'm still tired. On the way over here, Brett and I talked about just staying in tonight. But you all have fun, wherever you go."

"Well, no one seems interested in going out." Emily Nicole pouted. "I was just trying to suggest something fun, but I'm beat from skiing, too."

"Why don't we head back to the house and hang out there?" Damien suggested. "We've got a big enough group that we'll have fun wherever we are. The bars in the house are stocked, and that pool and hot tub in the living room have been calling my name."

Everyone agreed, so they got the check and headed back to the house.

It was supposed to be a "chill night." But Savannah suspected that with this group, that wouldn't be possible.

chapter 22: *Courtney*

When Courtney had mentioned at après-ski that she and Brett were staying in tonight, it hadn't been an invite for everyone to join them. The plan had been to make cookies with Brett, watch a movie and then read until she fell asleep—all before everyone else got back from a late night out on the town. Now their romantic night in had turned into a small house party.

Five minutes after getting back to the house, the splashing, giggling and shrieking started in the living room. At least Courtney had her room to herself, since Peyton was on her date with Zack. She'd told everyone she was tired and was going to sleep (nine o'clock wasn't too early to say she was going to bed, was it?), but she really just wanted some alone time to read. So she changed into her pajamas, took the books she'd bought out of their shopping bag and skimmed over the back-cover blurbs again. They were so different. One was a sweet love story, and the other was a futuristic adventure.

She settled on her bed, opened to the first page of the sweet love story and started to read. She didn't even finish the first paragraph before someone knocked on her door.

She laid the book on her stomach, careful not to crease the spine. "Who is it?" she asked, trying not to sound annoyed.

"It's Brett," he said. "Can I come in?"

She relaxed at the sound of his voice. "Of course," she said, putting a bookmark inside the book and setting it down on her nightstand.

He strolled inside, already changed into a bathing suit and T-shirt, his eyes locked on hers as he sat on the end of her bed. Her heart jumped into her throat. They'd been together for weeks—how did being around him still affect her so much?

"Hey," she said, smiling.

"Hey back." His deep green eyes studied her, and then he was hovering over her, his lips crushed against hers. His hand caressed the back of her neck, and she curved her body into his, never wanting this moment to end. "They're asking about you out there...wondering if you're going to come out and socialize," he said, his lips brushing hers. "I told them I would find out."

"I don't know." She untangled herself from Brett's arms and sat up, pulling her legs up to her chest.

"You don't have to," he said. "Trust me, I would rather lock the door and stay here with you."

"Then why don't we do that?" She went to kiss him again, but he stopped her. The rejection made her heart sink, and she pulled back, wrapping her arms around herself. Did Brett not want to be with her?

"We could," he said. "But Madison's the one who asked about you."

"You're kidding," Courtney said, although there was no reason for him to joke about that.

"Nope," he said. "It sounded like her way of saying she wanted you to join everyone."

"It does." Courtney sighed. Months ago she would have assumed this was the first step of a cruel joke. But everything was different now. "I guess I should go out there for a bit. But this is all so awkward. I don't know what to say to her. I haven't had much of a *chance* to talk to her yet, since our group is so huge."

"I'll be right there with you," Brett said. "And maybe it'll be easier to talk to her tonight, since we're all hanging out in the house."

He was right. And hanging out with the group could be fun. The One Connection guys were fascinating—she liked listening to their stories about life on the road and how they got from living in a small town in England to where they were today. Emily Nicole, Evie and Savannah were extremely chatty and giggly together, but Courtney would have Brett with her, and he would never let her feel out of place. And after Madison had specifically asked about her, Courtney would feel awful if she snubbed her.

"I'll hang out with everyone for a little," she said. "But I have to change into my bathing suit. Meet you out there?"

Brett kissed her again, and while Courtney wished she could stay in that room with him forever, he left her alone to change. Luckily Rebecca had told her and her sisters that swimming, especially in hot tubs, was a thing in Aspen, because otherwise Courtney never would have thought to pack a bathing suit on a ski vacation. She stared at her options and finally settled on a simple green bikini, pulling on a cover-up over it. She smoothed it out, took a deep breath and stared at the door.

She would be fine. Brett would be there with her the entire time, and Madison *wanted* her to come hang out. Maybe she would even enjoy herself.

She headed to the living room to find that a few bottles of alcohol had already been opened, and Perry, Savannah, Brianna and Damien were in the pool, splashing each other and laughing. Madison, Oliver and Emily Nicole were pouring drinks at the bar. Brett was lounging in the hot tub, with Noel and Evie of all people, the three of them involved in a conversation. Noel and Evie sat with their bodies angled toward each other, their legs touching. Evie giggled at something Noel said, and he nudged her shoulder with his, watching her with complete fascination. Even though Brett was sitting with them in the hot tub, they were in their own little world.

What was going on with those two? If Courtney snagged a second alone with Savannah on this trip, she planned on asking.

"You made it!" Emily Nicole smiled and waved at Courtney, a bottle of wine in her hand and a half-finished glass of it in the other. Courtney wasn't sure why Emily Nicole was so excited to see her, but it probably had something to do with the cocktails the girl had inhaled at après-ski and the wine she was drinking now. "Just in time for Never Have I Ever."

"Just in time for *what*?" Courtney joined them at the bar and poured herself a Sprite. Oliver held up a bottle of vodka, offering her some, and she shook her head no.

"You've never heard of Never Have I Ever?" Madison asked.

"No…"

"It's a game," Emily Nicole explained, refilling her wineglass to the brim. "We'll all sit around in the hot tub, and everyone puts ten fingers up. Then we go around in a circle, each person saying something they haven't done. If you've done the thing said, then you put a finger down and drink.

If you haven't done it, then you do nothing. The person who has all their fingers down first loses."

"Or wins." Oliver laughed. "Depends on how you look at it."

"It's not complicated." Madison took the wine from Emily Nicole and poured herself a glass. "It's a drinking game, so it's usually played with alcohol, but we won't tell everyone that your drink is only Sprite."

"I don't care if people know I'm only drinking Sprite," Courtney said.

"Right—of course not." Madison pressed her lips together, and adjusted the strap of her bathing suit. "I didn't mean it like that."

"I know," she said, and she felt bad if she sounded snippety, since she suspected Madison was only trying to be nice. "Maybe I'll just watch everyone else play."

"We go around clockwise, so if you sit next to me, I'll go first," Madison said. "That way you can go last and watch everyone else to get the hang of it."

Which was how five minutes later Courtney was sitting in the hot tub with the entire group, playing Never Have I Ever. As promised, Madison was on her left. Brett was on her other side, his leg against hers. If they'd been able to put their hands under water, she was sure he would have held hers, but they had to have one hand up for the game, the other holding onto their drink.

"I'll start," Madison said. "Never have I ever…had over ten thousand followers on Instagram."

Perry, Noel, Savannah, Emily Nicole and Oliver (who was apparently "Instagram famous" for his hotel heir party-boy ways) put a finger down and drank. Courtney only had Instagram to follow Savannah, so she didn't have even close to ten thousand followers. She didn't drink. Madison nodded at her, as if to say, "See...look how easy that was." Courtney nodded back, and they shared a smile, but she quickly looked away.

Next up was Damien. "Never Have I Ever...taken a day off from skiing to hang out at a bookstore," he said, smirking at Courtney and Brett.

"Way to purposely target us," Brett joked, putting a finger down and sipping his drink. Courtney did the same, which earned another nod from Madison. At least she was playing the game correctly.

Damien laughed and held his hands high. "All's fair in Never Have I Ever."

They circled around the group, saying fun things to target people, like "never have I ever recorded a song in a studio," "never have I ever gone to The Goodman School," and "never have I ever been a California resident." The game was simple, and Courtney was surprised to find that she was having fun.

They got back around to Emily Nicole, who had been taking such large sips of her wine that she'd already poured herself another glass. "Let me think of a good one." She raised an eyebrow and placed her glass on the ledge, smiling conspiringly. "Never Have I Ever...taken my top off in a hot tub in Aspen. Oh, wait..." She lowered her shoulders under the bubbles, pulled off her top, and held it in the air as if it were a prize. "Now I have!"

"Omigosh." Brianna gasped, covering her mouth with her hand. "No way."

"It's about time things got more interesting around here." Emily Nicole laughed.

"I like the way this girl thinks," Perry said. "The question is—will you *keep* it off?"

"Do you dare me to?"

"Yes." He held her gaze. "I dare you."

"Then I will." She flung the top onto the ledge and shrugged, although she stayed under the bubbles—where no one could see anything—and took an extra-long sip of her wine.

"Any other takers?" Perry said, glancing at Savannah. Courtney's hand tightened around her cup—she was *not* letting her little sister take her bathing suit top off in front of everyone, especially not to get the attention of a guy.

"Nope," Savannah said casually, although Courtney could tell from the way her voice wavered that she felt uncomfortable. "I haven't had half as much to drink as Emily Nicole."

"Let's hurry this game up, then," Perry said, taking a long sip of his drink.

"It's your turn," Noel said. "Although do all the lads get to put our fingers down and drink, since none of us are wearing tops?"

"Hell no," Oliver said. "Let's not make it too easy for us to win."

"Good point," he said, and the game resumed.

Perry had never gone to a real high school (he was homeschooled), so everyone but Noel got a finger down for that. Savannah had never been in a relationship for longer than two months, which made Perry, Noel, Damien, Madison, Emily Nicole and Brett put fingers down.

When had Brett been in a relationship for longer than two months? Was he referring to his relationship with Courtney? She *wanted* to put her finger down—since she and Brett had been official since December—but Savannah was the only one here who knew about that, so she didn't budge.

She made sure not to glance over at Brett and give anything away, glad when they moved on with the game. Oliver had never gotten all As for an entire semester at school, which got Courtney and Madison down another finger. Next up was Brianna.

"Never have I ever had sex," she said, her cheeks turning red.

Courtney looked around, curious about who would put a finger down. It ended up being Oliver (not surprising), Damien, Emily Nicole, Noel, Perry and Brett.

She focused on the water, unable to look at Brett. While they hadn't discussed it, he'd hinted to her that he wasn't a virgin. But seeing it come out in front of everyone made her stomach drop. Because as much as she cared about him—she was falling in love with him, although she hadn't yet said it out loud—she would never be his first. It wasn't his fault, but it didn't make her feel good, either.

He reached under the water and squeezed her hand, as if he could read her mind, which made her feel a little better.

"You're a virgin?" Perry asked Savannah.

"Yeah," Savannah said, and the way he looked at her—as if this disappointed him—made Courtney want to slap him. What had he expected? Savannah had just turned sixteen.

"Interesting," he said, although he sounded like he thought it was anything but.

After that conversation, Perry's body language shifted—previously he'd been angled toward Savannah, but now he was pointed toward Emily Nicole, who was on the other side of him. The shift was so visible that it made *Courtney* hurt—she couldn't imagine how Savannah felt. Even Damien glared at Perry as if he were a piece of scum.

They continued around the circle, and finally it was Courtney's turn. Perry was now blatantly flirting with Emily Nicole, and Savannah was so spaced out that it was like she wasn't there anymore. Courtney had the sudden urge to say something that would shock everyone, and hopefully distract her sister. What better way to do that than one-upping Emily Nicole's crazy stunt earlier?

"Never have I ever been naked in a hot tub in Aspen," she blurted, which made everyone stop any side chat and stare at her. Her cheeks heated—had she *really* just said that? If she hadn't poured her Sprite herself, she would have suspected someone had spiked it.

She was so shocked with herself that she didn't pay attention to who put their finger down. She just knew Savannah wasn't one of them.

"It's clear what needs to happen now," Perry said.

"What?" she asked.

"You need to get naked in the hot tub."

Courtney did a double-take to see if he was serious. He was.

"No way." She shook her head. "I said I've *never* done it. Not that I *will* do it."

"No one would be able to see anything," Emily Nicole said. "The jets are on, which would hide everything, and the lighting's pretty dim."

"Says the girl who's already taken her top off." Perry looked at Emily Nicole in approval. It was as if Savannah had disappeared off his radar.

"I have an idea," Emily Nicole said. "Let's say I do it, and Brett does it. Then would you do it, too?" With that, Emily Nicole pulled off her bottoms and tossed them into the pile with her top. "Just for thirty seconds—then put it back on. You can take it off while you're still in the water. No one will be able to see anything."

It was true—now that Emily Nicole was back in the water, it was impossible to tell she was naked. Plus, the way Perry was eyeing up Emily Nicole and acting like Savannah didn't exist made Courtney so *angry*. She wanted to do something—anything—to get the attention away from Emily Nicole.

She also wanted to shock everyone.

"If Brett does it, I'll do it."

"Are you sure?" Brett watched her, concerned. "I don't mind, but don't feel pressured because of everyone else."

"I don't feel pressured," Courtney insisted, because she didn't. What she felt was…daring. Like someone else's spirit was in her body. Which made her think of her twin. Her chest panged with the thought of Britney, and how she would never get to know her—this sister who would have had her face, but been a completely different person. If Britney were alive, would this be something she would do? Courtney's gut told her that yes, it would be. Besides, she had the rest of her life to act mature and responsible. What was wrong with trying to live a little? "I'll do it."

"If Courtney does it, I'm doing it," Brett said.

"I'll time you." Perry motioned to his watch. "Thirty seconds—no less—and then you can put your bathing suits back on. You ready?"

Courtney took a deep breath, trying not to overthink what she was about to do. "Yes."

Which was how seconds later, Brett's bathing suit and her bathing suit were on the ledge behind them, and they were both naked in the hot tub. Courtney sank lower in the water, so it came up to her chin. *No one can see anything*, she repeated to herself, although it didn't make her feel any more comfortable. Maybe she should put it back on now, before the thirty seconds were up?

Perry stayed focused on his watch. "Fifteen seconds to go…" he said. Then he pushed himself out of the hot tub, grabbed Courtney's, Brett's, and Emily Nicole's bathing suits, and ran up the stairs to his loft.

Courtney froze and wrapped her arms around herself, covering up even though the jets hid everything. She'd never felt more exposed in her life.

"Come on, man!" Brett yelled. "Not funny. Bring the bathing suits back down."

"If you want them, come and get them!" Perry said over the balcony.

"That's your friend," Damien said to Noel, his dark gaze unwavering. "And you're both here as guests. Get him to bring the bathing suits back down here—now."

"Don't get all worked up." Emily Nicole laughed, slurring her words. How much had she had to drink? "If that's how Perry wants to play it, fine by me. I'll get them back myself." And then, despite being naked, she stood up, got out of the hot tub and ran upstairs, dripping water behind her.

Minutes passed while they waited for Emily Nicole and Perry to return with the bathing suits. Courtney curled herself in a ball, clenching her teeth so hard that her jaw hurt. She didn't want to move, she didn't want to look at anyone and she didn't want to be stuck here.

"They're not coming back, are they?" she finally said.

"I'll go see what's going on." Noel got out of the hot tub, grabbed his towel and hurried up the steps.

It didn't take long for him to return. "Perry hid your bathing suits," he said. "He's up there with Emily Nicole, and they..." He glanced at Savannah, his eyes shining with pity. "They don't seem to be going anywhere anytime soon."

"What do you mean?" Savannah asked, her voice small. "Is Perry hooking up with Emily Nicole?"

"They're...busy." Noel shifted his feet and focused on the floor. "I know you fancied him. I'm sorry."

"It's fine." Her eyes filled with tears, and she wiped her hand at her cheek, as if splashing water on her face would hide that she was crying. "I actually have a headache. I must have stayed in the hot tub for too long. I'm going to bed."

Damien called at her to wait, but she didn't listen, hurrying off to her room instead. Courtney stared at where she'd disappeared, wanting to follow her sister and talk to her. She wanted to tell her what a jerk Perry was, and that she deserved so much better than him.

But she couldn't, because Perry had run off with her bathing suit, and if she got out of the hot tub, everyone would see her naked. She wrapped her arms tighter around herself. What had she been *thinking* by going along with all this?

"I'll go talk to Savannah," Evie said, pulling herself out of the hot tub.

"Thanks." Courtney smiled at Evie, because if anyone could cheer up Savannah, it was Evie. She would probably do a better job at it than Courtney, actually.

"Do you want me to come, too?" Damien asked, lifting himself out of the hot tub.

"No." Evie put out a hand to stop him. "It's best if it's just me. But don't worry… Savannah and I have been best friends for years. I've got this."

Damien frowned and settled back into his seat, his forehead creased. "All right," he agreed. "Let me know if there's anything I can do."

"I will," she promised.

"Evie," Noel called after her, and she stopped to look at him, her eyes wide with hope. "I'm sorry about Perry. He gets rather…wild when he drinks. If I'd known what he was planning, I would have stopped him."

"It's not your fault," she said. "I know that."

"Thanks." He ran a hand through his already messy hair. "I'm glad."

"Do you think you'll still be out here later?"

"Most likely." He glanced upstairs. "Since Perry seems… busy in our room. Why?"

"Because I didn't have much to eat this afternoon," she

said, wringing her hands together. "So I'll probably get hungry and grab some food later."

He beamed. "Then you can count on me hanging around the kitchen for the rest of the night."

Evie smiled back at him, and rushed up to the room where she was staying with Savannah. Once she shut the door, no one said a word.

This night certainly hadn't turned out as anticipated.

"Perry's really not going to give our bathing suits back, is he?" Courtney asked.

"It's okay." Brett wrapped his hand around hers, and then looked around at everyone else. "You'll all give us space while we get our towels on, right?"

"Yeah." Madison, surprisingly enough, was the first one out of the hot tub. "We'll hang out in the kitchen while the two of you cover up."

Everyone followed her there, and soon enough, Courtney and Brett were the only ones left. Naked. In the hot tub. Next to each other.

Courtney moved her hair over her shoulder, unable to look him in the eye.

"So." He ran a hand through his hair. "I guess we should grab our towels?"

"Yeah, we should." She lifted her eyes to meet his, and gasped at the fire that blazed within them. He rested his forehead on hers, his hand caressing her cheek, and she wanted so badly for him to kiss her, to run his hand over every inch of her body. But she couldn't be thinking about this stuff right now. Not with everyone a room away, able to walk in at any second.

"Okay." He swallowed. "I'll turn around while you get yours first."

"Okay." Her heart pounded so hard she could barely

breathe, and when he turned around, she hurried to grab her towel, wrapping it tightly around herself. "You can get out now," she said. The water sloshed as he got out of the hot tub, and she studied the fireplace in an extreme effort to not turn around.

"All right," Brett said, placing a hand on her shoulder. "Why don't I walk you to your room? I'll make sure that no one tries pulling your towel down as a joke. I don't think they would, but it can't hurt, just to be safe."

Courtney wanted to say "okay" again, but she'd said that over and over again, so she just nodded. They made their way back to her room in silence, dripping water on the floor, and he walked inside with her. Courtney shut the door and locked it.

She turned back to Brett, and his green eyes blazed with such intensity—such *desire*—that her heart leaped into her throat.

"Thanks for walking me back." She pulled her towel tighter around herself. "I can't believe I did that. I should have known someone would do something stupid…"

"It was a dick move," Brett said. "I'm done with Perry for the rest of the trip. But no one saw anything—trust me, I never would have let anyone take advantage of what happened. I care about you too much for that."

The next thing she knew, his lips crushed against hers, and he'd sandwiched her between the door and his body. She breathed him in, her head swimming with dizziness. It would be so easy to lose herself to him. But there was still one thing holding her back, and she broke the kiss, looking questioningly into his eyes.

"What's wrong?" His thumb brushed against her cheek, pushing a stray strand of hair behind her ear.

"This is all just new to me," she said softly. "I care about you so much—more than I've ever told you—and I trust you with everything."

"I care about you, too." He paused, watching her closely. "It's more than caring for you. I'm falling in love with you. I knew it from the moment I kissed you on the dance floor at the grand opening, but you were so unsure about us and I didn't want to scare you away. But I'm done hiding it. I love you, Courtney Diamond, and it's about time you knew it."

Her breath caught, his words making her dizzy. This was the first time someone who wasn't blood related to her had *ever* told her they loved her.

And it was absolutely perfect.

"I'm hoping you feel the same, but the way you're leaving me hanging is making me nervous," he said. "What are you thinking?"

"I'm thinking that… I love you, too," she said, smiling. "And I've also known I was falling for you since that first week, but it got so confusing from there. I'm sorry for holding back. Since I've met you, you're all I've been able to think about. Every moment when I'm not with you, I'm waiting for the next time we can be together again. It's just that…"

"It's just what?" His fingers grazed her lips, sending heat rushing through her body.

Courtney closed her eyes, unable to focus with him touching her like that. But she needed to get it out, so when she opened them again, she pulled back so she could think. "I couldn't help comparing myself to everyone in the hot tub tonight," she started. "And I'm a little…inexperienced. *Very* inexperienced. Our kiss this summer was my first."

"I don't see how that's possible." He smiled, as if he found her endearing. "Either those guys in California were blind to what they were missing, or you have very high standards."

"When I said I didn't have time for anything but school,

work and homework, I meant it," she said. "Whenever a guy was interested in me, I kept my distance. I couldn't afford the distraction."

He laughed. "And here I was hoping that you had high standards."

"Well, that, too."

"None of this changes how I feel about you," he said. "I love you, Courtney Diamond, whether you've kissed one guy or fifty."

"Fifty?" Her eyes widened. She couldn't imagine having kissed that many guys. Although she knew it happened— Peyton had a friend who kissed thirty guys just in sophomore year. "I wouldn't be *me* if I'd kissed fifty guys."

"I know that," he said. "And I like how picky you are about who you kiss. I'm glad that I was your first."

"I am, too." She swallowed. "And I know I wasn't the first girl you've kissed. Or even the first girl you've dated. But when we were playing Never Have I Ever…you put a finger down for having had sex before."

"I did." He nodded.

"Who was it?" she asked softly. "Or if it was more than one person, who were *they*?"

"Only one other person," he said, and she relaxed a little at knowing that. "My ex-girlfriend from my old school. At the time I thought I loved her, but knowing what I feel now for you, I didn't."

Courtney's cheeks flushed. "What happened between you two?" she asked, taking his hands in hers.

"I'd had a crush on her since middle school," he said, his eyes far off, as if seeing it all again. "I'd built her up to be someone she wasn't. For the first few weeks we were together, she was fun and upbeat. Then her true self came out. She talked about her friends behind their backs, and was constantly judging people. She brought negativity with her everywhere she went. Eventually I had enough and ended things."

"But not before losing your virginity to her."

"You have to understand…it wasn't bad between us all the time," he said. "There were lots of times when we were happy together. But she liked reminding me how she could have her pick of so many guys, and she'd chosen me—as if I should have been so grateful for that. I thought having sex would bring us closer, and that it would get her to drop that attitude. But it didn't. Maybe someday she'll find someone who makes her want to be a better person, but that person wasn't me. *She* wasn't the right person for me. But you are. She's in my past, and what I felt for her was nothing compared to what I feel for you. Because I love you, Courtney. So much more than I ever thought it was possible to love another person."

Her heart swelled, and she kissed him again. The curves of their bodies fit perfectly together, as if they were made for each other. They traveled to the bed, and she pulled him down on top of her, pressing her hips against his. Only the towels were between them, and her body throbbed at the re-alization. She wanted the towels to be gone. She wanted to feel his skin against hers.

"We need to stop." His breathing was heavy, and he pulled back to look into her eyes. "You're driving me crazy, and I don't want anything to happen between us that you're not ready for."

"I'm ready." Her breath caught, and she kept her eyes locked on his. "I love you, I trust you and I want to be with you."

"And I want to be with you," he said. "More than anything. But I don't want you to do anything you might regret."

"I love you, Brett," she said, strong and steady, tracing his cheekbone with her thumb. "And I want to show you how much. I want you to be my first. Here. Now."

He kissed her again, slower this time. If a kiss could say *I love you*, this one would. Her heart raced so much that it felt about to burst. His hips pressed against hers, and she wrapped her legs around his waist, needing to be closer to him. This was the closest she'd ever been to anyone, and she wanted more.

"Courtney," he murmured, burying his face in her neck, his lips caressing her skin. "I want to be with you, too. But I need to get protection first. And it's in my room."

Her cheeks heated. This was all new to her, and she'd never had this conversation with anyone. But this was Brett. She trusted him, and she could be up-front with him.

"I've been on the pill since December," she told him. He opened his mouth, but she continued before he could speak. "After we talked about officially dating—even though it was in secret—I figured it would be responsible to go to a doctor and get a prescription. But I agree that we should be safe in every way possible. And you actually don't have to go to your room, because Peyton brought condoms with her. They're in the top drawer of the nightstand."

"Okay." He nodded and rolled off her, his towel completely gone now. Her heart sped up, and she watched him open the drawer and rummage with the packaging. It didn't take long until he was kissing her again, his body hovering on top of hers.

"Are you sure you're ready?" he asked, his eyes so full of love that she couldn't imagine being anything *but* ready.

"I'm sure." She unfastened her towel, letting it slide off so he could see every inch of her. He took a sharp breath, and she pulled him down to meet her, losing herself to him completely.

chapter 23: *Peyton*

Aspen with a local was *so* much better than the snooty places in Aspen that Peyton had seen so far this trip. It also helped that the local she was with was Zack, since he was the hottest ski instructor in town. Well, most of the ski instructors were hot—skiing was quite the workout, so they had incredible bodies—but Zack was also *fun*. And after the intensity surrounding whatever had gone on between her and Jackson, it was nice to have some fun.

As Zack had mentioned, their first stop was a place called White Onion. What he hadn't mentioned was that Wednesday was their official "Beer Pong night." The bar was in a narrow building that resembled a saloon from the Old West, and it was crowded with local ski bums dressed in jeans and hoodies. It was also the first time Peyton had walked inside a building in Aspen without people staring at her to figure out who she was. Because apparently, when you're hanging out with the guys from One Connection, people automatically assume that you're a celebrity, too.

Zack had introduced her to his friends, and the beer pong began. He and Peyton paired up, won the first round and were on to the second.

"Who would have guessed that the Diamond heiress would be kicking my ass at beer pong tonight?" Zack's friend Ryan asked from across the table.

"I've only been an heiress since last summer." Peyton held the ping-pong ball at eye level and focused on her target— the only cup left. They would win if she made this shot. She took a deep breath and sent the ball flying in a perfect arc, straight into the cup.

Ryan stared at the cup, his mouth dropping open.

"I might not play sports, but I *rock* at beer pong!" She pumped her fist in the air, and Zack gave her a high five.

"Now that we've won two games in a row, what do you say we hit up our next stop of the night?" he asked.

Which was how a few minutes later, he was leading her down the steps to a club called Belly Down. It had free entry on Wednesday nights, which, according to Zack, was why it was the best night for locals.

The music inside was loud, the lights were dim (minus the spotlights on the stage) and the dance floor was packed. Tons of people said hi to Zack as he led Peyton through the crowd—he was one of those guys who knew everyone. There were tables on tiered levels around the sunken dance floor, and unlike the tables at clubs in Vegas, which you had to pay an exorbitant amount of money for, they were on a first-come, first-served basis. Luckily, Zack knew a group who had taken over a table, and there was just enough room left for him and Peyton to join them.

"So, do you all ski all day and stay out all night?" Peyton asked the group.

"First chair, last call!" Zack said, clinking his glass with a friend.

"What does that mean?" she asked.

"What it sounds like," he said. "Being at the chairlift when it first opens in the morning, and staying out until the last call at the bar. It's the true ski bum lifestyle."

"Sounds great," Peyton said, although she only halfway meant it. She was enjoying learning how to ski, but she couldn't imagine doing it all day, every day.

The DJ switched to a song Peyton loved, and she pulled Zack onto the dance floor, which was so packed that they had no choice but to dance with their bodies pressed against each other. She wrapped her arms around his neck, doing her best to lose herself in the music. Some of his friends joined them, and the night passed in a blur of dancing, with the occasional break so Zack could grab a drink.

It would have been perfect, except that whenever Peyton closed her eyes, she imagined it was Jackson she was dancing with, not Zack. She *should* have been able to get Jackson out of her mind with someone as hot as Zack interested in her, but it wasn't working. And it was frustrating as hell.

Eventually the crowd thinned out, and she and Zack headed back to the table.

"You sure you don't want another drink?" he asked. "It's last call."

"I'm sure," Peyton said, gulping down her water. "I'm still not used to the altitude here." Which was true, but she also just didn't feel like drinking anymore. Thinking about Jackson had put her in a weird mood. Because Zack was hot, and cool, and the type of guy she would have been all over months ago…but her feelings for him were only lukewarm. What was *happening* to her?

Zack and his friends ordered another round, and the lights

inside the club came on—universal bar language for "it's al-most closing time." Which was too bad, since Belly Down was one of the coolest clubs Peyton had been to in months. Sure, the clubs in Vegas were great, with their celebrity DJs and extravagance, but Belly Down had a perfect mix of club vibe and bar vibe, and she liked how laid-back everyone was. If she lived in Aspen, this would be her favorite hangout.

"I guess this is the end of the night?" she said.

"No way!" Zack said. "The best way to end the night is by grabbing a slice at New York Pizza."

"It's the best pizza in Aspen, and it's only a three-minute walk from here," Ryan added. "We're all going—you should come."

Peyton's stomach growled. "After all that dancing, I'm defi-nitely hungry," she said. "And I love pizza."

Even though she wasn't as into Zack as she'd hoped she would be, what was the harm in grabbing pizza? Especially since they'd be with the group.

The New York Pizza building had a sign in front with its name on it. The door opened to a single flight of stairs leading to the second floor, where they were greeted with the deli-cious smell of freshly baked pizza. It was by-the-slice counter style, and there was a long line, but the restaurant must have had the late-night crowd down to a science, because it didn't take long to get their slices. One of the girls in their group had already claimed a table, and once they all had their pizza, they sat down to feast.

"This is the biggest slice of pizza I've ever seen," Peyton said, shaking red pepper flakes onto a slice that was so huge that it was falling off the plate in both directions.

"It's also probably some of the best pizza you've ever tasted," Zack said.

She took a bite, and sure enough, the pizza was delicious.

It had the perfect mix of cheese, tomato sauce and crunchiness. "You're right," she said once she finished chewing. "It's perfect."

She finished off the slice, talking and laughing with Zack and his friends, glad she'd come out with them tonight. They were fun, and spending time with a completely new group of people was helping her get her mind off of Jackson.

Once they'd all finished their pizza, they walked down the stairs and Peyton said her goodbyes. She would probably never see them again, but she promised she would add them as friends online so they could keep in touch. She hated saying goodbye forever. It felt so permanent. And who knew where life would take her in the future?

"Hey." Zack placed his hand on her arm, holding her back as everyone walked away. "I know it's late, but do you want to come back to my place? Have some dessert?"

Peyton pulled away and wrapped her arms around herself, although her jacket was warm enough that it wasn't necessary. Months ago, she would have said yes. But she didn't *feel* anything for Zack. He barely knew her. And since she was leaving in a few days, there wasn't going to be much time to change that.

Going back to his place and hooking up with him wasn't going to help her get over Jackson. It would probably just make her feel worse.

"Thanks for the invite," she said. "But I'm just going to head home."

"You sure?" he asked. "I bought some wine for us tonight. I was hoping we would have more time alone together to get to know each other." He took a step closer, watching her with intensity, as if he were about to kiss her.

"Listen, Zack." She pulled back before he had a chance to make a move. "I had a lot of fun tonight. But I sort of…"

She glanced up at the stars to gather her thoughts—she wasn't used to explaining her feelings to people. Her instinct was to make up an excuse, get out of there and never see him again. But Zack was a good guy. He deserved to know the truth.

"You're sort of..." he repeated what she'd started to say, waiting for her to continue.

"I'm not over someone else." She shoved her hands in the pockets of her jacket and shuffled her feet. "It's a long story, and I don't want to get into it, because it doesn't end well. But I'm not over him." She let out a long breath, feeling freer than she'd felt all night. "I've had a great time with you, and I'm glad you showed me the local side of Aspen. This was the best night I've had here so far. But it's been a long day, and it's late, so I'm just going to head back now."

"Okay," he said with a shrug. "Thanks for letting me know."

"That's it?" Peyton tilted her head, bracing herself for more.

"That's it," he said. "You're into someone else. I get it."

"Oh," she said. "Thanks."

"No need to thank me." He laughed. "What'd you expect me to do?"

"I don't know," she said, running a hand through her hair. "I thought you might get angry. I mean, I've been spending all this time with you, and I never mentioned this other guy. I would be pretty annoyed if I were you."

"I'm not happy about it," he said. "Because I thought—and still think—that you're a cool girl. But I don't want to hook up with someone who's thinking about someone else, ya know?"

"Yeah," she said. "Definitely."

"Anyway." He cleared his throat. "Do you want me to call you a cab?"

"I actually have a driver waiting." She motioned to where

her bodyguard was standing on the end of the block, blending into the background.

"Has he been following us all night?"

"He has to," she said. "That's his job. He's not just a driver—he's a bodyguard." After the words were out of her mouth, she realized how strange they sounded. What normal seventeen—*almost* eighteen—year-old had a bodyguard? "Anyway, are you sure you're okay to drive?" she asked. "If you're not, my driver can drop you off at your place."

"I've been pacing myself all night, and I sobered up during pizza," he said. "I didn't want to be hungover tomorrow. Hungover skiing's the worst. You still on for a lesson tomorrow?"

Was she? That was a good question.

"I don't think so," she said, relieved once she'd spoken the words. "I came out here to spend time with my sisters, so I'm gonna stick to the original plan and take a group lesson with them. Or maybe just hang out with them around town tomorrow—everyone was pretty beat after skiing today. I wouldn't mind sleeping in."

"Well, you have my number," he said. "If you change your mind, let me know."

"Okay," she said, although she knew it wasn't going to happen. "Thanks again for taking me out tonight. I really did have fun."

"No prob," he said. "I had fun, too. I hope everything ends up working out for you."

"Thanks." She glanced at her bodyguard, who was waiting for her next to the car. "I guess I'll see you around."

She turned and walked away, not looking back. Even though she'd let Zack down, she couldn't help but smile—

because while opening up and telling him the truth hadn't been easy, it was the right thing to do.

And if Jackson had witnessed what she'd just done, she knew he would be proud.

chapter 24: *Madison*

Madison rolled over in bed and glanced at the glowing numbers on the clock. Two-thirty. After the bathing suit theft, everyone else had called it a night. Well, everyone except for Emily Nicole, whom Madison had been stuck rooming with, and who still hadn't made it back from Perry's room.

But despite the lack of her loud-mouthed and apparently wild roommate, Madison had been tossing and turning since getting into bed. She kept replaying the conversation she'd had with Oliver at Ajax Tavern. She was glad that they were friends again, but her feelings for him were stronger than that, and she couldn't make those feelings go away. She wasn't sure what to do. She wanted to tell him, but she was afraid. Because she feared that if he knew, it would ruin their friendship forever.

She hated the thought of losing him again.

She wanted to take a sleeping pill, but it was too late to take one without it making her sleep too late tomorrow. And being this restless was making her *more* restless, so she gave up trying to sleep, got out of bed and headed to the kitchen to make some tea.

She stopped in her tracks when she saw Savannah sitting at the kitchen table in her pink pajamas, hunched over her laptop. Savannah frowned at what she was reading, as if it upset her.

Madison ducked behind a wall, trying to be as quiet as possible. She should go back to her room. Because if she had to meet someone late at night in the kitchen, Madison would have preferred it to be anyone but Savannah. The youngest Diamond sister had every reason to hate her.

But Savannah had been through a lot tonight, and while it all still felt so new to Madison, Savannah was her *sister*. She should be there for her. So she stepped forward, slapping her feet extra loudly on the hardwood floor to warn her of her approach.

Savannah looked up, her eyes widening when they met Madison's. Her lips formed an O of surprise, and she clicked something on her laptop, pushing it away. "Hey," she said. "I thought I was the only one still awake."

"I couldn't sleep, so I came in here to make some tea." Madison pointed at the Keurig. "I'll be out of your way in a few minutes."

"You don't have to get 'out of my way,'" Savannah said. "You can stay here. If you want."

"Okay." Madison made her cup of tea and joined Savannah. She wasn't sure what to say, and she didn't want to force her to talk about Perry if she didn't want to, so she asked, "What were you looking at on your computer? You seemed pretty focused on it."

"Just YouTube stuff." Savannah shrugged.

Madison blew on her tea, watching the steam rise up. "For someone who has a YouTube channel taking off, you don't sound too excited about it."

"I'm excited about it," she said, although she didn't sound convincing. "I'm getting a ton of video views."

"But it's not happening like you imagined?"

She blinked and rubbed at her eyes. "No, not really." Her voice caught, and she sniffed, glancing up at the ceiling. "I'm sorry… I don't want to cry."

"Don't be sorry," Madison said. "We don't have to talk about it if you don't want to."

"It's fine." Savannah swallowed. "It's just that people online can be so *mean*. I can't stop myself from looking at their comments, and it hurts."

"You just have to ignore them." Madison made sure to sound strong, even though she knew it was harder than that. "Having people talk about you is the price you pay for putting yourself out there and being popular. Trust me, I know."

"True." Savannah twisted a strand of hair around her finger, staring at her computer screen. "Most people are nice, but every time I see something negative, I wonder if this whole YouTube thing is worth it."

"Of course it's worth it." Madison sat forward and placed her hands on the table. "I've seen your videos—you're amazing. People who say anything else are just jealous."

"That's easy for you to say." Savannah closed her laptop and pushed it across the table. "You've never put videos of yourself singing online for the entire world to rip apart."

"Maybe not," Madison said. "But you've seen campusbuzz. People talk about me on there all the time."

"Yeah." Savannah focused on stirring her hot chocolate. "People do say a lot of mean things about you on there. And about me and my sisters, too. How do you not let it affect you?"

"It stung at first," she admitted. "But you have to put yourself above it. Since I don't want to see it, I don't go on campusbuzz. Problem solved. It's tempting to look, but I never do. Which is why I thought it was ridiculous when you and Peyton thought I was behind that one post about the three of you."

"I really am sorry about that." Savannah brought her hair over her shoulder. "It was just that Peyton saw you take the picture that ended up in that post, so it made sense when she told me you wrote it."

"As long as you know now that I didn't write it, it's fine," Madison said. Which was true, but she also didn't want to talk about it. Because talking about it meant thinking about Oliver, which reminded her of how confused she was about her feelings for him. "I guess with your YouTube channel, it comes down to one question—how badly do you want this?"

"Want what?" Savannah asked. "To be a singer?"

Madison nodded.

"More than anything," she said. "It's my dream. If I didn't have singing…I don't know what I would do."

"Then you have no other option," Madison said. "You *have* to ignore the people who put you down. Look at the guys in One Connection. They have tons of fans, but there are also people who don't like them. They don't let it stop them from doing what they love and making music."

"That's different," she said. "They're *One Connection*."

"It doesn't make them any better than you," Madison said. "Don't ever forget that. They weren't always famous. Everyone has to start somewhere. If you let people bring you down now, you'll never know how high you could climb. And you owe it to yourself to try."

"You're right," Savannah said. "Thanks." They shared a hesitant smile, and she added, "But after tonight, Perry's not interested in me anymore. Everything was great between us this morning. Now it's a mess."

Madison sipped her tea, quiet for a few seconds. It was

over between Savannah and Perry—that was obvious, after what had happened in the hot tub. But what could she say that wouldn't come across as insensitive? To make sure that Savannah wouldn't regret opening up to her?

"You deserve better than him," she finally said. "Sure, he's famous, but he's a jerk."

"I know he was a jerk tonight," Savannah said, her eyes sad. "But he's been so nice to me until now. He's been texting me since we met at my Sweet Sixteen, and when we were on the chairlift today, he told me he believed I have real talent and that he wants to help me get on *Teen American StarMaker*. I thought he cared about me."

Madison curled up in her chair, waiting for Savannah to throw in another "but." Instead, Savannah played with the ends of her hair, waiting for what seemed like...advice. Like she was asking for help from a sister.

Or more like a sister replacement, since Peyton was out with that ski-instructor boy toy of hers, and Courtney was "otherwise occupied" with Brett. But it was the first time any of the Diamonds had made an effort to let Madison in. How could she not take it?

"Please don't tell me you would give Perry the time of day again," she said, since it was the same advice she would have given a close friend. "I don't care what teen reality show he says he can get you on—if he was *actually* interested in you, he wouldn't have stopped paying attention to you after finding out you were a virgin. And he *definitely* wouldn't be in his room with Emily Nicole doing who the hell knows what right now."

Savannah's eyes were glassy, and lower lip quivered, as if she were about to cry again.

"I don't mean to be harsh," Madison said. "But you deserve someone better than Perry. And I think you know that, too."

"Maybe." Savannah sniffed and pulled her knees to her chest. "And honestly…it's not even Perry that I'm actually upset about."

"You're more upset about the bitches on YouTube?"

"No," Savannah said. "It's another guy. Someone I've known longer than I've known Perry."

"Who?" Madison asked, although she had a feeling that she knew the answer.

"No one." Savannah wouldn't meet Madison's gaze. "Well, it's someone, obviously. But it doesn't matter, because I had a chance with him a while ago and I messed it up. He doesn't think of me like that—at least not anymore."

Madison chewed the inside of her cheek. "You're talking about Damien, aren't you?"

"Yeah." Savannah glanced down the hall and lowered her voice, even though Damien was sleeping and his room was far enough away that he wouldn't be able to hear them. "But please don't tell anyone? He only sees me as a friend, and I don't want to embarrass myself again like I did over the summer. I can't be rejected by him twice."

"But since the night of your Sweet Sixteen party, it's looked like you were more into Perry." Madison shook her head, genuinely confused. "And didn't you choose Nick over Damien at the grand opening of the Diamond, and ignore Damien for the rest of the night, even *after* he asked you out?"

"I guess." Savannah's cheeks turned pink. "But that happened *after* you kissed Damien. He wanted you more than me. So I thought if I tried to move on with other people, I would get over him. But it didn't work."

Madison took a deep breath. She'd apologized to Savannah before, but she had to try again. "I really am sorry about what happened last summer," she said. "I shouldn't have kissed Damien that night. But someone I liked had just rejected me, and it hurt a lot. I knew Damien had feelings for me, and after I saw him with you, I wondered if maybe I could return those feelings. But I didn't, and it blew up in my face. Damien and I never would have been good together. I knew it, and now he knows it, too. I promise that we're truly just friends now."

"I believe you," she said. "Especially because Damien sort of said the same thing."

"So you know it's true. You're the one he wants to be with."

"No." She shook her head. "I believe that you and Damien are only friends. But not that he's interested in me. If anything, he likes Brianna now. He's been spending a lot of time with her on this trip, and they're always sitting next to each other."

"Brianna?" Madison laughed. "No way. Damien's known Brianna longer than he's known me. He doesn't see her as anything but Oliver's little sister."

"So how come he's always with her?"

"Because he's comfortable around her," she said. "Come on, Savannah. Give yourself some more credit. Damien skips lunch with our friends to help you with your YouTube stuff, and he ditched his family vacation in California to come here for *you*. He wouldn't have done all that if he only saw you as a friend."

"But if he was interested in me, wouldn't he have made a move by now?" she asked. "He wasn't exactly shy about going for what he wanted when we first met."

"Because he didn't *know* you then, so he wasn't risking anything by trying," Madison said. "Take it from someone he used to be interested in. He flirts a lot, but if he's *really* interested, he won't make the first move. That night at Luxe, I was the one who kissed him, remember?"

"You weren't subtle about it, either." Savannah cracked a smile. "From what I heard, you basically pounced on him."

"Yeah, well, I'd had too much to drink that night." She

shrugged and sipped her tea, which was starting to get cold. "It wasn't one of my finest moments. But that's all in the past. What I'm trying to say is that if you're interested in Damien, you need to let him know. Otherwise he'll go on thinking you have feelings for Nick, or Perry, or someone else."

"Being obvious didn't work for me over the summer," she said. "And then I thought that I was clear about my feelings for him last semester when we were working together on my YouTube channel."

"Did you *tell* him your feelings?" Madison asked. "Or did you expect him to pick up hints?"

"Hints, I guess." She pressed her lips together, then sat up straighter. "But if he likes me, shouldn't he be the one to make it happen?"

"Please don't tell me you're going to follow those old-fashioned dating rules." Madison rolled her eyes.

"They're not old-fashioned!" Savannah retorted. "Every website says that guys like the chase, and you should let a guy come to you, or else you're going to come off as too aggressive and make them lose interest. If they don't come to you, you're supposed to ignore them. No calling, no texting, no interacting with anything they do online." She counted each one off on her fingers. "Then if they like you, they'll come bouncing back."

"How many websites have you consulted about this?" Madison asked.

Savannah glanced sideways at her computer. "A few."

"And how's that been working out for you?"

"It hasn't."

"Exactly." Madison crossed her legs and smiled. "Stop looking up dating advice on the internet. No website knows your exact situation. But I know Damien, and here's what I think—

he's one of the most confident guys I know, but even he has to feel overshadowed by Perry Myles."

"I guess," Savannah said, picking at her nails. "But it's hard to think of Damien being intimidated by anyone."

"Like I said, he's confident, but come on." Madison laughed. "This is *Perry Myles* we're talking about. Imagine if Damien had a thing with Ariana Grande, or Taylor Swift, or someone like that. Wouldn't you feel intimidated, too?"

"'Intimidated' would be an understatement," Savannah said. "I dream of their level of success. If Damien got involved with either of them, I would probably give up all hope that he would ever notice me."

"Exactly." Madison finished off her tea.

"Not that it matters," Savannah said. "Since Perry was playing me the entire time."

"What he did tonight was pretty crappy."

They sat in silence for a few seconds, and Madison watched as Savannah stirred her hot chocolate. It must be cold by now, but that didn't stop her from drinking it. The entire house was quiet—more peaceful than it had been since they'd arrived—and Madison was glad she'd joined Savannah..

"I should have known better than to get involved with Perry," Savannah said. "But come on, he's *Perry Myles*. Even my agent told me I would be stupid not to see what might happen with him. That's part of how this all began. Then when he started replying to my texts, and saying he wanted to see me again, I got caught up in the excitement. But if you're right about Damien actually having feelings for me this entire time, then I'll feel like the biggest idiot ever for messing that up."

"You can still fix this," Madison said. "I truly believe that Damien cares about you—but you have to let him know how you feel."

"If I have a chance with Damien—and I trust that you

mean it when you say I do—I don't want to miss out on that, either," Savannah said. Then she frowned. "But he's barely paid attention to me this entire trip. He hasn't talked to me one-on-one at all. It's like I don't exist."

"Because you've been spending so much time with Perry," Madison reminded her. "But tonight, in the hot tub, Damien looked like he wanted to punch Perry in the face."

"Really?" Savannah brightened.

"Really." She scooted her chair forward. "Seriously, Savannah, you *have* to tell him how you feel. If you don't, then you guys will keep having these misunderstandings, and it'll be so much of a mess that you won't be able to fix it."

"You're right." She chewed on her lip. "But if I tell him how I feel, and he says he doesn't feel the same way, it'll be awkward being in the house with him for the rest of spring break. So I'll tell him toward the end of the trip. Okay?"

"I think you should do it as soon as possible, since I'm positive he'll be happy when you tell him," Madison said. "But I can understand wanting to wait until the end of the trip."

"And I don't know *what* to do with the One Connection guys," she said, burying her fingers in her hair. "I don't want Perry here anymore, but I can't just kick him out. Can I?"

Madison raised an eyebrow—she couldn't imagine Savannah kicking Perry out, although it was an amusing thought. "It's Adrian's house, and Perry's a guest here," she said. "You can do whatever you want."

"I'll think about it." Savannah sighed and sat back in her chair. "Anyway, enough talk about Perry. You and Oliver have been spending a lot of time together recently… What's going on between the two of you?"

Madison shifted in her seat. She hadn't talked about her feelings for Oliver with anyone yet. It was almost as if, by not putting her feelings into words, they didn't have to be real.

But Savannah had just opened up about Damien. If Madison wanted them to become closer—to really try seeing what having sisters was all about—she would have to put herself out there, too.

"If I tell you, promise you won't say a thing?" she asked. "To anyone?"

"I promise," Savannah said.

"Okay, here it goes." Madison sat cross-legged on her chair, making herself comfortable. "I care about Oliver a lot. I wouldn't have invited him here if I didn't. But the first day we were in Aspen—when everyone went skiing and I spent the day in town with him—he told me he was upset because I hadn't tried harder to stop him from getting in the car the night of your party. I said that he shouldn't blame me—that he's responsible for his own actions—but I can't stop wondering if maybe he's right. That I should have done more." Her throat tightened, and she blinked away tears. "All I did was tell him not to drive, and I was so upset that night that I just…let him go."

"His accident wasn't your fault," Savannah said softly. "It was a hard night for you, too. Peyton told me that she'd just told you about the bet. And you knew about us being sisters, but couldn't tell us. I can't imagine what that was like."

"It was awful," Madison said. "After Oliver left, I cried in the bathroom for most of the night. And I hate admitting this, because I shouldn't forgive him so easily…but even *after* knowing about that bet, I still have feelings for him."

"If it helps, when Peyton and I first told him about the task she'd come up with for him, he said he could never hurt you like that and there was no way he would do it," Savannah said. "From what I saw, he really cares about you. More than it seems like he cares about *anyone* else."

"That's almost the exact same thing he said to me before leaving your party." Madison sniffed and wiped away a tear.

"Maybe because it's true," Savannah said.

"Maybe." She smiled, although her chest panged with doubt. "Everything's been so hard since the accident. He wouldn't talk to anyone for weeks. Now things are finally starting to feel like they're getting back to normal between us, and I don't want to mess up our friendship."

"I get that," Savannah said. "But what was it you told me about Damien? That you believe he has feelings for me, but that I need to be honest with him about how I feel, or else nothing will ever happen between us?"

"Yeah." Madison nodded.

"Then you should take your own advice and do the same with Oliver."

Madison jerked back and studied Savannah. Savannah had seemed so fragile and naive before, but now her eyes gleamed with strength, her fists curled with determination. "I sound like a hypocrite, don't I?" she asked.

"Maybe a little." Savannah smiled. "But when anyone's wrapped up in the emotions of their situation, it's easier for someone else to see what's really going on than for them to see it themselves. And I wouldn't tell you that I thought Oliver cared about you if I didn't believe it."

"Thanks," Madison said, although she still wasn't sure what to believe. The advice she'd given Savannah was right because she *knew* Damien. Savannah didn't know Oliver. Their situations were so different. "I'll think about it."

Then the front door opened, and Peyton rushed inside. She was so loud that she could have woken up everyone in the house. Her cheeks were red, her hair a mess—Madison could only guess what she'd been up to with that hot ski instructor of hers all night.

"Is everyone else sleeping?" Peyton asked, throwing her bag onto the kitchen island.

Madison looked to Savannah to take the lead.

"Oliver, Brianna, Evie, Noel and Damien are sleeping," Savannah said. "Courtney and Brett are still in the room you're sharing with Courtney, so you might want to steer clear from there tonight."

"They're not..." Peyton shook her head, her eyes bulging. "No way. She would have told us if she was sleeping with him."

"Maybe they're just talking?" Savannah squeaked. "Or sleeping. Not as in *with* each other, but you know...just sleeping."

"We'll find out tomorrow," Peyton said. "I bet they were just talking and fell asleep."

"You could stay in my room tonight," Madison offered. "Emily Nicole's been upstairs with Perry, and it doesn't seem like she's leaving anytime soon."

Peyton looked back and forth between the two of them, tossed her jacket on the table and plopped in the chair next to Savannah. "Why do I have a feeling that I missed a lot while I was out?"

Savannah and Madison shared a knowing look, and then told Peyton everything that had happened, up through their conversation about Damien. They left out the part about Oliver, which Madison appreciated, since Savannah had promised to keep it secret.

"Wow," Peyton said once they were done, leaning back in her chair. "First of all, Perry Myles is a jerk. You deserve better than him. Now, on to Damien. I wasn't his biggest fan when we met him last summer, but now I agree with Madison— you should tell him how you feel." She turned her gaze to Madison. "Thanks for being there for Savannah."

"Of course." Madison had a feeling that, coming from Peyton, those words meant a lot.

"Now you have to tell us about your night," Savannah said. "How did it go with Zack? Since you got home so late, I'm guessing you hit it off?"

"It didn't go quite as you might think," Peyton said, and then she launched into the tale of her night.

Madison settled back in her chair to listen. For now, only one thing was certain—after tonight, things were definitely going to be interesting tomorrow.

www.campusbuzz.com

Who's hooking up with who on the Diamond ski trip?!
Posted on Thursday 3/12 at 12:05 PM
Ok sooo...we all saw the pics of Savannah and Perry on the ski lift. But then last night, Perry posted a selfie with Emily Nicole, and they looked SUPER close, with no Savannah in sight!

1: Posted on Thursday 3/12 at 12:33 PM
he prob got bored of Savannah and went for her friend instead! LoL

2: Posted on Thursday 3/12 at 1:01 PM
OR he found out that Savannah and Damien have been hooking up for MONTHS. they spend so much time together it's gotta be happening!!!

3: Posted on Thursday 3/12 at 1:15 PM
you also forgot that Peyton and Oliver—both known for sleeping around—are there, too. I don't even wanna KNOW what's going on in that house...

4: Posted on Thursday 3/12 at 1:59 PM
What happens in Aspen stays in Aspen?

chapter 25: *Savannah*

While everyone got ready the next morning, Savannah pretended to be cheery and happy—purposely avoiding asking if Emily Nicole had ever made it back to her room last night. Then, as Savannah had been dreading, Perry decided to stop being patient with her on the easy trails on Buttermilk and ski with Emily Nicole on Ajax instead. At least Courtney, Peyton, Evie and Noel took a lesson with her.

She'd also been dying to ask Courtney about what happened last night with her and Brett, but she knew her sister well enough to wait until they were alone.

Now they were at après-ski, and Savannah was acting like she was happy and everything was fine. But when Perry sat next to Emily Nicole and was touching her and flirting with her, Savannah's eyes welled with tears. He was rubbing last night in her face. So what if Savannah's agent had asked her to become friends with Emily Nicole, and also asked her to flirt with Perry? Savannah *couldn't do it anymore*. Emily Nicole was *not* her friend, and Perry Myles was *not* interested in her. And she didn't want to be around either of them for one second longer.

"Okay, that's enough." Savannah slammed her fists onto the couch, glaring at Perry and Emily Nicole. Everyone stared at her, stunned into silence.

"What's up?" Perry didn't move his arm from around Emily Nicole's shoulders.

"I can't sit here and watch this anymore," she said. "I want you, Emily Nicole and Noel to leave."

"Pardon?" Noel's eyebrows shot up. "You want us to leave the restaurant?"

The way he said it made Savannah feel like an oversensitive kid.

"I don't own the restaurant, so I can't ask you to leave it." Savannah crossed her arms. "But you *are* staying in my dad's house—because *I* invited you—and I don't want you staying there anymore."

"Come on, Savannah." Perry removed his arm from around Emily Nicole's shoulders and cracked his knuckles. "Lighten up. We're all just having fun. That's why we're here, right?"

"You can't want us to *leave*!" Emily Nicole widened her clear blue eyes as if she were so innocent. Which, after last night, Savannah knew she wasn't. "We have two more days left of the trip."

Savannah glared at Emily Nicole. Her, Perry and Noel leaving was exactly what she wanted. They were all just using each other for publicity and fame, and it was so fake. She would be much happier once they were gone.

"Actually, she can, since it's Adrian's house, and you're her guests," Madison chimed in. "If Savannah doesn't want you there anymore, then you have to leave. Right?" She looked at Courtney and Peyton for affirmation.

"If that's what Savannah wants, then yes, they need to

leave," Courtney said, at the same time Peyton said, "Hell, yes."

Savannah held her gaze on Perry's, unwavering now that she had her sisters backing her up. Perry actually turned his eyes away from hers, and while it was only a small victory, her body felt light from the thrill of it.

"It's settled, then." Damien clasped his hands together. "The three of you should go back to the house and pack your things. Or tell your guards to pack for you—whatever you need to do. It shouldn't take too long. Once we get back from dinner, we expect you to be gone."

"This isn't fair." Evie leaned toward Noel, her cheeks bright red. "Noel didn't do anything wrong."

Savannah's mouth dropped open. Why was Evie standing up for Noel? Evie was *her* best friend, and she'd seen everything that had happened last night. Her sisters had backed her decision…why couldn't Evie? Unless Evie had never truly forgiven Savannah for their fight on the night of her Sweet Sixteen?

"Noel might not have done anything wrong," Madison said, as cool and composed as ever. "But he's here with Perry, and if Savannah wants them both to leave, then they both need to leave. End of discussion."

"Right." Savannah somehow kept her voice steady after the blow from Evie. "I invited them so we could have fun, and this isn't fun anymore."

"We can't just *leave*." Emily Nicole slumped forward. "Where are we supposed to go?"

"You'll figure something out," Oliver said casually. "If you need a hotel recommendation, check out The Little Nell. They're usually booked way ahead of time, but maybe you can use your connections to get a room."

"You can't be serious." Perry chuckled and brushed his fin-

gers against Savannah's knee. "You're taking this too personally. We're all just trying to relax and hang out. And I won't
be able to recommend you for *American StarMaker* if you go
through with this."

He was giving her that trademark look of his—the one
that made girls all over the world melt—and his words made
her heart twist. But she yanked her knee away from his hand,
refusing to be fooled by him again. His being famous didn't
give him a right to use her and treat her like dirt.

"I can audition for *American StarMaker* like everyone else,"
she said. "I'll go to an open casting call."

Emily Nicole's jaw dropped open, hurt swirling in her eyes
as she looked at Perry. "You offered to put in a word for Savannah on *American StarMaker* and not me?"

"It's nothing personal." Perry shrugged. "You've got a great
YouTube presence, your voice is good—especially after some
help from auto-tune—and your vids are fantastic. You just
need to keep doing what you're doing, and your fan base will
grow. But Savannah's got raw talent that would get her far
on the show."

"Hold on," Emily Nicole said. "You think she's a better
singer than me? And you would put a word in for her over
me…even after last night?"

"You girls need to stop taking all this so personally." Perry
ran his fingers through his hair, making it look more messy-
perfect than before. "Both of you are cool, all right? So let's
chill out, be friends and enjoy the rest of this trip."

Savannah's temper blazed. "You've been texting me and
acting like you cared about what was going on in my life, and
now you're telling me you just wanted to come here to 'chill
out and be friends'?"

"Well, yeah," Perry said. "What'd you expect? I text a lot
of people."

Her hands shook, and she felt like the biggest idiot. What *had* she expected? For him to want to be her boyfriend, after a few hours hanging out at a party he'd been paid to attend, and some text messaging? It had been so exciting to think someone as famous as him was interested in her that she'd forgotten everything else. Like how she'd only let herself get involved with Perry because her agent had pushed her to talk to him. And how she cared about Damien more than she'd *ever* cared about Perry.

Her stomach churned when she remembered how Damien had watched her flirt with Perry all week. It was no better than how she'd felt watching Perry flirt with Emily Nicole. She'd ruined her chances with Damien. Because no matter what Madison had said, he couldn't still be interested in Savannah after these past few days.

"I don't know what I expected." Savannah clasped her hands together so no one would see how they were trembling. "But this isn't fun anymore, and I want to spend the last days of this trip with my sisters and my friends. So we're going to go to dinner, and like Damien said, we expect you and your stuff to be out of the house when we get back."

"Fine." Perry jutted out his chin. "I was ready to jet out of Aspen, anyway. There's a party in LA tonight that sounded like it could be fun. What do you say, Noel? Let's text Lara and let her know to expect us?"

"If Savannah wants us to leave, then we'll leave," he said. He turned to Savannah. "Sorry that we messed up your holiday."

His brown eyes were huge, and he seemed sincere. So she nodded and said nothing. What was she *supposed* to say to that? That she was okay with what had happened last night? Because she wasn't okay with it, and she was done pretending. She was just glad they were leaving.

"What about me?" Emily Nicole asked. "You can't kick

me out. I have nowhere to go. My mom thinks I'm spending the entire break at your house, and I can't go home because she's out of town, and I can't get a hotel room by myself. She'll freak."

Savannah studied Emily Nicole. Every time she looked at her now, she thought of her running naked from the hot tub to spend the night with Perry in the loft. But her forehead was creased, her eyes glassy, and she looked so lost. Maybe she'd gotten as caught up in the attention of the guys as Savannah had. And with Perry and Noel gone, what more could Emily Nicole do to her?

"Fine," Savannah said. "You can stay."

"Thank you." Emily Nicole breathed out a long breath. "I owe you one."

"Well, I guess that's our cue." Perry threw a wad of cash on the table and stood up. "We'll be flying to LA before you all get back from dinner. It's been an…interesting past few days. And Emily Nicole? Thanks for last night."

He winked, and then he and Noel were out the door.

Savannah didn't say much during dinner. Her eyes felt hot, her body felt numb and she worried that if she tried to pretend that everything was okay, she would break down crying in public.

When they got back to the house, Perry and Noel were gone, as promised. It was like they'd never been there at all. Even their room was spotless, thanks to the maids that came to the house every day while they were out. Now, everyone watched Savannah, like they were waiting to see what she would do next.

"I need to talk to you." Savannah grabbed Evie's arm and pulled her toward the stairs. "Let's go to our room."

"Okay." Evie followed Savannah up and shut the door behind them. "I was caught by surprise earlier," she said, wringing her hands together. "I didn't realize you were going to ask them both to leave…"

"'Caught by surprise'?" Savannah threw her bag onto the bed and glared at the girl who was supposed to be her best friend. "Everyone else—even *Madison*—took my side when I asked them to leave. And then you took the guys' side. Why would you do that?"

"I didn't take the guys' side," she said softly. "Perry's a jerk—you were right to ask him to leave. But he's not the same person as Noel. Noel didn't do anything wrong…"

"They're both in the same band!" Savannah raised her voice. "They were here together. I had to ask Noel to leave, too. And he's probably also a jerk, so whatever. I'm glad they're gone."

"Noel's not a jerk." Evie leveled her gaze with Savannah's, and Savannah stilled, shocked by how intense Evie was being about this. "He's a good guy. I know you were involved in all of your drama with Perry and Madison and Damien and didn't have time to notice, but Noel and I clicked from the moment we met. We got along really well this entire trip."

Evie and Noel together? Savannah couldn't wrap her mind around it. Except…on the first night in Aspen, Noel *had* talked to Evie a lot. Savannah had assumed he was just being friendly. When they were skiing, Noel and Evie rode the chairlift together, but Savannah thought they'd been stuck together because everyone else had someone to ride with. They'd also been sitting next to each other at meals, and they'd been next to each other in the hot tub last night… Savannah's lips parted as it all came together. Noel had been flirting with Evie this entire time.

And Evie was only going to get hurt by it.

"Perry and Noel are players," Savannah said. "They're going to get back on tour, have girls throwing themselves at them in every city, and they're never going to think about either of us again. It sucks, but it is what it is."

"You don't know Noel," Evie said. "How can you say that about him?"

"I don't know." Savannah sighed and fell down onto the bed. "This is all such a mess, and I hate it. I'm sorry."

"I know. But I like him a lot." Evie sat down next to her and leaned into the pillows. "He got my number, and he promised to keep in touch. He's already texted me saying he was so happy we met this week and that he can't wait to see me again."

Savannah stared at the ceiling, her entire body empty and numb. She said nothing. Because Evie clearly liked Noel, and nothing Savannah said would bring her to her senses. Only time would do that.

"I'm sorry Perry ended up being a jerk," Evie said. "And that Emily Nicole chased after him."

That was enough to make Savannah crack a smile. "It's not your fault," she said. "I don't think I even liked Perry that much, anyway."

"You just liked the idea of dating someone famous?"

"Yeah, I guess." She sat up, grabbed a small decorative pillow and hugged it to her chest. "He's hot, and I love watching him sing, so it was fun to get so much attention from him. I loved it every time he Tweeted me, or commented on my Instagram, and when fans speculated about us. It made me feel special."

"But you didn't actually like *him*?" Evie asked.

"I'm a huge fan of his," she said. "You know I've followed One Connection for years. So I felt like I knew Perry, but I guess that's different than having real feelings for him."

"Better to find out what an ass he is sooner rather than later, right?"

"Maybe." Savannah's heart felt like it had been run over all over again, and she played with the seams of the pillow. "I just hate how he ditched me for Emily Nicole in front of everyone. It was so embarrassing."

"The way he ditched you in front of *everyone*?" she asked. "Or the way he ditched you in front of *Damien*?"

Savannah groaned. "Is it that obvious?"

"Only because I've known how you feel about Damien since you first moved to Vegas," Evie said. "And I don't think Damien would have come on this trip if he didn't return those feelings."

"That's exactly what Madison said." Savannah shifted so her legs were under her. "But I'm not sure if I believe it."

There was a knock on the door, and Savannah turned to look at it. "Who is it?" she asked.

"It's me." Emily Nicole opened the door and poked her head inside. "Can I talk to you? Alone?"

Emily Nicole seemed so innocent now, in jeans and a fluffy light blue sweater, but Savannah couldn't unsee her being naked and running up the steps to do who knows what with Perry. What could Emily Nicole possibly say to fix this?

She turned to Evie, as if Evie could tell her what to do.

"I can stay here if you want," Evie said.

"No," Savannah decided. "It's fine. I can talk to her for a few minutes. Then I just want to be by myself."

"What should I tell your sisters?"

"Tell them I need time alone with my iPod," Savannah said. "They'll know what I mean."

"Okay," Evie said. "Good luck." She scooted past Emily Nicole and out of the room, leaving her and Savannah alone.

Emily Nicole closed the door and sat exactly where Evie had been. She pulled her hair over one shoulder, then rubbed her hands over her jeans, as if she didn't know where to start.

Savannah just stared at her, waiting. Emily Nicole had wanted to come in here—it was up to her to begin this conversation.

"Thanks for letting me stay," Emily Nicole said.

"I couldn't kick you out when you had nowhere to go."

"Still." She swallowed. "Thanks. What I did last night... I was really drunk. I know that's a crappy excuse, but it's true. Perry was flirting with me all week, and he made it seem like he liked me, and I've had a huge crush on him for so long... I'm sorry."

"You knew I liked him." Savannah fought back tears and ran her hands through her hair. "I told you about our texts, I told you about how I thought he liked me, and you saw how he backed off last night when he realized I was a virgin. Then you *slept with him*. And you're only here because *I* invited you. How could you do that to me?"

"That's what I wanted to tell you," Emily Nicole said. "I know it looked bad, and no one has any reason to believe me, but I didn't sleep with him."

"You ran up to his room naked and spent all night with him." Savannah laughed—thinking about it hurt like hell, but Emily Nicole's denial was so ridiculous that it was funny. "You really expect me to believe you didn't sleep with him?"

"I didn't sleep with him," she repeated. "You saw how much I had to drink last night. We did kiss, but I passed out pretty soon after I got up there. It's embarrassing, and I hate it, but that's what happened. I swear it."

Savannah's eyes widened. "He didn't...try anything while you were passed out, did he?"

"No!" Emily Nicole's mouth dropped open in horror, and she held her hands out. "Nothing like that. I wish he'd woken me up and helped me back to my room, but I just slept up there. I promise."

"Okay," Savannah said, since Emily Nicole seemed so sincere. "But if that's true, then what was that about when he left—when he thanked you for last night?"

"He was being a jerk," she said. "Is that so surprising?"

"No," Savannah said. "I guess not."

"Anyway." Emily Nicole pulled at the sleeves of her sweater. "I was hoping that since you're letting me stay, it might mean that we can still be friends."

"I don't know," Savannah said, shifting uncomfortably. She barely *knew* Emily Nicole. They'd had a blast when they were making that video together, but after last night, did Savannah really know how far Emily Nicole would go to climb to the top? She wasn't sure. "I'll think about it."

"Okay." She lowered her head. "I really am sorry."

"I know." Savannah believed her, but it was all so fresh right now that she wasn't sure what to do. "But it's been a long few days, and I'm really tired."

"All right." Emily Nicole stood up and headed for the door. "Thanks for listening."

The door shut, and Savannah was finally alone. She let out a long breath and allowed all of the sadness and frustration to wash over her. This trip had been awful, and she just wanted it to be over. But it wasn't just the trip. Her life was spinning out of control and she couldn't keep up.

Whenever her emotions took over to the point where she couldn't think straight, one thing always made her feel better—music. So she grabbed her iPod, locked herself in the bathroom, curled up in the empty Jacuzzi and selected her "sad songs" playlist. The first notes blasted from her earbuds, and the tears immediately streamed down her face. All the hurt, rejection and frustration poured out of her. Songs came and went, until Savannah had cried so much that her eyes burned, the tears dried in salty streams on her cheeks. She wasn't sure how long she stayed like that, curled up crying in the bathtub, but enough songs had passed that it had to have been at least an hour.

The song she was listening to ended, and she heard footsteps on the bathroom floor. She paused her iPod and forced her eyes open. Damien sat down on the marble ledge next to the tub, his eyes full of concern.

He must think she was so pathetic, crying in the fetal position in an empty Jacuzzi.

She pulled the earbuds out of her ears, not moving from where she lay on the cold porcelain of the tub. "How did you get in here?" she asked. "I locked the door."

"The bathroom lock isn't designed to keep out criminals." He reached into his pocket and held up a coin. "I used this to wedge it open."

"Oh." Savannah sat up and pulled her legs toward herself, wrapping her arms around them. "Okay."

"You'd been in here for a while, and you weren't answering when anyone knocked," he said. "Your sisters told me to give you time, but you were in here for so long. I wanted to make sure you were okay."

She stayed where she was, unmoving. But he waited, watching her, apparently expecting a response.

"Does it *look* like I'm okay?" She sat up, unable to meet his eyes.

"No, it doesn't." He sat down next to her, close enough that she could feel electricity hum between their bodies. "So, is this normally what you do when you're upset?"

"Listen to depressing music, curl up in a bathtub and cry?" She chuckled at how sad it sounded. "Yeah, I guess."

"Why?"

She twisted her hair around her finger. "When something's

really bothering me, I just like to get it out." She couldn't believe she was talking about this, here, with Damien. But he'd sounded genuinely curious, so she continued, "I like to completely give in to the emotion. If I pretend I'm not sad—if I try smiling through it, and pretending like everything's fine—it makes it worse. When I give in and let it out, I feel better."

"Interesting." He nodded. "I've never thought of it that way, but it makes sense."

"I don't understood how going out and pretending to be happy is helpful for *anyone*," she said. "But by letting myself feel everything, I'll wake up tomorrow morning refreshed and ready to start the day with new possibilities."

"So you're going to get over Perry in one night?"

"There's not much to 'get over.'" Savannah shrugged. "I never really knew him at all. I thought I did, because I follow his Twitter and Instagram and his interviews, but none of that's *real*. He was basically…a person I'd imagined in my mind. And I can't be interested in a person I dreamed up. Especially when…" Her cheeks flushed, and she broke away from Damien's gaze.

"Especially when what?" He studied her with so much intensity, as if his gaze could pull the confession out of her.

Savannah swallowed, her tongue feeling thick. Last night, Madison had been so convincing when she'd told Savannah to be honest with Damien, and Savannah had felt ready. Now she was so terrified that she couldn't think.

Maybe it would help if she reminded herself about what Madison had said. How she thought that Damien was truly interested in Savannah, because he was no longer trying to make the first move. Because he hated the possibility of rejection. How if Savannah wanted to know if there could be anything between them, she had to be brave and tell him how she felt.

He'd already seen her at her lowest point—lying in the

bathtub with tears, and probably mascara, running down her face. What did she have to lose?

"I'm not upset about what happened with Perry because he's never really been the one I was interested in," she said. "It's you. It's been you since the first day I came to Vegas, when you knocked on my door and introduced yourself."

He watched her in wonder, as if that had been the last thing he'd expected her to say. "I don't understand," he said, shaking his head.

"What's not to understand?"

"Where do I even start?" he said. "Over the summer, you chose Nick. Then when the school year started, you friend-zoned me. And at your Sweet Sixteen party, you spent most of the night flirting with Perry."

"I know." Savannah's eyes teared up again, and she buried her head in her hands. "I was talking with Perry as a fan—I honestly didn't think he would remember me or that I would ever hear from him again. But then he texted me. And after all those months of thinking you weren't interested in me, I figured if I was going to try moving on with someone else, it might as well be Perry Myles." She shrugged. "But it all ended in disaster."

"A disaster that started the night Madison kissed me at Luxe," he said. "It feels like that happened in another life."

"It really does," Savannah said. "She finally apologized, and told me she never should have kissed you."

"I wish I could say that I wish Madison hadn't kissed me," Damien said. "But I can't."

Savannah's stomach fell, and she took a sharp breath inward. "What?" she said. "I thought you didn't have feelings for Madison anymore. Now you're glad she kissed you?" She moved to stand up, but Damien put his hand around her wrist, stopping her.

"I don't have feelings for Madison anymore," he said, his eyes blazing with so much intensity that Savannah could barely breathe. "But it was the night she kissed me—well, the morning after she kissed me—that it started to sink in that Madison and I were never going to be good for each other. So while I hate the way it went down that night, I'm glad Madison kissed me. If she hadn't, who knows how long it would have taken for me to realize that she isn't the one for me? I might not have been as quick to see what was in front of me the whole time."

"Do you mean…me?" Savannah swallowed, hoping she wasn't taking his words the wrong way.

"Yes." He smiled, and her stomach felt like it was free falling in a million different directions. "Of course I mean you."

"But when you were first interested in me—the week I moved to Vegas—it was when you still had feelings for Madison," she said. "We barely knew each other."

"When we first met, I thought you were hot, and I asked you out," he said. "Then the Madison stuff happened, and I thought you'd chosen Nick, so I went on that summer teen tour. But it wasn't Madison I was looking forward to seeing when school started—it was you. When I got back to town, I was hoping you would reach out to me, but you didn't. That drove me crazy."

"The phone *does* work two ways," Savannah reminded him. "You could have reached out to me."

"That's why I went to that volleyball party," he said. "I knew you would be there. We hung out, and I started helping out with your YouTube channel so we would have a reason to spend time together. That was when I really realized I was falling for you. You have a good heart, down to the very core of it, and you see the world with so much hope and light. You believe in yourself, you think the best of everyone and you thought the best of *me*. You trusted me to help you spread the word about your YouTube channel. I've had tons of friends all my life, but none of them have ever believed in me like you have. You're beautiful, Savannah, and I've never felt as happy around anyone as I do when I'm with you."

Savannah's lips parted, and she saw herself through Damien's eyes. Not as the naive girl with her head in the clouds who worried too much about what other people thought about her, but as someone full of light and hope. Someone who could place her trust in another person and help him see himself in a new way.

"If you've felt this way for so long," she said, "why did you never tell me?"

"I was going to, on the night of your Sweet Sixteen party," he said. "I was waiting until the end of the night, since I knew you were busy with recording for the show and mingling. But Perry Myles was hanging all over you, and we didn't get a moment alone together. Then there was Oliver's car accident. He may be a jerk sometimes—well, a lot of the time—but I've known him since preschool. Seeing him like that was rough. When the doctors weren't sure if he would make it, I wasn't thinking about anything else. Once he woke up and they said he would be okay, you were on that family trip in Italy."

"And when I got back home, everyone knew I was texting with Perry." Savannah shook her head, marveling at how oblivious she'd been.

"Yep," he said. "So I backed off."

"I'm so sorry, Damien." She held his gaze, hoping he believed her. "You've always been the one I wanted, but I had no idea you felt the same, and I didn't want to be that girl who couldn't get over the guy who only saw me as a friend. So I tried to move on. But it's always been you. It's been you this entire time."

"So you would have chosen me over Perry Myles?"

"Of course." Savannah rolled her eyes. "Perry's a player. I always knew that—*everyone* knows that. I wish I hadn't—"

She didn't have time to finish the sentence, because the next thing she knew, Damien's lips were on hers. He kissed her slowly, as if he were exploring the depths of her soul. His hand cupped her cheek, his fingers tracing the dried lines of salt where tears had been pouring down her face, and it was like he could take away all the pain and betrayal from earlier. The crazy thing was…it worked. Everything that had happened today and last night didn't matter anymore. In fact, Savannah was *glad* it had happened, because it had all led to this moment.

His fingers traveled through her hair, brushing it off of her face. "You know," he said, his lips grazing hers. "You don't need the hair extensions, or the sparkly makeup, or the fancy clothes. I noticed you the day you arrived in Vegas, before you had all that stuff, when you were first walking down the hall of the Diamond. You shine, Savannah, because of who you are inside."

"Thank you," Savannah said, smiling. "But I have the hair extensions, and the sparkly makeup and the 'fancy' clothes because *I* like them. Not because I'm trying to please anyone else. They make me happy."

"I was trying to give you a compliment." He chuckled and moved to kiss her again, but Savannah placed a hand on his chest, stopping him. "What?" he asked. "Is something wrong?"

"No," she said. "Everything's perfect. But what you just said about me…you really mean it?"

"Every word."

"But what about next year?" The question tumbled out of her mouth. "You're going to college, and I'll still be in Vegas."

"I'll still be in Vegas, too," he said.

"What?" She tilted her head. "You're not going to college?"

"No," he said. "I'm going to college. But I got into UNLV, and they have a great publicity and marketing program. I love Vegas. I don't plan on moving anytime soon."

"In that case..." Savannah took a deep breath. "Do you want to be my date to Adrian and Rebecca's wedding? I know it might be too much, too soon, and that Adrian can be intimidating, but I have a plus one, and I haven't asked anyone yet—"

"Savannah Diamond," he cut her off, her name sounding like music when he spoke it. "Are you asking me out?"

"Maybe." She smiled shyly. "Are you saying yes?"

"Yes," he said, kissing her again. "Of course I am."

chapter 26: *Courtney*

The morning after Perry and Noel jetted out of town, breakfast was the most peaceful meal they'd had since arriving in Aspen. Courtney, Brett, Brianna and Madison gathered early in the kitchen and made pancakes and eggs for everyone. Well, Madison sat at the kitchen table and *watched* as the three of them cooked, but she was smiling, chatting and laughing—an entirely different person than the standoffish girl from last summer.

And Brett…well, Courtney felt closer to him than ever. She'd never given much thought to when she would lose her virginity—she'd always assumed it would happen in college—but being with Brett had been perfect. Every time he looked at her, she could feel how much he loved her, and how much she loved him.

She hadn't told her sisters yet, and while the drama of the One Connection boys leaving had distracted them, she knew from the way they watched her that they suspected something was up. She couldn't keep it from them for much longer, but for now, it was nice having it be just between her and Brett.

Evie wandered into the kitchen, followed by Emily Nicole, Peyton and Oliver. Savannah and Damien were the last two to join them—from their *own* bedrooms. They must have slept late because they stayed up so late talking last night. So late that Courtney had gone to bed before she could talk to Savannah about what had happened with Perry.

She was happy to see that Savannah looked bright and cheery—completely opposite from how sad she'd been yesterday. Maybe Courtney had been wrong last summer, when she'd thought Damien was a sleazeball. Or perhaps he'd changed and grown up in the past few months.

Breakfast was on the table and ready for them to dig in, when Savannah's phone blared the latest One Connection hit.

"I need to change my ringtone." Savannah silenced her phone and glanced at the caller ID. "It's Grandma. I should probably get this."

Courtney nodded, unsure of why Grandma would be calling now. She had called twice since spring break had started, but in the afternoon, between après-ski and dinner, since she knew they were skiing during the day. Whatever it was must be urgent.

A pit formed in Courtney's stomach. This must be about Mom. Had she relapsed last night? Gone to a bar and gotten drunk? Driven after drinking and hit something—or someone? As much as Courtney wanted to believe in her recovery, she wouldn't put it past her.

Courtney gripped the edges of her chair as Savannah picked up the phone. Hopefully she was wrong, and Grandma was simply checking in to say hi. Mom had been doing so well recently. If she'd relapsed, it probably had to do with how

Courtney still hadn't forgiven her about keeping Britney a secret. Then it would be partly Courtney's fault.

Her emotions must have been plastered on her face, because Brett placed his hand over hers. She managed a small smile, hoping to express her appreciation for his support, and he squeezed her hand, letting her know that he was there for her no matter what.

"She wants to talk to you." Savannah held her cell out to Courtney. "She wouldn't tell me what it was about…just that she tried your phone first, but you didn't pick up. She sounds… well, she doesn't sound good."

Courtney took the phone from Savannah—her case was blinged out in Swarovski crystals, the sunlight from the window bouncing off it like a disco ball. "Hi, Grandma," she said, her mouth so dry that her tongue felt like sandpaper. "Sorry I didn't pick up when you called… I was making breakfast and left my phone in my room. What's going on?"

"I have some bad news." Grandma sounded lifeless, and Courtney was positive that this was serious. Even in the worst of times, when Grandma had broken the news that Mom was going to rehab and Courtney and her sisters would be moving away, she hadn't sounded this hopeless. "It's probably best that you step out of the room, away from the group."

Courtney made her way into the billiard room, which had gone relatively unused all week, except for a few nights ago when Oliver had hosted a pool tournament that he'd won. Savannah, Peyton and Brett followed her inside, shutting the door. They watched her expectantly, as if asking for permission to stay. Courtney nodded that it was fine.

"Are you somewhere you can talk?" Grandma asked.

"Yes." Courtney braced herself on the edge of the pool table. "Savannah, Peyton and Brett are here, too." She put her phone on speaker and laid it on the green felt surface.

"Brett?" Grandma sounded confused, and Courtney wondered why. Then she realized—she'd been so concerned about keeping her relationship with him secret that Grandma had no idea how close they were.

"Rebecca's son," Courtney clarified. She wanted more than anything to add, *my boyfriend*, but now wasn't the time to drop that news. How had she kept so much from Grandma? They used to be so close.

"Can I talk to you and your sisters alone?"

Brett squeezed her hand, giving her an encouraging smile. "I'll be in the kitchen," he said, quietly enough that Grandma couldn't hear.

"All right." She watched him back away, his eyes not leaving hers until he reached the doors and let himself out. She wanted to pull him back inside and tell him to stay. But then her sisters were by her side, Peyton sitting on the edge of the pool table, and Savannah leaning against it, her eyes wide as she waited to see what Courtney would do next.

As much as she would *like* for Brett to be there with her, she didn't *need* him with her. Because she had her sisters. Whatever Grandma was about to tell them was clearly a family matter. Brett would be there for her afterward. Her sisters would be here with her now.

"It's just the three of us," Courtney said. "Me, Peyton and Savannah. What happened?"

"There's no easy way to tell you, so I'm just going to say it," Grandma said. "Aunt Sophie passed away in her sleep last night."

Courtney gasped, her hand flying to her mouth. Aunt Sophie was doing okay when they'd visited in January. Yes, she was low on energy, and was having trouble getting around, but she hadn't seemed like she was close to…dying.

She'd known this day would come, but she hadn't expected

it to happen this fast. Aunt Sophie couldn't be gone. What could Courtney possibly say? She couldn't make this better. She couldn't bring Aunt Sophie back. She couldn't turn back time so she could be with Grandma during these last few days, instead of vacationing in Aspen. She wished she could. But she couldn't.

"I'm so sorry, Grandma." Savannah spoke first, her words filled with so much raw honesty Courtney's heart broke even more.

"If we'd known she was getting worse, we would have been there with you," Courtney finally said.

"I know you would have," Grandma said. "But you know that Aunt Sophie had her bad days and her good days. I didn't want to worry you this time, especially since a few days ago, she had a burst of energy and we were able to have dinner together at a vineyard..." Her voice faded, as if recalling the memory hurt her. "I didn't think the past few days were more than another setback. I wouldn't *let* myself believe anything else. Then this morning, I thought she was sleeping in for longer than normal, and I didn't want to wake her, because she needed every second of rest she could get. It was your mother who eventually realized..."

An image popped into Courtney's mind of what it must have been like for her mom to walk into Aunt Sophie's room and realize that she wasn't going to wake up. A wave of dizziness hit her, and she gripped the pool table to keep steady.

"We'll fly out today," Peyton said. "It'll be a few hours before we're there. Is Mom with you?"

"Yes." Grandma's voice was so hollow that goose bumps rose up along Courtney's arms. "She just came out of the kitchen, with sandwiches."

"Good," Peyton said. "You need to remember to eat. Can we talk to her?"

They transferred the phone, and all Courtney could think about was how she couldn't believe that Aunt Sophie was gone. How could Grandma be so healthy, and have had a twin who got so sick? It wasn't fair.

Just like when Courtney and Britney had been kidnapped all those years ago, Britney had been the one who died. None of it was fair. It just *was*.

They talked with their mom for a few minutes, and she told them about the funeral plans. It was going to be small—the immediate family, plus some of Grandma's and Aunt Sophie's friends.

"One last thing," Mom said. "The graveyard where Sophie will be buried…our family has been using it for generations."

"That makes sense," Courtney said.

"It's where Britney's buried."

"Oh." She picked at a piece of felt on the pool table. Why hadn't she ever asked where Britney had been buried? Since finding out about her, the pictures in the baby book had been the way Courtney had chosen to mourn her lost sister.

But maybe it was time she faced this.

"I just thought you should know that she's there," Mom said.

"Okay." Courtney's head spun so much that she wasn't sure what else to say.

"I'm going to let you go now so you can get your stuff together and tell your friends goodbye," Mom continued. "And while I wish the circumstances were better, I'm looking forward to seeing you."

They clicked the End Call button, and Courtney stared at the phone, unable to believe this was all happening.

"I knew Aunt Sophie was sick, and that she didn't have long," Savannah said, her lower lip trembling. "But I still feel like we're going to walk into Grandma's house, and Aunt Sophie will be there, alive."

"Yeah," Courtney said. "But when we get there today… she won't be."

She was stating the obvious, but she didn't know what else to say. What had Mom and Grandma done when they'd realized Aunt Sophie wasn't just sleeping? Called 911, even though they knew she was past saving? Sat with the body, as if hoping they'd been wrong and she might still wake up?

Courtney couldn't let herself dwell on these details…it wouldn't help. So she stood up straighter and put on a brave face for her sisters. "Come on," she said, leading the way back to the kitchen. "Let's tell everyone that we're leaving."

When they'd filled their friends in, everyone reacted differently. Madison had said to let them know if they needed anything, and she'd sounded like she meant it. Oliver had offered to charter a plane to fly everyone else back to Vegas, and to buy Emily Nicole a ticket back to LA. Damien had offered to go to the funeral with Savannah, and Brett had offered to go with Courtney, but since Mom had been clear that they were keeping it small, they told them to go back to Vegas with Oliver and that they'd see them when they got home.

Courtney was in a haze the entire time they traveled to California. When they finally arrived, it was like she'd entered some strange parallel universe. Grandma had less energy than ever, and she spent most of that day and the next watching TV, staring blankly at the screen. Mom, surprisingly, buzzed around the house, managing arrangements for the funeral.

Now they were under the tent in the graveyard, watching the coffin lower into the spot beside Aunt Sophie's husband. It was the last moment Aunt Sophie's body would be above ground. Behind the lenses of her sunglasses, Courtney's eyes filled with tears.

Grandma sobbed, and Courtney squeezed her hand to let her know she was there. She wished she'd had more time to get to know her great-aunt. That conversation in January was the only one-on-one conversation they'd ever had, when Aunt Sophie had urged Courtney to forgive Grandma and Mom. Hopefully she trusted that Courtney would eventually heed her advice. But if there was any reminder that life didn't last forever, this was it.

At the end of the ceremony, everyone stepped forward individually to scoop up a small amount of dirt with a gardening shovel and toss it on top of the coffin. When it was Courtney's turn, she picked up the shovel, scooped up dirt and tossed it inside. It landed on the coffin with an echoing *plunk*.

She grabbed her second scoop, and her thoughts wandered to Britney. To how all those years ago, Grandma, Mom and Aunt Sophie had gone through similar steps while burying her twin. As the third shovelful of dirt landed on Aunt Sophie's coffin, it was like she was putting Britney to rest, too.

The ceremony ended, and the few people who were there said their goodbyes and condolences. Eventually only Courtney, Peyton, Savannah, Mom and Grandma remained.

Mom stepped up beside Courtney, both of them staring at Aunt Sophie's burial site. "Would you like to see Britney's grave?" she asked.

Courtney stared ahead, running her fingers over her key necklace—the one Grandma had given her for her birthday, the one that unlocked the trunk that held her and Britney's baby book. She didn't feel ready. How would she ever be ready for this? But this was something she had to do. So she nodded to her mom to lead the way. Her sisters followed, and Grandma stayed behind to say her final goodbyes to Aunt Sophie.

Britney's grave was a few over from Aunt Sophie's, the marker the same gray concrete as most of the others in the cemetery. Yellow mustard flowers were growing nearby, so Courtney picked one and placed it on top of her sister's gravestone. She read the dates—the ones showing that Britney had lived for only six months—and knelt next to it. The rain from that morning soaked through her tights, and she shivered, goose bumps rising on her arms. Her fingers traced the dates etched on the stone, and then traveled to the text underneath, where it said *Beloved sister and daughter.*

It was so unfair. Unfair that Britney had lived only six months, and unfair that Courtney hadn't known about her existence all this time. How many times had Mom snuck away to come here to visit Britney? So many years had passed when Courtney, Peyton and Savannah could have been visiting Britney here, too.

Courtney sniffed and wiped away a tear that had fallen past her sunglasses. She placed her palm on the damp ground in front of the headstone. Only a few feet away, her sister's body was buried, frozen forever at six months old. Her sister, who would never have the chance to grow up—whom Courtney would never have a chance to know.

She would never forget how Mom and Grandma had kept Britney's existence from her and her sisters. But they were her family, and the time she'd spent not speaking to them could never be regained.

She stood up, wiped the grass from her knees and rejoined Mom, who'd been standing behind her and her sisters. Together, they observed Britney's grave in silence.

"Thank you for bringing us here," Courtney finally said.

"After all these years, you deserved to come," Mom said. "I'm sorry I didn't tell you the truth sooner. It's one of the many things I would change about the past, if that were possible."

"We can't change the past."

"No," she agreed. "But I am sorry. For everything."

"I know," Courtney said. "And I don't want to keep blocking you and Grandma out. I want to move forward."

"You mean…you forgive me?"

"Yes." Courtney's voice was stronger than it had been all day. "I forgive you. But there can't be any more lies. Adrian swore there weren't, and I want to hear it from you, too."

"No more lies," Mom repeated. "You know everything. I promise." She stepped forward, wrapping her arms around Courtney. Courtney froze—her mom rarely hugged anyone, or showed any affection. She usually only hugged Savannah, and that was only on good days.

But Courtney hugged her back, and as they rejoined Grandma, a hopeful feeling swelled in her chest.

Perhaps this could be a fresh start for them all.

chapter 27: *Peyton*

They flew back to Vegas on Sunday night, since school would be starting back up tomorrow. It had been a long day, and while Peyton normally loved staying up late, she couldn't wait to get into bed and pass out. But, of course, Adrian and Rebecca were waiting for them when they got home. Rebecca had even brought cookies from the Diamond Café.

Adrian settled onto the couch, picked up a cookie and popped a piece of it into his mouth. He rarely ate anything unhealthy—Peyton couldn't recall ever seeing him eat dessert—so he must really be in need of comfort food.

He finished chewing and said, "I know this has been a hard weekend for you. I spoke with your mom and offered to come out to California for the funeral, but she wanted to keep it to her side of the family. I had to respect her request."

"You spoke to Mom?" Peyton hadn't thought that her parents had spoken at all since the divorce. She'd assumed that Grandma had always been the one to talk to Adrian.

"Yes, I spoke with your mom," he said. "I wanted to express my condolences. I didn't know Sophie well, but she was at our wedding. She was a kind woman."

Peyton nodded, unsure what else to say. Since finding out that Aunt Sophie had passed away, everything felt like a blur. Flying to California, seeing Grandma so distraught, the funeral, visiting Britney's gravestone and Courtney forgiving Mom and Grandma. It had been a long few days. She rubbed her eyes and yawned, wanting to collapse into bed.

"The three of you look exhausted," Rebecca said.

"Yeah." Courtney studied her cookie, which she'd only taken a small bite from.

"We just wanted you to know that we're here for you if you need to talk," Adrian said. "And we completely understand if you need a day off from school tomorrow."

"Hold up." Peyton was about to take a bite out of her cookie, but she paused in midair. "Are you giving us the okay to skip school?"

"Yes," Adrian said. "Although Rebecca and I would like you to join us for brunch."

"Okay." Peyton didn't need more than a second to think about it. Apparently her sisters didn't, either, because Savannah agreed, and Courtney did, too. Courtney had never skipped a day of school in her life, so she must have been really wiped out.

"What time should I make brunch reservations for tomorrow?" Adrian asked. "Eleven?"

"Eleven?" Courtney's eyes bulged. "Isn't that late for breakfast?"

"It's *brunch*, and eleven is perfect." Peyton glared at her sister to be quiet.

"I would rather do eleven, also," Savannah said. "I need to catch up on sleep."

"Eleven it is," Adrian said, getting up from the couch. "See you girls then. Sleep well."

"And remember, if you need anything, we're right next door," Rebecca added.

Once they were gone, Peyton collapsed onto the couch. Courtney and Savannah both took out their phones, their gazes glued to the screens.

"Damien's been texting me like crazy since we got back," Savannah said, typing furiously. "I'm going to stop by his condo before going to sleep."

"And I want to stop by Brett's, too." Courtney looked at Peyton, guilt splashed on her face. "I don't want to abandon you, but you do look like you could pass out and sleep for twelve hours straight."

"I could." Peyton ignored the jab at how tired she looked, since she knew she looked like shit. The circles under her eyes had gotten so dark that no amount of concealer would make a difference. "And I get that you want to see Brett. But it's been *days*, Courtney. Aren't you gonna tell us how it was?"

"How what was?" Courtney blushed and picked at her cuticles.

"Your first time with Brett," Peyton said nonchalantly. "Which I assume went well, since when I was packing I couldn't help noticing the *multiple* condoms missing from the box I'd brought. All in extra large, I might add. Wasn't expecting that one."

"Omigosh." Savannah gasped, her mouth dropping open. "Please don't tell me you've thought about the size of Brett's…" She pressed her lips together, as if she couldn't bring herself to say it.

"Penis?" Peyton supplied. "Nope, not something I sit around thinking about. But I had to take stock of what was missing to resupply—after all, it's important to be prepared, which is apparently a lesson Courtney learned this weekend— and it was hard to miss. So tell me…" She crossed her legs and turned to Courtney. "How was it? You can't lose your virginity and not tell us. That's against the code of sisterhood."

"It was the night we played Never Have I Ever in the hot tub, wasn't it?" Savannah asked. "I knew Brett walked you back to your room, and that he stayed the night, but I thought you were just *talking*. Because if you'd lost your virginity, you would have told us. Right?"

"I swear I was going to tell you both," Courtney said, before they had a chance to get in another word. "But we never got any time alone in Aspen, then we went back to California for the funeral…and it was a personal moment, you know?"

"I guess," Savannah mumbled. "I just thought you would have told us before now."

"I liked having those few days when it was only me and Brett who knew," she said. "And even though I'm telling you now, please don't ask me to spill every detail. Because those are for me and him only. Okay?"

"But you're happy with your decision?" Peyton asked. "You don't regret it?"

"I don't regret a single moment." Courtney smiled. "Well, I regret taking my bathing suit off for that stupid game in the hot tub. But everything else that happened that night?" She gazed out the window, her expression dreamy. "I wouldn't change a thing."

"You're in love with him, aren't you?" Savannah clasped her hands together, her eyes shining.

"Yes," Courtney said. "I am."

"But no one knows the two of you are together except for me and Savannah…and everyone else who was with us in Aspen," Peyton said.

"Madison, Oliver, Brianna, Damien, Evie, Emily Nicole…" Courtney counted off everyone who stayed in the house—

minus Perry and Noel, which was probably for Savannah's benefit. "They all know?"

"Of course they know," Peyton said. "Every time you and Brett look at each other, it's obvious that there's something up between you two."

"I thought we were being subtle," Courtney said, although she didn't sound like she believed it.

"You look at him with your whole heart in your eyes," Savannah said. "You were *not* being subtle."

"And you have to know that you can't keep it from Adrian and Rebecca forever," Peyton added. "Remember what happened with me and Jackson? Adrian finds out *everything*."

"I know." Courtney sighed. "But I want to wait until after the wedding. I don't want to add to Rebecca's stress."

"She has an entourage planning the wedding for her," Peyton said. "All that's stressing her out is keeping to whatever fad diet she's trying this month, and deciding which headpiece and what jewelry go best with her dress. As if choosing between a tiara and a veil is some huge decision. It's a headpiece, not a life crisis. Just *pick one* already."

"She does have all those magazines and websites reporting on the wedding," Courtney said. "They'll be critiquing everything she wears, and everything she does."

"If I ever get married, I'm going to elope," Peyton decided. "Months of worrying about stupid party details is *so* not worth it."

"Hey!" Savannah said. "I spent a lot of time worrying about the 'stupid party details' for my Sweet Sixteen, and it was a blast."

"I don't get how that stuff is fun." Peyton rolled her eyes.

"You don't give Rebecca enough credit," Courtney said. "She's trying really hard, and she wants you to like her."

"I don't give her enough credit?" Peyton shook her head.

"You're the one who thinks she 'can't handle' finding out about you and Brett. And after everything that's been kept from us recently, I would think you'd want to be honest with her and Adrian."

"I'm just trying to be considerate," Courtney said, although her voice was small, as if even she knew it was an excuse. "Anyway, I told Brett I would be at his condo soon."

"And Damien's texted me five times in the past fifteen minutes," Savannah said. "You don't mind if I stop by his place? It'll only be for a little bit."

"It's fine," Peyton said, although her chest felt hollow. If she texted Jackson and told him about this weekend, would he want to talk to her as much as Brett and Damien wanted to see Courtney and Savannah? She had no idea. And she wasn't even excited about her eighteenth birthday this week, because age was only a small problem now compared to the distance. "I have some stuff I have to do before going to bed, anyway."

They left without asking what "stuff" she had to do, and Peyton went back to her room, opened her computer and got to work.

The next morning at brunch, they talked about what had happened in Aspen (only the basics, since Adrian and Rebecca didn't need to hear about all the drama), and about Aunt Sophie's funeral. Once they'd finished eating and were picking at the remains of their food, Peyton brought a folder out of her bag. Stuffed with papers, it was red and unlabeled, with no signs of what could be inside.

"What's that?" Rebecca eyed the folder as if it were a bomb.

"Just something I've been looking into for next year." Peyton shrugged and placed it on the table. "I threw it together last night."

Courtney widened her eyes. "You've been looking into something for next year?" she asked. "Since when?"

"A few weeks," she said. "It's just something I'm thinking about. I thought Adrian might want to see it."

"I would like to see." He eyed Peyton, clearly curious, and pulled the folder toward him. Inside was the colorful stack of papers that she'd printed out last night. The one on top had a heading in large, bold letters that said *Gap Semesters*. Underneath the title, in smaller font, it said *Empowering three-month programs*.

"What's this?" Adrian asked, his fingers grazing the papers.

"It's some stuff about gap-year programs," Peyton said. "A friend mentioned it to me, so I looked it up. I didn't think I would like it, but it actually sounds kind of interesting."

"What's a gap year?" Savannah asked.

Rebecca leaned closer to Adrian, and read off the first sheet of paper, "It's a year between high school and college that you spend traveling, volunteering and learning in real-life situations." She smiled, and turned back to Peyton. "A friend of mine has a daughter who did one of these."

Adrian skimmed through the first few pages. "Interesting," he said. "Does this mean you'll go to college after this gap year?"

"I'm not sure yet." Peyton poked her food with her fork. "I don't know if I definitely want to do the gap year or not. But it sounds like it could be cool."

After all, soon Courtney would go off to college, and Savannah would probably want to move to LA. Her sisters were going to do amazing things with their lives…and Peyton would be left behind. Her throat tightened at the thought of it. She wished she had something that drove her like academics did for Courtney, and singing did for Savannah. But she didn't.

A year traveling the world—where she could start fresh,

away from everyone she knew—might be exactly what she needed to figure out what *she* wanted.

"These sound amazing," Courtney said, reading through the papers. "Latin America, the South Pacific, Asia, Africa, Spain, India...so many choices. I wouldn't be able to pick just one."

"I don't know which to pick, either," Peyton said. "Maybe you can help me."

"Of course." Courtney smiled. "I would like that."

Adrian placed the packet he'd been checking out down on the table, and he looked surprisingly pleased. "I'm going to look into this further," he said. "But from what I've seen so far, it sounds like a decent option."

"In the meantime, you should send your deferral in to UNLV," Rebecca said.

"About that," Peyton said. "I know the gap year says I have to defer college to go. And I'll do that. But if I still don't want to go to college after the gap year, then I'm not going. Okay?"

"But you'll consider it?" Adrian asked.

"Some of the stuff I read online said that gap years help students realize what they want to study in college," she said. "If that happens to me, then yeah, I'll think about it."

"I think that sounds like a great plan," Rebecca said, her eyes shining as she looked at Adrian.

"Cool," Peyton said. "You can keep the folder. I printed all that stuff out for you."

"Thank you." Adrian tapped the folder thoughtfully. "I have to admit, this caught me by surprise, in a good way. I'm glad to see you figuring out a direction for next year."

"I never said I was definitely going," Peyton reminded him, although the more she thought about the gap-year programs, the more she wanted to go.

"I know." He nodded. "And speaking of next year, there is something important I want to discuss with all of you."

"What?" Savannah asked. "Nothing bad, right?"

"Nothing bad," he assured her. "But I'm sure you remember that last summer I told you that you would be living in Las Vegas for one year, and that after the year was up, you could choose if you wanted to stay, or move in with your grandma and mom."

"Yeah." Peyton nodded along with her sisters. So much had been happening recently, and it felt like they had so long until they had to make a decision. But it was almost April. Summer would be here soon. It was crazy how fast this year was flying by.

"I do have custody at the moment," Adrian said. "But since your mom hasn't had any setbacks since returning from rehab, if you want to move back to California, that's your choice. I'm not going to keep you here against your will."

"I can't leave here," Savannah said quickly. "Not after Damien and I finally started dating. I'm staying."

"I don't really want to leave, either," Courtney said, placing a hand gently on Savannah's shoulder. "But what about what Mom and Grandma want? We can't do anything without talking to them first."

"I'm going wherever they go," Peyton told Adrian. Although did it really matter what she chose, since she might be traveling next year, anyway?

"You don't need to make a decision right now," he said. "Nothing needs to be final until summer. I just wanted to make sure it was on your mind, so you could start thinking about it."

"We will," Courtney promised.

"Anyway," Rebecca said, taking out her iPad and opening up the wedding folder. "Have you decided if you're bringing dates to the wedding? Because I'd like to finalize table assignments…"

chapter 28: *Madison*

Madison's first day back at school after spring break was absolutely awful. She'd hoped to see Savannah, Courtney and Peyton, so she could say *something* to them about their aunt, but they weren't there. But honestly, she wasn't even sure *what* to say to them. Madison knew nothing about their mom's side of the family. How was she supposed to be their sister—to ever be close to them like they were with each other—with so much standing between them?

To make things worse, Oliver had disappeared during lunch again. He'd flown them all back from Aspen, and as they went their separate ways, Madison had asked him to find her before lunch so they could sit together. He'd said he would. But then he was nowhere to be found. So she'd had lunch with her friends, smiling and laughing and ignoring the hole in her heart that Oliver had caused by acting like she didn't matter to him at all.

Once last period ended, she gathered her stuff from her

locker and headed out to the parking lot. She couldn't wait to get back to the condo and have some time to herself.

She'd made it past the fountain when someone called her name. Oliver. Her heart leaped, and she turned to face him, her hand clenched around the strap of her tote bag. He was standing outside the door, so casual in his Ray-Ban Wayfarers, his dark hair in his favorite "messy but styled" look. Minus the brace on his knee, the weight he'd lost and a few light scars on the left side of his face, he looked the same as he had before the car accident. But the energy that normally surrounded him was gone. It was like something was constantly on his mind, worrying him, and he didn't know what to do about it.

"Hey." She kept her voice cool, even though her insides warmed at the sight of him.

"Hey."

"What's up?"

"Sorry to catch you while you're in a rush." He stuck his hands in his pockets and shifted his feet. "But I was hoping to see you before you headed out today."

"I'm not in a rush," she said, even though she'd been storming over to the parking lot as if she couldn't get out of here fast enough.

"Want to sit for a minute?" He motioned to the wrought-iron bench next to the bubbling stone fountain. Madison had always loved that bench. It looked like it had come straight out of a fairy tale.

"Sure." She sat down, placing her tote at her feet.

He sat next to her and rubbed the back of his neck, as if he didn't know where to start. "I've been wanting to talk to you all day."

"So you avoided me?" she asked. "If you wanted to talk to me, that's not a good way to go about it."

"I wanted to talk to you alone," he said. "I knew you would

be with our friends at lunch. I couldn't sit there, knowing there was so much I wanted to tell you, but not being able to say any of it because everyone else was listening. I texted you three times during last period, and you never responded, so I rushed out here to make sure I caught you before you left."

"Oh." She glanced at her bag, where she'd stashed her phone beneath all her stuff. She'd been in such a crappy mood that she hadn't checked her texts for hours. "I haven't checked my phone since lunch."

"Figured as much." He smiled. "I know you avoid people when you're upset."

"I'm not upset," she said. "I was just busy."

"You asked if I would sit with you at lunch, and I said I would," he said. "You tried to be casual about it, but I know you, Mads. You cared."

"Fine," she admitted. "Of course I cared. I thought that after Aspen, we would be back to where we used to be. I thought I would have my best friend back. But then you disappeared again, and I worried that we would be back to where we were before spring break—back to when you were pushing me away."

"I don't want to push you away." He leaned closer to her, and her heart raced so much that she could barely breathe. "I've just been thinking a lot about our talk at Ajax Tavern, and I wanted to apologize again."

"About what?" She watched him closely, curious about where he was going with this.

"About how I blamed you for the accident."

"You apologized for that already."

"Not as much as I should have," he said. "Blaming you for the accident…that was messed up of me. You tried to stop me from driving, but I lashed out to hurt you, knowing it would make you back off. That was my fault. I'm lucky to have you in my life, and I'm not going to take you for granted again. I promise."

"Thank you." She laid her hand on top of his to show him how much she meant it. But she wanted more than this small touch—she wanted him to kiss her again. She wanted to know if he cared about her as much as she did for him. She *needed* to know.

"Why do I feel like there's something else on your mind?" he asked.

Her cheeks heated, and she looked down at her lap. What if she told him how she felt, and he didn't feel the same? She could lose him forever.

But Savannah had been honest with Damien, and now they were together. Didn't Madison deserve that same happiness?

"At Savannah's party, you said your feelings for me were real." She lifted her gaze to his again, wishing his sunglasses were off so she could see his eyes. "Was that true? Or were you telling me that so you wouldn't upset me more?"

"It was all true," he said. "But I never should have told you that, because it doesn't really matter." With that, he pulled his hand away, and her heart felt like it had been smashed.

"How could you think that?" Her chest felt hollow, and she traced the spot where his hand had rested on hers. She wanted to reach for him again, but she didn't. It would hurt too much if he moved away. "Of course it matters."

"No, it doesn't," he said. "Because in less than a year, you'll have been accepted by early decision to Stanford and will be getting ready for California. You'll get there, meet a genius science major and fall in love with him. And I'll still be here, going to UNLV. Because let's face it—even though my grades are picking up, I'm not Ivy League material. And even if I were, it's not my scene. But it's yours. And you're going to do amazing there."

"Hold up." She ran her fingers through her hair, trying to make sense of what he meant. "You're saying that your feelings for me don't matter because of something that may or may not happen a *year and a half* from now? Because you think I'll fall for a Stanford science major who doesn't even exist?"

"Yeah, pretty much," he said. "Isn't that what you've always wanted for yourself?"

"We have over a year until we go to college," she said. "This just sounds like another excuse. If you were lying about having feelings for me, I wish you'd just tell me the truth." She stood and grabbed her tote bag, ready to get out of there.

But before she could walk away, his hand was on her arm, stopping her. Heat surged from the spot where his skin touched hers, and although she knew she shouldn't, she waited for him to say something. Anything to prove she was wrong.

If he didn't, she was turning around and going home. She couldn't think past collapsing on her bed in tears, but she would survive. She always did.

"I'm not lying to you," he said. "Everything I said was 100 percent truthful. I couldn't have been more honest." He pushed his sunglasses onto the top of his head, his gaze glued to hers, his eyes begging her to believe him. "I'm falling for you, Madison. Hell, I already *have* fallen for you. And I hate the thought of you eventually leaving and forgetting about me."

She fell back onto the bench, dropping her bag on the ground. "I could never forget about you," she said softly. "Because I'm falling for you, too. I have been ever since the first time we kissed last semester. And remember, we have a year and a half until I go to Stanford. That is, if I get *into* Stanford. I'm still applying to UNLV as a backup."

"You'll get into Stanford," he said. "And when you do, you're going. You're not staying here so you can be with me and miss out on your dream school."

"Whoa." She held her hands up. "If I get into Stanford, I'm going to Stanford. But there are these great things called planes that'll let us visit each other on the weekends. And—in case you've forgotten—our families own their own planes. So I don't see why such a short flight would be a problem."

"I just don't want to hold you back."

"Then be honest with me," she said. "Why did you want to talk to me today?"

"Because…" He paused, as if searching for the right words. "Since we started talking again, there's been a distance between us, and I hate it. I can't lose you, Mads. You're the most important person in my world."

Her heart leaped into her throat, and it took a few seconds for her to speak. "You're not going to lose me," she said. "I promise."

"Good." He relaxed for the first time since they'd sat down. "You have no idea how long I've wanted to hear you say that."

"Really?" She smiled and leaned into him. "How long?"

"Since middle school," he admitted. "I never thought you felt the same, so I pretended that I only wanted to be friends."

"And this entire time, I had no idea." She tilted her head, thinking about all the time they'd spent together. "I never thought you saw me like that. You always seemed interested in every girl *except* for me."

"You couldn't be more wrong." He draped his arm around her shoulder and pulled her closer. "Yes, I tried to be interested in other girls, but none of them held my interest for long because they couldn't compare to you. You're the one constant in my life, Mads. No matter what stupid thing I do, you stick by me, and you think the best of me. No one else believes in me like you do—not even my family. And I think you're absolutely amazing. You go for what you want no matter who tries to stop you. You're smarter than anyone else in our grade. You speak your mind, you can always make me smile and you're beautiful. For me, there's never been anyone else. It's always been you."

His words left her breathless, and without thinking about what she was doing, she crushed her lips against his. His hand cupped her cheek, and he kissed her back hungrily, as if he couldn't get enough. She never wanted this moment to end.

But like he'd said, they had a year and a half until college. That was a long time. And she didn't want to rush one moment of it. So she broke the kiss and forced her eyes open, the intensity of his gaze taking her breath away.

"You're the only one for me, too." She felt like she was in a daze, like this was too perfect to be real. "But I never let myself think about the possibilities between us, because I was afraid that if I did, you would break my heart. I just wish it hadn't taken you landing yourself in the hospital for me to realize how much I needed you."

"You knew before then." He smiled and captured her hand with his. "Remember Thanksgiving? You were the one who kissed me..."

"Hey." She gave him a playful shove. "What about on Halloween? Before Larissa interrupted us, you were totally about to kiss me."

"You think so?" he challenged. Then his lips were on hers again, silencing her so she couldn't answer. This kiss was sweeter than before, and she felt so happy that she wanted to melt into him. "I was pretty bummed when you left on Halloween," he said. "The rest of the night sucked without you."

"Last semester was rough." She traced patterns on his arm, loving being able to touch him whenever she wanted. "You got me through it."

"I hated seeing you so upset." His forehead rested against

hers, his eyes shining. "But I have an important question for you."

"Oh, yeah?" she asked. "What's that?"

"How would you like to be my date to Adrian and Rebecca's wedding?"

"Wouldn't you technically be *my* date?" she teased. "Since I'm the daughter of the groom."

"Come on." He held her hand tighter. "Don't leave me hanging here."

"Yes," she said, and he brightened the moment she'd said it. "I would love to be your date to Adrian and Rebecca's wedding."

He kissed her again, and for that moment, everything was perfect.

www.campusbuzz.com

Adrian and Rebecca's Wedding Weekend!
Posted on Wednesday 4/1 at 5:12 PM
Who else has been following the TV specials about Adrian and Rebecca's wedding this weekend? It's so so so romantic—high school sweethearts reunited. My mom keeps saying that it's just like William and Kate, only in America <3

1: Posted on Wednesday 4/1 at 5:24 PM
I heard they were keeping it small? like, only the family and close friends?

2: Posted on Wednesday 4/1 at 5:47 PM
The ceremony will be small, but the reception is going all out!

3: Posted on Wednesday 4/1 at 6:15 PM
why are you all even talking about this on here? the only people from school who are going are Peyton, Courtney, Savannah, Madison, Brett, Damien, and Oliver...

4: Posted on Wednesday 4/1 at 6:45 PM
I get why most people on that list are going (the girls and Brett are obvious, and Oliver's family is close friends with the Diamonds) but why Damien?

5: Posted on Wednesday 4/1 at 7:00 PM

Damien is Savannah's date! The two of them have been together since spring break!

6: Posted on Wednesday 4/1 at 7:23 PM

Speaking of Savannah, I heard she went to LA a few days ago to audition for American StarMaker, and that she got a callback. I always knew that girl had talent—can't wait to watch her on the show this summer!

chapter 29: *Savannah*

We'll be there in ten minutes! See you soon!

Savannah paced around the lobby of the Diamond, rereading the message on her phone. Finally, a limo pulled around the front, and a flash of red hair reflected through the window. Before the bellman even had a chance to reach for the door, Savannah ran outside to greet her friend.

"Evie!" she said, wrapping her in a hug the moment she stepped out of the limo. "I'm so glad you made it."

"You know I couldn't miss the big wedding weekend," Evie said, smiling brighter than Savannah had ever seen. "I'm seriously so excited. And thank you again for giving me a plus one."

"Of course," Savannah said. She glanced back at the limo, watching as a guy stepped out wearing dark sunglasses, a baseball hat, and a hoodie pulled over his head. No one would have been able to tell it was Noel from One Connection unless they specifically knew to be looking for him.

"Hey, Savannah," he said, his hand sliding easily into Evie's. "Thanks for letting me come so last-minute."

"Anytime," she said. "Just don't break her heart, okay? I don't want to have to kick you out of the hotel..."

"Don't worry." He smiled. "She's in safe hands with me."

"I know," she said. "When I heard you were flying here for the two nights this week you have off from tour, I knew it meant you weren't playing around."

"Very true." He nodded, and then yawned. "Speaking of which, I have massive jet lag. Do you mind if I lie down so I'm ready for the rehearsal dinner tonight?"

"Not at all," Savannah said. "This weekend is going to be crazy—I'll have so much family stuff—so this might be one of the only times Evie and I have to catch up."

Which was how she and Evie ended up at the Diamond Café, at Savannah's favorite table in the back corner, talking over mugs of Signature Hot Chocolate.

"So, what's been going on with you and Damien?" Evie asked, her eyes shining. "I saw that you're Facebook official."

"Everything's amazing with me and Damien." Savannah smiled. "We've even been double-dating with Oliver and Madison."

"Really?" Evie raised an eyebrow. "Is that...weird?"

"Sometimes." She shrugged. "But Damien, Oliver and Madison have known each other for so long, and they're all really comfortable around each other, so it's not as awkward as it could be. It's actually pretty fun. We go to dinner, and the movies, and bowling."

"Bowling?" Evie crinkled her nose. "That sounds boring for Vegas."

"Oliver's trying to tone down his partying," Savannah explained. "And between keeping up with school, recording new videos, managing my YouTube channel and working with my new songwriting coach, I don't have the time to stay out late at parties, anyway."

"Speaking of YouTube, I can't believe you got that callback last weekend for *American StarMaker*," Evie said. "Well, I *can* believe it, because you're an amazing singer, but I remember us watching that show together at my house every summer. And now you might be on it!"

"It was just a callback," Savannah said. "It doesn't mean I'm on the show."

"I know," she said. "But it's one step closer."

"True." Savannah couldn't help from smiling. "I don't want to get my hopes up, because I might not get through this round of auditions, but it is pretty awesome."

She wasn't the only one who thought so, because later, when she was at lunch at the Grande Café with her sisters, Mom and Grandma, it was one of the first things that came up. They'd all gone with her to LA for the auditions and hadn't stopped talking about it since.

"I have to admit, I was worried for you before you stepped onto that stage," Mom said as she used her small lobster fork to scoop out the claw.

"I was so nervous, too," Savannah said. "I could barely eat toast and jelly that morning, my stomach was such a mess. But then when I stepped out on the stage and started singing, being up there felt so right."

"You should have seen the group of us jumping up and down backstage when the first two judges pressed the button that they wanted you to continue on to the next round of auditions," Courtney said. "Well, you *will* see it when they air it. It was a pretty incredible moment."

"Remind me what comes next?" Grandma asked.

"I'll go out to LA at the beginning of the summer for the next round of auditions," Savannah said. "It's the *American*

StarMaker boot camp week. It's at a hotel, and from what I've seen on the show, it's intense. There's usually about thirty people there, and half of us won't make the cut. Based on that week, the judges will decide which half of us will move into the house and be on the show, and which ones of us will go home."

"And you did it without Perry Myles's help," Peyton said.

"I'm glad I did it on my own," Savannah agreed. "Although I felt bad that Emily Nicole didn't make it past the first round of auditions."

"Whatever." Peyton rolled her eyes. "She may have an established fan base from being on YouTube for years, but you're way more talented than her."

"At least when we were in LA, we got past what happened in Aspen and are friends again," Savannah said.

"What happened in Aspen?" Mom asked.

"Oh…nothing," Savannah said, sharing a knowing look with her sisters. "Just girl drama. We're over it now."

"Well, I'm sorry your friend didn't make it through the try-outs, but you deserve this," Grandma said. "You've got a real shot at making it onto the show, and maybe even at winning."

"Thanks," she said. "But I don't want to get ahead of myself. I still have to get through boot camp week."

"We know." Grandma smiled. "But you were the best. You'll make it. And even if you don't, you're still a star to us."

"You *have* to say that," Savannah said, laughing. "You're my family."

"We believe in you," Mom said. "But with all the contestants living in a house together and being filmed all the time, we're also worried about you."

Savannah stopped twirling her pasta, dreading what was coming next. "What are you worried about?" she asked, sitting up straighter. "You're not going to keep me from doing the show, right?"

"We just want you to really think this through," Grandma said. "We know how stressed you were during the filming for *My Fabulous Sweet Sixteen*, and you'll be on camera even more for *American StarMaker*."

"I know." Savannah stabbed her pasta with her fork. "Which is why after the wedding, I'll be working with that publicist Adrian hired, to make sure I'm ready. I can handle this."

"I'm sure you can," Grandma said. "But if you decide you want to have a normal summer here with your sisters and friends, none of us will think less of you for it."

"And *turn down* this opportunity?" Savannah's eyes widened. "No way. I'm going to LA this summer. I'm going to be great on camera, and I'm going to do everything I can to win that competition. Plus, since Courtney and Brett are doing that summer program at UCLA, they'll be there to support me through all the live performances."

"We know you can't turn this down," Mom said, and Savannah could finally breathe again. "We're excited for you, too, but we just worry about you sometimes. I've seen that show before—you need to remember to stay out of the drama, and focus on the competitions."

"I watch the show, too, Mom," Savannah said. "I know what to do. And I'm going to rock it."

"We'll be rooting for you the entire time," Grandma said.

"Thanks." Savannah took a big bite of her pasta, not wanting it to get cold.

"Let's not have this be all about Savannah, since we're celebrating Peyton's eighteenth birthday today, even if we are a week late," Mom said. "So, Peyton, what are your plans for the summer? Are you spending time in LA, too? At the rate your sisters are going, perhaps your grandma and I should move out there as well."

"It's just for the summer," Savannah said, although her stomach fluttered at the thought that LA could be something more permanent in her future.

"I'm not going to LA," Peyton said.

"You're doing the Summer at Sea program, right?" Courtney asked.

"Yeah." Peyton shrugged, as if the program were no big deal.

"I thought you didn't want to go away for the summer?" asked Grandma. "That you were going to enjoy your summer until your fall gap-semester program started?"

"Well, I'm not allowed to live in the *American StarMaker* house with Savannah, or the UCLA dorms with Courtney, and staying here by myself would suck," Peyton said, picking at her chicken with her fork. "So I did some more research and found something called Summer at Sea. Apparently it's like living on a cruise ship for the summer, and you learn from 'real-life experiences' while traveling. It doesn't sound too bad."

"It actually sounds amazing," Courtney said. "You get to cruise through Europe—and get academic credits for doing it. I definitely want to go the summer before I go to college."

"It sounds nice," Grandma said, smiling. "And speaking of the next few months, your mom and I have something important we'd like to tell you."

"Okay." Savannah fidgeted and sipped her water. "What's going on?"

"Since the funeral, we've done some talking," she started. "When Sophie was in such a fragile condition, we didn't want to uproot her, since we worried that the stress of moving to another state would have been too much. But now that..." She choked on her words, and Savannah and her sisters looked down in respect for Aunt Sophie. Grandma took a few sips of water, composed herself, and continued, "Now that we have more freedom about where we can live, your mom and I have decided to move to Las Vegas. We'll be in the suburbs, away from the Strip, but we've chosen a house in a community close to your school."

"So we won't have to choose between California and Las Vegas?" Savannah asked. "We'll all be living in the same city?"

"Yes, we will, but you still have a decision to make," Mom said. "Peyton will be traveling for her gap year, but you and Courtney will need to decide if you want to continue living in the penthouse at the Diamond, or move in with me and Grandma. The house has enough bedrooms for each of you to have one of your own." She took a deep breath, and continued, "I would really like for you to come live with us."

Savannah opened her mouth to say yes, because she wanted to make her mom happy. But was leaving the Diamond what *she* wanted? She loved living here—the feeling of being in an enchanted wonderland forest every time she walked through the lobby, the incredible food at the restaurants like the Grand Café, the Diamond Café, Adagio and the Diamond Steakhouse, and the easy walk to the gym and the pool. There were also the room-service breakfasts with Rebecca and Adrian, and the spa days she'd had with Rebecca—who she was enjoying spending time with. The Sundays she and her sisters had been spending with Adrian had helped them get to know him, too.

And, of course, she loved having Damien a few doors down. Since UNLV was so close by, Damien was going to keep living in the Diamond next year while going to school. Then there was Madison. While they'd gotten off on a bad start, they'd had that breakthrough in Aspen. Savannah liked this "new" Madison much better than the one she'd first met over the summer. She wanted to live near her, and get to know her.

"I don't know right now," Savannah finally said. "I'm glad that both of you will be living in Vegas, and no matter what, I'll be spending a lot of time at your house. But I love the Diamond, too." Her stomach dropped at the thought of how disappointed Grandma and Mom must be that she wasn't jumping at the opportunity to move back with them, so she looked to Courtney. Courtney always had answers. "What do you want to do?" she asked. "I want to be wherever you are."

Courtney took a deep breath and looked at Mom and Grandma. "I'm glad that you both are moving to Vegas, too," she said. "It makes this decision easier. Because as much as I never thought this would have been possible, I love the Diamond. I'm happy here."

Mom ran her fingers over her hair, smoothing it down. "Does that mean you want to keep living in the condo instead of moving in with me and Grandma?"

"I would like to," Courtney said, unable to meet Mom's eyes. "Especially since like you said, you'll be living so close by. We'll still see each other a lot. What about you, Savannah?"

"I want to live in the condo, too," Savannah agreed. Mom sank back in her seat and frowned, so she added, "I'm so happy you're both moving here, and I'll see you all the time and stay at the house with you over some weekends. But if it's okay with you, I want to stay at the Diamond."

Nobody said anything for a few seconds. Savannah played with her napkin. Maybe she should take it back and say she would move in with Mom and Grandma?

But she didn't want to promise anything she would regret.

"It's your decision," Grandma finally said. "If you want to stay in the condo, then we understand."

"And you're welcome to stay at the new house with us whenever you want," Mom added, although she did look disappointed.

Maybe Savannah should rethink her decision? After all, Mom and Grandma's new house wouldn't be *too* far away from the Diamond. She would still be able to see Damien, and Madison, and Adrian.

Then she looked around at the places she'd grown so used to over the past few months. The green-and-white Victorian drapes in the Grande Café, the delicious brunches of fluffy pancakes and cinnamon-roll French toast, the energy from the groups gathered around gambling tables as they tried to hit it big and the stream of people walking through the colorful halls, ready for their next adventure.

When Savannah envisioned next year, she saw herself here, in the condo she'd moved into that Fourth of July all those months ago. She wanted to continue her Sundays with Adrian, to keep getting to know Rebecca during their spa days, to grab hot chocolate at the café with Courtney no matter what the hour, to work out with Madison in the gym, to walk over to Damien's any time she wanted. Living in Las Vegas had taken some getting used to, but right now, she was the happiest she'd ever been in her life.

She was happy that Mom and Grandma were moving close by, and she would visit them as often as she'd promised.

But the Diamond was her home.

chapter 30: *Courtney*

The Five Diamond Steakhouse was packed for the rehearsal dinner—which included celebrities, European royalty, business partners from China and well-known hotel moguls and their families. Mom and Grandma were there, too. Courtney had feared the worst, knowing that Mom hadn't seen Adrian since moving away from Vegas all those years ago, but beyond a casual greeting and congratulations, Mom stayed by Grandma's side all night.

Among the business partners there was the familiar face of Logan Prescott, Oliver's dad. He and Adrian had officially worked out their differences and were going ahead with their original plans for the new hotel in Macau. And Oliver's mom, Ellen Prescott, had been beaming at Oliver and Madison all night, as if she couldn't be happier that they were there together.

"It's complete crap that Ellen Prescott is happy that Oliver and I are together," Madison said quietly to Courtney over dessert.

"Really?" Courtney tilted her head in confusion. "Why do you say that?"

"You know how much she wanted Oliver to date you or your sisters—you saw it when she tried setting you up with him last summer, as if it were a Jane Austen novel." Madison huffed. "But now that Adrian has claimed me as one of his daughters, Ellen couldn't be happier that Oliver and I are together. She thinks it'll be good for Logan and Adrian's business partnership."

"Maybe," Courtney said, although she suspected Madison was right. "Or maybe she's just glad that you're both happy?"

"You talking about my mom again?" Oliver asked from his seat next to Madison. He smiled when he looked at her, his eyes shining with something that Courtney hadn't expected from the guy who until now, she'd thought was a huge jerk—adoration and love.

"Yep." Madison stabbed her salad with her fork. "She only likes us being together because I'm now one of Adrian's daughters."

He placed his silverware down and held Madison's gaze. "None of that matters," he said. "Because I would be with you no matter whose daughter you are, and I don't care who approves of us or not."

Madison grabbed his hand, and whispered something in his ear that made him smile. Watching them made Courtney's heart flip. They were so happy, and they could show everyone how perfect they were together without worrying about their parents trying to rip them apart. Courtney wanted that for herself.

Her gaze met Brett's over the table, his forest-green eyes filled with so much emotion that she could barely remember to breathe. She couldn't keep their relationship secret any longer. They loved each other, and she shouldn't have to feel guilty about that. Which was why, when dinner ended and only the immediate family remained, Courtney pulled Brett aside to talk to him.

"Hey." He eyed the hand that she'd rested on his forearm, as if worried someone might see. "What's going on? You've been off in your own little world all night."

"I don't want to keep us secret anymore," Courtney said, the words coming out in a rush. "I want to tell Adrian and Rebecca the truth."

"I don't want to keep us secret, either." Brett smiled, and Courtney wanted to kiss him right then and there. "I never wanted to keep us secret, but I didn't want to push you to tell them before you were ready."

"I'm ready now," Courtney said, holding her gaze with Brett's.

"*Right* now?" He ran a hand through his hair. "But they're getting married tomorrow."

"Yes," she said. "Tomorrow will be a fresh start for all of us, and I don't want that to begin with a lie. If I stand up there as a bridesmaid, and I still haven't told them, I'll feel like I'm going behind their backs. Haven't there been enough lies and secrets in the past few months? Don't they deserve to know the truth?"

"They do, but I'm not sure if *now* is when I would have chosen to tell them…" His eyes darted over to where Adrian and Rebecca were standing, and apparently they took that as a cue to join them, because that's exactly what they did.

"Is everything all right over here?" Rebecca glanced back and forth between Courtney and Brett. "You both seem worried about something."

Courtney swallowed, her voice stuck in her throat. She wouldn't tell them now if Brett didn't want to. But Adrian and Rebecca were watching them expectantly, and Courtney played with her necklace, unsure what to say.

"We actually have something we want to tell you." Brett took Courtney's hand and nodded at her. She froze, her heart racing, her mouth going dry. It had been a lot easier to think about telling them when they weren't standing right in front of her.

"All right…" Adrian raised an eyebrow, waiting for them to continue.

Courtney wished she'd had time to plan this out. Now Peyton and Savannah had moved closer, listening in, both of them nodding and watching her expectantly. Brett squeezed her hand, letting her know he was there. This was it.

She swallowed down her anxiety, and forced herself to speak. "I know that last summer, Brett and I promised that we wouldn't date, since we're going to be stepsiblings," she said, unable to look Adrian or Rebecca in the eyes. "But we spent a lot of time together in the fall semester, and in December— on the night of Savannah's birthday party—we started dating in secret. We've been together since. I hated going behind your backs, but we *love* each other, and we don't want to hide it anymore. I know that the timing right now isn't the best, but it didn't feel right for the wedding to happen tomorrow without both of you knowing the truth."

Her heart stilled, the blood draining out of her face as she braced herself for Adrian's and Rebecca's reactions. They were going to be so disappointed in her. They would repeat why her and Brett dating was a terrible idea, and it would be hard, but there was a small amount of comfort in knowing that she'd told them the truth.

Instead, to her surprise, Rebecca smiled, and Adrian let out a short laugh.

Courtney blinked, making sure this was actually happening. "You're not mad?" she asked.

"No, we're not mad," Adrian said. "I'm actually glad you finally said something. It took you long enough."

"You knew?" Brett sounded as astonished as Courtney felt.

"Yes, we've known for a while," Rebecca said. "We realized when we saw the two of you together in Italy in December."

Courtney's mouth dropped open. "You *saw* us together?" she asked. "And you didn't say anything? What did you *see*?"

"Nothing like that," Rebecca assured them. "We just couldn't help but notice all the time you spent together, and the way you look at each other."

"And you're okay with it?" Brett asked. "Just like that?"

"We did mean what we said last summer, about how dating a future stepsibling isn't something that either of us advised," Adrian said. "But we both know what it's like to love someone you can't, or shouldn't, be with." He shared a smile with Rebecca and continued, "Sometimes, no matter how hard you try, those feelings can't be controlled. And while the circumstances aren't ideal, after seeing how happy the two of you make each other, we fully support you being together."

"And we're happy that you told us, instead of us having to sit you down and drag it out of you," Rebecca said.

"So you mean that during all these weeks, we didn't need to be being so secretive about our relationship?" Courtney asked. "We could have just told you the truth?"

"Yes," Adrian said. "Although, since we did specifically ask for something like this not to happen, we don't blame your hesitation in being honest with us. It took us seeing you together to realize we were wrong. And we're sorry about that."

"Thanks." Courtney could barely get the word out, she was so shocked that this was all happening.

"So I guess you figured out that Courtney and I are going

to be each other's dates tomorrow?" Brett asked, pulling her closer.

Courtney leaned into him, warmth traveling through her chest at how amazing it felt to not have to hide her love for him anymore. They no longer had to worry that they were doing something wrong—to *feel* like they were doing something wrong. The realization made her feel lighter than she had in months.

"We had that figured out a while ago." Rebecca smiled.

"I can't believe it," Courtney repeated.

"I can," Savannah chimed in. "You should see the way you both look at each other. Someone would have to be blind not to notice."

Courtney's cheeks heated, and she held Brett's hand tighter.

"Well, as happy as we are for both of you, we should all head back to our condos and try to get some sleep," Rebecca said. "Remember, we do have a wedding tomorrow."

chapter 31: *Peyton*

Peyton was usually stubborn about dressing in her own style—iron-straight hair, dark smoky eyes and black clothing—but this was Rebecca's big day, and since she was a bridesmaid, her hair and makeup was being done in the same style as her sisters. Her nails, which she'd been painting black for the past two years, were now smothered in a French gel manicure. She'd even agreed to have the blue streaks in her hair removed for the weekend, although she planned on redoing them as soon as possible.

After hours sitting in the spa, her hair being attacked by hair extensions and curling irons, her face bombarded with airbrush machines, makeup brushes and itchy eyelash extensions, Peyton's stylist turned her chair around. At the sight of her reflection, Peyton took a sharp breath inward. She couldn't believe that was *her*.

Her hair fell in soft curls, secured by a braid around the crown of her head. Her makeup was all gold and pink, her skin smoother and more radiant than ever. She looked like a summer fairy princess about to step into a magazine cover shoot.

"Wow, Peyton," Savannah said from the chair next to hers. "This could be a new look for you—you look like a high-fashion model. Tyra Banks would be freaking out over your perfect bone structure."

Peyton studied her face in the mirror. "It looks good for the wedding, but it's not *me*. I'm not giving up my own style."

"Figured." Savannah shrugged. "I just wanted to let you know how pretty you look."

"Thanks." Peyton smiled at her youngest sister, whose hair and makeup was done in the exact same way, the curls and light makeup making her look like a fresh young pixie. "You look gorgeous, too."

Rebecca's complicated updo was taking longer than the bridesmaids' simpler style, so it was soon time to part ways, although Rebecca's mom would be by her side for the entire day.

"You're going to look absolutely beautiful," Savannah said to Rebecca. "I still can't believe that *Yumi Katsura* custom-designed your gown for you…and that it's going to be in *Vogue!*"

"Thank you." Rebecca smiled, her cheeks flushed. "You girls look beautiful, too."

Savannah's stylist placed her hand on her shoulder to get her attention. "Come with me," she said, leading all the bridesmaids into their connected suite. They were helped into the gold silk dresses made by… Peyton glanced at the label one more time. J. Mendel. Another designer Savannah had fawned over while they were getting fitted.

"I know you weren't happy about the color, but the dresses do look pretty," Courtney said to Peyton after they were dressed.

"At least it's not pale pink or purple." Peyton adjusted the

beaded strapless bodice, and let her stylist slip a dainty diamond bangle on her wrist. "By the way, I still can't believe
you told Adrian and Rebecca about you and Brett."

"I know," Savannah chimed in. "I can't stop thinking about
it. But you look so much happier now that you don't have to
keep it from them."

"I feel happier, too." Courtney beamed. "Like we all have
a fresh start."

The three of them chatted easily, like they always did. The
only one of them not in the conversation was Madison. She'd
been quiet all morning, and now she was having a hushed
conversation with her stylist.

It was strange that this girl, whom Peyton barely knew, was
her sister. But Madison had ended up being nicer than she'd
seemed last summer. She might actually be fun.

Peyton never thought that this would happen, but she
wanted to get to know her better.

She took out her phone and snapped a selfie. "We should
take some sister photos before the craziness begins," she said.

"Do you want me to take them for you?" Madison asked.

"No," Peyton said. "You should be in them."

Madison tilted her head, as if she couldn't believe Peyton had
asked. She clasped her hands in her lap and glanced at Courtney and Savannah, who watched her expectantly. "Really?"
she asked. "Are you sure?"

"Of course," Peyton said.

"Thanks," she said, standing up to join them. "I would
like that."

For the next few minutes, the four of them posed around
the dressing room as the stylists snapped pictures of them with
their iPhones. They laughed, made silly faces, joked around
and wrapped their arms around each other—like sisters.

They were perfecting their most ridiculous duck faces when

someone knocked on the door. Savannah giggled, and they broke their poses.

"Come in," Peyton called out to whoever was out there.

She expected it would be Rebecca, but it was Adrian who stepped inside the bridesmaids' suite, as sleek as ever in his tuxedo. His blond hair was styled back perfectly, his eyes shone and his face was glowing. This was the happiest and most laid-back that Peyton had ever seen him.

"I'm glad that the four of you are ready early," he said, holding up a shopping bag he'd carried inside. "Because I have something I want to give you."

Peyton eyed the bag, curious about what it held.

"I know that Rebecca carefully picked out every detail of your outfits today." He sat down on the couch, and they all sat down around him, making sure not to wrinkle their silk dresses. "But I asked her if it was all right to give you these to wear. She agreed the present was perfect, and that they would look beautiful with your dresses."

"What are they?" Savannah asked, leaning forward as if she would get a peek.

He pulled four small velvet boxes out of the bag, and handed one to each of them.

Peyton opened hers and gasped. Inside were gorgeous diamond earrings—studs that sparkled everywhere the light hit. They were elegant, but simple enough that they wouldn't clash with Peyton's style. She'd never owned anything so beautiful.

"I thought that the four Diamond sisters should have matching diamond earrings," Adrian explained.

"I love them," Savannah said, taking them out of the box and fastening them in her ears. She walked over to the mirror and looked at them from the side, admiring how they sparkled. "Thank you so much."

"They're perfect," Courtney agreed. "Thank you. And thank

you again for being so understanding about what Brett and I told you last night."

"I'm just glad you don't feel like you have to keep secrets anymore," he said. "As Rebecca said, we're both happy that you and Brett were honest with us."

"Rebecca's a great person," Courtney said. "I can't wait to see you marry her." She tried to put her earrings in, but struggled without being able to see what she was doing, so she got up and joined Savannah at the mirror.

"You didn't have to buy these for me." Madison blinked, her eyes glassy, as if she were about to cry. "But thank you for including me with the rest of the family."

"Of course," he said. "You're part of this family. All of you are." Adrian smiled at her, and turned his attention back to all of them. "I'm sorry that I wasn't a part of your lives until recently. I thought keeping my distance from you was for the best, but I was wrong. Seeing you through this year showed me how much I've missed. So while today is about my love for Rebecca, it means more than that to me. It's about all of us becoming a family."

Peyton swallowed back tears, willing herself not to cry. Adrian would never be able to make up for the time he'd lost with them, but the earrings held a promise—a bright, sparkling promise of new memories to come.

She realized she was still holding the box, and that she was the only one who hadn't put on her earrings. But while she knew her thoughts shouldn't be on herself today, she still felt like an outsider. Because with Courtney and Brett's relationship finally being accepted by Adrian and Rebecca, Madison and Oliver unable to keep their hands off each other, Savannah and Damien looking so happy together and the big wedding happening today with Adrian and Rebecca...Peyton felt a little left out. Maybe she was never meant to find love.

"Is something wrong?" Adrian asked, his voice surprisingly gentle.

"No, nothing's wrong," she lied. "The earrings are very pretty."

"I'm glad you like them," he said. "And I have some news that might put a smile on your face. A *real* smile."

"Okay..." Peyton waited, a bit nervously.

Adrian ran his hands over his pants. "Over the past few weeks—since your eighteenth birthday—I've been reconsidering my decision regarding Jackson."

Peyton's heart leaped. "What about him?"

"With your plan to take a gap year, you'll need a guard around at all times who's able to go undercover as a fellow student," Adrian began. "And while I do still worry about Jackson's feelings for you affecting how he does his job, he's one of the best. It wouldn't be a stretch for him to pull off nineteen or twenty in a gap-year setting."

"No way." Peyton's head spun so much that everything blurred around her. "You don't mean..."

Adrian held a hand up so he could continue. "I discussed the idea with Jackson, along with my concerns, and he promised that protecting you would be his top priority. I had my people talk with the owners of the programs you're considering, and everything is settled. Jackson will be undercover as a gap-year student, serving as your guard to make sure you're protected at all times."

"Are you serious?" Peyton asked, her eyes wide.

"Of course I'm serious," he said. "Consider it my birthday present to you. I trust that you're okay with this?"

Peyton clutched the jewelry box to her chest. "Yes!" she exclaimed, sounding as giddy as Savannah on a shopping spree. "Of course I'm okay with this. It's the most perfect present ever."

She jumped up from the couch and wrapped her arms around her father in a hug. She wasn't normally a hugger, but she didn't know how else to express how much this meant to her. He hugged her back tightly, and she squeezed her eyes shut, not wanting any tears to escape.

"What changed your mind?" she asked, letting go and stepping back.

"Rebecca calls it 'wedding fever.'" He laughed. "This is one of the happiest days of my life, and I want you and your sisters to be happy, too. Plus, the practicality behind the arrangement was impossible to ignore."

"Of course," Peyton said, unable to stop smiling. She put on her earrings, amazed that she would be spending all of next year with *Jackson*. It made her want to explode with happiness.

"I have more good news for you, too," Adrian said. "I wanted it to be a surprise, but we have so much more to do today with the photo shoots and the press interviews, so I thought you should know now."

"What?" Peyton asked, watching him expectantly. How could anything make her happier than what she'd just learned?

"Jackson will be attending the wedding, and the party planner was able to arrange it so he'll be at your table for the reception, as your date."

"You mean he's here? Now?" Her stomach jumped into her throat, and she glanced at her phone, lying on the table. "How long has he known about this? Why hasn't he told me?"

"His coming to the wedding was very last-minute," Adrian said. "After Rebecca and I saw how happy Courtney and Brett were at our acceptance of their relationship, and now that you're eighteen and a relationship with Jackson is no longer a potential legal issue, we wanted to see you just as happy. So we had Jackson catch a flight this morning. He's not here yet, but he'll arrive in time for the ceremony. We specifically asked him to let it be a surprise, so hopefully you don't hold it against him that he hasn't personally contacted you to share the news.

"But," he continued, glancing at his watch, "we have a long day today, and I need you girls to have your head in the game. We should be heading to the lobby now to begin taking the photos. And I must say, the four of you look beautiful." He held his arm out, offering it to Peyton. "Are you ready?"

Peyton took his arm, and Savannah was quick to take the other. With Madison and Courtney close by their sides, the five of them left the bridesmaid suite together.

The majority of the day was a boring string of photo shoots, hair and makeup touch-ups and interviews. Peyton's stomach tumbled the entire time with the anticipation of seeing Jackson.

Once all the photos and interviews were finished, she and her sisters were escorted back to the bridesmaid suite so the stylists could freshen them up. Savannah and Madison chattered away a few chairs over, but Peyton's mind was such a jumbled mess that she needed a break. She closed her eyes as her hair was sprayed into place, her legs bouncing in her seat, and sipped the espresso that had been brought to her.

Courtney came over and sat down in the seat next to her. "Are you nervous about seeing Jackson?" she asked.

"Yes," Peyton said, tapping her nails on the armrests. "What if when we see each other again, the spark between us is gone? What if Jackson was right, and I only thought there was something between us because we weren't allowed to be together?"

"I don't think that will happen," Courtney said. "But if it does, at least you'll have closure. It's better than wondering forever."

"You're right." She took a deep breath and popped a piece of gum into her mouth. "These past months when I thought

I would never know what could have happened between us have been driving me crazy."

"I've never seen you get this worked up over a guy." Courtney smiled. "I can tell how much you care about him."

"Yeah," Peyton said. "I really do."

Once they were freshened up and ready to go, the wedding planner came into the dressing room to escort them to their places. The guests were already seated, although it was difficult to see anything with the doors closed. Peyton tried to peek, and while she could just barely spot Mom and Grandma in the back, she couldn't see Jackson.

Could he have backed out last-minute and decided not to come?

"It's impossible to see everyone from this angle," Courtney said to her quietly. "But Jackson's there."

"You see him?" She stood on her tiptoes to get a better view.

"No," Courtney said. "But Adrian said he'll be here. He wouldn't have told you that if he wasn't sure."

Peyton lowered her heels, took a deep breath and tried to relax. But even though she was about to walk down an aisle in front of celebrities, famous entrepreneurs and royalty, she was more nervous to see Jackson—the young bodyguard from Omaha, Nebraska.

If he was even there.

"Do just what we did in the rehearsal," the wedding planner reminded them, handing them each a huge bouquet. "Smile, take your time walking down the aisle and hold your bouquets at belly-button level. Make sure your arms don't droop. And Peyton, untuck your hair from behind your ear. It's supposed to fall softly around your face."

"Sorry." Peyton moved her hair back into place.

The wedding planner nodded, and the first notes from the

string quartet rang through the air. The officiant was the first to walk down the aisle, followed by Adrian, his best man—a famous Hollywood actor who had been friends with Adrian for years—and then Brett.

Next up were the bridesmaids. Since she was the oldest, Peyton had to go first, and she stepped through the doors to the outside terrace.

The designers had turned the patio into a flowered wonderland. Pink and purple bouquets in wrought-iron stands lined the pews, and purple flower arrangements that must have been seven feet tall stood against the hedges. The altar was taller than some of the surrounding trees, consisting mainly of woven vines that came together in a dome at the top, with sheer white drapery flowing from the center down the edges. A golden chandelier hung from the middle. Above it all, the gleaming gold tower of the Diamond Residences rose overhead, as if keeping watch over the ceremony.

Peyton felt the eyes on her when she entered, and her vision blurred, but she steadied herself and walked down the rose-petal-covered aisle. She tried to smile and not rush, despite wanting to hurry to the front so everyone would stop watching her.

Finally she made it, and she took her designated spot. She faced the audience, and that was when she saw him.

Jackson sat in the third row, his hazel eyes lighting up when they met hers. He wore a pressed tux as sleek as the ones worn by the attending celebrities, and his hair had grown out from the shorn buzz cut he'd kept while working as her guard. It was long enough now that she would be able to run her fingers through it, and it made him look younger. It was perfect for going undercover as a college student.

He beamed at her, and her breath quickened—she wanted to run to him and wrap her arms around him and tell him how happy she was that Adrian accepted them being together, and that he was here. But while she normally didn't mind making a commotion, this was her father's wedding, and a proper greeting would have to wait until later. So she smiled at Jackson with the promise of speaking to him soon, and watched her sisters walk down the aisle.

The song changed to "Here Comes the Bride," the guests stood and Rebecca made her way down the aisle on the arm of her father. In her floor-length, white lace wedding gown, her hair curled in a half-down, half-up bundle on her head, and a dainty headpiece of woven diamonds, she fit the press-given title of the "Duchess of Las Vegas" perfectly.

Adrian watched Rebecca with so much love and adoration, and her gaze was on him the entire time. She joined him at the altar, and when he took her hands, it was clear that she was the only person in the world he was seeing. During their vows, Adrian talked about how Rebecca was his first love in high school, and that while their lives had diverted for a time, it had allowed them to grow as people. He said he believed that it was meant to be between the two of them, that she was his one true love, and that he couldn't wait to start the rest of his life with her. Peyton's eyes watered, and she blinked away the tears, hoping no one had noticed.

Rebecca shared a similar story, about how Adrian had always held her heart. She promised to love him always, and to love his family, as well. She glanced at Peyton and her sisters at that part, and Peyton smiled back at Rebecca, promising herself to stop being so hard on her new stepmother and to give her a chance.

Adrian and Rebecca exchanged rings, were pronounced man and wife, and they kissed. They floated back down the aisle, and Peyton and the rest of the wedding party followed them out, just as they'd practiced last night. The doors closed behind them, and Adrian and Rebecca shared a longer kiss. Once they broke off, the members of the wedding party walked up to them, hugging them and offering their congratulations.

"I'm really happy that you're a part of our family now," Peyton said to Rebecca, picking at a stem of her bouquet.

"Thank you, Peyton." Rebecca beamed, and pulled her into a hug. "You have no idea how much that means to me."

Brett was the next to offer his congratulations, and Peyton stepped back to join her sisters.

"So, you finally decided to give Rebecca a chance?" Savannah asked.

"She's part of our family now, so I figured it couldn't hurt." Peyton shrugged, not wanting to bring *too* much attention to her change of heart, and Savannah smiled.

"If you're in the wedding party, please follow me to the bridal suite," the wedding planner announced. "There's champagne and hors d'oeuvres waiting for you." She held up her hand to lead the way, but Peyton glanced behind her, her heart pulling her back to where the guests were filtering out of the ceremony.

"Would you mind if I meet you there in ten minutes?" Peyton asked Adrian. "There's someone I need to see."

"And I think that young man is looking forward to seeing you, too." He nodded. "But please make it brief—we want you there for the champagne toast. You'll have plenty of time to spend with Jackson at the reception tonight."

"I'll be quick, I promise." Peyton handed her bouquet to Courtney and held up her dress slightly to make sure she didn't trip on it. "I'll see you all soon."

She waited behind a column, twisting her hands and trying to blend in, despite the gold bridesmaid dress. Since Jackson was in the third row, it took a while for him to make it out, but he finally did. His eyes scanned the area—he was clearly looking for someone.

"Jackson," Peyton called in a loud whisper. His gaze met hers, and she smiled, motioning for him to join her.

"Is there a reason why you're hiding behind this column?" he asked, his hazel eyes dancing with amusement.

"I only have a few minutes, but I had to see you before going back to the bridal suite for the toast." Peyton studied Jackson, unable to believe that he was here, and her thoughts came out in a jumbled rush. "I'm so sorry about everything," she said. "I never wanted to get you fired, or for you to risk your career for me. You're one of the few people I've ever opened up to, but I was only thinking about myself, and I messed up. I hope you can forgive me, but it won't feel real until I hear it from you."

"Of course I forgive you." He laughed and took her hands in his, as if the idea of *not* forgiving her was ridiculous. "I was upset at first, and I wasn't sure what to do, which is why I needed time to think everything over. But I wasn't angry at you—I was angry at myself. Our relationship was supposed to be professional, and I let myself fall for you. I told myself that the move to New York was for the best, but as hard as I tried to get over you, I couldn't. You've been on my mind every day since the last time we saw each other. You proved to be more distracting to me when I was away than you ever could have been if I were here, because I didn't want your protection left in anyone else's hands but my own."

Her heart raced at his words. Could it really be true? It had to be. He wouldn't have said that if he didn't mean it.

"I've thought about you every day, too." Peyton blinked away a tear and gripped at the fabric of her dress. "But I had no idea you felt the same. If I did, I would have fought to be together no matter what."

"Which is exactly why I didn't tell you," he said. "Besides the fact that nothing could happen between us until you turned eighteen, you were just getting to know your father. He would never have supported us being together until you were of legal age, and I couldn't let myself be responsible for ruining your relationship with him."

She released her grip on her dress, letting it fall over her shoes, and straightened her shoulders. "You wouldn't have ruined my relationship with Adrian," she said.

"I would have driven a wedge between you two," he insisted. "But a few weeks ago, Rebecca called me. She told me that you were looking into doing a gap-year program—I'm glad you liked my suggestion, by the way—and that you would need an undercover guard. She couldn't promise anything at the time, but she said that if you decided to do that program, and if I was still interested in working for your family, she would talk with Adrian about hiring me for the job."

"And you told her you were interested?" She already knew the answer, but she wanted to hear it from him.

"Without hesitation."

"Wow." Peyton's skin tingled, and she smiled. This was actually happening. But despite her happiness, guilt twinged in her chest.

"What's wrong?" Jackson asked.

"I had no idea Rebecca was doing all of that," she said. "I wish I'd known earlier."

"She didn't want to get your hopes up, in case she couldn't get Adrian on board with the plan," he said. "It was only last night that he gave the official go-ahead. From there, he arranged for me to fly out here and tell you the news myself." He watched her, his eyes serious. "What are you thinking right now? You *are* glad I'm here, right?"

"I'm just wondering how long it's going to take for you to

kiss me." Peyton smiled. "Everyone's waiting for me in the bridal suite, so I don't have all day—"

He pressed his lips to hers, and she melted into him, everything else fading into the background. But what if someone saw? Her breath caught, and she almost pulled away... then she remembered that they didn't have to hide anymore. They were allowed to be together.

And he would be by her side for the next year as they traveled the world.

chapter 32: *Madison*

The moment that Madison walked into the ballroom for Adrian and Rebecca's wedding reception, she knew it would be a blowout that made Savannah's Sweet Sixteen party look tame.

Red-and-gold embroidered cloths covered the many tables surrounded by golden chairs, dozens of giant spherical bouquets hung from the ceiling, trees with dangling diamond lights lined the walls and a gigantic stage fit for a concert had been assembled at the front. Country superstar Luke Bryan opened the show, followed by Tony Award–winning Broadway stars Idina Menzel and Kristin Chenoweth. They both sang separately, and then performed their much-anticipated duets from *Wicked*.

The six-course meal, planned by renowned Chef Bart Messing from the Diamond, was absolutely delicious. Each course came paired with fine champagne or wine, so by midway through dinner, every guest was sufficiently tipsy.

Finally, out rolled the eight-tiered wedding cake, all-white frosting with delicate flower designs on each level. Madison had inhaled every bite of the meal, and she was so full that her bridesmaid gown felt considerably tighter than it had that morning. But it was fine, because this was one of her two "cheat meals" this week. Of course, she shouldn't eat this much food *all* the time, but she was learning not to beat herself up over a slice of cake.

Adrian and Rebecca stood up from the table to cut the first piece, leaving Madison, Courtney, Peyton and Savannah alone with their dates. Madison played with the diamond earrings that Adrian had given her and smiled.

"I can't believe everything that's happened in the past year," she said, looking around at everyone at the table. "Who would have thought we would all be sitting here together today?"

"Last year feels like a lifetime ago," Peyton said. "We were living in that small apartment in Fairfield, and Mom was out of a job. If I knew I would be here now…" She looked around the room, with the twinkling lights, beautiful flower arrangements and celebrity guests, and shook her head. "I never would have believed it. I especially wouldn't have believed that I would be *happy* here."

"I knew I would love it here the moment I stepped inside the Diamond," Savannah said.

"This year hasn't been easy," Courtney said, her eyes distant. "It's probably been the hardest year of my life. But it's been the best year of my life, too."

"Because you met me, right?" Brett nudged her shoulder, and they looked at each other in the same way that Adrian and Rebecca had been looking at each other all day—with complete and total love.

"Yes." She blushed. "But mainly because this year brought me, Savannah and Peyton closer together. Back in Fairfield, even though we shared a room, our lives were so separate.

This past year, we've become more than sisters—we've become friends."

The three of them looked at each other and smiled. Madison's throat felt tight, and she sipped her water, not wanting to cry. She'd already cried while watching the wedding ceremony earlier. The stylists had fixed her makeup afterward, but she didn't want to mess it up again. Plus, she hated crying in front of people.

"I hope that someday you'll feel that close to me, too." Madison's voice was timid, and she wasn't sure if she should have said it at all. But then Oliver's hand found hers under the table, giving her a surge of strength. "I feel like this wedding's a new start for us. And I'm really happy to have the three of you as sisters."

"I never would have believed it after last summer, but I'm happy to have you as a sister, too," Savannah said. Courtney and Peyton agreed, and before Madison knew what was happening, a tear snuck its way out and slid down her face. She pretended she had an itch and wiped it away.

Luckily, all attention turned to Adrian and Rebecca, who held a giant silver knife over the cake. They cut the first slice, and applause echoed through the room.

Madison looked over at Oliver, only to find that he'd been watching her the entire time, his eyes dark with intensity. She leaned closer, her nose brushing his cheek, and asked, "Is everything okay?"

"Yes." He swallowed, then lifted his hand so his thumb caressed her cheek. Electricity stirred between them, and his gaze was filled with so much longing that Madison's heart jumped into her throat. "I just... I love you, Madison," he said. "I know it might be 'too soon' to say it, but I don't care, because I love you, and I want you to know. I *need* you to know."

Her breathing slowed, and even though there were a thousand people in the room, Oliver was the only one she saw. And he loved her. She'd wanted him to say those words for weeks, and she smiled, repeating them in her mind. Oliver really, truly loved her.

"I love you, too," she said. "So much." She brushed her lips against his, and he kissed her back slowly, as if she meant everything to him. This kiss felt different—full of promise for a future between them. There were a lot of things about her future that Madison couldn't be sure of—if she would get into Stanford, how her relationship with her parents would change, getting to know her sisters and what Adrian's role would be in her life moving forward.

But the one thing she did know, that she trusted above all else, was that Oliver—her best friend, her boyfriend, her first love, her *true* love—would be there for her through every second of it.

epilogue: Brianna

At the wedding reception, Brianna Prescott was stuck at a table to the side full of other hotel owners and their families. Her dad sat next to her, and Ellen Prescott—aka the step-monster from hell who hated Brianna just because she had dared to be born—sat next to him. Ellen would never sit next to Brianna. She couldn't even *look* at Brianna without shooting her icy, hateful glares.

When Adrian and Rebecca were up on stage cutting the wedding cake, Brianna stared longingly at the table in the front and center, where Oliver, Madison, Peyton, Courtney, Savannah, Brett, Damien and Jackson sat. They were smiling and laughing nonstop, and Brianna wished she were sitting with them instead.

Actually, she wished for more than to just be *sitting* with them—she wanted the glamorous, fun life that they had in Vegas. Instead, she was stuck at an all-girls boarding school in middle-of-nowhere Pennsylvania. She'd rarely had the chance to be around guys, so just talking to them usually made her clam up. She'd never even been kissed.

She'd wanted to change that on the trip to Aspen. She'd hoped that Damien Sanders—Oliver's best friend for years— would finally notice her. But Damien didn't see Brianna as anything more than Oliver's little sister. He had eyes only for Savannah. And Savannah was so bubbly and fun that Brianna couldn't help but like her. The entire *country* was going to fall in love with her once she was on *American StarMaker* this summer.

When Brianna had gotten back from Aspen, she'd told her dad that she wanted to come live with him in Las Vegas. But Ellen Prescott wouldn't hear of it. And Brianna's mom hated Las Vegas—she called it an evil city full of sin, and believed it would be the worst thing on earth for Brianna to live here.

But once she turned eighteen, she would get the first chunk of her trust fund. Then no one would be able to control her anymore. She would have the glamorous life in Vegas that she wanted. She just had to get through two more years of boarding school in the middle of nowhere.

Then, come college, it was UNLV or bust.

www.campusbuzz.com

High Schools > Nevada > Las Vegas > The Goodman School

FIRST DAY OF SUMMER BREAK!
Posted on Saturday 6/6 at 10:28 AM

FINALLY IT'S HERE—SUMMER BREAK HAS STARTED!
This has been one hell of a year. When Savannah, Courtney, and Peyton moved into the Diamond, I knew people
would be talking about them, but I had no idea how much
they would shake everything up.

Who would have thought that Damien would ever get
over Madison...and now he's seriously dating Savannah?!
And that Savannah would go from a wanna-be YouTube
star to being on American StarMaker? Or that Brett would
fall for one of the Diamond girls, and that their parents
would be okay with them dating? (Brett and Courtney
ARE the cutest couple, though.) Or that Peyton would go
from hooking up with Oliver, to having a secret relationship with her bodyguard, and that Oliver would finally realize that he's been in love with Madison since middle
school? Because come on, we've all seen the way Oliver
looks at Madison. They totally compete with Courtney and
Brett in the cutest couple category.

This summer will definitely be interesting. And always
remember: What happens in Vegas stays in Vegas...but
that doesn't matter when you live there ;)

★ ★ ★ ★ ★

Acknowledgments

I can't believe The Secret Diamond Sisters trilogy has come to an end! I hope you've all loved reading about Savannah, Courtney, Peyton, Madison and all the other characters in this series.

This series wouldn't be where it is today without the help of so many people.

Natashya Wilson—you have believed and loved this series from the beginning, and that has meant so much! Your amazing ideas and insight have guided me to make this story what it is today. Thank you so much for believing in me and in the Diamond Sisters.

Lauren Smulski, Nancy Fischer, Siena Koncsol, Lisa Wray, Bryn Collier, Erin Craig, Amy Jones, Ashley McCallan, Michelle Renaud, Mary Sheldon and everyone else on the Harlequin team who has helped with this series—thank you.

Danielle Barclay and Cameron Yeager, for doing so much and working so hard to spread the word about this series. You're both amazing!

Molly Ker Hawn, for believing in this series from the first draft.

Kevan Lyon, for believing in my writing and in my future!

Brent Taylor, for your constant support from the beginning. You are one of the smartest, most determined people I've ever met.

Sasha Alsberg, for spreading her love for this series online! You rock!

Dallin Porter, for creating and managing The Secret Diamond Sisters fan pages on Instagram, Twitter and Facebook.

Lindsay Cummings and Claire Kovarik, for being such amazing author friends, and for always being there to talk.

My incredible Street Team, for your enthusiasm and involvement with the series.

My family—Mom, Dad, Steven, all the grandparents and extended family, for your unconditional love and support. Special shout-out to my mom for coordinating my events, and for helping out so much with the series!

And, of course, to the fans—knowing that you're excited to read my stories is what keeps me inspired. I hope you loved the final book in The Secret Diamond Sisters trilogy!

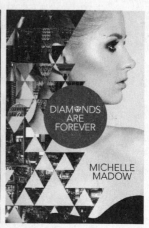

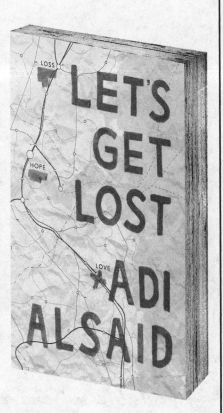

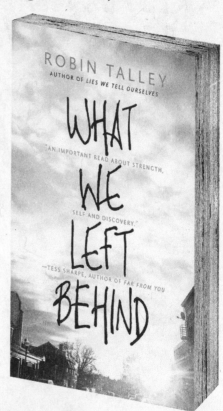